Florence Marryat

Her Lord and Master

Anatipos

Florence Marryat

Her Lord and Master

Reprint of the original, first published in 1872.

1st Edition 2023 | ISBN: 978-3-38212-761-9

Anatiposi Verlag is an imprint of Outlook Verlagsgesellschaft mbH.

Verlag (Publisher): Outlook Verlag GmbH, Zeilweg 44, 60439 Frankfurt, Deutschland
Vertretungsberechtigt (Authorized to represent): E. Roepke, Zeilweg 44, 60439 Frankfurt, Deutschland
Druck (Print): Books on Demand GmbH, In de Tarpen 42, 22848 Norderstedt, Deutschland

HER LORD AND MASTER.

A Tale.

BY

FLORENCE MARRYAT,

[MRS ROSS CHURCH,]

AUTHOR OF "LOVE'S CONFLICT," "VERONIQUE," ETC. ETC.

"By pride
Angels have fallen before thy time."

LONDON:
FREDERICK WARNE AND CO.
BEDFORD STREET, STRAND.

CONTENTS.

HER LORD AND MASTER.

CHAPTER I.

IN LORD CLEVEDON'S CHAMBER.

It was past midnight—and at the close of the London season. Half the weary world was sleeping, whilst the other half (the true labouring class) was toiling to procure the amusement of itself and friends.

At a house in Park Lane, the numerous lights, sounds of music, and gay figures that flitted continually across the open windows, showed that some festivity was taking place; whilst the long train of carriages in waiting, with patient servants slumbering at their posts, was no proof that the assembly was likely to break up soon. A few night-wanderers, attracted by the glare, and curious perhaps to gain some insight to a world of which they had only heard, were hanging about the palings on that side of the house which looked into the park, and grumbling to each other that Heaven's gifts were so unequally divided, and that some had all the riches and the pleasure, whilst others, homeless like themselves, looked on from afar, with empty stomachs and repining hearts.

But all was not so bright as it appeared in the house in Park Lane. The reception chambers might be brilliantly illuminated, but there were other rooms beneath the same roof, where the light burned dim and low, and pain and sickness were causing a very different scene to be enacted. In an apartment richly hung with maroon velvet, and furnished in the style of Louis Quatorze—an apartment sufficiently secluded to enable its occupant to remain undisturbed by any noise which might go on beneath him—a man was sleeping in an arm-chair. Not an old man, by any means, and yet so aged from the effects of frequent and acute suffering, that his hair and beard were nearly white, and the long thin hands which lay passively upon his knees were shrunk and wrinkled. At a first glance he seemed to be alone, for the shaded lamp upon the table threw its mild beams upon no other living creature. But his attendants had only left him when he appeared disposed to sleep, and were in the ante-chamber, napping themselves, but ready to start up at the least summons of their master.

For this was the owner of the house himself—the man whose purse-strings must undraw to pay for all the merriment going on below—Robert, Earl of Clevedon, and his sickness was not a thing of yesterday. For months he had been resting in that arm-chair, unable from the painful nature of his disease to sleep in a recumbent posture, until even those nearest to him had begun to fancy that so lingering a complaint must end in convalescence. And yet the death-like appearance of his handsome face, and the listless heavy manner in which his wasted body pressed the pillows, might have forewarned them that Nature was almost tired of the warfare, and ready to lay down her arms.

Presently, the door of the bed-chamber was pushed noiselessly open, and, stepping in the cautious manner with which we approach sleepers, a girl, apparently of about nineteen years old, passed over the threshold and drew near the arm-chair of the slumbering man. Robed in white satin, with her fair arms and neck discovered, and pearls twisted in her hair, she seemed a strange apparition to visit a sick-room at midnight; but unconscious as heedless of the fact, she dropped quietly into an adjacent seat, and with clasped hands and parted lips, which betrayed a very sorrowful anxiety, gazed earnestly upon the features of the sleeping earl.

And at this juncture, a stranger, with permission to observe her undisturbed, would have been less struck perhaps with her beauty than with the lofty patrician order of its merit. Fair as she was, almost to a fault (for the slight bloom which mantled on her cheeks had been called forth by excitement, and would vanish with the morning), the Saxon hair, blue eyes, and delicately-moulded features, so common to our English aristocracy, attracted less notice than the high brow, oval face, and curled upper lip; which last, though obviously formed by nature for the purpose, had been materially assisted in its heavenward direction by the excellent opinion entertained by Lady Ethel Carr of herself, her accident of birth, and everything belonging to her. The stately way in which she carried her aristocratic little head, showed that she considered herself as something superior to the rest of the world; and a glance at her pretty, supercilious mouth was sufficient to prove that the sorest point on which she could be wounded was her pride. And yet there was nothing cold about the expression of her face; on the contrary, proudly as she could repel the advances of strangers, or check the familiarity of inferiors, there was at times a passion in her glance not often found in eyes of that colour; and at the moment when we are first introduced to her, she seemed to have forgotten every feeling but that of filial love.

In a few minutes Lord Clevedon stirred uneasily, and then, with a slight sigh, opened his eyes and fixed them on his daughter.

"Ethel! is that you?"

"Yes, dear papa; I hope I have not disturbed you."

"What are you doing here, my dear?"

"I only ran up to see how you were going on. I feel uneasy when we are separated for so many hours. Go to sleep again, dear father; I shall be quite satisfied now I have had a look at you."

"How goes the night, child?"

"It is past two o'clock."

"Not later? I had hoped it was almost dawn;" and, with a look of resignation, the sick man slightly changed his position. "I suppose your party is not over then, Ethel?"

"Not yet; but I daresay it soon will be."

"You had better go back then, my dear; your mother may miss you."

"No fear of that, papa; Lady Clevedon is better engaged."

There was a half-hidden bitterness in this reply which did not escape her father's notice.

"You have not been enjoying yourself, I fear, Ethel."

The tears rushed to his daughter's eyes. She rose hastily from the chair on which she was seated, and flung herself upon her knees beside him.

"Enjoying myself! whilst you lie here; how could I? It is a shame there should be any joy in the house, any merry-making, even the semblance of it, whilst you——O father!" and here Lady Ethel's utterance was impeded by her sobs.

"Hush, hush!" said Lord Clevedon, soothingly, as he placed his hand upon her bowed head; "a long illness like mine, child, cannot be permitted to interfere with all the duties we owe to society. My wife occupies a high station in the world, and greater sacrifices are expected from her than would be from a woman of a lower rank. She does not belong entirely to me; I could not expect it."

"You expect far too little," murmured Lady Ethel; "you think of every one before yourself."

"Not so!" replied the earl, with a faint smile. "Are we not all to be packed off to Nice next week for my especial benefit, and is it not sufficient to set a whole household travelling at this time of the year for the sake of one old man? Meanwhile, Lady Clevedon owes something in return for the attentions of her friends and mine, which she is very properly trying to pay off. I would not have had put off her *réunions* this season for any consideration. How many guests have you to-night—on an average?" he continued, with a view to diverting her attention from himself.

"About two hundred, I should think—perhaps more," said Lady Ethel, indifferently, as she rose from her kneeling position, and stood before the glass drying her eyes.

"The Marquis de Lacarras is amongst them, I suppose?"

"Yes."

A quick observer might have seen the scarlet flush which mounted to the face of Ethel Carr, as she replied to this simple question: it would have taken a still quicker one to note the look, made half of pain and half of patience, with which the earl received her answer.

"And *your* friend, Ethel, the gallant colonel of artillery, is he there also?"

"*My* friend!" returned the girl, recovering from her slight confusion; "who dares to call Colonel Bainbridge by that name?"

"I understand you like him."

"From Lady Clevedon, father; she was your informant, I presume?" and Ethel's lip curled to its highest extent.

"Or that he likes you—which is it, Ethel?"

"*Voilà une autre chose,*" rejoined his daughter, haughtily, as she coaxed a stray love-lock to lie smoothly on her forehead. "Colonel Bainbridge may admire me; I know nothing about that, and care less; your footman may do the same, sir, and the admiration of one man is likely to bring forth as much fruit as the other. It is impossible, even for me, to avoid the adulation of the herd: it would be another thing to encourage it."

"Come, come, Ethel!" said Lord Clevedon, with some degree of reproof; "you are going too far in speaking like this. Were you agreeable to the proceeding, there would be nothing extraordinary in your marrying a man like Colonel Bainbridge. He is a gentleman; and the king cannot be more."

Lady Ethel stared at her father with unmitigated surprise.

"But your daughter may require more, sir," she said; "and you need not expect she will ever so far forget what is due to her birth and station in society as to sink the name of Carr in that of Bainbridge," with withering contempt.

"The Bainbridges are a very wealthy family," resumed Lord Clevedon, in a musing tone, "and it would not be the first time a woman has exchanged her noble name for the means of maintaining it. Remember that you have no dowry, Ethel; that when you marry you will take your husband literally nothing."

"*Nothing,* father?" she repeated interrogatively, with a satisfied glance at the lovely features reflected in the mirror.

"Ah, child! I know what you are thinking of; but beauty is a gift common to peer and peasant alike, and of small value in the matrimonial market. You know I am not rich, Ethel; in fact, for a man in my position, I am exceedingly poor; and after my death there will be no separate provision for yourself. Carrhampton and Temple Grange are entailed estates: they both go to your brother Temple, with little enough for the poor child to keep them up on, long as his minority may last; for I regret to say that I am deeply involved in debt. This house, then, and furniture, with the income derivable from her own marriage settlements, is positively all I have to settle on your mother. Were I certain of her remaining as she is, I should feel differently on the subject, for, in any case, she will enjoy the interest of her son's money till he comes of age; but, as it is, Ethel"—with a deep sigh—"Gertrude is young, you see, and very much admired, and it is impossible to calculate on what may happen."

"I understand you, father, and it is no news to me; you have often told me the same thing before; and if it must be so, it must. But no circumstances, however unfortunate, are likely to influence me in making a match below my station in life."

"But what I want to convince you of is, that birth is a mere accident, and no man, who is a gentleman, can be beneath you. I have been obliged to leave you dependent on your mother, Ethel; and you do not always get on well together. The thought often makes me feel unhappy."

"We get on well enough, father; don't let that distress you; but as for this man Bainbridge—"

"*Colonel* Bainbridge," mildly interposed Lord Clevedon. "Colonel Thomas Bainbridge, I believe his name is."

"Yes," rejoined Lady Ethel, with supreme indifference; "perhaps so, the name fits the man. As for this Colonel Thomas Bainbridge, then, I tell you truly, sir, that I would rather starve as Lady Ethel Carr than owe my means of support to him."

"Not if you learned to love him, Ethel?"

"My eyes are not likely to look on the ground long enough to learn to love him," she replied, insolently.

Lord Clevedon regarded his rebellious daughter for some moments in silence, and when he spoke, the sadness of his tone was almost solemn.

"Ethel, that pride of yours will some day be brought down. I pray that when it is, your life's happiness may not be overwhelmed at the same time;" and then, as though fatigued with the discussion, he added: "You had better go back to your visitors now, my dear; your long absence will be remarked upon; and I think, if left to myself, that I could sleep again."

Lady Ethel bent down and kissed him almost mechanically, for her ruffled feelings had not quite settled down into their proper place; but, as she was leaving the apartment, Lord Clevedon called her back.

"My child," he said, with affectionate earnestness, as he drew her towards him, "try to be more like your own dear mother who is gone before us; she was so meek and gentle, Ethel. And if I should leave you, dear—if I should join her sooner than you anticipate—don't forget what I have said to you to-night."

Then all the girl's pride melted beneath her alarm.

"Father! Father, dearest! what do you mean? You do not feel worse, father; not weaker than you felt yesterday, or the day before?"

"No, no, my dear! indeed not. What have I said to frighten you? But death is near at hand for all of us, Ethel, and surely nearer for the weak than for the strong."

Lady Ethel shuddered. To her the name of Death conveyed no notion but that of a dark grave and narrow coffin, and all the soul-repellent horrors with which we invest our funeral solemnities. Her heart had never realised the perfect happiness of ransomed souls set free from the chains of earth and sin; or the burst of choral singing with which the gates of pearl are thrown open to admit another angel to the Presence that redeemed it. She had no power to look beyond the signs of our mortality.

Her cheeks blanched, and her frame trembled when Lord Clevedon mentioned his probable decease, but it was more from fright than misery. She did not believe it possible that his surmise was correct, but she shuddered to remember that such a horrid thing as death must inevitably come to every living creature, and would have obliterated the knowledge altogether if she could.

"Papa, papa, what are you thinking of? what are you saying?" she said, imploringly; "pray don't speak like that. We shall be at Nice, you know, next week, and then Dr Chalmers says that you are certain to get well again."

"Perhaps so, my child; as God pleases," replied the earl, gently. And then, with a blessing, he once more dismissed her. And hastily drawing her handkerchief across her eyes, Lady Ethel quitted the apartment.

CHAPTER II.

LADY ETHEL'S LOVERS.

But she had scarcely crossed the threshold of his chamber, before the softness which had played about her features as she listened to his last words disappeared, to be replaced by a bearing in which offended pride was the predominant feeling. For the tenour of her father's conversation returned upon her memory, and she recalled from whom it was he had derived his information of the Colonel's predilection for herself.

"She would see me married to a tradesman," thought the girl, bitterly, "in order to gratify her own ambition to get rid of me; but if Lady Clevedon imagines that a Carr will be turned out of her father's house to enter any but one equal to it, she is very much mistaken."

And the remembrance of a title as ancient as the Earl of Clevedon's, and which she had reason to expect would, before long, be offered for her acceptance, sent the same conscious blush to her fair forehead which had crimsoned it before, and dispelled much of the ugly feeling which was lingering there.

The suite of reception rooms to which Ethel Carr now took her way were gorgeously furnished with white and gold, and hangings of pale blue satin, in the same old-fashioned style as the bed-chamber. They were profusely decorated, moreover, with hot-house flowers, and crowded with a large and brilliant company, in the midst of which, surrounded by the *élite* of her visitors, sat their hostess, Gertrude, Countess of Clevedon.

In age not over six-and-twenty, with large, clear, grey eyes, fine features, rosy complexion, and an abundance of auburn hair, Lady Clevedon, in the estimation of many of her friends, was considered a handsomer woman than her step-daughter. But a certain coarseness in the outlines of her figure, the sparkle of her eyes, and the appearance of her open mouth, with its full red lips, deterred men of refinement from paying her the admiration which she exacted from the crowd.

Physically beautiful she certainly was; but there was less intellect than vivacity written on her face, and more cunning than cleverness depicted in her character. And yet, like many women of her type, she drew simply because she stooped to draw; and the men who now hovered round the ottoman on which she was reclining, and vied with one another in engrossing her attention, were some of the most flattered and sought after of her acquaintance.

Conspicuously amongst them shone the Marquis de Lacarras, the mention of whose name had called forth a sigh from the lips of the Earl of Clevedon. This gentleman—even in an assembly where many were handsome, most were young, and all fashionable—was the possessor of sufficient beauty, youth, and mode, to command universal notice. And, perhaps, his manifold attractions were increased rather than diminished by the fact of his nationality, which was not sufficiently prominent to raise any great barrier of distinction between him and his associates. Descended from one of the oldest and most noble families of France, and bred and born in the land of his fathers, Victor de Lacarras had yet been educated in England, and formed most of his early friendships with sons of our country.

From this circumstance, he had been accustomed to pass much of his time here, and on becoming his own master, had so associated himself with English manners and people as to be more than half an Englishman himself.

There was no subject connected with our national customs, laws, or amusements, on which the Marquis de Lacarras was not as well informed as any of his neighbours. He was to be met with on every race-course in England, kept his house in town, his hunters in the country, and his yacht at Ryde; spoke the English language as fluently as he did his own, and never troubled Paris excepting during the season.

Notwithstanding which, he retained all the grace and polish peculiar to a well-bred Frenchman, knew intuitively by which delicate flattery each woman's ear was to be gained, and had always the plea of foreign extraction to fall back upon when he found that he had gone too far.

Finally, Victor de Lacarras was what is called by his own sex a very lucky man. His black, almond-shaped eyes, which could be soft as velvet or hard as steel, as fickle nature dictated to him, were sufficient of themselves to take female hearts by storm, had they not been set in a handsome face, and joined to a supple, well-knit figure.

But it is sorry work to attempt to describe beauty. Easy enough to write down a list of features, and say that, amalgamated, they looked well; but expression is not to be caught in so many words, and without expression life is wanting.

The expression of the Marquis was generally an indifferent one; in repose, he appeared tired of the world and its pleasures, which was perhaps the reason that with him to appear interested was to pay the highest compliment of which he was capable.

On the present occasion, although he hung conspicuously over the Countess of Clevedon, and even took the trouble to draw off her attention from her other guests, he seemed more listless and indifferent than usual, and his dark eyes roved constantly from the contemplation of her neck and shoulders to the door of the apartment in which they were sitting.

No such feeling of *ennui*, however, possessed his fair hostess, for she was all sparkle and flutter at his monopoly of her, and would leave any question unanswered to listen to the faintest murmur from his languid lips.

It was at this juncture that Lady Ethel descended the broad staircase leading from the upper story.

A group of men and women, who had been unable to find seats within, or who preferred freedom and flirtation to foul air and *chaperones*, were clustered on the landing, whispering in couples, or being "eloquent in silence."

They fell apart as she appeared, making way for her to enter, and with a faint smile and inclination of the head she passed through them into the crowd beyond.

"Very lovely! Don't you think so?" suggested one young lady to her companion, as the white satin train swept over the threshold of the drawing-room.

"H—m!" said the companion meditatively (he knew that an unqualified "yes" would anything but please the fair querist), "some people might think her so, but she's not my style; she is far too cold and statuesque-looking to please me."

At this qualified commendation the young lady felt that she might safely push her argument.

"Oh! but I assure you Lady Ethel Carr has been considered quite a belle this season; and at the last drawing-room it was remarked that she was the prettiest woman there."

"Indeed! then *you* can scarcely have been present," returned her cavalier gallantly.

"How *can* you?" was the curt but expressive rejoinder, and then, as though to change so personal a subject, the lady continued: "But I believe what you said respecting Lady Ethel's appearance is perfectly true as regards her character. Everybody says that she is terribly cold."

"Of course! perhaps you will believe me another time."

"She does not get on well with other girls. They complain of her being so uncommunicative and reserved. Not a bit like dear Lady Clevedon, is it?"

"No!—There's a pretty woman now, if you like," replied the gentleman, forgetting for a moment his *rôle.* "Such life—such colouring! She is worth two of her step-daughter."

"But don't you consider her just a little too stout for beauty?" inquired his listener dubiously; and then he saw that he had overstepped the bounds of making himself perfectly agreeable, and declined to carry on the discussion any further. Meanwhile the subject of their remarks had gained the inner drawing-room.

A cloud, mingled with an expression of contempt, passed over her face as she surveyed the group upon the ottoman; and turning quickly to one side, as though to avoid the sight of it, she ran straight upon a tall, dark man, who was leaning against the wall and contemplating her with grave earnestness.

He started; seized a chair, and stammeringly asked her if she would not take it; whilst Lady Ethel, scarcely knowing what to answer, accepted the proffered courtesy, and found herself the minute after in possession of a seat, at the back of which stood sentry the man of whom she had spoken with such scorn—Colonel Bainbridge.

And now, at the risk of wearying my readers with description, I must devote a few lines to the notice of this gentleman, who will play no mean part in the story which follows.

Thomas Bainbridge, a man of thirty, but one of the youngest colonels in the service of artillery, was the only child of a very wealthy Birmingham manufacturer, who, having amassed a large fortune, had for many years past retired from trade, and lived on an estate which he had purchased over the Border.

His son having evinced a strong ambition to serve her

Majesty, Mr Bainbridge had considered himself justified in consenting to his wishes; and proud of seeing his child in a position superior to his own, had forwarded his career by every means in his power.

At first, Thomas Bainbridge had not found it all smooth sailing in the army; and there were hours when he had wished heartily that he had chosen a more humble occupation. It is a well-known fact, that sons of our wealthiest tradesmen are to be found in the best regiments of the service, but it is quite as indisputable that they do not always find their position to be a bed of roses; and young Bainbridge's experience had been no exception to the rule; yet he had outlived almost the remembrance of it. If, in the first years of his military career, there had been found spirits coarse and ungentlemanly enough to taunt him by a covert allusion to the calling of his father, that time had passed away, and at the present moment there was not an officer in the length or breadth of England who would not have been proud to shake Colonel Bainbridge by the hand.

And this change had not been effected by any lavish display or distribution of his riches, for he lived as quietly as any subaltern; it had been wrought solely by himself and his behaviour.

In fact, Thomas Bainbridge *was* a gentleman; and when Lord Clevedon called him so, he only paid a natural tribute to his mind and manners, which all who knew the man would have been ready to acknowledge due.

Little by little, without any forward pushing or eager desire for introduction to those above him, he had silently worked his way upward in society, until he not only carried men of high birth back with him each year to spend the shooting season at Cranshaws, but what is far more worthy of note, found himself a welcome guest at their houses in return, and on the visiting-list of such leaders of fashion as the Earl and Countess of Clevedon.

But it is not to be supposed that Colonel Bainbridge carried any mark about him by which it might be recognised that he was not of aristocratic birth; on the contrary, he was a far finer-looking man than many of the sprigs of nobility by whom he was surrounded; and his manners, though rather grave and silent, were equal to the best of them.

Of unusual height and bulk, and bronzed like a Moor from the Indian sun, beneath which he had passed several years of service, the healthy, uncontaminated blood which he had derived from a race to which luxury was unknown, betrayed itself in his muscular limbs, thick hair and beard, and fine white teeth. His eyes, not large, but searching, were of a dark brown, his nose was prominent, and his mouth (although this latter feature was concealed by a heavy moustache) clean cut and decided. As to his character, if this tale is to tell anything, it may be left to speak for itself.

CHAPTER III.

THE WHISPER ON THE BALCONY.

Lady Ethel, having accepted the chair which Colonel Bainbridge offered her, felt very uncomfortable at his close vicinity.

Her breast was still heaving with indignation at the thought that he presumed to aspire to her hand, or that her father should encourage so ridiculous an idea; and she was determined to say nothing that could further the notion that he was in any way agreeable to her.

And so she continued to sit before him in dignified silence, like a beautiful statue; whilst he gazed at her from above, thinking sadly that the sooner all this was ended, and he had put miles between himself and his folly, the better. But at last he ventured to bend down to speak to her, for people were chatting together on all sides, and the silence between them had become oppressive—almost remarkable.

"Shall you be at the opera to-morrow night, Lady Ethel?"

She jerked her head slightly as his voice struck her ear, but she answered him without any appearance of annoyance.

"I am not sure. Our engagements at present depend so much upon papa."

"Lord Clevedon is better, I trust?"

"Yes! he's better; at all events, he is no worse."

"The season is fast drawing to its close, and town will be

nearly empty, I suppose, next week. Is there any chance of our seeing you on the moors this year?"

Lady Ethel lifted her brows in unaffected astonishment. The man would be sending them an invitation to his father's house next, she concluded. Her answer was delivered with some asperity.

"Not the slightest! We shall be at Nice, I hope, this time next week."

"Have you ever visited Scotland? Have you seen the Lammermoors when the heather is in bloom?"

"No! and I cannot say I wish to do so. I have never had the slightest desire to cross the Border."

She delivered this so curtly that he sighed. It was the merest fragment of a sigh, more worthy to be called a long breath than by that name; but she heard it, and it irritated her, for it betrayed the interest which the manufacturer's son dared to feel in what she thought, and it urged her to say more than she intended.

"The fact is, I hate Scotland, and everything connected with it;" and then, aware of the extreme rudeness of her speech, she added, "You must forgive my plain speaking, Colonel Bainbridge, but the truth will out."

"Yes!" he said softly; and then he bit his lip hard, and said no more.

Meanwhile she sat, red with conscious shame, and fanning herself violently, whilst she wondered how she should make her escape from him, for the crowd seemed to increase instead of diminish, and they were hemmed in by a throng of silken skirts.

"I suppose you like it as you live there," she went on presently, feeling that she must say something by way of apology; "but I have never been used to the country, you see; I have lived all my life in a town, and have no fancy for trees, and grass, and all that sort of thing! How intensely hot it has become here! Those windows can never be open, surely!" And, without further preface, she started from her seat and commenced to edge her way towards the other end of the apartment.

Colonel Bainbridge looked after her in troubled silence. At another time, he would have sprung forward to execute her orders, or accompany her across the room; but, at the present moment, he saw plainly that her move had been effected to avoid himself, and he was too delicate to follow her. So he remained behind, in the same position as she had found him, but with a sadder heart.

Meanwhile, Lady Ethel gained her object in escaping unmolested, and passed out of the drawing-room into a wide balcony enclosed with glass, the windows of which had been thrown open to admit the evening air. It was a lovely night; the dark blue July sky was studded with stars, and the light breeze, which scarcely stirred the passion-flowers trained against the casement, blew refreshingly upon her heated face and neck. She placed both her arms upon the window-sill, and leant out as far as she could, whilst something very like a sob rose in her throat.

Ethel Carr was angry—but more with the force of circumstances than herself. She knew she had spoken rudely to a gentleman, who had never given her the slightest cause of offence, unless a silent and respectful admiration could be interpreted as such. Yet she did not blame her own pride as the reason. She considered her behaviour had been forced upon her by the absurd pretensions of the man himself, the interference of her step-mother, and her poor father's ready acquiescence in everything that Lady Clevedon did or said. Still, she was too much of a gentlewoman to feel easy at what had occurred; to which sensation an intense though unacknowledged jealousy of the conversation which was being carried on by the group upon the ottoman, added its share of excitement—excitement which would have probably ended in tears, had not her reverie been interrupted by the sound of footsteps, which followed her into the balcony.

At that sound, Lady Ethel's unshed tears disdained to fall, and the arms which rested on the window-sill commenced to tremble; for the girl knew intuitively that the presence which now stood beside her was not that of Colonel Bainbridge.

"All alone?" said the voice of the Marquis de Lacarras, after a moment's pause. "Lady Ethel Carr must have something very pleasant to meditate upon, to prefer her own company to the worship of her numerous admirers."

"She has!" was the sarcastic reply. "She is meditating on the sweetness of this life and the love we bear our neighbours, and the truth and honesty of what the world calls society! Are not such thoughts sufficient to make one enamoured of solitude, Monsieur?"

Monsieur pulled a passion-flower from its stem and said nothing. He had scarcely expected to receive so earnest an answer to his idle question. When he replied, he seemed to have grown earnest too.

"I cannot allow there is so much fault to be found with the world, Lady Ethel. The present assembly, for instance: what have we done wrong? We have been chatting and laughing together, and making ourselves agreeable, and"——

"And pretending we are the dearest friends," she interrupted him, "whilst, in reality, there is not one of us who cares a straw for the welfare of the other."

"Do you think so?" he said, in a low voice. "If *I* might speak—I could vouch that there is one, at least, whose whole heart—whose every hope—is centred in his neighbour."

His neighbour was silent. Her face was still turned from him, for she had not changed her first position; but a mist rose before her eyes which made the stars she gazed on look blurred and indistinct, and her heart beat so rapidly that she could count its loud and impulsive throbs. This was the moment she had been waiting for for weeks, that she had watched, as it were, recede and approach—approach and recede, until hope deferred had made her sicken with anxiety; and now that it had come, she felt as though she could not bear to remain still and listen. But yet she leant there, her whole frame shaking with nervous emotion, and her beautiful face, from which all trace of pride had fled, turned up to the cold, passionless stars.

Presently, a hand came creeping softly upon hers, a fine and white, though not effeminate hand, on which, even in the midst of her agitation, she could not help looking down with fond admiration.

"Am I very presumptuous?" whispered the Marquis, in whose English there lingered just sufficient of his native accent to make the words sound more caressing than when pronounced boldly.

Still Lady Ethel answered nothing, because she could not have trusted her own voice to speak; and Victor de Lacarras so favourably interpreted her silence, that in another moment he had thrown his disengaged arm about her waist and drawn her closely to him.

"Ethel!" he exclaimed, passionately, "there is more than one person here to-night who cares a straw for the welfare of the other;" and if her heaving breast and closed eyes, swimming in tears, told truth, Monsieur le Marquis was correct.

"Say!" he went on presently, with all a lover's fervour, "say only that you have seen my love, that you do not despise it, that you sometimes think of me and my affection as not unworthy of you!"

"O Victor! can you doubt it?" she murmured, reproachfully; and then he bent down, and laid upon her lips the first kiss which she had received from any man, except her father.

And there was a long pause between them, whilst they stood locked together, and looking in each other's eyes.

"My darling!——" commenced the Marquis presently; but at that moment there was a visible commotion amongst the occupants of the drawing-room, and Ethel, gazing timidly from the shelter of her lover's arms, watched the crowd give way to permit the entrance of Dr Chalmers, who appeared desirous of gaining the presence of her step-mother.

"Oh! hush!" she said, in her surprise, "what can be the reason that Dr Chalmers has been sent for at this time of night? My father must be worse!"

"No! no!" he answered, soothingly; "there is no chance of that! Ethel, let me once hear you say that you return my love!"

"Yes—yes! you know I do," she uttered, hurriedly, as she disengaged herself from his clasp; "but, Victor, dearest, let me go. See! Dr Chalmers is leading Lady Clevedon from the room. I am certain that some harm has happened to my father."

She darted from him as she spoke, carrying her flushed face and tearful eyes as marks for comment through the crowded room; yet no one stayed her progress, or asked the reason of her visible alarm.

For the intelligence which would so soon be hers had already spread like wild-fire through the fast thinning ranks of fashion. The Earl of Clevedon's heart complaint had reached its climax, and his attendants had found him as his child had left him—peacefully reposing in his arm-chair—but never to wake again this side the grave.

CHAPTER IV.

MAGGIE HENDERSON.

CRANSHAW CASTLE, or Cranshaws, as the estate of Mr Bainbridge was generally called, was situated on the Scottish moors, a little north of the county of Roxburgh.

The *nouveaux riches* are usually supposed to be dissatisfied with anything to reside in under a castle or a court; but it was not the fault of Mr Bainbridge that his possession bore that high-sounding name, for it had neither been built nor baptized by himself.

He had bought it as it stood, with its many hundreds of adjoining acres, and had been anxious at first to alter its pretentious title, but finding that the place was too well known to admit of such a change, suffered it to remain as its former owner had left it. For Mr Bainbridge was in all things a most humble and retiring man, desirous of nothing more than to avoid publicity, and proud of nothing less than of his self-made fortune. And if any modern erection deserves the name of castle, Cranshaws was that place. Built in the style of the twelfth century, with careful regard to every peculiarity of the architecture of that period, and backed by a noble plantation, it stood, with moat and drawbridge, on the brow of one of the highest undulations of the moors, frowning down upon the smiling valley beneath, and the river which ran rippling through its bosom. But the frown of Cranshaws, like the frown of one pretending to be angry, was but a make-believe, for the house itself was furnished in a light modern style, and the approach to it lay through a beautiful flower-garden.

All the ground inside the moat was dedicated to flowers and smooth-shaven lawn, the especial property of Mrs Bainbridge;

and the faces which were to be daily seen there were as smiling and contented as the valley they gazed on.

For, if he could help it, Mr Bainbridge allowed no one about him to be unhappy; and he was so good a man, and so faithful a Christian, with a temper so equable and serene, that it was difficult to live with him and not catch the infection of his kindly spirit.

He was a universal philanthropist, exercising benevolence in a thousand little ways which were never made public; spending far more of his wealth on the relief of his fellow-creatures than on his own comforts, and never thanking God so fervently for the good fortune He had sent him as when it had been the means of furthering religion or alleviating distress.

For miles before you reached Cranshaw Castle, you drove through the property which belonged to it, and Mr Bainbridge took good care there should be no want within his precincts. He was about the only remaining landlord in those parts who refused to adopt the new hay-cutting and reaping machines, because the use of them threw so many poor Irish, who had crossed the Border expressly to find work at harvest time, out of employment.

And no labourers were better paid, or horses and cattle better kept, than on the farm at Cranshaws.

But there were impunities (or what some people would consider such) attached to these good things. No man who drank, or ill-used his wife, or was a Sabbath-breaker, was retained at work on Cranshaws; and, by the same rule, Mr Bainbridge was very particular about the behaviour of his servants and the members of his own family. They had every comfort and luxury which they required, and in all innocent amusements the master of the house took a cheerful and ready part; but he was most strict with respect to their attendance at church and prayers, and the way in which they spent their Sundays, even to the conversations they maintained on that day. And his opinions on these subjects he diffused freely, both to guest and relative alike, which made a visit to the castle to be felt by many as somewhat of a restraint. At the same time, there were found a few (and amongst them some of the wildest and most careless spirits, whom Colonel Bainbridge took home with him to his father's house), who admired the old man, not only for his sentiments but the rigour with which he maintained them.

His own family consisted of his wife, himself, and their son Thomas, who was seldom at Cranshaws, except for the shooting season and Christmas; but with his accustomed benevolence, Mr Bainbridge had offered a home to the maiden sister of his wife, and to his own orphan niece. And these two had lived so long at Cranshaws (which had been in the possession of its present owner for more than twenty years), as to have become part and parcel of the family and place.

Miss Letitia Lloyd (better known as Aunt Letty), that she might not feel herself to be a visitor, had always been deputed a share in her sister's housekeeping, and she divided with Mrs Bainbridge the love of blooming Maggie Henderson, who had grown up amongst them from a child of three years old to be the pet and darling of the household. The aunts vied with each other which should wait on and caress their niece the most, whilst Maggie returned their affection with all the warmth of a very genuine heart.

Aunt Letty boasted that she had instructed her in drawing, music, and French, whilst Mrs Bainbridge had reserved to herself the direction of her general education, and made her a good housekeeper and needlewoman.

These simple-hearted, old-fashioned women had sincerely imagined that, having the time, they had all the requisite capability of imparting to their niece the information they had themselves received—which idea had been strengthened by Mr Bainbridge's often-expressed dislike to boarding-schools for young ladies, and their own disinclination to introduce a stranger as governess to the family circle. If there had been two or more girls to educate, they argued, it would be different, and their duty, perhaps, to endure the inconvenience; but "only little Maggie," surely the brains of Aunt Letty and Aunt Lizzy combined must be sufficient to make her as accomplished as it was necessary she should be. Accordingly, "little Maggie," having been put through the routine of morning lessons when she felt so disposed, and excused the same whenever she desired to fish in the river or ride her pony or accompany her uncle round the farm, was at eighteen years of age about as unaccomplished a girl as it was possible to find in her station of life.

She could ride and fish, and shoot at a mark, and walk over the moors for hours together without feeling fatigued; but her general knowledge was very small, and she had no idea of pronouncing French, or of fingering a piece of classical music; above all, she had never mixed in what is termed good society, and her very misty notions of the ways and manners of the fashionable world were derived from the remarks she occasionally heard fall from the lips of her cousin's regimental friends.

Once or twice Colonel Bainbridge had commented on Maggie's deficiencies to his aunt and mother, and then the two good creatures had looked at one another, and commenced to fear that they had made a mistake in not confiding the girl's education to some one more competent to conduct it than themselves. But an appeal to Mr Bainbridge invariably met with the same reply.

"Not accomplished enough!" he would exclaim. "Tell Thomas to mind his own business. The child can read, and write, and sew, and what more would you have? We have no need for French and German on the moors, and I should be sorry to see Maggie mixing in the society where they are needed. Let us be content with the station of life in which God has placed us; the girl will do her duty there, or I am much mistaken!"

And, as far as outward appearance went, there seemed every probability of his prophecy being verified, for Maggie Henderson was no ordinary character.

Younger by a year than Lady Ethel Carr, she had already twice the command over her feelings than was evinced by that young lady, and her naturally high temper had been brought into such control, that seldom, if ever, did its ebullitions disturb the equanimity of the quiet household at Cranshaws.

They might disturb her own soul, but on the surface there appeared nothing but sorrow for a nature as yet imperfectly subdued, but which, with few exceptions, was most bright and sunny.

This effect might, in a great measure, have been owing to example and the method by which she had been reared, for it is difficult to dwell amongst those who live in the presence of another world, and not be imbued with a deep sense of the responsibility of living.

At the same time, Maggie Henderson owed much to her own energetic spirit, to her warm heart, impulsive feelings, and desire to evince her gratitude to those who had supplied the place of parents to her.

By nature she was quick and clever—always ready to see a joke, and very fond of making one; but she had her serious moments when the young heart was too full to laugh and be merry, although it overran with joy and gratitude.

These were Maggie's dull hours, as some considered them, for her Aunt Lizzy's cares were directed more to her bodily than her spiritual comforts; and her uncle, good man as he was, was of too blunt and rough a temperament to penetrate the finer sympathies of his little niece's mind.

But there was one person in Cranshaws who always understood Maggie, to whom the girl had no shame in disclosing her most sacred feelings, and from whom she never met with anything but the keenest sympathy in return, and that one was dear Aunt Letty.

It was on a brilliant afternoon in the beginning of August, that these two, the aunt and niece, were seated on the lawn which bordered Cranshaw Castle, beneath the shade of some far-spreading trees.

Aunt Letty, a pale, delicate-looking woman of about fifty years of age, whose simple cap enclosed a patient face, on which suffering had left its traces, sat on a low garden-chair employed in needlework, whilst Maggie Henderson, with a book in her hand, lay stretched upon the grass beside her.

She was a fine, healthy girl, with brown eyes and hair, a complexion like blush roses, and usually a most animated expression, but at that moment a serious mood seemed to have stolen over her, for the humid eyes were looking far away into the incalculable distance, and her laughing mouth was firmly closed.

It was a lovely scene that lay before her, for the farm of Cranshaws, with all its unsightly buildings and enclosures, was situated some half a mile distant on the other side of the castle, and she gazed only upon the pleasure grounds, the moat and drawbridge, the sloping wood which clothed the side of the hill, and then the sparkling river with its salmon-fall, and the miles of heather-covered moor which, far as her eye could reach, stretched out in purply undulations; whilst the only sounds to be heard were the distant bark of a sheep-dog, or the sharp chattering cry of the grouse, as they were startled by it from their coverts.

But Maggie's thoughts were occupied with none of these things.

"How glorious it would have been," she exclaimed, suddenly, after a long pause, and alluding to the subject of which they had been reading, "to have lived in those times, Aunt Letty! Fancy being tortured and dying for the faith; ah! after all, suffering is the true heritage."

Aunt Letty did not immediately respond—she had outlived the enthusiastic age when martyrdom appears a desirable thing; perhaps, too, she had experienced her share of it, and had no wish to recommence the warfare.

"We should be very thankful that we have been spared such a trial, Maggie. It must have been a fearful time for them, poor creatures! Reading of it only makes one feel inclined to thank God that their sufferings are over" ——

"But they could not have felt them, aunt," replied the girl, turning her glowing eyes up to Miss Lloyd's face; "not as they would have felt them under ordinary circumstances, I mean; the triumph must have made them almost insensible to pain. And then," she added, in a lower voice, "I think, when they knew for certain that they were so very near seeing *Him*, the joy of their hearts must have quite overpowered the weakness of their flesh. For, only fancy what it must be, Aunt Letty, to know assuredly, that within a few minutes it will come to pass. Oh! I should die with anticipation before they had half expired!"

Aunt Letty patted the blooming cheek laid against her knee, with a very happy and contented look in her own face.

"It would be great joy, my darling, too great to bear, perhaps, were it not in general mercifully hid from us. But it is not absolutely necessary it should be preceded by a life of suffering!"

"Don't you think so?" said the girl, thoughtfully; "now it seems to me, Aunt Letty, that all the saints and apostles of old glorified Him by unhappy lives or violent deaths; and that, if our paths were all sunshine, it would seem as though He had forgotten us, or had nothing for us to do for Him!

The Bible says, you know, that He chasteneth every son in whom He delighteth."

"I know it does, my dear, and also that His chastenings are not grievous; and yet I should be sorry to think your life was not to be a sunny one. You are not destined for a martyr, my little Maggie!"

"I am not good enough for one, you mean, auntie. Yes! I know that well enough; still, I have often wished that I lived in those days, that I might have some means of knowing how much my faith is worth. Aunt, I *think* that I could do it;" and Maggie's eyes sparkled at the idea of testing her strength of mind.

"I think so, too, Maggie! I think you are capable of doing everything that is right—with His help!" Miss Lloyd added, reverently; "only sometimes a very happy life, free from all trouble and care, is a greater trial to our faith than misery. Sorrow draws us nearer to Him as our consolation, but prosperity and affluence are only too likely to make us forget from whom they come. Your future is likely to be a very bright one, Maggie; but cling close to Him through it all, and you will be safe."

"Oh! I will—I do!" exclaimed the girl, fervently. "How could it be otherwise, Aunt Letty, when everything that I possess has come from Him!"

And then there was silence between them for the space of some moments, during which Aunt Letty raised her hand to brush away a tear that came gently coursing down her cheek.

CHAPTER V.

AUNT LETTY HEARS A SECRET.

THE pause at last became almost too long; it threatened to break up their pleasant intercourse.

"Aunt, shall I go on reading?"

"No, dear, not yet awhile; I would rather talk, if you have no objection. Your uncle has been speaking to me of your cousin Thomas. He received a letter from him this morning!"

Maggie turned her head away directly, and looked out over the moors.

"Did he?"

"Yes! and he purposes to be at Cranshaws on the eleventh. He brings two friends with him this time: Captain Grant and Sir Charles Hammond. You remember Captain Grant, Maggie?"

"Oh yes, Aunt Letty, quite well; he was here last season—such a lively, good-tempered young man! Don't you recollect the day we went for a picnic, and our letters were brought out to us on the moors; and he received one that required immediate attention; how cheerfully he left us all, although he had been enjoying himself so much before, and went home to write the answer? I always liked Captain Grant from that day; I thought it so good of him."

"Yet he is not a religious man," said Miss Lloyd, thoughtfully.

"Religious? No; certainly not, if you take the word literally; for religion means strictness. But I think there is more deep feeling amongst young men than you give them credit for, Aunt Letty. This Captain Grant, for instance, I remember observing how reverently he used to behave at prayers, or church, although he might have been laughing only the moment before; and he always joined in the hymns when we sung on Sunday evenings."

"But you don't consider that those qualities, however promising, are sufficient to make a good husband, Maggie?" said Aunt Letty, anxiously.

The girl burst out laughing; she had evidently no tender memories connected with the name of the promising captain; and her mirth seemed to clear away the shade of trouble which had gathered on her aunt's brow.

"I really can't say, Aunt Letty, for I never sat down seriously to consider; but I should certainly suppose it requires something more than good-nature, and a gentlemanly desire to accommodate himself to the habits of those around him, to enable a man to guide wife and children aright through the intricate ways of this world. It must be no easy matter, and a heavy responsibility. Poor Captain Grant has,

I fancy, enough to do to keep himself straight just at present." And Maggie's light laugh again rippled over.

"Not like your cousin Thomas, my dear. He is so good and steady as to be competent to be the guide of any young woman. Don't you think so?"

Miss Lloyd had expected to receive a ready answer in the affirmative; but her niece's eyes had dropped upon the ground instead, and the colour deepened in her cheeks.

"We have no doubt but that he will make his wife happy, have we, Maggie?"

"No! Aunt Letty," came at last, but in a very subdued voice.

"Your uncle has been talking very seriously to me about Thomas, this morning," continued Miss Lloyd, nervously (for she was anxious to sound Maggie Henderson upon a certain subject, and had not the least idea how to set about it); "he naturally looks forward to his own death as an event which at past seventy cannot be so very far distant, and is desirous to see his son comfortably settled before that time, and prepared to take his place here as soon as he shall be gone. For Cranshaws is very dear and familiar to all of us now, Maggie! We should not like to see it let, or pass altogether into a stranger's hands."

"Oh no!" replied the girl, quickly.

"Then it follows, that Thomas must look out for a wife who shall be contented to live here with him all the year round, and not be continually sighing to go to London for the season, or spend the winter abroad."

"I should think there must be many such," said Maggie Henderson; "he will not have to search far."

"Many who would accept the terms, my dear, but not many, I fear, who would keep them afterwards. And your cousin, having travelled a great deal, will require, perhaps, a particularly home-loving wife to induce him to settle down contentedly as the landlord of Cranshaws. And yet it is his father's great wish that he should do so. *You* have never found the place dull, Maggie, have you?"

"O Aunt Letty! how can you ask me such a question of my own dear home?" and Maggie's brown eyes glowed with affection. "Dull! no! I should think not. No one has ever been happier in a place than I have been at Cran shaws. I love every inch of the ground, every tree in the plantation. I would not exchange that view of the moors, and the river with its salmon-fall—(do you remember when I caught the big salmon there, Aunt Letty, and he quietly walked down stream with my line and the first joint of my rod?)—for all the finest sights that London or Paris could afford me. No more than I would exchange you, my own sweet aunt, who has taught me the best of all my little knowledge, for the grandest friends that I could meet there!" And Maggie ended her harangue by throwing herself into Miss Lloyd's outstretched arms.

"Then, my little Maggie would be quite content to spend and end her life at Cranshaws?" whispered the elder lady as she pressed her niece to her; "she would not think the pleasures here too limited, nor the society too insignificant and small?"

"I? No—of course not," stammered the girl, half-raising a burning face from the shelter of her aunt's breast; "but I do not suppose, Aunt Letty, that when *it* happens—that is, when he is married—any of us will continue to live on here."

"Not if he were to choose you as the mistress of Cranshaws, my darling!"

"*Me?*" she exclaimed, hurriedly. "Has Cousin Thomas spoken of it, Aunt Letty?"

"No—no," said Miss Lloyd, in a soothing voice, as she stroked the head of brown hair which was again buried in her bosom; "not yet, dear; but he is very likely to do so, for his father wishes it, and I should like to know your thoughts upon the subject, Maggie."

But to this insinuation there came no reply.

"Should you object very much to the idea?" demanded Miss Lloyd, after a moment's pause—"that is, if all went well, and your cousin was willing to accede to his father's desire; would it be disagreeable to you to look upon him as your future husband, Maggie?"

"O Aunt Letty! don't ask me—don't ask me. I don't know what to say."

The blushing face was still concealed from view, but Miss Lloyd could feel the rapid pulsations of Maggie's heart as it pressed against her knee, and knew by the heaving of her shoulders that the girl was undergoing violent emotion.

"Maggie, my dear! I have not wounded you?" she said, anxiously.

"No!" came presently in a tremulous and broken voice; but the agitation continued, and there was nothing to be done but to wait till it had subsided. When that occurred, Maggie Henderson voluntarily passed a handkerchief over her face, and lifted two shy, tear-swollen eyes to meet those of her aunt. One look was sufficient to reveal her secret.

"My darling," said Miss Lloyd, as she kissed the crimson cheeks, "I had no idea it had gone so far as this. I am so happy, Maggie."

"I don't know why I should feel so ashamed to think that you have guessed the truth," resumed Maggie in a very low voice; "but I could not bear that any one but you should know it, Aunt Letty. And yet there is no real reason to be ashamed, is there? for I could not help it! He has always been so good and kind to me; so thoughtful of my wants and attentive to my wishes, that it was natural I should grow to miss him, and think Cranshaws quite a different place when he is not here. And now, this new idea—of which I assure you I had never dreamed as possible—it seems so wonderful, so startling—and that uncle should desire it, too—I can hardly believe that it is true."

"It is not so strange when you come to think of it, my dear. Your uncle has but one child to provide for, but he looks on you as his own daughter. It is natural he should wish to see your interests united with those of Thomas. Has your cousin never hinted at such a probability to you?" inquired Aunt Letty, who was becoming curious to hear if anything which could be construed into a love-passage had passed between the two.

"Oh no! never—indeed, he has not!" asseverated Maggie, who appeared to imagine that blame would attach to him if he had done so. "We have never talked of such things: how could you think so, Aunt Letty?"

"But your cousin is always very kind to you, my dear; is he not? Very affectionate in his speech and manners."

"Yes!" said the girl, with that quick colour, which was her chief attraction, flying to her cheek, "and he never likes to go out shooting or fishing without me, you know. One day, when they were going far, uncle said I should be a nuisance to them; and *he* said—my cousin said that"——

"What did he say, darling? you need not feel bashful with me."

"He said," replied Maggie, with a hanging head, "that he should not have half the pleasure in his sport if I were not there."

"Nor will he have half the pleasure in his life if you are not there," exclaimed Miss Lloyd, enthusiastically. "Maggie, my child, I congratulate you; I could not conceive a future of greater happiness than that which is opening before you. Thank God for it."

"But, Aunt Letty," rejoined the girl, timidly, "it is not a settled thing, you know; he has said nothing, and" ——

"But he will, my child, he will. Thomas is a good man and a good son, and when he sees that his father's hopes are set upon this marriage, he will do his duty and make us all happy. Leave it in God's hands, and it will come right in the end: you may depend upon that."

"But I would never marry him unless he" —— and the sentence remained eloquently unfinished.

"My darling! who could live with you and not love you?" exclaimed Aunt Letty, unintentionally concluding it; and then, with a promise to preserve her niece's secret with the strictest fidelity, even towards Mr and Mrs Bainbridge, she embraced her several times, and gathering up her sewing materials, passed into the house, leaving Maggie by herself upon the lawn.

She was glad to be so left, for her head was still whirling with the unexpected announcement made to her, and she wanted a little time to collect her thoughts before she mixed with the family again.

It was the fourth of August, and on the eleventh he was to be there; and when he had seen and spoken to his father, he might speak to her. What should she say to him? The summer sun was beginning to decline and throw long shadows athwart the unshaded moorland, and turn its purple glory into the richest brown. The sheep which had been lying sheltered all day in the heather and the fern, were commencing to bestir themselves again, and speckle the hillside with dots of white. Stray hares and rabbits thought it time to peep out of their hiding-places, and she could see the trout leaping in the clear stream below.

And even as she thought how peaceful and how dear the landscape was to her, and that she might live her life out amidst its quiet beauties, and beneath the protection of one who was worthy of all her love and reverence, a little bird began to sing shrilly from a neighbouring bush, and Maggie's heart ran over.

Not in tears: there seemed too much certainty for them: but in a burst of gratitude to the Giver of all good, who had mapped out her present life as He had done the smiling scene before her.

She had a powerful voice, with tones as clear and dulcet as a bell; and as she pealed forth a verse of the grand hymn—

"Holy, Holy, Holy, Lord God Almighty,
All Thy works shall praise Thy Name in earth and sky and sea,"

the strain attracted the notice of Mr Bainbridge, who was in the shrubbery close by.

"What! my little Maggie!" he ejaculated, "all alone, with no one but the birds to listen to your singing? Well, never mind, we shall have an audience for you in a few days; for here is a second letter from Thomas, asking house-room for another of his friends. I was just going in to speak to Aunt Lizzie about it."

"I don't want an audience," said Maggie, shyly, as she rose and slipped her arm through that of her uncle.

"So much the better, my dear. Songs like yours are never lost, for they have listeners up there"—pointing with his finger to the blue arch above them—"and a chorus too, I reckon, if our ears were only quick enough to catch the sound of it. Ay, and He pays His singers too, as a Royal King should do. Stick to your songs, my daughter; they're the only ones worth learning, for they'll endure when Time itself has passed away."

Kind and fatherly as the manner of her uncle always had been, it was the first time he had actually addressed her by the name of "daughter," and as the unwonted term of endearment struck her ear, connecting it with the circumstance which she had just heard, Maggie's quick start of pleasure and surprise resolved itself into a quick sigh of full contentment.

CHAPTER VI.

COLONEL BAINBRIDGE AT CRANSHAWS.

No further allusion to the subject of her future prospects passed between Maggie Henderson and her Aunt Letty; and an occasional glance of intelligence on the part of the elder lady was the only intimation by which she conveyed that she had not forgotten the revelation made to her. But, after a while, even this furtive token of sympathy grated on the girl's feelings. In the first heat of her surprise at the proposition made to her, she had divulged far more than she intended—the secret which she had sacredly guarded for many months beforehand; and though it was only to Aunt Letty she had betrayed it—Aunt Letty, who had been the depository of all her little joys and troubles since her days of infancy, who had heard all her secrets thitherto, and was as true and as safe as the rock of Gibraltar itself—yet, that she should have disclosed her love to any one—the love which, up to that moment, had neither been asked of nor offered to her—was a cause of burning shame, and an episode upon which she could not look back without feelings of deepest annoyance.

She was only a country-bred girl, lacking in most of the requirements of fashionable society, but she possessed a refinement of character too often found wanting in the highest circles. Her tell-tale cheeks and eyes, unused to practise concealment where all about them was done openly, had foolishly blurted out her preference for her cousin before her aunt; but Maggie was terribly angry with them for doing so, and would have scorned to let them repeat the same story when in his presence. She was up to no one of the thousand little ways by which a woman of the world will let a man know he is agreeable to her, and she would have opened her brown eyes very wide, could she have been initiated into many scenes that take place between members of Belgravian coteries, who have no intention, and in many cases no power, of becoming more than lovers to each other (if triflers in search of mere excitement may be called by such a name).

Maggie's simple, old-fashioned notions, derived from the

homely experience of Aunt Letty and Aunt Lizzie, did not carry her beyond the exploded ideas, that it is the peculiar province of man to make love to woman; that an engagement deliberately entered into is sacred as a marriage, and that marriage itself is a death to illegal admiration and excitement, and a resurrection to all the domestic virtues which can be crowded into one female form. And, feeling like this, she was horribly ashamed whenever she remembered that she had overstepped the privileges of her sex, in making that revelation to Aunt Letty.

But there was no remedy for it now, and no comfort, excepting in the thought that she had not wilfully done wrong, and Miss Lloyd's promise of secresy was sacred.

Yet her distress and nervous anxiety increased as the time for Colonel Bainbridge's arrival drew near; and she seemed to realise how much easier, if disappointment came to her, it would have been to bear it all alone; so that, when she greeted her soldier cousin, she was, in reality, looking paler and less well than she had done for some time before.

Colonel Bainbridge, in company with his friends, arrived to the day appointed, for he was as particular in private as in professional matters, and, quite unspoiled by the hospitality which had been extended to him abroad, would have been ashamed to upset the regularity of the home management by giving himself any of the airs of a fine gentleman.

He did not notice the unusual timidity and quietness of Maggie's welcome, nor the subdued expression in her face; on the contrary, fresh from contemplating the waxen-like delicacy of Ethel Carr's complexion, and the trained grace of her movements, his little cousin's appearance and manners struck him as being far too robust and noisy for those of a young lady, and the fashion of her dress seemed equally to offend him.

"I say, mother!" he exclaimed, abruptly one day, as he followed Mrs Bainbridge into her private sitting-room, "when are you going to let Maggie have some new things?"

Mrs Bainbridge, who, with the traces of considerable beauty, and without being positively unladylike (her father had been a curate), was still one of those stout rosy-complexioned, countrified dames, whom one never suspects of having any blue blood concealed about their persons, deposited her comfortable self in an arm-chair; and then regarded her son over her spectacles with unmitigated surprise.

"New things, my dear Thomas! new clothes, do you mean? Why, your cousin had no less than four dresses made last month, and I believe the one she is wearing this morning is put on for the first time."

"Really? Well! I don't know how it is, I don't pretend to understand such things, but it doesn't look right to me. Ought not ladies' dresses to have some bobs and tails behind now-a-days, and little crinkley things all round the edge of the skirt?"

Lady Ethel's dresses being the only ones the man had ever taken the trouble to observe, had been made somewhat after the fashion he attempted to describe, and the remembrance of them was still running sadly in Colonel Bainbridge's head. But "bobs," and "tails," and "little crinkley things," were a paraphrase of the last Parisian mode, and a flight of dress-making altogether beyond the comprehension of his worthy mother.

"My dear Thomas!" she exclaimed, more amused than interested, "I really don't know what you are talking about; Maggie's dress appears very neat to me, and very suitable for a girl of her age, and Jeanie Ransom, who came over from Borthwick expressly to make it" (Borthwick was the nearest town, distant about ten miles from Cranshaws), "said that she was cutting all the ladies' dresses now exactly in the same style. And I know that Jeanie has the fashion-books regularly from London. What fault can you have to find with it?"

"Oh, none, mother! it is very suitable for her, as you say; and, after all, it signifies little what one wears in the country—only I should have liked Grant and Hammond to see Maggie at her best; and don't you think she is just a little brusque in her manners for so young a girl—a little off-hand in her way of answering, and so on? I may be too particular, but it strikes me so."

"Towards the other gentlemen, Thomas?—well, perhaps she may be, but I am sure you always find her considerate enough with yourself."

"Oh yes! I have no complaint to make on that score! Maggie is most affectionate and kind; she is a thoroughly good, honest little creature, and I love her dearly, which is, perhaps, the reason I perceive her faults sooner than I should those of another person."

"You can scarcely call it a fault, Thomas. In my time it was considered a *desideratum* in young women not to be too forward in their manners."

"Oh, by Jove! and so it is now. But Maggie certainly wants a little polish—she 'll never get a proposal if she sets her face so determinately against small talk."

"Our Maggie will not go begging for a husband," said Mrs Bainbridge, with an oracular smile.

"No! not if I can prevent it," rejoined her son, heartily; "she is too good for that." And then he sauntered off to join his cousin in the garden, whilst his mother hurried away to repeat the important conversation which they had held together to his father, for with her all his anxiety about Maggie's dress and behaviour tended to but one point—a conviction of the particular interest he took in her.

That he was interested in her was indisputable, though in a very different manner from what his parents imagined. From his boyhood he had seen this girl growing up beside him, like a younger sister, and his earliest memories of Cranshaws were associated with her bright face and winning ways. After a service of three years in India, he had returned home, about a twelvemonth previously, to find his childish playmate changed into a woman, but ready to extend the same affectionate welcome to him as of old. He had thought then (with the memory of the pallid faces he had left behind him fresh in his mind), that he had seldom seen a more attractive countenance than that of his country cousin, and if Colonel Bainbridge had ever stood in danger of falling in love with Maggie Henderson, it must assuredly have been at the moment of his return. A great deal of innocent but affectionate intercourse had taken place between the cousins at that period, but his stay at Cranshaws was necessarily limited, and when he quitted it to rejoin his battery at Woolwich, he left behind him an impression which, even at that date, he would have been shocked to discover.

Since which time he had mixed much, as has been said, in good society, and had his eyes opened wider and wider to poor Maggie's deficiencies.

He did not love her less; on the contrary, the more intimately he came to know her character, the more estimable he perceived it to be; but his organs of sight and hearing, rendered fastidious by the ultra-refinement of the circles in which he moved, began to be shocked by the rusticity of her address, and the obsolete, not to say vulgar fashion of her clothes.

Every one knows what a dress, let the materials be what they may, turned out by a country dressmaker, looks like—how it bulges out wherever it ought to lie flat, and turns all a woman's curves into squares, and makes its unfortunate wearer appear about as easy as though clothed in a suit of armour. Miss Jeanie Ransom's productions (although she did come all the way from Borthwick to make them) were no exception to the general rule, and Colonel Bainbridge's mind, already filled with a fairer and more fashionable image, had no leisure to bestow on the dissection of the generous, self-denying, womanly heart that beat beneath those ill-made coverings of silk and merino.

Yet he was pleased to hear his friends speak in warm terms of Maggie's bloom and youth, and as he gained her presence on the occasion alluded to, and threw himself beside her on the grass, the old brotherly feeling returned so strongly upon him that he longed to make her a confidante of the anxiety then preying upon his spirits.

This impulsive, tender, and compassionate little heart, he thought, which was always ready to listen, even to a beggar's tale of misery, would be so sure to sympathise with the prolonged pain of suspense occasioned by his uncertain hopes.

The girl changed colour as she saw his tall figure issue from the French windows of his mother's morning-room, and advance towards her, but Colonel Bainbridge was too indolent or too uninterested to observe the action.

"A glorious morning, Maggie!" he exclaimed, as he stretched his huge limbs lazily on the smooth sward; "but almost too warm for tramping over heather. I feel sadly inclined to waste a few hours in your company instead."

She did not appear to notice the indifferent compliment his words conveyed, but inquired, anxiously:

"Have you a headache, Cousin Thomas?"

For Colonel Bainbridge's altered looks had been the subject of universal comment since his arrival at Cranshaws, and he had been compelled in self-defence to attribute them to the effect of the late hours he had kept during the season.

"A mere trifle, Maggie!—I did not sleep well last night. What a lovely prospect we have from here! It is a thousand pities that Cranshaws is not nearer some good town. It is terribly isolated."

"But Borthwick is not much more than an hour's drive," replied Maggie, "and you can get everything there that you can possibly want."

Colonel Bainbridge laughed.

"Bah! my dear child! why, Borthwick is nothing but a stupid little pottering country town. I don't suppose there's a pair of gloves fit to wear to be procured in the place. No woman of fashion could dress herself from a hole like Borthwick."

"Oh no! I suppose not. I know so little about such things," said Maggie, timidly.

"But *you* are happy at Cranshaws, are you not?" he resumed presently. "It is pretty lively here, I suppose?—for the country, that is to say—during the summer and autumn weather. In the winter it must be unbearable."

"I never find it so," replied the girl, whose heart had commenced to beat very rapidly at his question, so significantly like that of her Aunt Letty; "but I have always lived here, you see."

"It might be vastly improved," he went on, dreamily; "there is no croquet-ground, and the paddock at the back of the castle would be just the place for archery. It was a mistake of my father's not having a billiard-table on the lower floor; that stupid orangery, which is no good at all and little ornament, just takes up the room required for it."

"He would have had little use for it, you see, cousin, as he never plays billiards himself, and your visits are so few and far between."

"But we shall change all that, perhaps, by and by, Maggie," he said, with a bright glance upwards. "I suppose you think I am such an old bachelor, there is no chance of my ever marrying; but more wonderful things have come to pass before now."

"Oh yes! I know," she answered, confusedly, as she bent her eyes upon the work in her hands.

"Heaven forbid I should wish to oust the dear old people from their places; but Cranshaws may own a younger mistress some day; and if that ever happens, I shall make it as bright and pleasant for her as I can. It would be a jolly place to live in for six months in the year."

"Uncle and aunt have lived in it all the year round," suggested Maggie, who could not help thinking what his parents would say to hear him speak so lightly of his obligations towards Cranshaws.

"Ah! yes—but then they are old people, who have never been used to mix in gayer scenes; you could not expect a young girl to be contented with what makes them happy. Now, tell me the truth, Maggie: do you really believe that a girl, say of your own age, could settle herself as my wife, down here at Cranshaws, and live through all the weary round of spring, summer, autumn, and winter, year after year, without wishing for something a little livelier than the company of her husband, and the prospect of these everlasting moors?"

"Oh! I don't know. I really can't tell," faltered his blushing cousin. But at that moment the voices of Sir Charles Hammond and his other friends were heard in search of him, and he rose to join them in their morning's sport.

"Think well of it, then," he answered, laughing, as he rose to his feet, "and let me have your deliberate conclusion. A great deal may depend upon it, Maggie; you don't know but what I shall be guided by your answer in one of the most important occasions of my life."

And so he left her, jestingly on his part it is true, but with a firm conviction on hers that Aunt Letty's surmise was correct, and that she should very soon be told that her cousin's future happiness was bound up in her own. And, thinking on his final words, Maggie shed tears of excited joy and gratitude.

CHAPTER VII.

A DECIDED REFUSAL.

It was but a few days after the circumstances just detailed that Mr Bainbridge called his son into his study.

"Can you give me a few minutes of your time, Thomas?"

"Certainly, father!" and in a second the door was closed behind him.

They were a great contrast, this father and son; for Mr Bainbridge was a small, stout man, with the rounded shoulders acquired from stooping over a desk, and plain unaristocratic features; and as he sat opposite his noble-looking offspring, whose personal appearance had been all derived from the other side of the house, a stranger would have found it hard to believe they were so nearly related to each other.

Yet there was *that* on the face of Mr Bainbridge which almost beautified it; which certainly made his friends forget that it was homely, and which, joined to its kindly expression, impressed all who saw it; and that was the stamp of a settled and abiding peace, such as had never softened the dark features of his son. Indeed, as they now appeared, notwithstanding his disadvantages of age and person, the father looked almost the younger of the two, for in many a tussle with the world and thought, the brow of Colonel Bainbridge had gained deep furrows, which Time, and a heart at rest with God and itself, had smoothed out of the forehead of the other.

And this fact seemed to strike Mr Bainbridge, as though almost for the first time, as he lifted his eyes and contemplated the careworn expression of the man who had thrown himself into a chair beside him.

"My boy," he said, affectionately, as he touched his hand, "there are more lines in your face than there should be at your age. You are not concealing anything from us, Thomas; you are in good health, are you not?"

"Perfectly so, father," replied Colonel Bainbridge, rousing

himself. "I have the strength of a lion and the appetite of a horse—if that is sufficient to satisfy you."

"The reason goes deeper, perhaps?" said the old man interrogatively, for to see the day when his son should feel as he did, was all he cared to live for; but we know what Englishmen are when any one, even a parent, attempts to probe their most sacred feelings. Colonel Bainbridge sat bolt upright in his chair, affirmed that if anything was to blame for his wrinkles, it was the climate of India, and putting on a look of the most perfect indifference, begged that he might hear for what purpose his father had desired to speak with him.

Mr Bainbridge returned to his desk with a sigh, but still with a degree of satisfaction. Here was, perhaps, the very remedy for his son's waning youth and premature cares; the means, too, by which Heaven designed to lead him into the way of peace. He entered on his self-imposed business with alacrity.

"I have just been looking over these papers," he said, "the title-deeds to the little farm of Brackenhaugh, our Maggie's single possession, you know. It's a poor place, very poor indeed; and we've only been drawing a pound an acre for the best part of it, for many years past. But Taylor, who held it up to Lady Day, has just vacated, and Robson, the Glasgow manufacturer, wants to take it on lease for the next fourteen years. He has two other farms about there, and Brackenhaugh divides his property. Only he won't give even as much rent as Taylor did, but promises, on the other hand, to use the ground for arable purposes. Now, my difficulty is this. Brackenhaugh ought to bring in a higher rent than Robson offers us, and so Maggie will be losing by it for the next fourteen years; but still the place wants draining and a dozen other improvements, and if I let it again to a sheep-grazier, the property will go on deteriorating till it's worth nothing at all. Robson will do his duty by it, for he's an affluent man and an honest one; and if Maggie is cheated out of part of her rent, she will profit by the loss in the end. But I should like to have your ideas on the subject, Thomas, for two heads are better than one; and it's hard to choose for another person."

Colonel Bainbridge had listened to this harangue with the

utmost astonishment. It was the first time in his life that his father had appealed to him for advice about anything connected with agriculture; and, considering that he had chosen his profession at an early age, and followed it closely ever since, it was but natural he should know nothing of such matters.

He remained quiet till Mr Bainbridge had finished speaking, and then, as might have been expected, he replied:

"I am really so totally ignorant of everything concerning the business of a farm, that I am afraid I can be of little service to you. I have never even seen Brackenhaugh, you know; so my opinion, if I had any, would be utterly worthless."

"Don't you think it is time you began to think of such things, Thomas?" said the old man, gently. "I may be called home at any moment; and if Cranshaws is not to run to waste after my death, you will be compelled to superintend the farm yourself."

"I trust that contingency is a very long way off," replied his son, affectionately.

"That is as *He* pleases, Thomas, though, whenever you are master here, I hope that you will be a good one. Not that that was my reason for introducing the subject of Brackenhaugh to you this morning," continued Mr Bainbridge, a slight degree of nervousness becoming apparent in his movements; "Maggie's interests are very dear to me, Thomas, and I should like to feel that you hold them so, and in the same degree."

"I do," exclaimed the younger man, firmly. "Have I ever given you reason to think otherwise, sir? I am as fond of Maggie as though she were my sister, and you may rest assured that I shall never divide her interests from my own." (This he said, thinking that the old man was troubled by the idea of what would become of his orphan niece after his own death.) "All whom you leave behind you," continued Colonel Bainbridge, "will become sacred charges to me, and I shall guard their happiness with the greatest care."

"I am sure of that, my son. But Maggie is the only child of my only sister: her poor mother used to be the plaything of my boyhood, as she has been of yours, and when she lay dying, she said I had made death easy for her by the promise that I would rear Maggie as my daughter. Now, I feel as though my deathbed would be easier if I could see her future lot decided before I lie down upon it."

"It may be," said Colonel Bainbridge, encouragingly. "Maggie leads rather a secluded life here, but I should think she was a girl who attracted a good deal of admiration."

"I don't want to see her married to a man who only admires her," replied the other, impatiently; "my fondest wish, Thomas, is to leave her settled *here* at Cranshaws."

"At Cranshaws?" repeated Colonel Bainbridge. At first he had some indistinct idea that his father desired to oust him from his heritage, and settle Cranshaw Castle on his cousin instead; but the moment his eyes met those of Mr Bainbridge, the truth flashed on his mind. "Do you want me to marry her?" he said, quickly; and then, struck by what appeared to him the absurdity of the idea, he burst out laughing.

Nothing could have grated so harshly on the feelings of the elder Bainbridge as that undisguised and hearty laugh. Had he been a worldly man, I should have said that he considered Maggie Henderson to be perfection; but, even as it was, he believed her to be as innocent and free from the taint of sin as is possible to a fallen creature, and that any man could ridicule the idea of an alliance with her was incredible to him.

Had his son looked surprised or thoughtful, or protested against his chances of success, or a becoming love for his young cousin, hope still might have remained behind, and persuasion have done much, but in that genuine mirth all concealment was impossible. It was evident at once that Maggie Henderson could never reign at Cranshaws.

Colonel Bainbridge saw that he had hurt his father's feelings, and hastened to apologise.

"My dear father, I am so sorry that I laughed, but pray dismiss that idea from your mind for ever. It can *never*, *never* be! I could as soon think of marrying old Hetty the henwife, whom I have known ever since I was put into jackets. Maggie and I are far too much like brother and sister to become anything nearer. It would be impossible!"

"I am sorry for it!" was all that Mr Bainbridge said in reply.

"*She* knows nothing about this, I hope?" resumed his son, anxiously.

"Oh no!" was the prompt reply, for it must be remembered that Miss Lloyd had never even mentioned that she had spoken to Maggie on the subject.

"Thank heaven for that!" ejaculated Colonel Bainbridge, "or it would have broken up all our pleasant intercourse. Father, I can't imagine what should have put such an idea in your head."

"It seemed feasible to me, Thomas; she is a sweet, loveable girl, and I suppose you will marry some day?"

A dark shade passed over his son's face.

"Perhaps so! but it is not at all certain. Anyway, I should have thought with your sound sense, that in the event of my marrying, you would have seen the advisability of my extending instead of contracting the family circle."

"Of raising it, you mean, Thomas!" rejoined Mr Bainbridge, quickly.

"Well, yes, father, of raising it," was the honest reply. "I am not ashamed of my birth, as you know; but your wealth and my profession enable me to take a higher stand in society than you have done, and to choose a wife in accordance with my improved position."

"You are ambitious of getting one with a handle to her name, perhaps, Thomas."

"She will make you none the worse daughter-in-law for that circumstance, if I am," was the hasty reply.

"I was rather afraid of that when I heard you had got amongst the aristocracy," said Mr Bainbridge, with a sigh. "I am not like many self-made men, Thomas; I don't rail against the aristocracy, and think it unfair that some should be born to a high station and others to a low. I know that God appoints our different conditions, and that what He does cannot be wrong. But yet I should be very sorry to see you take a wife from amongst them, and bring her home to Cranshaws to look down upon your mother, and aunt, and cousin."

"I should never bring home any one but a *lady*, sir," interposed the colonel, with marked emphasis.

"Ladies can be very bitter sometimes," replied his father, "when they don't fear God. The higher classes are exposed to more temptations in that respect than we are, Thomas; the flattery they meet with, the requirements of the society they move in, and the demands made upon their time, leave them in general little leisure to devote to serious things. Now, my dear boy, you know that I can't control you in this matter, and that I should not wish to do so if I could. But promise me one thing: that you will never bring home a careless, irreligious woman to be the mistress of Cranshaws."

Colonel Bainbridge moved uneasily in his chair. The only creature whom, at that moment, he would have made mistress of himself and his possessions, he knew nothing of, except that she was beautiful and that her image haunted his imagination. And yet he believed that, however careless in speech, she must be at heart religious (does not every man try to believe so of the woman that he loves?); and was sincere when he replied that he would never take a wife who was not, at the least, as pure and innocent as his cousin Maggie.

"Nobody is pure in this life," said Mr Bainbridge; "and the world's interpretation of innocence is very different from that of Heaven. Here, every woman is called innocent who has not grossly sinned. You are not a religious man yourself, Thomas (I wish to God you were), but you have been brought up, to the best of our ability, to know the signs of a religious life; and I conjure you, as you value your own happiness and our honest name, to marry no woman in whom they are absent. I have no more to say to you at present. I suppose your mind will never be altered on the subject we have discussed this morning?"

"I am sorry to have disappointed you, father; but it will never be altered. No thinking could bring me over to the idea—it is quite impossible."

"Very well, my son. Let us say no more about it. I trust, when you choose for yourself, that you may get as good a wife and Christian as that girl will make."

And then the conversation was concluded, and never again renewed between them.

But the disappointment which fell upon Aunt Letty and Aunt Lizzy, when Mr Bainbridge made the upshot of the interview which he had held with his son known to them, is not to be described.

Thomas had positively refused to take their Maggie as his wife; had even laughed at the idea of such a thing—it was incredible to them.

"He must have some other attachment," concluded Aunt

Lizzy. "Nothing less could make a man indifferent to Maggie."

"I am not so sure of that," replied her husband; "but I am afraid that Thomas is ambitious—that he hopes to marry higher; and connections entered into for worldly motives seldom turn out happily."

Aunt Letty said nothing; she remembered the words which had passed between her and Maggie in the garden, and her heart was bleeding for her darling.

"It is lucky our dear Maggie knows nothing of all this," resumed Mrs Bainbridge, presently; "if *her* feelings had been concerned in the matter, it would indeed have been a disappointment, though time and her good sense would doubtless have worked a cure."

"He who permitted the sorrow would Himself have provided the remedy," said her husband, confidently. And Aunt Letty laid up his words in her heart, and crept away to her own room to comfort herself with them as best she might.

She felt terribly guilty in the matter, as she realised how much more hard it would be for the girl to bear up bravely against her disappointment, knowing that the cause was patent to another. She longed to see Maggie undeceived and put out of pain at once; but she dared not speak to her upon the subject again—it would be too sore a wounding of her darling's pride. She could only pray that her eyes might be soon opened to the truth, and strength given her to bear the sight of it.

And, meanwhile, the glorious August and September days went on, and Maggie Henderson lived through them, a little anxiously, perhaps, but still quite undismayed by the prospect of the life that lay before her.

CHAPTER VIII.

LADY ETHEL IN DEEP WATERS.

Lady Ethel Carr felt the shock of her father's sudden death deeply.

It startled, frightened, terrified her, and for the first few weeks she was like some wild creature taken captive—flying from side to side to find an outlet for her sorrow, and driven back from all points on herself and her own miserable thoughts.

And then she sank into a state of apathy, from which nothing seemed to rouse her, and it was sad to see so young a creature sitting hour after hour with her mournful eyes fixed upon the blank wall of her apartment, and turning a deaf ear to the solicitations of her attendants, that she would take either food or rest.

Yet her despair was not unnatural, for she had no hope with which to brighten it. Unable to remember her mother, and her father having been the only one of the home circle who had engaged her affections, she felt as though in losing him she had lost everything. It was the first time Death had stepped in between her and any one she loved, and it was all so dark and terrible, she did not dare even to think of it.

She told herself, of course, and in a manner she believed, that her father had been taken from earth to heaven, and that some day she should meet him there.

But in Ethel Carr's ideas (as in the ideas of so many of the young and careless) Heaven, instead of being a happy home to which she might be called upon to journey any day, was a very vague, misty, unsatisfactory sort of a place, where, by some means or other, everybody would be united at last, to spend eternity in a fashion which she had no hesitation in affirming would be abominably dull; but which was an event so far off in the future, having nothing in common with our present existence, and only connected in her mind with doomsday and the end of the world, that she never troubled herself to think of it seriously at all.

Meanwhile, her father—her dear, dear father whom she had loved so much—had been taken from her, and hid in that dark, dreadful grave, of which she could not think without a shudder. He had disappeared, as it were, into impenetrable blackness, and she could only remember that in this world she should never see him more.

But, through all her misery, Ethel's pride continued to reign paramount. She was cold and stately in her grief as the marble statues which adorned the corridors; she disdained to ask for sympathy, and there was no one found bold enough to offer it to her.

Lady Clevedon, whose part it should have been, was too much occupied with her crape and bombazine, and the most correct style in which to clothe the youthful earl, to have any leisure to bestow on her step-daughter; and bitterly as Ethel was grieving, perhaps even at that moment she would have resented any attempt at comfort on the part of her father's widow as an infringement on her rights as chief mourner. For between these two women there existed, and always had existed, an antagonism which was none the less deadly because it hid itself beneath a mask of smiles and caresses and endearing appellations.

Lady Clevedon had been jealous of her step-daughter from the first, of her superior influence over the earl, and the lofty, dictatorial air which she had never been persuaded to abandon; whilst Ethel viewed her young step-mother in the light of an interloper, and her beauty as a fatal snare by which her father had been unfortunately betrayed.

And, added to this, there had lately sprung up a fresh source of rivalry between the two, which threatened to be more dangerous still.

With these feelings towards Lady Clevedon, it was very bitter for poor Ethel, when the will was read, to learn that, with the exception of a small marriage dowry, she had been left entirely dependent on her step-mother. She had heard her father say so on the night of his death, and on several occasions beside, but she had attached small meaning to his words, or rather she had imagined she should be free from all authority but that of a husband before they would be put into effect; now she felt as though the circumstance were almost more crushing than the blow which had preceded it.

The Earl of Clevedon had died very much in debt, to which the extravagance of his Countess had largely contributed, and his landed property descended by entail on his infant son, who was but two years old. There was little doubt, therefore, that the young mother would be amply provided for whilst the child's minority lasted; and if, on its cessation, her charms were still left "blooming alone," she had always her marriage settlement to fall back upon. But Lady Ethel Carr, at once the fairest and the proudest of her sex, was commended to her kind affection and maternal care.

Under other circumstances, this would have been the most pleasant and natural position in which to leave an orphan girl; but to Ethel Carr it was intolerable pain.

She had several offers of a home made her, from relatives on both sides of the house; but her proud spirit saw no difference in one form of charity from another, and she resolved to abide by the lot her father had chosen for her. She had but one comfort in prospect—but one star shining on the dark horizon of her future—and that was that Victor de Lacarras would release her from her bondage before long. Had it not been for that hope, she would almost have died from disappointment and wounded pride.

But the first wildness of her grief over, her heart returned with yearning fondness to the scene which had passed between them on the balcony, and she cherished the words which he had then spoken as a sure pledge that he would be the champion of her future life. She knew it was not the moment that such assurances should be repeated or exchanged; but with her own ears she had heard the avowal of his love, and she was satisfied.

As soon as the Earl's interment was completed, Lady Clevedon proceeded, as had been pre-arranged, to Nice. A house had been engaged there for the winter, and she thought she could not do better than spend the first months of her widowhood abroad, where Lady Ethel Carr of course accompanied her. They quitted London immediately after the funeral, and without seeing any of their friends again, for which the Countess had her own reasons, and Lady Ethel was, comparatively speaking, glad.

She would not have cared to meet the Marquis de Lacarras after what had passed between them, as an ordinary acquaintance. She preferred to live upon the memory of that scene, and to wonder how long it would be before it was repeated.

Could she have overheard a conversation which took place about that time between Victor de Lacarras and one of his club-friends, Lady Ethel would have been better able to come to a decision on the subject.

The name of the club-friend was Colonel Hartley, familiarly known amongst his intimates as "Paul Pry," on account of the wonderful facility with which he wormed out other men's secrets, and the interest he took in everybody's business but his own.

He was an elderly man, much made-up, both by tailor and hairdresser; and he attacked the Marquis on the day after Lady Clevedon left town; and as he was standing in one of the club windows, thoughtfully regarding the traffic which went on in the street below—

"Well, De Lacarras, and so you have lost your friends!"

"What friends?" demanded the Marquis, turning an indifferent gaze upon the speaker.

"Why the Clevedons, to be sure. No Temple Grange shooting for you this season, old fellow, whatever you may have secured by next. Queer will, that of the earl's, though, wasn't it?"

"In what way?"

"Do you ask me in what way? I should have thought you would have been the last man to dispute it. Why, in leaving Lady Ethel Carr without a halfpenny. I know it's the case, because Hogden, the earl's solicitor, is doing a little business for me, and I've seen him since the reading of the will."

"I daresay Lady Ethel will survive it."

"And you?"

"I have no possible interest in the matter: what should make you appeal to me?"

"Oh! come, Marquis," exclaimed Colonel Hartley, with one of his most Paul Pry-ish looks; "it is of no use trying to hoodwink me. Everybody knows what was your attraction in Park Lane this season; and that, had it not been for this melancholy circumstance, we should have seen you a Benedict before Christmas."

"Everybody knows a great deal more about me than I

know myself then," rejoined De Lacarras, with an expression of annoyance; "and if your report is correct, Hartley, you may contradict it as soon as you like."

"You are *not* engaged to Lady Ethel Carr?"

"*Engaged!*" (Victor de Lacarras delivered the word with as much emphasis as if he had been accused of some dishonourable action). "Do I look like a man who is *engaged?* I should like to meet the person who has been spreading such folly abroad."

"I should certainly never have taken you for a marrying man," said his companion, who began to draw in his horns at the other's manners.

"*Marrying man!*" repeated De Lacarras, contemptuously. "Now look here, Hartley, judge for yourself if it is likely. Every one knows my circumstances; that I'm a regular beggar, without sufficient money to keep up my title, and in debt all over the world. How could I, in the name of all that's reasonable, dream of marrying a girl like Ethel Carr, who, by your own showing, has not a halfpenny? It bears absurdity upon the face of it."

"But you have not been unfavourably received in that quarter, Monsieur de Lacarras, if rumour speaks true," ejaculated old Hartley, with a meaning look.

The Marquis turned away to the window with a smile which meant even more than his friend's look—such a smile as men of the world put on when taxed with gallantries which they have not the strength of mind to deny—such a smile as is death to the hopes of any woman who has been led to place her trust in them.

"That may be so," it said, as plainly as though he had spoken; "but it is not my part to boast of it." And then the men separated, Victor de Lacarras to think how fortunate it was that he had not committed himself by proposing to Ethel Carr before learning her penniless condition, and Colonel Hartley to spread several reports concerning them, by no means beneficial to her character or his.

CHAPTER IX.

AT TEMPLE GRANGE.

It was not a long time before the Countess of Clevedon wearied of the monotony of Nice. Six months had been considered the shortest period for which she should observe her retirement; but long before that time had expired, she announced her determination to return to England and take up her quarters at Temple Grange.

"I am quite sure that Nice does not agree with Alured," she said, in explanation to her step-daughter, and alluding to her son; "besides which, my spirits require cheering, and at the Grange I can ask some of my sisters down to spend their Christmas with us."

And cordially as Lady Ethel Carr disliked the Countess's sisters (who were all a degree faster and more flirting than herself), she acquiesced readily in her decision, for she also was becoming, not tired of Nice, but weary for news of Victor de Lacarras.

She had grown fond of the quiet, peaceful spot which had ministered to her first sorrow, and in a measure taught her to overcome it; but she longed to hear again that voice, the music of which was ringing in her ears by night and day, and to receive the re-assurance that her lover loved her. For the memory of that interview, which had been interrupted by the fatal tidings of her father's death, was a sacred memory to her; she had lived on it for months past, and would have staked her life upon its repetition.

She was not surprised that she had received no letter from the Marquis, or at least she told herself so. She told herself that it was far more delicate, and honourable, and forbearing in him not to press his suit at a time when he must know that her heart was sore, and occupied with graver things. He had heard her confess she loved him—and at the recollection of what she had said on that occasion, and his passionate rejoinder, Lady Ethel's cheeks would flush scarlet with mingled shame and pleasure—he must be certain she should never change her mind; and was satisfied to wait, as she was, until the proper period for a renewal of his courtship had arrived. And yet—and yet—that waiting time was sometimes marked by very anxious tears.

It was December when they arrived at Temple Grange. Everything around was looking bare, grey, and desolate; and Mrs Mowbray, the Countess's favourite sister, was confined to her bed with an attack of bronchitis, and powerless to rise and dance attendance on her.

These circumstances combined to ruffle the equanimity of Lady Clevedon's temper, and she was loud in her complaints of the dulness of everything about her.

"I *must* have a few people down, just for Christmas and the New-Year," she said, when the state of affairs became patent to her; "my sisters won't thank me for asking them here without a man to speak to, and Dr Chalmers says that if I don't take more care of myself I shall be seriously ill. And no wonder, such a time as we have been moping at Nice."

"Is it not rather soon?" inquired Lady Ethel, alluding to her step-mother filling the house with company, when she had so recently been made a widow, although her own heart was throbbing at the idea that *he* might be amongst the intended guests.

"Not at all!" was the pettish rejoinder. "We mustn't have any dancing or theatricals, or anything of that sort, of course; but, otherwise, there is no reason on earth why we should not see a few friends in a quiet way. With that dear child depending entirely on me, 'it is of the utmost importance,' as Dr Chalmers says, that I should not permit my health to suffer, which it most assuredly will do if I cannot shake off this dreadful depression. I shall only ask my sisters and the Marchmonts, and two or three men; and I shall tell them that they are to expect no gaiety, for it is to be quite a family gathering."

Lady Ethel asked no further questions, for she knew that Lady Clevedon had guessed her *penchant* for the Marquis de Lacarras, and was too proud to evince any interest on the subject of his being one of the invited. But she had not many days to wait in suspense.

"They will both come," laughed the Countess, lightly, as she threw two envelopes across the breakfast-table to her a few mornings after. "I thought as much." And Ethel, recognising on one the emblazoned cypher of Victor de Lacarras, took up his letter with a trembling hand, and perused the brief courteous sentences in which he accepted her step-mother's invitation.

The flush which they called forth had not yet died away when she turned to the second letter, and with a sudden start read the signature of Thomas Bainbridge.

"That *horrid* man! Whatever made you think of asking him?" she said, abruptly.

"Really, Ethel! That is a polite way to speak of one of my friends. I asked Colonel Bainbridge because I like him, and he likes me. Is not that a sufficient reason?"

"Certainly, if it is the case; but I was not aware that your mutual acquaintance had progressed so far. I cannot say I acquiesce in your opinion. The man is beneath us, in birth, and station, and everything."

"Ah! you must make allowances for me, Ethel; my blood is not so blue as yours, remember; I am but a commoner myself, so I can sympathise with Colonel Bainbridge. Any-way, let us hope that his residence at Temple Grange for a few weeks may not have the power to contaminate you."

"Were he to take up his residence here for ever," replied Lady Ethel, haughtily, "it would make no difference to me. He and I have nothing in common, and should be no better acquainted at the end of five years than five days."

"Poor Colonel Bainbridge!" said Lady Clevedon, with mock compassion. "It is well my sisters have a higher opinion of him than yourself, or I should feel inclined to ask him to postpone his visit. But Harriet writes me word that he is still considered *the* match *par excellence*, and seems quite excited at the prospect of meeting him here."

"I trust that Miss Trevanion may derive all the advantage from his acquaintance that she desires," replied Lady Ethel, as she rose from the breakfast-table.

Meanwhile, Colonel Bainbridge did not at all consider him-self an object for compassion. He was in a state of the utmost delight at the unexpected invitation he had received to Temple Grange, and feverishly anticipating the moment when he should go there. Since his return from Scotland, he had been working steadily with his battery at Woolwich, often heaving a sigh as he thought on the events of the season past; and wondering if, in the coming one, he should meet with Lady Ethel Carr again. He felt how visionary were his hopes respecting her, but he told himself that if she would not marry him, no other woman should.

And in the midst of this vague, unsatisfactory train of thought, came Lady Clevedon's note, like an earnest of success, inviting him to join a family gathering at Christmas time, and in her country house—the first, too, which she had assembled since her husband's death.

What man, hoping as he did, would not have been startled by such a proof of interest? He had been but one of hundreds who had partaken of Lady Clevedon's hospitality during the past season, and if his silent admiration of Lady Ethel Carr had been observed (and he had reason to believe the Countess had observed it), there was the greater reason that he should not be singled out to meet her in the privacy of home life. Unless, indeed—and here a hope, faint as to precedents, but strong enough to make the man's brain reel, would interpose itself, and turn his future into one great glory. He had been going down to Scotland as usual, to spend his Christmas week; but he wrote and made his excuses for not doing so at once. He told the truth; the Countess of Clevedon had invited him to spend a short time at Temple Grange, and he should be sorry to lose the opportunity of doing so: he did not seem to consider that any other reason was required for breaking faith with the home circle. At Cranshaws, his announcement was received with various feelings.

Mrs Bainbridge, notwithstanding her disappointment, was proud to think her son should be associating with such grand people; but Mr Bainbridge read the title with a sigh; and Maggie's face (which had been growing very pale and thin since his visit in the autumn) turned just a shade paler as she tried to console herself with the promise in his postscript that he would try to get another fortnight's leave, and run down to see them in the spring instead. So true it is, that seldom can one reap joy in this world without entailing sorrow on another. On the day that Victor de Lacarras was expected at the Grange, Ethel Carr did not know herself. She, ordinarily so quiet and self-possessed, accustomed to stamp on her emotions with the iron heal of pride, was almost alarmed to find her feelings had outstripped her will, and that she was as nervous and trembling as the most ordinary creature born. She had never realised till then, she said, with a frightened look at her pale anxious features in the glass, how much she cared for him. She felt as though she could not walk down into the room to meet him; and yet she knew that not only must she do so, but that the eyes of her step-mother and her step-mother's sisters would be fixed upon her the while, eager to mark her agitation, and delighted if she publicly displayed it.

That thought alone was sufficient to nerve her for the coming interview, and perhaps Lady Ethel Carr had seldom looked lovelier or more defiant than when she emerged from her dressing-room that evening, and set her foot on the staircase which led to the apartment where she knew the company to be assembled.

The deep mourning robes which she still wore for her father set off the transparent delicacy of her skin and the beauty of her golden hair to the greatest advantage; whilst a soft flush, called forth by anticipation, relieved the pallor which her face had too often displayed since his death. She would not yield to the inclination which called on her to pause and try to calm the rapid beating of her heart, or still her trembling nerves; but passed swiftly on until she reached the ante-chamber to the drawing-room. Even as she stood upon the threshold, she saw a figure quickly leave the side of Lady Clevedon and advance towards her. She felt the pressure of his hand, and heard him utter a few ordinary words of greeting, but she never could remember afterwards how she had met him; for at the sound of his voice a sickly faintness assailed her, which made her fear lest she should fall, or betray what she was feeling. And perhaps she might have done so, had not a wholesome correction awaited her upon the other side.

"I trust that Lady Ethel Carr has not quite forgotten me," said a voice from that quarter; and turning with relief to any distraction from the immediate presence of Victor de Lacarras, Ethel placed her hand almost eagerly in that of Colonel Thomas Bainbridge.

CHAPTER X.

SPORT TO HER AND DEATH TO HIM.

THE dinner, and evening that followed it, passed much in the manner that such entertainments do, where the gathering is small and private, and the conversation becomes general.

The Miss Trevanions, by forwardness and much talking, contrived, as they usually did, to monopolise the lion's share of attention; and, after a due amount of coffee and drawing-room ballads, the party separated for the night, without its having been possible for any two of its members to exchange a quiet word with one another. And yet, somehow, Lady Ethel felt disappointed at the result of the meeting to which she had been looking forward with such ardour, even whilst she was angry with herself for feeling so.

The Marquis de Lacarras had met her as any other gentleman of her acquaintance would have done; as he had been used to do whilst her father was alive; and under the circumstances she could not have expected him to do more. It would have been wrong, indelicate, unseemly; she would have been the first to blame him if he had dared to make any open demonstration of his attachment to her; so she said, with the quick eagerness of a woman to deny any imputation of coldness in the man she cares for. Victor would take a proper opportunity to renew the conversation which had been interrupted; in a few days all would be right between them, and she would be enabled for ever to silence the insinuations and stop the sneers concerning him, which she had so often found it hard to bear from the lips of Lady Clevedon. And so Lady Ethel went to sleep that first night very full of happiness and trust. But, when day after day slipped away without the Marquis making the slightest effort to see her alone, or the remotest allusion to what had passed between them, her pride took alarm, and she asked herself whether it were possible she could have been mistaken.

Was the scene which had taken place upon the balcony, and every particular of which she so vividly remembered, only a delusion of her fevered brain? Had Victor de Lacarras never really told her that he loved her, and asked for the assurance of her affection in return? and had she been dwelling for all these months upon a mere chimera, the product of her vain imagination?

Lady Ethel, with her face buried in her hands, sat down in her own room, seriously to consider this. Oh, no! it was not fancy, her memory was too clear, her love too real, she could never have invented so much happiness.

She saw again the balcony lighted only by the stars, watched the white hand creeping on her own, heard the low fond tones, and felt the warm kiss laid upon her lips.

It was not fancy; she had passed through and felt all this; she had been deceived and made a fool of; she was of all women the most miserable.

Now it necessarily happens in a small coterie such as was assembled at Temple Grange, that there is little privacy for any one. There is no seclusion so perfect as that of a large crowd, where each individual is occupied with his own concerns, and too busy to pry into those of his neighbour; but in a family party, separation means estrangement.

Consequently, Lady Clevedon, who was most particular in impressing on her guests that she was living in the utmost seclusion, and could not hear of anything like gaiety, took care that whether they rode, or drove, or walked, each one should share in the amusement! but if it happened, as it very often did, that her "poor head ached," or her "poor heart felt heavy," and she claimed the privilege of bereavement to be left behind, she generally managed that the Marquis de Lacarras should be her companion.

"You are so good, you will not mind staying with a stupid creature like myself," she would say, on such occasions; and Victor de Lacarras, with all a Frenchman's fervid politeness, would affirm that he had no pleasure equal to that of waiting on the wishes of his amiable hostess.

Lady Ethel was not annoyed at this: she had none of the petty jealousy which would keep a man for ever loitering by her side, and she knew that the manner of the Marquis, like that of many foreigners, was *empressé* towards every woman with whom he happened to be brought in contact. But when she found that he never attempted to break the Countess's chains in order to remain with her, and that his services appeared to be always engaged either by her step-mother or the Miss Trevanions, her mind, loath to give itself up to the despair which was fast coming on it, passed into another phase of feeling, and she clung to the idea that it was by Lady Clevedon's means that the Marquis was prevented coming to an understanding with herself. She remembered how, even during her father's lifetime, her step-mother had vied with her in attracting his attention, and she believed that she was doing all she could to come between them now.

Lady Ethel knew that she was proud, that many called her cold and reserved, and she was aware that she had never gone one step out of her way to afford Victor de Lacarras the opportunity for which he might be diligently seeking. On the contrary, on more than one occasion, fearful of her conduct being misconstrued, she had purposely avoided being left alone with him. She might have been wrong; thinking the matter quietly over in her chamber, she decided now that she was wrong; and that if such an accident occurred again she would not shirk it.

A large conservatory opened from the drawing-room at Temple Grange; and two days after she had arrived at this conclusion, Lady Ethel was standing on its threshold, looking at the bright array of winter flowers, when the Marquis de Lacarras approached her leisurely.

"A splendid show of camellias," he said, following her glance.

"Yes! is it not?" she answered, in the nervous tone with which she always now addressed him; "and the nearer you look at them the more beautiful they appear," with which words she stepped into the conservatory. It was a long one, and Lady Ethel walked slowly to the end of it, and back again; but Victor de Lacarras had not followed her. When she returned to the drawing-room, Lady Clevedon was sitting there alone.

"So your invitation was not accepted," she said, with a sarcastic laugh. "Upon my word, Ethel, I did not give you credit for so much forbearance. I should feel just a little piqued with the indifference of *Monsieur le Marquis* if I were you."

The hot blood rushed to Ethel's cheek and brow, and she

was about to give an angry rejoinder, when her words were checked by the re-entrance of the Marquis himself, accompanied by Colonel Bainbridge.

"My dear Lady Clevedon," he exclaimed, addressing his hostess, "we come to ask a favour of you. We have got up a scratch-race in the park below—just a couple of hurdles, you know, and a ditch of water; but we shall derive no pleasure from our little burlesque unless the ladies honour us with their presence, and encourage us with their smiles. Pray let me conduct you to the scene of action; the Miss Trevanions have already gone on under the charge of Major Marchmont."

"What, *Monsieur!* is it to take place immediately?" she said, laughing. "Indeed, then, you must manage your race without me, for it is much too cold to stir out this morning, in my estimation. But here is Lady Ethel, who, I am sure, will be only *too pleased* to accept your escort; you can offer her your arm instead."

Lady Ethel, who had been standing, flushed and indignant, by the table whilst Lady Clevedon was delivering her emphasised harangue, now drew back with a gesture of refusal.

"Many thanks, *Monsieur*," she said, as she bowed in acknowledgment of the Marquis's extended arm; "but Ethel Carr prefers to choose her cavaliers to having them chosen for her, even by so good a judge as Lady Clevedon;" and with a smile that was too openly scornful to pretend to be in play, she passed him by, and placed her hand upon the coat-sleeve of Colonel Bainbridge.

The Countess burst into a loud laugh, whilst Victor de Lacarras bit his lip and looked annoyed, and Colonel Bainbridge, colouring with pleasure at the unexpected preference shown to him, led his beautiful companion from the room.

The glance of displeasure with which the Marquis had viewed this act on the part of Lady Ethel did not escape her notice, and prompted her to follow it by many of the same sort. If he choose to neglect her, she said passionately to herself, he should at least be made to see that there were others ready to take the place he had abandoned.

And since between Colonel Bainbridge and himself there had always been a very apparent though unavowed dislike, no less than because the former was always near at hand to aid her in her scheme of retaliation, it came to pass that he was made the tool of Lady Ethel's revenge, and from having studiously avoided his company it might almost be said she courted it. Her heart, burning with resentment at the slight put upon her by the altered conduct of Victor de Lacarras, she thought of nothing and no one but herself and her own wrongs, and in self-defence she used the first weapon which came in her way. That Colonel Bainbridge, cherishing the feelings which he did for her, should have been that weapon was unfortunate for him and for herself. And yet she scarcely thought of the great evil she was doing him; nor was she conscious of the consequences she was drawing down upon her head until she was roused to a sense of the situation in which she had placed herself by receiving an offer of marriage from him.

It was after an evening of great excitement on all their parts—an evening during which Lady Clevedon had entirely appropriated Victor de Lacarras, and flirted with him in a manner so open as to call down censure on herself from even the lenient lips of Mrs Marchmont, and in the sight of which, Ethel Carr, deaf and blind to everything but what concerned the man whose ungenerous behaviour was eating out her heart, had permitted Colonel Bainbridge to say more, and to go further, than she had ever suffered him before—that she found a note, in his handwriting, placed upon her dressing-table.

Half fearful of what it might contain, and yet scarcely believing in her intolerant pride that he would presume to make her an offer of marriage, Lady Ethel tore the letter open, and read as follows :—

"DEAR LADY ETHEL,—If you deem me presumptuous in addressing you on a matter which lies very near my heart, you must blame the kindness which has emboldened me to do so ; but after the events of the last few days, and especially of this evening, I feel that I can wait no longer to ascertain my fate ; for every extra moment of suspense becomes a purgatory to me. I cannot remain at Temple Grange unless it is as your accepted suitor. Am I to go—or stay ?—Believe me, yours always, THOMAS BAINBRIDGE."

CHAPTER XI.

THE RIVALS.

When Lady Ethel read this letter it was late at night; the guests of Temple Grange had separated for their respective chambers an hour before; and had she not, in a vain endeavour to shake off the restless anxiety which oppressed her, been loitering and laughing in the room of Mrs Marchmont, she would have received it on first going up-stairs.

She was alone—her sleepy maid was nodding in the ante-chamber, waiting for the sound of her mistress's bell—and no one was witness of the feelings with which she perused it.

And it was as well, for those feelings were very bitter. She had been thinking much more leniently of Colonel Bainbridge lately; but this letter changed all the current of her thoughts. She was not generous enough to observe what a manly, straightforward proposal it was, nor to remember that her encouragement had forced it from him, but a mighty, unwomanly indignation, and a hot sense of having been insulted in her father's house by the man whom Lady Clevedon had chosen to invite there, rose up to choke all thoughts more befitting the situation and her sex.

She was hard, contemptuous, crushing, in the first knowledge of his presumptuous hopes, and her angry heart cried out against Victor de Lacarras as the accomplice by whose cruel conduct this indignity had been brought upon her.

Everybody was, in Lady Ethel's mind, to blame, except herself, and her resentment knew no bounds. As for Colonel Bainbridge and his probable suffering, those were matters left out of the question altogether. Her first impulse had been to tear the letter into shreds, and cast it to the winds; her next, to show her step-mother what had come of her insisting upon asking people to the house who did not know how to preserve their station in society, and the stern means by which she intended to teach them the lesson. Always impulsive, when her weak point had been interfered with, without further reasoning, Ethel flew down the broad staircase and into Lady

Clevedon's dressing-room. But it was unoccupied, excepting by the servant working patiently by the fire, who, in answer to the young lady's excited inquiry, replied that her mistress had not yet come up-stairs.

It was all the better—so thought Lady Ethel—for her stepmother would be alone; and what she had to say to her was not a subject fit for listeners.

Her light feet scarcely sounded on the rich carpets she traversed between that chamber and the drawing-room, which had been deserted, as she thought, so long before.

But, as she gained the doorway, the low murmuring of voices reached her ear, and without further preface, she drew aside the heavy *portière* and stood upon the threshold.

At the scene she witnessed there her heart seemed as though it turned to stone; for on one of the low sofas which had been wheeled near the fire, there reclined easily the form of the Marquis de Lacarras, whilst by his side, still in her evening dress, her hand clasped in his, and her wealth of auburn hair laid caressingly upon his shoulder, sat her father's new-made widow—Gertrude, Countess of Clevedon.

Lady Ethel stared at them without speaking a word; yet that undefinable instinct which makes us *feel* without knowing that we are observed, caused the pair upon the sofa to turn their heads and quickly change their position. But before they did so, Lady Ethel had dropped the *portière* and was gone.

"Who was that?" said the Countess sharply to her companion.

"It was Lady Ethel Carr," he rejoined, moodily, and then they drew apart from one another, and there was silence between them for a little space. It was interrupted by Lady Clevedon's nervous laugh.

"I shall have to make some excuse or other to her, I suppose, to-morrow morning?" she said, inquiringly. "Can you help me to one, Victor?"

"There is no occasion to ask me," was the quiet answer; "you know that you are much cleverer than I am."

The Countess sighed, gathered up a shawl which had fallen off her shoulders, impatiently, and holding out her hand, affirmed it was high time that all respectable people bid each other good-night.

The Marquis took the proffered hand, released it without sc

much as a pressure, and turned on his heel towards the smoking-room; whilst his fair hostess walked off to her own apartment, and rated her maid for her stupidity and awkwardness until she drove the unfortunate menial into giving her warning.

Meanwhile, Lady Ethel Carr was creeping—creeping slowly, like one who has received a severe blow on the head, and is blinded or dizzy from the shock—back to the shelter of her own room.

She passed through the ante-chamber, mechanically letting fall the sentence, "I don't want you," to the servant as she went, and then she locked her door and sat down by the dressing-table (still in a kind of stupor), and spread out her hands upon her lap, and tried to understand what was this misfortune that had overtaken her.

I have drawn her as a vain and arrogant girl—as one whom many would call heartless; but in this hour of her deep humiliation, every head should be uncovered before her.

O women! women possessing not only hearts and souls, but warm, full life, and the natural impulse to be loved, I appeal to you if there is any life so cruel, any death so hard to bear, as the life which has been robbed of the affection which was all in all to us, and the death of hopes which we had considered to be certainties. No man can understand this grief as we can, for we were made for them, not they for us; and love us as they may, we never can fill up every chink and cranny of their lives, as their affection does for ours. And we are so utterly powerless to do more than sit down, and cry our eyes out over their inconstancy.

When Lord Clevedon died, his daughter thought she had lost everything; but in this moment of discovering that her lover was untrue to her, she felt that she had never yet known what it is to be really poor. Up to that moment she had hoped against all hope; now hope was done, and love, and life, and everything finished. She had seen his perfidy with her own eyes.

When Lady Ethel's meditation reached this point, a vivid picture of her own deserted and desolate condition rose up before her mental vision, and struck with pity for what lay in the future, she cast herself prostrate on the floor, and gave vent to an exceeding bitter cry.

Oh, that her life were ended; that she could die of grief just where she lay; that she might never more see the hateful light of day, nor hear the voices of her fellow-creatures! How could she ever bear again to go through the monotonous routine of daily existence: to listen to the song of birds, or walk amongst the flowers: how could she support the intolerable pain of living? O Victor! Victor! And the mere mention of his name brought down a flood of tears which did not cease until nature was well-nigh exhausted.

For an hour or more the wretched girl lay on the floor, moaning quietly to herself, or giving way to fresh bursts of sorrow, as memory recalled to her what she had lost. And then there came a lull. With a sudden effort, Lady Ethel rose to her feet, and staggeringly approached the mirror. Was it her own image she saw reflected there? or had a midnight ghost sprang up to personate her? Her eyes were bloodshot, her eyelids dark and swollen, her face ghastly pale, and down her fair smooth cheeks the tears seemed already to have cut two little channels for grief. As she gazed at the effect of her unusual emotion, the idea struck her that in a few hours all the world of Temple Grange would see them too, and become masters of her secret. That thought was sufficient; in a moment her predominant passion had sprung into full play; and Lady Ethel, ashamed of her weakness, even though no eye had been witness to it, hastily bathed her burning features in order to eradicate the traces of her grief. She would not allow *him* and—and—Lady Clevedon (this last name brought out with a dry, hard sob) to have the pleasure of triumphing together over her crest-fallen and woe-begone demeanour.

If it killed her, if she died of suppressed agony the moment afterwards, she would yet appear at breakfast on the following morning, and look them both straight in the face, and make them believe she had never been more happy.

Happy! Merciful God! and everything connected with happiness was over for her!

O Lady Ethel! pray! If every friend in this world had forsaken you, you have still the Best, and the Highest, and the Nearest of all Friends left; and One Who takes far greater interest in the blighting of these wretched earthly affections than His creatures give Him credit for.

But the girl could not pray, she did not even think of praying; from first to last of that long night of agony, a wild mention of the name of the Almighty was all the appeal she made to Heaven for help in her distress.

How was she to escape from the life-long misery of seeing them together? That was the next question that came to torture her.

She could act her part for a few hours, for a few days, perhaps for a few months; but could she trust herself to act for ever? to live in the same house with him, as the husband of her step-mother—in the position of his *daughter*—and at the thought, so sadly ludicrous, so unnaturally probable, an hysterical laugh rang sharply on the night air, to be followed by a tremendous burst of passion. It should *never* be!—and her foot stamped, and her pale features kindled beneath the rising storm—he had insulted her enough already; they had combined together to outrage her most tender feelings; they should never have the satisfaction of seeing her heart daily trampled on.

But how to escape from it! she, who was tied down in miserable dependence upon Lady Clevedon's pleasure: how was it possible for her to evade the hourly pain which her step-mother would so well know how to inflict upon her?

At that moment, her eye fell upon the letter which contained Colonel Bainbridge's proposal, in which he made her the offer of his heart, a matter she was perfectly indifferent to—of his home, the refuge she was seeking. Lady Ethel's breast heaved, and her breath came quickly. Was it possible she could accept it? She sank into a chair, and taking the crushed letter in her hand, smoothed it out and read it over carefully. She was still gazing at it in a vacant stony manner, when the first rays of morning streamed through her bed-room window and looked upon her pale and careworn face.

Then she rose; and with the same fixed expression as though she were walking in her sleep, deliberately summoned her maid to her assistance, and having first refreshed herself with a warm bath, proceeded to make a most elaborate toilet.

CHAPTER XII.

CASTING THE DIE.

THERE were various feelings at play in the hearts of those who assembled round the breakfast-table at Temple Grange that morning. Lady Clevedon, especially, would have been puzzled to explain exactly what she felt. She was half-nervous at the idea of encountering her step-daughter (for she had never yet arrived at the knowledge of Lady Ethel's character, and was uncertain whether she would resent the blow her pride had sustained by an open show of resentment or indifference), but at the same time she experienced all a woman's triumph at the defeat of her rival. For that was the real position in which she stood to her late husband's daughter. For months before Lord Clevedon's death, she had viewed the attentions of the Marquis de Lacarras to Lady Ethel Carr with the keenest jealousy, and had done all in her power to divert their tendency. And her first thought on becoming a widow had been how best and easiest to secure them for herself. But the game was not yet in her own hands. She had met the Marquis in the corridor that morning, and with a pretty pout of injured innocence, accosted him with the complaint :

"You have made me quite afraid to meet Ethel again, Victor ; I am sure she will repeat that story everywhere. You have compromised me most terribly."

"If so, it will be for the last time," he replied, carelessly, "for I return to town this afternoon ;" and then Lady Clevedon had been ready to contradict all that she had said, in her endeavours to make him stay.

But the Marquis was determined, for he would rather any *contretemps* should have happened than that Lady Ethel Carr should have witnessed his familiarity with her step-mother.

He was a wild, dissipated man, careless and unthinking, but his heart had never so nearly approached loving any woman as it had done the daughter of Lord Clevedon. Had her father lived, he would doubtless have proposed to her—in fact, he was on the point of doing so when they were interrupted in the balcony; and notwithstanding he had congratulated himself since that he had not gone so far, of late—and especially since Lady Ethel had bestowed so many of her smiles on Colonel Bainbridge—he had nearly arrived at the conclusion that he *did* care for her, and that, fortune or no fortune, he must tell her so again.

And now, by one act of folly, he had ruined all his chances of success, for he knew the girl's disposition too well to believe she would ever forgive such a direct insult to her affection.

Why had he ever permitted it? The Marquis de Lacarras pulled his silky black moustache thoughtfully through his fingers, and was unable to answer the question.

Ah! why indeed? Why was he not stronger than ninety-nine out of a hundred of his fellow-men, subjected to the same ordeal? He was weak, and selfish, and irresolute by nature; and "the woman tempted him!"

A man requires to be something more than stoical to push away the head that uninvited is laid upon his shoulder; to disengage his hand from the soft clinging clasp of feminine fingers; and, reminding their owner to be a little less free with him, run the risk of being called a "brute" and a "bear," amidst tears of disappointment for his pains. Women seldom forgive the man who dares to read them a lesson on the virtue which should be their own peculiar province; and Victor de Lacarras was not sufficiently bold, nor sufficiently particular, to care to draw down such resentment on his head.

Besides, the Countess of Clevedon was a very pretty woman—and uncommonly fond of himself—and since no one would be the wiser, no one could be the worse. So had he argued at the moment, and so would he have argued to the end of time, had not the fact of his folly having had a spectator entirely changed the aspect of affairs. *Then* he was a fool; Lady Clevedon an *intriguante;* and the sooner he turned his back on Temple Grange, and the chance of getting himself into a scrape, the better.

And so much more uneasy even than Lady Clevedon was he at the idea of seeing Lady Ethel again, that when the breakfast had proceeded half way without her having made her appearance, he would have escaped to the shelter of his own apartment had it not been for the fear of meeting her alone upon the stairs. So he kept his place in moody silence, refusing to smile at his hostess's most brilliant sallies, and making a great pretence of being occupied with the contents of his plate every time a footstep approached the door.

There was another person at the table that morning who awaited Lady Ethel's approach with nervous solicitude, and that one, as may be supposed, was Colonel Bainbridge. It was the licence with which she had permitted him to address her the last few days, and the bright looks she had cast upon him, which had emboldened him to write to her; but he had done so while in the flush and excitement of her unexpected notice; and by the cold morning light, his boldness appeared very like unpardonable presumption.

Did she consider it so? Was this unusual delay in her appearance an indication of her consent to, or her refusal of, his wishes; and would her eyes as they met his shed an encouraging forgiveness or paralyse him with their scorn?

His whole heart filled with these perplexing questions, Colonel Bainbridge sat on thorns till he should learn his fate; showing but too plainly, by his inattentive and distracted manner, that his thoughts were not with the business in hand. But, even as he pondered, the dining-room door flew open suddenly, and she was in the midst of them.

The meal had been a dull one until then, for the Countess's gloom had proved contagious, Mrs Marchmont looking tired, and the Miss Trevanions annoyed at the listless and absent demeanour of their cavaliers.

But with Lady Ethel Carr the vapidity dispersed, for she came forward so springily, and with such a well-acted smile upon her countenance, that brightness seemed to enter the room with her. At her approach, the men of the party rose to their feet, but she motioned them to their places again with a light wave of the hand.

"Pray don't disturb yourselves. I don't deserve it, for I know that I am shockingly late. Good-morning, Gertrude. I hope you slept well. Good-morning, Mrs Marchmont. *Monsieur*, we will shake hands when breakfast is concluded," and then she nodded smilingly to the rest of the company and took the chair which Victor de Lacarras placed for her. She had noticed each one there by word or look excepting Colonel Bainbridge; but as she was about to seat herself, she felt that he was still standing, and involuntarily raised her eyes to his. Something in their expression, something betwixt humble pleading and a man's demand for his rights, touched the best portion of her nature, and for the first time a sense of the wrong she was about to do him excited her compassion, and rising, she stretched out her hand across the table, and put it into his.

A quick flush of pleasure kindled the bronze features of the soldier, as he reverently accepted the honour done him; and the Marquis de Lacarras turned his head the other way, and pretended he had not witnessed the compliment she had denied to himself.

Meanwhile, Lady Ethel's tongue ran on glibly.

"A beautiful morning, is it not? We really must not waste it in-doors as we did that of yesterday. Gertrude, cannot you devise some plan to amuse your guests? We have done nothing but yawn and look at each other day after day. Could we not make up a riding party somewhere? You are fond of riding, Colonel Bainbridge, of course,—a soldier always is;" at which appeal the man she addressed coloured again furiously, and said he should be only too pleased to accompany Lady Ethel Carr anywhere.

Lady Clevedon looked at her step-daughter with amazement, and indeed any one cognisant of the facts related would have done the same. She had expected to see her pale and dejected at the very least; or if she smiled, do so in a forced and unnatural manner; but nothing could appear freer and more unconstrained than the behaviour of Lady Ethel. Her dress, too, which bore tokens of having been arranged with the utmost care, was lighter than any in which she had hitherto appeared; her black robes being relieved by mauve-coloured ribbons, whilst knots of the same shade were interwoven with the golden glories of her head. She looked more like a triumphant victor than a fallen rival; and as the Countess regarded her smiling face, she was almost disposed to question whether she had not been mistaken all along, and there had ever been a *penchant* for Monsieur le Marquis de Lacarras lurking in her step-daughter's heart.

Some one remarked that the beauty of the morning would

not last, and that some one else had prognosticated the approach of rain.

"In that case," exclaimed Lady Ethel, "we really must invent some entertainment for in-doors. Gertrude, is it quite impossible that we should get up a dance this evening? Christmas comes but once a year, remember."

"I am surprised at your asking it," returned the Countess somewhat indignantly, for she would have been better pleased had her step-daughter appeared less gay; it robbed her of so much of her victory; "when you know the circumstances under which we are assembled here, and the proviso I made with my guests respecting gaiety."

"Ah! forgive me! I forgot that the days of mourning were not ended," with an arch look across the table. "But we young ones really want something occasionally to keep our spirits up. Don't you find it very dull here, Colonel Bainbridge?"

She was still torturing them all round—causing Lady Clevedon to look daggers, whilst her guests tittered against their will; covering Colonel Bainbridge with confusion by her pointed queries, and making Victor de Lacarras remember every second that she had lifted the *portière* to the drawing-room the night before—when the breakfast came to a conclusion, and the company broke up into little groups and sauntered out of the room, leaving her standing there—with the exception of one other—alone.

Then all the forced spirit and *diablerie* died out of the girl's face; and she withdrew into one of the embrasured windows, sick at heart and trembling with indecision; for she knew that the hour was come, and her fate was in her own hands.

It was not a second before Colonel Bainbridge joined her.

"Lady Ethel, let me have my answer," he said, frankly; "suspense is so difficult to bear."

But she leant her head against the panelled wall and closed her eyes and answered nothing. She had thought that she had quite made up her mind; that she was determined to accept the relief his letter offered her, but now that it had come to the point of saying "yes" or "no," her courage failed her, and she felt as though she *could* not put the sign manual to the death of all her hopes.

Her silence threw cold water on the fire of his expectation, and when he next spoke his manner had become much more subdued.

"You received my letter?"

"Yes."

"Then be merciful, and if there is no hope for me, put me quickly out of my pain. You don't know—you cannot understand"—here his voice sank at least two tones lower—"what I am suffering."

"I cannot—I mean, I"——

"You mean that I have made a fool of myself, only your heart is too tender to tell me so. Lady Ethel—if it is the case—only say that you forgive me; that you can make allowances for my presumption and do not despise my love—an honest one, I swear to you—and I will try to be content with your decision."

But still she had no words in which to tell him that he was mistaken. Again and again she tried to find her voice, but her powers of utterance seemed to have forsaken her, and the syllables died away upon her trembling lips. At last the man before her, perceiving her prolonged distress and futile efforts to say what she wanted, accepted her silence as a sign that hope was over for him.

"Lady Ethel, I see it all. There is no need for you to speak—I thank you for your great forbearance—I shall leave Temple Grange this afternoon."

So he said huskily in his deep manly voice, whilst two thirsting eyes were fixed upon her now pallid countenance, drinking in each detail of the beauty they never expected to look upon again.

She raised her own, scared and half-irresolute; and at that moment, as though to strengthen her decision, the Marquis de Lacarras, with his hands in his pockets and a cigar between his lips, sauntered leisurely upon the terrace which ran outside the window. At that sight the angry light which flashed into her face would have been apparent to any but a lover. And all her determination seemed at once to return to her.

"Colonel Bainbridge, stay one moment! I wanted just to tell you"——

"Don't be afraid of wounding me," with a sad smile; "I

am very strong, remember, and can bear misfortune as well as most men."

"But this—you may not think it so; it is, that you must not go away; there is no need; I"——

"Ethel! is it possible that you would give me hope? has my great fear misled me?"

"You can stay at the Grange as long as ever you like. I—I—accept your offer, Colonel Bainbridge."

CHAPTER XIII.

THE NEWS TRAVELS NORTH.

It would be difficult, without giving a digest of his character, to explain how this sudden and unexpected fruition of his dearest hopes affected Colonel Bainbridge.

In the first place, then, he was no universal lover, which circumstance arose, most probably, from the fact that his feelings were deeper than those of most men. Without being that odious hybrid, a male prude, he had never been very open to the attacks of the other sex, chiefly because his mind was occupied with matters of deeper importance. But he had always entertained a wholesome reverence for women—a reverence which made him believe the best of them—and hold the old-fashioned creed that the virtuous of their sex were not to be approached or spoken of with undue lightness or familiarity. A pure woman, whether as maiden, wife, or mother, was in his eyes as something sacred; and therefore it is not to be wondered at, that for many months he was contented silently to worship Ethel Carr. He had not frittered away his honest heart upon a score of women—knew nothing of their nature—had not been used, in fact, to being courted, and did not therefore recognise the signs of indifference which she exhibited towards him. Had he gone through but one such scene as took place between her and Victor de Lacarras upon the balcony, Colonel Bainbridge would have known better. But for a man, and respecting women's ways, he was most innocent. Lady Ethel's coldness he called purity, almost persuading himself he would not have it otherwise, and he regarded her beauty much as we do that of a perfect statute set upon a shrine, as something to dream of, and long after, but not to touch. And when, encouraged by the sudden warmth that came into his statue, he poured forth the story of his love, and found, as he thought, that she was responsive, his happiness knew no bounds—he was like one delirious with joy.

Not a doubt crossed his mind as to the motive for her acceptance of his offer; it was her extreme goodness, her sweet tender nature and undue appreciation of his worth, doubtless, that had prompted her, for the sake of his great love, to overlook his deficiencies of birth and station and character; but that the heart he considered so valuable a prize was burning away with rage and jealousy and disappointed passion, and that she had only accepted his proposal in order to rid herself of the continual presence of a faithless lover, never entered his ideas for a moment.

Lady Ethel had said that she would be his wife. In a few months, this peerless creature (in his eyes the fairest and most stately of all womankind) was to become his own possession; to set up in the highest niche to which he could elevate her, and worship with all the strength of his noble generous heart to his life's end; and Thomas Bainbridge was more than grateful for her condescension. And if, as day succeeded day, and her reserve became, if anything, greater than it was at first, he experienced just the shadow of a disappointment, he consoled himself with the idea that it was the bashfulness of a girl's first love that made her shrink from any contact with him, and that he would not have seen her free and forward (like the sisters of Lady Clevedon for instance) for all the world.

Yet, men "about to marry" would do well to mistrust the feelings of that woman who, after having confessed a preference for them, shrinks from the circling embrace of their arm —the pressure of their hand. Nature may teach her modesty; but modesty and love are not incompatible, and love casts out fear.

Colonel Bainbridge, at the period spoken of, would have scouted the morality of such a sentiment. To him, timidity and reserve appeared such beautiful and desirable things just then, particularly as Lady Ethel Carr had so large a stock of them on hand.

He wrote home, to convey the news, in a perfect fever of delight. Totally forgetful, in the exultation of success, of the conversation which had taken place between them in the autumn, he dilated largely, in a letter to his father, on the extreme beauty, high birth, and aristocratic connections of his *fiancée*.

Mr Bainbridge was alone when he received this epistle, and it troubled him greatly.

He seemed to have had a foreboding all along that it would come to this—that his son's large expectations and position in society would be found sufficient to purchase him a wife, who considered that she lowered herself by becoming his; but it was no less a disappointment to him.

All his little schemes about Maggie, his hopes of gaining a daughter for his old age, instead of losing a son, were dashed to the ground at once; for he was too sensible and clear-sighted to suppose that a Lady Ethel, reared in the hot-bed of folly and fashion, would ever be contented to sit down quietly in the domestic circle at Cranshaws, and call him and his good dowdy old wife by the names of father and mother.

No! he must give up that idea once and for ever. Thomas was no longer a boy, and he trusted he had chosen for his own happiness; but that that happiness would henceforth be separate from theirs, was without doubt. So that it was with a grave face he called Mrs Bainbridge to read her son's communication, and pass her opinion on it.

It was much more favourable than her husband's. Woman-like, the good mother was dazzled by the reported beauty and the high-sounding title, and began to think at once what the people of Borthwick would say when they heard of Lady Ethel Bainbridge. She was not at all dismayed, either, at the notion of entertaining a town-bred young lady at Cranshaws Castle, and even went so far as to wonder if her intended daughter-in-law had any unmated brother that would do for Maggie.

"It is the best thing that could possibly have happened to Thomas," she concluded, oracularly; "and it may be the making of his cousin. Maggie will marry a lord, next, my dear—mark my words."

"Oh! I hope not—I trust not," replied the old man, fervently. "It is bad enough to lose Thomas; but I couldn't part with my little Maggie yet awhile. Pray don't put such notions into the child's head, Elizabeth; she must wait till I am gone before she leaves Cranshaws."

"Nonsense!" exclaimed his wife, who was not to be reasoned all at once out of her conceit. "You would never be so selfish, surely, as to tie the poor girl down to a dull country house, when she might have the chance of getting a title. When Thomas is married, Lady Ethel will doubtless invite Maggie to stay with them in London, and there is no saying what luck may not be in store for her. But come along, my dear, and let us go in to breakfast, and tell the good news to them at once. I am sure, if I set them guessing, it would be hours before they discovered our secret." And dragging her husband with her, Mrs Bainbridge descended, all pomp and flutter, to the breakfast-room, where Miss Lloyd and Maggie were waiting for them.

Maggie Henderson was certainly not looking well. The sickness of deferred hope had robbed her cheek of much of its bloom, and her figure of its roundness. The neighbours said she wanted change of air, and her uncle and aunt had more than once urged a trial of the remedy upon her; but Maggie was resolute to stay at Cranshaws, and had been allowed to have her way. She performed all her duties as regularly as theretofore; was constant in visiting amongst the farmpeople, reading to her uncle, and teaching in the Sunday school; but the vivacity and spirit which had formerly characterised every movement was gone, and a dull listlessness had taken its place. She was as gentle and as good as ever—rather more so in fact—but her bright smile was less often witnessed, and her gay laugh had ceased altogether. She was suffering the tortures of silence and suspense, than which there is no agony more intolerable; and the hopes which she had almost thought herself authorised to cherish were being slowly starved to death. Yet no one guessed the cause of her altered looks and manner, except Aunt Letty—Aunt Letty, who, unknown, shed tear for tear with her darling, and watched each change in her condition with the anxiety of a mother.

They were already seated at the breakfast-table, when Mr and Mrs Bainbridge entered the room.

"Such news, my dears!" exclaimed the latter, exultingly, as she received their morning kisses. "Now, just try to guess what it is—but you never will, it 's quite impossible."

"Blossom has calved," ejaculated Miss Lloyd, alluding to the expected *accouchement* of a favourite heifer.

"Cousin Thomas is married!" said Maggie Henderson, with the intuition of affection; but she was scarcely prepared for the immediate answer.

"Yes, you are right! Only fancy, your guessing it so

quickly, Maggie. He is not married, though, but going to be, which is the same thing, and to the daughter of an earl. I never was so astonished in my life."

"I hope it may turn out well," remarked Mr Bainbridge, as he sank with a sigh into his chair. Maggie said nothing, but walked away and seated herself behind the tea equipage, to attend to which was her peculiar province. Aunt Letty's eyes involuntarily followed her there, but there was something in the girl's face that forbid scrutiny, and she re-turned her attention to her sister.

"You surprise me greatly, Lizzie," she said, in a voice which shook with agitation. "Surely it is very sudden. Has Thomas written to you himself about it?"

"He has written to his father; here is the letter," replied Mrs Bainbridge, as she produced it; "and I fancy from what he says he must have been courting the lady for some time past. He writes very enthusiastically about her appearance, which he describes as perfect."

"A lover's folly," ejaculated her husband, impatiently. "We had better leave that until we can judge of it for ourselves."

"But, my dear, Thomas would never be guilty of an un truth, and he says distinctly that she is very beautiful. Just listen here: 'It would be impossible for me to describe her loveliness to you; it must be seen to be appreciated. She is a thorough blonde, with blue eyes and golden hair, and very perfect features, and was considered to be the belle of last season.' He could scarcely say more than that, I think."

"She must be very handsome," replied Aunt Letty, with a furtive glance every now and then towards the tea-urn; "but you have not told us her name, Elizabeth."

"Lady Ethel Carr," said Mrs Bainbridge, with great unction, "the daughter of the Earl and Countess of Clevedon. 'Her father is dead,' Thomas says, 'and her little brother, only eighteen months old, is the present earl; but her mother is still the Countess:' nothing can rob her of that."

"And it is quite a settled thing, then; you are sure that Thomas will marry her?" demanded Aunt Letty, presently.

"As sure as one can be of anything in this world, I suppose," replied her sister. "They are engaged to each other, at all events; and Thomas says it is probable the marriage will take place shortly, but that it will be quite private on account of Lord Clevedon's recent death."

"Which will prove very convenient in this instance," said Mr Bainbridge, with what was, for him, a most unusual degree of sarcasm, "as it obviates the necessity of asking one's country relations to take part in the ceremony. I see that Thomas particularly mentions that none but the immediate members of Lady Ethel's family will be present. It is just as well. You and I would be quite out of place there, wife, amongst earls and countesses."

"Now, my dear, I think you are hard upon our boy. Thomas has never been ashamed of his parents yet; he has been a good son to us; and surely we may trust him to choose a wife for himself."

"Yes, he has been a good son, and I thank God for it; but he has made a mistake in this matter, as he will find out to his cost by and by."

"Well, I can't think why you should set your face so much against it, when most people would be delighted at the prospect of such a match. Aunt Letty, you have said nothing yet upon the subject. Don't you think it appears a most desirable connection?"

"If Thomas is really attached to the lady," commenced Miss Lloyd in a tremulous voice. She was waiting nervously for some sign or sound of agitation from behind the tea-urn; but, except for the clatter of the sugar-tongs and tea-cups, all there was as still as death.

"Attached, my dear! attached is no name for it; if one may judge from his own words his affections seem to be most deeply engaged. And, then, fancy what a thing it will be for Maggie there to have a cousin brought up with such advantages; why, as I was telling Mr Bainbridge, it may be the making of her. We shall have you coming out as a London belle next season, Maggie."

"Never! whilst I have a voice in the matter," exclaimed her uncle, energetically; and then Mrs Bainbridge abandoned dangerous ground, and confined her conversation for the rest of the breakfast hour to speculating which room she should give up to the married couple when they visited Cranshaws; and whether it ought not to be completely re-furnished and decorated for the reception of so aristocratic a bride.

Meanwhile, Maggie Henderson had raised neither eyes nor voice; and, fortunately for her maiden pride, both Mr and Mrs Bainbridge were too much occupied with their own reflections to pass any on her silence.

All she hoped—all she prayed for—was that she might be enabled to preserve her equanimity unbroken, until she had gained the privacy of her own room. And, therefore, she would not trust herself to speak or look up from her occupation, but went on mechanically with her duties, trying even not to think or understand, until she had earned the luxury of doing so.

Aunt Letty, who was feeling the occasion almost as cruelly as the girl herself, after having made one or two futile attempts to turn the conversation into a less painful channel, sat, pale and anxious, on her chair, answering her sister's questions in monosyllables, and longing for the moment when she should rise from table and release them.

It came at last. Mrs Bainbridge shook out her ample skirts and stood upon her feet; Mr Bainbridge, with his hands beneath his coat-tails, took up a station on the hearthrug; and Maggie, turning the key of the rosewood tea-poy, fled, like a lapwing, to the upper stories.

There Aunt Letty quickly followed her. She feared lest the strong restraint the girl had placed upon her feelings all through the breakfast-time, should result in an hysterical or fainting fit. She did not yet half know the strength of Maggie's character.

She reached her bed-room just as she had entered it. Maggie was leaning on the chest of drawers, as though to support herself; her face was very pale, and she seemed to have some difficulty in breathing; yet, as she caught sight of her aunt's anxious countenance, she tried to smile.

"Aunt Letty! will you leave me quite alone for a little while—no! not *alone;* I never can be that—but, by myself—I shall be all right again in an hour or two."

And so Miss Lloyd retreated, having offered neither comfort nor caress, and left the girl alone with God and sorrow. Where even her love feared to intrude, curiosity must not seek to enter.

CHAPTER XIV.

MAGGIE'S STRENGTH.

It was noon when Maggie's pale face peeped into her Aunt Letty's bed-room door.

"Has anybody been inquiring for me?" were her first anxious words.

"No one, my darling! Your uncle went out on the farm directly after breakfast, and Aunt Lizzie has been engaged all the morning with her housekeeper. O Maggie! I am so deeply grieved about this business!"

Her niece closed the door and drew nearer to her, but she answered nothing.

"I do so feel for you, my darling! so young, so full of life and happiness! to have all your prospects blighted in this manner; it seems too cruel to be true."

"*All* my prospects, aunt? Is that the comfort you draw from your own teaching?"

"All your worldly prospects, dear; though I trust, indeed, that even they may only be blighted for a while. You will get over this disappointment after a time, Maggie, and find some one who will appreciate your affection more than Thomas does; at least I hope and pray so."

At this allusion Maggie started.

"Aunt Letty! tell me one thing; tell me the truth. Did uncle ever speak to him about—about what he so much wished?"

Her niece's anxious eyes were staring her full in the face, and Miss Lloyd, even had she dared, could not have evaded the inquiry.

"My darling! I believe he did—just mention it, but your cousin's affections were, doubtless, even at that time engaged; and so he could scarcely have been expected, you see, Maggie" — with a yearning look into the girl's countenance, over which an expression of the deepest pain was passing.

"Of course not! don't say anything more about it, Aunt Letty. It may make it a little harder, but there is only one thing left for me to do now, and that is to try and bear it as well as I can. And you must help me, dear; not hinder me."

"*Hinder* you, Maggie! when I would sacrifice all I have to give you any comfort or pleasure."

"I am sure you would, and therefore I have the more confidence in asking you, as a favour, to speak to me henceforward as little on this matter as may be. I have been thinking it well over, Aunt Letty, and I am sure my best plan will be, if possible, never to mention it again. I have spoken too openly and too freely of it already."

"But, my dear child," exclaimed Miss Lloyd, in whose eyes to discuss and weep over a misfortune appeared the very "luxury of woe;" "what will you do if you have no one to whom you can sometimes unburden your heart? it will kill you, Maggie, never to speak of what is weighing on your mind!"

"I have always one Friend to whom I can unburden it," replied the girl, simply.

"Look here! Aunt Letty!" she went on presently, finding that her companion made no response to her last words; "I should like to tell you exactly what I think about this matter; and then we will consider the subject a forbidden one.

"No one is to blame, remember. My cousin certainly is not; and I—I hope I have not done very wrong in encouraging feelings for which he had given me no sanction—therefore, that thought must make it easier to bear than if it had been otherwise, and I have been thinking even this morning how small a trouble it appears besides those that some people are called on to endure."

"The back is fitted to the burden, Maggie, and this is an overwhelming trouble to invade your quiet, inexperienced life."

"Aunt Letty! do you want to make me more discontented and rebellious than I am? If you knew what wicked thoughts I have entertained during the last few hours, you would see no occasion for it. But, in the midst of my ingratitude, I recalled a conversation which we had on the day—the day I first told you about myself (do you remember?) and I felt so ashamed—so bitterly ashamed."

"What was it, darling? it has slipped my memory."

"About the martyrs, and their dying for the faith; and I told you how I wished I had some means by which to ascertain how much my faith was worth; and as soon as I remembered that, Aunt Letty, I saw the purpose of this sorrow. It was as though He stood before me, holding out the cross for me to bear. Shall I shrink from it?"

Maggie's figure was drawn up to its full height, her hands were clasped together, her eyes were kindling with devotion.

Miss Lloyd regarded her with silent admiration; she felt her pupil had outstripped herself.

"And it seems to me, Aunt Letty, that since we *must* endure whatever pain He sees fit to send us, whether we will or no, the only way by which we can show our love to Him is to endure it cheerfully; to *lift up* the cross instead of letting it drag after us. And I have read somewhere," she added, in a lower voice, "that when we do that heartily, and with all the strength of our poor will, He always bears the heaviest end of it Himself. Crosses are ever so much lighter when we carry them in company, Aunt Letty," with a little wintry smile stealing over her young features.

"O Maggie!" exclaimed Miss Lloyd, in a tone which was almost reverential, "you are teaching me a lesson to-day which I shall not easily forget. My brave girl! I had no idea you were so lion-hearted; you are a little heroine, Maggie!"

But at these words Maggie looked up in a hurried fearful manner, as though frightened at the honours she was called on to sustain.

"*Brave! lion-hearted! a heroine!* O auntie! how little you know of the poor, weak, cowardly spirit I possess!" and to Miss Lloyd's surprise, in another moment she was sobbing in her lap.

"Let me cry, auntie! don't try to stop me; it is for the last time! we will forget to-morrow that this has ever been."

"Not forget it exactly, perhaps," she added, after a pause, as she rose to her feet and dried her streaming eyes; "but we must act as though we had forgotten it. I have so many duties here, Aunt Letty. I owe so much to those who have been like parents to me, that I should be worse than ungrateful if, in return for all their kindness, I permitted them to be unhappy on my account, or even to suspect that I was so upon my own. Therefore, unless this matter should be forcibly dragged before our notice, we will not talk of it again, will we?"

"Just as you please, my love. But oh! if I could only see you happy!"

Maggie pondered for a moment, and then slowly and deliberately she answered:

"*I am happy!* I never knew until this moment how much I owe to your teaching, dear, and to your example, without which I never should have realised that all you taught me was the truth. I suppose this will be a very heavy trouble to me; but I can say truly in the face of it, that I have lost neither the best Hope, nor the dearest Friend, that I possess."

"Thank God!" ejaculated Miss Lloyd, and when the girl had left her she thanked Him on her knees.

CHAPTER XV.

FROSTED WEDDING FAVOURS.

It was, perhaps, an hour after she had accepted Colonel Bainbridge's proposal, that Ethel Carr entered Lady Clevedon's morning-room.

"Are you disengaged, Gertrude? I want to speak to you."

There was so little difference between her age and that of her late father's wife that she always called her by her Christian name.

Lady Clevedon glanced up at the determined features of her step-daughter, and grew uneasy. She felt certain she had come with the intention of speaking to her of the occurrence of the night before, as it was not the first time Lady Ethel had taken her to task for light behaviour, and she had no wish to have scandal afloat about her in the early months of widowhood.

And so, on the principle that the first thrust has the advantage, and forgetful of the adage "*qui s'excuse s'accuse,*" she answered the simple query addressed to her with the warm remark—

"I know exactly what you have come to say to me, Ethel; and though it is altogether out of your province to mention the circumstance, yet as you *did* see us, I have no objection to tell you that the situation (though, doubtless, sooner or later, it must have occurred) was hurried on by the foolish interest I take in your affairs. I say foolish, because hitherto it has been a thankless task, as you well know."

At these words Lady Ethel stood amazed. She had sought Lady Clevedon with the sole intention of informing her of the alteration in her prospects; and to allude in the remotest degree to the conduct of the Marquis de Lacarras was the last thing to which her proud heart would have prompted her. Now, however, as her step-mother's last sentence struck her ear in her surprise, she ejaculated:

"*My* affairs!"

"Yes! yours. I know that you are very independent,

Ethel; but I have been left by your dear father in the position of a mother to you"—(Lady Clevedon could be so *very* motherly when it suited her purpose)—"and I should not have thought I was doing my duty—after all that passed last season, and what I have seen during his visit here—if I had not asked Victor what were his intentions concerning you."

"Concerning *me!*"

It would be impossible to describe how much force Lady Ethel threw into this sentence, nor how white and still she turned, like a living creature suddenly transformed to marble—all except her eyes, which glowed indignant fire on the woman who had prepared this insult for her.

"You spoke to the Marquis de Lacarras concerning *me?*" she repeated, after a slight pause. "Then I consider that you took a most unwarrantable liberty with my name, Gertrude."

"A liberty!" exclaimed Lady Clevedon; "what next? Do you suppose I was going to permit the man to hang about you as he did last season, causing your name to be connected with his own by every one who saw you, when I had very good reasons for suspecting that he meant nothing more by his attentions than the most ordinary politeness? *Your* eyes may have been blinded, Ethel; perhaps, under the circumstances, it was natural they should be; but mine were not!"

"With what object, then, did you ask the Marquis down to Temple Grange?"

Lady Clevedon commenced to play with an ivory paper-knife.

"I suppose it is not absolutely incumbent on me to divulge the reasons for everything I do to my step-daughter. One object, though, certainly was to discover how far he intended to trifle with your feelings."

"I am infinitely obliged to your ladyship for the interest you take in what concerns me," interposed Lady Ethel in a tone of sarcasm.

"Now it is of no use your being angry about it, Ethel, for to do so was my plain duty, and I put my own feelings in the matter entirely on one side." (And here Lady Clevedon bit her lip, and looked sideways at the paper cutter, and tried to get up a little natural confusion.) "I put the question to him last evening, and his answer—well, I suppose from what you saw that you guess what his answer was—and indeed he only seemed surprised that I should have ever imagined his affections were engaged in any other quarter. Of course I am sorry there should have been any understanding on the subject, Ethel, and I certainly should not have mentioned it so soon; but as it is"—— and here Lady Clevedon smiled at the paper-knife, and waited in malicious expectation for some token of her rival's discomfiture.

But if she expected to receive such a gratification she was disappointed, for Lady Ethel's voice, when raised in answer, was more than urbane—it was positively mirthful.

"Indeed, Gertrude, you have been giving yourself most unnecessary trouble on my account; for, in the first place, the situation in which I surprised you is not a sufficiently novel one to demand any explanation at your hands; and in the second, you could not pay me a worse compliment than by supposing I have the least desire to have been your substitute. I am afraid you must have wasted the valuable time of yourself and the Marquis de Lacarras to small advantage; for had you but left my affairs out of the question until this morning, I could have told you what I have just come to announce—namely, that I have accepted the offer of Colonel Bainbridge's hand."

Lady Clevedon for the moment looked confounded.

"Of the artilleryman! is it possible?" and then she burst into a laugh. "My dear Ethel, excuse my merriment, but your opinions concerning him must have changed so very rapidly."

"Opinions do change rapidly, sometimes."

"And it is really settled—*un fait accompli?* Well, I must congratulate you, for he is an uncommonly fine-looking man, and will be, they say, as rich as Crœsus. So, notwithstanding a few trifling disadvantages, I consider you are a lucky girl, Ethel."

"Of course I am. If my marriage only turns out as well as yours did, Gertrude, I shall have nothing to complain of."

"Ah! your poor dear father,"—with a sigh—"well, it was the will of Heaven, and we must not complain."

"I am sure I have never accused you of doing so, Gertrude!"

"When is your marriage to take place?" demanded Lady Clevedon, who thought it as well to change the subject. Lady

Ethel's news had quite put the idea of triumphing over her, *in re* the Marquis de Lacarras, out of her head; for being by no means certain of that slippery gentleman herself, it was a great object to get her step-daughter married and out of the way, and she felt that the more conciliatory she became the better it would be for her purpose.

At that question, recalling her to a sense of her situation, a shudder passed over Lady Ethel's frame; but her voice continued steady.

"I do not know—he has not yet spoken of it—but soon, I suppose; in a month or six weeks."

"Ah! so early?—but of course you will have everything very quiet, considering our mourning; and at this time of the year no one will be the wiser."

"Of course! you do not suppose I should wish to do anything to outrage your widow's weeds, Gertrude!"

At this dart Lady Clevedon reddened, but took refuge in her ready tongue.

"Am I to write to your guardian, Lord Morston, on the subject, or leave the colonel to communicate the news of his own success?"

"I think you had better speak to Colonel Bainbridge, and arrange such matters personally. I only came to tell you the mere fact that I am engaged to him. I leave all the rest to you." And Lady Ethel left the room as abruptly as she had entered it.

He had been spoken to about her—urged to confess the truth of his affection, the honour of his intentions—and he had denied that he had ever given her occasion to believe that she was dear to him. Oh! false—false—cowardly heart!

It was the remembrance of this fact that kept Lady Ethel's courage up during the wretched anticipation of the month that followed; for whenever she found her spirits drooping and her bravery at zero, she had but to recall the triumphant words and looks of Lady Clevedon to reanimate her resolution.

She was spared at this time the presence of either of her lovers; for the Marquis de Lacarras quitted Temple Grange on the day of her engagement, and Colonel Bainbridge, after a few blissful days at her side, returned to Woolwich and his duty, from which he did not expect to procure further leave of absence until the day before the wedding, which was fixed to take place in the beginning of February.

Lord Morston, who had the entire management of Lady Ethel's slender dowry, found everything concerning marriage settlements and pinmoney from the other side so easily and liberally arranged, that he was seen to rub his hands more than once over the voluminous epistles he received from Cranshaws, whilst he declared that "these Bainbridges" seemed "stuffed with gold, and he was sorry they had not another son that he might have secured for his own daughter."

Lady Clevedon, who, notwithstanding her jealous and intriguing character, had all a woman's love for purchasing articles of dress that were not to serve as foils to her own beauty, busied herself over the trousseau, that the *nouveaux riches* might not say the daughter of an earl came into their family unbefittingly attired; whilst Colonel Bainbridge, debarred from the sight of his beloved, let scarcely a day pass by without sending her some offering of gold, or gems, or enamel, which made everybody but herself lift rapturous eyes and hands.

But, though she heard and saw it all, she yet remained utterly cold—utterly indifferent. She hardly believed she was going to be married, though she often wished she could forget it; and yet there were moments when she caught sight of a well-known monogram on Lady Clevedon's correspondence, or heard her step-mother make some pointed remark relating to the past or future, or passed beneath the *portière* dividing the two drawing-rooms, or recalled the moonlight balcony in Park Lane, when Lady Ethel would have given all that she was worth to know that Colonel Bainbridge would return that very day and take her from a place fraught with such hateful recollections, and from society with which it was so difficult to keep the peace.

Miserable and lonely, feeding on her own heart, and apparently reckless what happened to her, so long as something or somebody—Death or the Colonel of Artillery, it was much the same to her—would come to dissipate the maddening current of her thoughts, Lady Ethel Carr saw the dawn break which ushered in her wedding-day.

CHAPTER XVI.

ANTICIPATION.

"THOMAS and his wife will be at the Borthwick Station at five o'clock this afternoon," announced Mr Bainbridge one morning, as he perused his letters at the breakfast-table, "and they bring a German maid and a lot of luggage, so I shall give orders for the close carriage and the waggonette to meet them, and you had better see after preparing them a good dinner, Elizabeth, for they ought to be hungry after such a long journey."

"They cannot be here till past seven," remarked Mrs Bainbridge; "for it will take Duncan more than an hour to find his way back over the moors these foggy evenings."

"Half-past seven, or thereabouts," replied her husband; "and now, look you, my dears," addressing all three of the women, "I have one word to say to you before this young lady makes her appearance amongst us, and that is, that I am not going to have any of the rules of the castle upset on her account. Our meals and prayers and hours for retirement must go on the same as usual, whether she chooses to take part in them or not; for I am a methodical old man of business, and cannot have all the regularity of my life disturbed because my son chooses to bring home a 'lady' for a wife to Cranshaws. Do you understand?"

"My dear! how can you talk in such a way?" exclaimed his wife, in a tone of remonstrance; "I am quite sure, from all that Thomas says, our daughter-in-law will never wish to do anything that is not pleasant and accommodating."

"I would not be too sure of our daughter-in-law until you see her," said the old man, quaintly. "As for Thomas, he is in love, and would think it only too delightful if Lady Ethel were to condescend to use him as a door-mat. You must not trust letters written in the honeymoon, my dear."

"They were married six weeks ago, yesterday!" remarked Mrs Bainbridge, who did not like her husband speaking so freely before her sister and Maggie Henderson.

She was correct in her statement, for it was as long ago as that since the wedding of which I spoke in my last chapter had been celebrated, and Colonel and Lady Ethel Bainbridge, after having made the inevitable continental tour, were about to pay a visit to Cranshaws.

It was the worst time of the year for Scotland, and Colonel Bainbridge was almost reluctant to take his bride there; but he was so full of pride of his new possession, and so anxious to show her to his parents, and Lady Ethel was so utterly indifferent where she went, that the journey was finally agreed upon.

"Why not?" she had remarked, when her husband hesitated on the propriety of her visiting Cranshaws in the winter. "I suppose they have fires there as well as anywhere else, and we certainly cannot stay in town at this season of the year;" and so, after much deliberation and cautions, privately addressed to his mother, on the extreme delicacy of his treasure, the day for their arrival was at hand.

Anticipation of their immediate appearance threw the women of the household into a flutter. The good-hearted, simple-minded creatures were so utterly ignorant of the customs and manners of high life, that they imagined the preparations for receiving a woman of rank should be made on a more luxurious scale than for a commoner article; at the same time, they knew their resources to be so great that they had no fear but that the bride would be fully satisfied. They little thought that the grand difference to Lady Ethel would lie, not in their surroundings, which were more sumptuous than what she had been accustomed to, but in themselves.

The sleeping-chamber, which had been newly decorated with blue and white hangings for her use, was visited by each one of them at least three times during that day, that they might re-examine the bed with its wealth of fine linen, lace-bordered pillow-cases, and fleecy-white Scotch blankets, or the dressing-table, covered with cut-glass and silver, and make sure that nothing more was needed for the convenience of the coming stranger.

Maggie Henderson flew about the house like a bird, and it seemed to her Aunt Letty afterwards as though she had never sat down once during the twelve hours. Now she was up-stairs with Mrs Bainbridge, turning over the contents of the linen-closet (for, with all her riches, the mistress of Cranshaws was too homely to delegate the duties of housekeeping to her servants), then in the hall, giving orders to the gardener for changing the exotics in the library, anon ringing for the housemaid to keep up the fire in the room appointed for the married couple; only once did Aunt Letty detect her in anything like a thoughtful mood, and that was as she was arranging a small group of hot-house flowers to be placed in a vase upon the bride's dressing-table. Then Maggie had certainly lost herself in a reverie, as she stood with clasped hands, and dim, sad eyes, silently regarding the bouquet she had made.

"O Aunt Letty!" she exclaimed, waking up with a start, as Miss Lloyd approached her, "do you think my flowers are pretty? I would have none but white ones, although the honeymoon *is* over," with a low laugh; "because I thought Cousin Thomas might like to see them." And then came a shade over the countenance, and the lips twitched a little. "Oh! how I do hope that she may make him happy."

"We all pray for that, my dear," replied Aunt Letty with assumed briskness; "and I think there is little doubt of it. But there is old Janet Burns down in the housekeeper's room, Maggie, waiting to speak to your Aunt Lizzie, and I am sure she is too much engaged to see her this morning. Could not you be her deputy, and hear what it is that the old woman wants?"

"Of course I will;" and Maggie turned from the dressing-table without another look, and ran down to the housekeeper's room.

But, as the evening approached, she grew decidedly nervous, although it was only to be detected by those who knew that the sudden laugh brought to a close with a spasmodic jerk, in which she continually indulged, was unnatural to her, and assumed to cover the intensity of her feelings.

The dinner hour was fixed for eight o'clock, two hours later than usual; and it had been decided in feminine conclave that, in order to pay a compliment to the bride, it was advisable they should dress with greater care than they were wont to do when by themselves. Aunt Lizzie and Aunt Letty, therefore, were closeted with much state in their dressing-rooms for half-an-hour previously; and it would have been sufficient for any keen observer to watch the erratic manner in which Maggie Henderson flew from one apartment to the other, and hear the rattling comment she kept up on all their little adornments, to discover that her mind was ill at ease in prospect of the meeting before her.

"Aunt Letty, you look charming! There is no colour suits you so well as grey; and that is the prettiest cap you have ever had. No, you must not wear that camellia in your dress; it is too deep, it kills the lilac of your ribbons. I do not care who gave it you, you must take this stephanotos instead; stephanotos is quite a bridal flower, you know. And now I must run and see how Aunt Lizzie is getting on. How well your dress hangs, Aunt Lizzie—Jeanie Ransom is getting cleverer every day—and your blue ribbons match it exactly. They might have been manufactured for the purpose. Won't you have some flowers? I have gathered you such a lovely tea-rose: we should all wear bouquets to-night, Aunt Lizzie; it is the orthodox thing, brides and flowers always go together. Now you are quite ready, and you couldn't look nicer. Such a dear, plump, soft old mother to welcome a daughter home. And poor Lady Ethel is like me; she cannot remember her own mother. I am sure you ought to seem like a real one to her."

Mrs Bainbridge turned round and folded the girl to her bosom, whilst something very like a tear rose in her eyes.

"My darling Maggie," she said; "I wish—oh, how I wish"—

Maggie thought she could guess what was in store for her, and struggled to get free.

"I will tell you what I wish, aunt; and that is, that these good people would be quick in coming. Don't you feel the pangs of hunger? I shall feel disposed to eat them both at one meal if they stop much longer on the road."

"I hear the carriage wheels," shouted Mr Bainbridge from the staircase; "Maggie, my child, come with me;" and unknowing what excuse to make for not doing so, the little martyr placed her trembling hand in that of her uncle, and descended to the hall, before the door of which in a few seconds drew up the carriage which had been sent to Borthwick station.

CHAPTER XVII.

BRINGING THE BRIDE HOME.

The servant in attendance threw down the steps, and Colonel Bainbridge quickly alighted.

"What the devil do you mean by being such a time coming over these moors?" he demanded sharply of the coachman, and without observing the presence of his father and cousin.

The coachman touched his hat, and said it was impossible to have done the journey quicker. He was an old servant of the family, who had known Colonel Bainbridge ever since he was a child, and as he remarked afterwards in the servants' hall, it was the first time "Master Thomas" had ever spoken angrily to him.

"Have you found the journey very tedious?" demanded Mr Bainbridge, coming forward.

"Yes, indeed! Ah, father! how are you, and Maggie too? I did not see you before. I should think we must have been an hour and a half, at least, jolting over these horrid moors, and my wife has been nearly shaken to pieces. This place is altogether too much out of the way; I thought we should never arrive," and then, with the same air of complaint, he turned to the open carriage door. "Come, Ethel, my dearest, we are really here at last."

A slight figure, much enveloped in velvets and sables, appeared upon the steps, and, having gained the ground, was passing rapidly through the lighted hall.

Her husband's voice detained her.

"Ethel!—my father!"

She stopped short, turned to regard Mr Bainbridge in his quaintly-cut old-fashioned costume with wide open eyes of surprise, and then with a faltered apology, held out her hand.

"I beg your pardon, I did not see you; I was only thinking of the fire."

Her father-in-law was about to bid her welcome in his hearty manner, when his son again interrupted him.

"The fire? of course, my poor child, you must be nearly frozen; this way, Ethel," and without further parley he led her into the drawing-room, and seating her before the blazing hearth, attempted in his blundering fashion to relieve her of her wraps.

Meanwhile Mr Bainbridge disappeared to hurry the movements of his wife and sister; and Maggie, unnoticed by either of the married couple, crept after them to offer her assistance.

"I wish you would leave me alone," she heard the bride say fretfully, as she entered the apartment. "I would rather go up to my own room at once. Where is Louise?"

"I will call her, dearest! O Maggie!" perceiving his cousin, "will you tell some one to send Lady Ethel's maid to her; and which room is to be ours?"

"The blue room, Cousin Thomas; the one to the right of Aunt Lizzie's;" and Maggie departed to execute her commission.

"Who is that girl?" she heard the bride say, as she left their presence. The question stung her; it proved how little *he* could have thought or spoken of her during his married life.

On the upper landing she encountered Mrs Bainbridge and Miss Lloyd.

"O Aunt Lizzie! they are come!" she breathlessly ejaculated, "and she is so cold, and she wants her maid, and Cousin Thomas asked me to fetch her, and she *is* so beautiful,"—with a wild desperate look in the direction of Aunt Letty,—"her hair is quite golden colour, and she has such a quantity of it, and"——

"Hush! hush, my dear," remonstrated Mrs Bainbridge; "Lady Ethel will overhear you, if you are not more cautious. You had better do as she desires, and join us afterwards. We are just going down to make her acquaintance."

But when Maggie, having ascertained that the German lady's-maid really understood what was required of her, returned to the drawing-room, she found the three elders of the family standing upon the hearth-rug by themselves, the bride and bridegroom having disappeared before they gained the apartment.

"Perhaps it is as well," Mrs Bainbridge was good-naturedly saying, in order to cover the little disappointment which they all felt; "for Thomas told his father that the dear girl is dreadfully tired and upset by her journey; and doubtless she is anxious to change her dress and make herself tidy before being introduced to us all. It is rather a formidable thing entering a strange family; at least, I remember *I* thought it so, my dear," with a tap on her husband's shoulder, "when you first took me to call on your mother at Birmingham. I had plenty of gowns to my back, but I must needs have a new one made to see the old lady in; and it was a grey merino, piped with blue satin, a very handsome dress,—(you haven't forgotten it, John?)—and I was so nervous that I spilt a glass of wine right down the front breadth."

But here Mrs Bainbridge's reminiscences were interrupted by the re-entrance of her son, with an expression which struck Maggie as being rather worried. But as he caught sight of his mother and aunt his face brightened; and he kissed them both most affectionately.

"Well, mother, and so here I am, you see, taken in and done for, at last."

"I trust you may be very, very happy, my dear," murmured his mother, tremulously; "and your dear wife, where is she? We are so anxious to see her."

"She will be down directly. I am sorry she should have left the room before you entered it; but she was nearly fainting from fatigue. I am afraid she is not very strong, mother," with a sudden overclouding of his countenance.

"Oh! my dear Thomas!—a young wife, and after such a long journey—we must make allowances. She will feel more like herself to-morrow. But, shall I go to her? will she think me remiss in remaining here?"

"Not at all—she would not expect it—besides which, here she comes!" he exclaimed, brightly, and going into the hall to meet her; in another moment glowing with the pride of possession, he stood amongst them with Lady Ethel on his arm.

"Here is your daughter, mother," he said, as he led her up to Mrs Bainbridge; "but she begs you will excuse her dressing for this evening, as she is really too tired to undergo any unnecessary exertion."

He spoke cheerfully, and the good ladies of Cranshaws, who had prepared all sorts of little kind welcoming speeches for their new relation, advanced to receive her, both metaphorically and physically, with open arms ; but there was something in the look and demeanour of the young stranger which checked their ardour, and after having taken courage to imprint a formal kiss upon the passive cheek which was not advanced one inch for their convenience, the conversation relapsed into the merest commonplaces.

And, indeed, a greater contrast than Lady Ethel presented to her husband's relations, in dress and style and manner, could scarcely be imagined, and was sufficient to freeze the warm impulses of those who had been ready to welcome her as one of themselves. Attired in the black velvet dress in which she had travelled (for she had not relinquished the mourning for her father), with a morsel of point lace carelessly tied round her slender white throat, and neither bow nor ornament in the piled masses of her hair, the negligence of her costume alone separated her more from them, than if her charms had been hidden beneath a panoply of silk and jewels; whilst her stately and composed demeanour and air of frigid uninterested languor (so unlike the blushing timidity which Mrs Bainbridge and Miss Lloyd had pictured to themselves), made the breach seem still wider. The very faintest of smiles passed over her face in reply to her new relations' good wishes and congratulations; and then Lady Ethel sank down into the chair which her husband placed for her, and shading her cheek from the fire with her delicate hand, left him to conduct the conversation unaided by herself, until the dinner was announced.

Every one felt it to be a relief when they were once fairly occupied round the table; but even then the bride remained as uncommunicative as before, and her silence threw such a damper over the whole party, that Colonel Bainbridge was obliged to talk much louder and faster than usual in order to cover the unpleasant impression made by the conduct of his wife. He spoke of Paris and Brussels, and the German baths, at which they had been whiling away their time: every now and then appealing for a confirmation of his words to Lady Ethel, with the hope of drawing her into the general conversation, and receiving a monosyllable in reply for his pains; and then he alluded to the house in Curzon Street, which had been taken and furnished for them by the liberality of Mr Bainbridge, but which would not be ready for their reception until the following May.

"You must come and see us then, mother," he concluded, warmly. "It is years since you have been in London, and you would enjoy the change."

"Oh, my dear Thomas!" exclaimed Mrs Bainbridge, flattered nevertheless by the invitation, "you will have plenty to do and to think of on first setting up house together, without encumbering yourselves with the trouble of looking after an old woman like me."

"I should be sorry to think we should ever have too much business or pleasure to permit of our devoting a little time to you, mother; and so would Lady Ethel, I am sure;" and as he spoke, Colonel Bainbridge glanced across the table at his wife, as though urging her to second his assertion.

But Lady Ethel was playing with a little pile of bread-crumbs at the side of her plate, and did not even appear to have listened to his words.

"And Miss Maggie, too," he went on rapidly with a kind look towards his cousin; "she should pay a visit to town during the season, were it only to say that she had seen the Row at four o'clock in the afternoon. Can you imagine any one being such a little rustic, Ethel, as never to have set foot further south than Birmingham in the whole course of her existence?"

"Your cousin?" said Lady Ethel, interrogatively, and forced to say something.

"Yes, little Maggie there; have you never been introduced to her yet? what a shame! Why, she's like a sister to me, and the right hand of Cranshaws; isn't she, father?"

"She is the greatest blessing that Cranshaws has ever possessed," replied the old man, fervently.

"A compliment to me," exclaimed Colonel Bainbridge, with mock distress. "Can't you find one word to say in my favour, Ethel?"

"Oh, my dear Thomas!" interposed his mother, taking his jest seriously, "you must not believe your father to be in earnest. Every one knows the good dutiful son you have been to us, and how thankful we are in your possession; and though I say it as should not say it, it will be your wife's own fault if she is not a happy woman."

At this little outburst of maternal pride, which was delivered with a cheerful nod across the table, Lady Ethel reddened, and Colonel Bainbridge laughed, though not quite easily.

"Come, come, mother; no more of that, or you will set me off blushing. We were talking of Cranshaws, were we not? I wish that Lady Ethel could have seen it first at a more seasonable time of the year: she will hardly be able to credit what a pretty place it is when the moors are covered with heather bloom." And then he rattled off again upon all kinds of subjects connected with the country and the farm, though every now and then his dark eyes stole across the table and rested longingly upon the fair creature whom he called his wife, as though yearning to extract a look of interest or kindness in return.

And Maggie, who was still as crimson as a peony, from the effects of the notice bestowed upon her, intercepted one of these glances.

It turned her cold, and sick, and trembling. She had never seen any look before which expressed such entire devotion to —almost worship of—its object, and she wondered that Lady Ethel did not appear more affected by it, that she could sit so immovable and quiet whilst it glowed upon her, with her own eyes fixed upon a painting on the wall.

Maggie seemed at that moment to comprehend for the first time how absorbingly a man's heart *can* love; and though it made her see how foolish she had been to imagine that her cousin ever cared for her, the very fact, by absolving him of all blame in her disappointment, made her resolve to do what she could to please him, by making herself agreeable to his idol. Her nature was sufficiently generous to confess that neither of these persons having borne an active part in giving her pain, should be held accountable for it; and sitting silently at the end of the long table, she prepared to offer up the first-fruits of her cheerfully-accepted sacrifice, by not only feigning, but studying, to feel an interest in what so greatly interested him, and trying to make his beautiful wife feel more at home amongst them than she appeared to do.

CHAPTER XVIII.

FIRST IMPRESSIONS.

It was with this intent that when the ladies found themselves alone in the drawing-room, Maggie, blushing up to her ears at her own audacity, ventured to approach the spot where Lady Ethel had thrown herself into a low chair, and ask if she felt less fatigued than she had done before dinner.

They were, comparatively speaking, alone, for Mrs Bainbridge had left the room upon some household business, and Aunt Letty, scared out of her affectionate intentions by the distant demeanour of the bride, had carried her knitting to the further end of the apartment.

The fair face, with its chiselled features and white forehead, over which a few locks of golden hair were negligently disposed, slightly turned towards the speaker, as her question was answered in the negative, and Maggie thought she had never seen any one so lovely as this new cousin in her life before. She looked so graceful, so elegant, so composed, so unlike any of the rosy, blooming, vivacious girls, who passed as beauties in that part of the country; so totally unlike herself.

Maggie's heart gave one great jealous throb at the conviction, but her next remark was no less sympathetic for the feeling.

"You look so pale, I am sure the dinner was a worry to you. Perhaps you are longing for your bed?"

"Thank you—I am very well as I am!"

"You will feel better to-morrow morning, I hope. I think most people arrive here too tired to enjoy themselves. It is a very pretty place by daylight. Are you fond of the country?"

"I can't say I am!"

"Oh! isn't Cousin Thomas sorry for that?" said Maggie, quickly.

"I really can't tell you—I never asked him."

"Because he is to live at Cranshaws, you know, when—when—it becomes his."

"Indeed!"

Lady Ethel's tone added so plainly the query "whether I choose or do not choose?" that Maggie's courage suddenly evaporated, and she felt she had said more than she intended.

Then followed a long pause between them, which was at last broken by Lady Ethel inquiring in a peevish manner—

"What do you do with yourselves all day here?"

"Oh! lots of things," was the hearty rejoinder; "there is always work, of course, about the house and grounds, and then there are all the farm people to be looked after, and we generally ride or drive out once a day. Aunt Lizzie does not often go further than the garden, unless there is something to be done in Borthwick; but Aunt Letty and I have each a little 'Sheltie,' and we go scrambling over the moors whenever we feel so inclined."

"And cannot you reach any place without crossing those dreadful moors?" demanded Lady Ethel with a look of genuine distress, beneath which Maggie's face fell.

"I don't think you will mind them so much after a little," she answered, timidly. "There are some beautiful walks amongst them, if you can manage to climb the hills; and if you like riding, my pony will take you anywhere; only, of course, it is not so pleasant now as it will be in the summer time."

"Who are your nearest neighbours?" was the next question.

"The Duke of Ramsay has a shooting-box about three miles from Cranshaws, but he only uses it during the season, and the Marquis of Booth keeps Herne Hall on the other side for the same purpose. The only real neighbours we have though, who live here all the year round, are the Appletons of Horse-ap-Cleugh, and Mrs Elliott of Burnside, but she is a very old lady, and never goes out anywhere."

Lady Ethel's silence was ominous.

"We don't depend upon neighbours in a place like this, you see," continued Maggie, who was anxious to defend the charms of her country home; "for there is always so much business connected with a large estate, that we have no time for paying and returning visits, and those friends who wish to see us come and stay here; indeed, if it were not for going to church, I don't think I should ever care to leave the grounds myself."

"And where may your church be?"

"Oh! only three miles off, at Mindon; such a dear little place, all covered with ivy, and it is not much bigger than double this room."

"Three miles across these moors!" said Lady Ethel, with a shudder, as she involuntarily wheeled her chair nearer to the fire, and placed her feet upon the fender-stool.

She remained thus musing for a while, and then, as though thought had suddenly become oppressive to her, sprang to her feet, exclaiming—

"I am really too tired to sit up any longer, and will go to my room at once. You must make my apologies to Mrs Bainbridge!"

But as she spoke the door opened, and her husband, accompanied by his father and mother, entered the apartment.

"Colonel Bainbridge! I was just going upstairs; my head aches dreadfully!"

He was by her side in a moment.

"My darling! I am so sorry; is there nothing I can do or get for you?"

"Nothing, thanks! Mrs Bainbridge will perhaps excuse my retiring so early."

"Of course, my dear; do just as you feel inclined," replied the old lady; "and I think myself that bed will be the best place for you. I will send you up a cup of strong coffee directly."

"Pray don't trouble yourself; I shall take nothing more. Good evening;" and with a bow that included the whole company, Lady Ethel was moving onwards.

"Ethel! my dearest! I am coming with you," exclaimed Colonel Bainbridge, as he followed her.

At that she halted, and turned her pale face towards them.

"I beg you will do no such thing—I would so much rather be alone; and you must have plenty still to say to your family."

Her voice and manner were so cold that they would have deterred most men, but they had not the power to deter him.

"I have nothing of interest in this world now in which you are not concerned," he answered, fondly, as he drew her arm within his own, and led her up the broad staircase to her room.

Then a blank seemed to fall on the party they had left behind, for this was the first time that they had been alone and together since their introduction to the bride, and each felt that all was not as it should be, whilst each was anxious to hide the fact from the others.

"Thomas seems perfectly devoted to her," sighed Mrs Bainbridge, with the slightest twinge of maternal jealousy.

"There is no doubt about her being very handsome," remarked the old man.

"Oh no! she is lovely!" said Maggie, with enthusiasm.

"But isn't it just a little singular, you know," put in Miss Lloyd, "for a wife to address her husband by his surname? I confess I should have been better pleased to hear her call him Thomas."

"Oh! that will all come by and by," said Mrs Bainbridge, with the superior intelligence of a married woman. "They have not been married many weeks, remember, and for my part I would rather see her too retiring than too forward—she certainly is a most beautiful girl," falling back upon the fact which was indisputably pleasant.

"Yes! and so aristocratic! She might be a princess from her appearance. How proud Thomas seems of her."

"So he may well be! He would never have found such a wife down at Cranshaws," at which Mr Bainbridge grunted dissent. "And, talking of that, I wonder if Lady Ethel has everything she wants—just run up-stairs, Maggie, and see."

But Maggie shrunk backwards.

"Oh no, aunt! they can't want me, and Cousin Thomas would be sure to ring if anything was wrong."

"My dear, what nonsense! Lady Ethel has probably not yet gone into her dressing-room. Just knock at the door, and ask her, with my love, if she has everything she requires."

Thus urged, Maggie started on her errand; but as she placed her foot upon the staircase she encountered Colonel Bainbridge. Again she thought (but it might have been her fancy) that his face looked troubled; but as he caught her eye he smiled.

"Well, Maggie! are you bound also for the Land of Nod?"

"Oh no! I was just going to ask if I could do anything for Lady Ethel."

"That's my kind little cousin! Yes! I wish you would;

perhaps your company might do her good." And then he added, in a lower and more confidential voice, "She's not quite the thing to-night, Maggie; she has been upset by travelling, and feels shy and timid amongst a lot of strangers. You are more of her own age; you must cheer her up, and make her feel at home."

"I will try," said the girl, softly; and with that she passed her cousin, and walking more slowly up the remainder of the staircase, knocked gently at Lady Ethel's door.

CHAPTER XIX.

GOOD NIGHT.

At first there was no answer; but after a second appeal Maggie thought she heard the words, "Come in," and turning the handle, entered the bed-chamber. What was her amazement at the scene she witnessed there! She had been prepared to find the bride thoughtful, and even dejected, at the strangeness by which she was surrounded; but she little expected to see Lady Ethel sitting by the table, with her head cast down upon her outstretched arms, and sobbing with all her might—a perfect rain of tears, as though she had lost all control over herself. For a moment Maggie stood still and watched her silently, for she was frightened at the sight of so much emotion, and hardly knowing what excuse to make for her own presence there, would gladly have crept away again without having been perceived. But the slight movement she made attracted the notice of Lady Ethel Bainbridge, who, raising her head proudly, and with the tears still glittering on her eyelashes, demanded what it was she required of her.

"O Lady Ethel," faltered the girl, "I am so sorry. I thought I heard you say 'come in.'"

"It is of no consequence," returned the other. "Have you a message for me?"

Her pride was wounded that this country-bred girl should have seen her in her hour of weakness; but as it was the case, she was too proud to let her know that she cared anything about it. And so she would not even raise her hand to brush away the tears from her streaming eyes, but sat there, with wet cheeks and humid glances, looking twice as beautiful as she had done before.

"Aunt Lizzie told me to ask if you have everything you want," said Maggie.

"Everything, I believe, except my maid, and I suppose she will come if I ring; or, if she does not, some one else will. Pray don't trouble yourself on my account."

"But it is no trouble, Lady Ethel, and I will send your maid to you. You may not like to see strangers."

"Thanks!" returned Lady Ethel, curtly; and then there was nothing for Maggie to do but to go. But yet she could not go. A feeling had come over her, she could hardly define what it was; but something which seemed to say that she must try what she could do to comfort Colonel Bainbridge's bride.

That Lady Ethel—that the wife of her Cousin Thomas—the object of so much love and devotion on his part, could be unhappy, was incomprehensible, and, had Maggie stopped to analyse the probable reason, would have seemed absurd; and yet her immediate conviction was that it was so.

Why, or wherefore, were puzzling questions reserved for the future, the present was alone before her; and in the present was a fellow-creature in distress, another woman suffering—and a wild notion struck Maggie's heart—suffering somehow much in the same way as she had done and was doing still herself. With that, every throb of envy and jealousy, which had been torturing her throughout the evening, died out of the girl's heart, and in their stead reigned a great womanly compassion and sense of pity.

And as that feeling gained predominance, Maggie lost her timidity, and going up to where Lady Ethel still retained her seat, she knelt down by the table, and with a sweet manner, half shy and half determined, said, gently—

"Don't cry, dear!—pray don't cry. It would make him—it would make us all so unhappy to think you were so."

Lady Ethel bent her sad eyes upon the speaker with surprise. It was not often she had heard a woman's voice appealing to her in tones of affection; not often that she had met so innocent and pure a glance upraised to her own, or encountered a stranger bold enough to plead with her as with a sister. She was generally excessively haughty and stern with any one who attempted to take a liberty with her; but there was something in Maggie's brown eyes—Lady Ethel did not recognise it at that moment, but it was the mysterious light of sympathy—which attracted her as she had seldom felt attracted towards any girl before; and instead of rebuking the familiarity of her appeal, she placed her hand before her own eyes, and commenced to weep afresh.

Yes! She had reason for her tears; for the glamour and excitement of her unhallowed marriage were wearing off, and leaving her (as any sensible person could have warned her that she would be left) stranded on a shore barren both of sympathy and affection.

That her husband loved and gloried and trusted in her, that he poured upon her hourly proofs of his passionate attachment, and thought no portion of his life worth living that was passed out of her presence, was only an aggravation of the punishment she had brought upon herself, as no *woman* will need to be informed; for the existence bereft of all that it holds dear is far preferable to that which is compelled to suffer caresses obnoxious to it.

All through that evening, during which Maggie had been silently putting up little prayers to heaven to help her to subdue the evil feelings of jealousy for the happy condition of her cousin's bride, with which her heart seemed filled to bursting, Lady Ethel had passed a hundred times through the last interview she had held with her poor father, and heard the answer that he had made to her insolent remark that she was not likely to look long enough upon the ground to learn to love a man like Colonel Bainbridge.

"Ethel; that pride of yours will some day be brought down. I pray that when it is, your life's happiness may not be overwhelmed at the same time."

Wandering about amongst German spas and Parisian society, with a handsome husband devoted to every wish, Lady Ethel had nursed her romantic sorrow for the treacherous desertion of the Marquis de Lacarras, without realising the whole of the bargain she had made with Colonel Bainbridge, for the satisfaction of her outraged womanhood. But to-day, when he had brought her home to his own people, whom he expected her to call *her* people—and, aware of their deficiencies, had striven so hard to conceal everything that was not just as she had been used to see it—this had been an awakening which she had never quite believed in, although she had talked so loudly on the subject.

And it had overwhelmed her. The child of folly and fashion, ruined by her own pride and self-indulgence, had had her eyes fully opened at last to the fate she had deliberately carved out for herself, and she shrunk from it as from a scorpion. She had no friends to turn to in her distress, for she had cut herself off from her own associates to enter a family which she felt could never be congenial to her; so it is no wonder if the gratuitous sympathy even of this little ignorant, unfashionable stranger seemed for the moment as something too sweet to be rejected.

But only for a moment: Lady Ethel had accidentally lost command of herself, but she had no intention of adding to it the loss of self-respect. And so she hastily dashed away her newly-risen tears, and answering Maggie's affectionate address with a deceptive laugh, said, lightly—

"Unhappy!—what nonsense! Pray don't take such an absurd idea into your head. I am only a little overcome by the fatigue of my journey, and shall be all right to-morrow."

Still Maggie lingered by the table. Her feminine tact told her that Lady Ethel's nonchalance was only assumed, and she longed to leave her more composed.

"I daresay the castle would look rather gloomy, seen for the first time at night," she said, thoughtfully. "It is large, you see, and difficult to light well, and my uncle has an old-fashioned dislike to introducing gas."

"Oh! it is not that, I can assure you!"

"I know it is not, but it all adds to it; and coming to the country too, to which you have never been accustomed, and amongst a lot of strangers, of course would make you feel a little lonely."

"Lonely, child! what should you know about being lonely?"

"I feel so sometimes myself," replied Maggie, simply, "even though I live amongst my best friends. We all have thoughts occasionally in which no one else can share—no one on earth, that is to say."

"Yes; I suppose so."

"And then the only way to get comfort is to take them straight to Him."

"What did you say?"

"To take them to our Saviour," said Maggie, in a low voice, though she grew very red the while, for she had perceived from Lady Ethel's foregoing question that the freemasonry which exists between all those who hold a common interest in a common good was wanting here.

"Oh! yes—of course," replied the bride, indifferently; and then she added—"If you are really going to be so kind as to summon Louise for me, I wish you would do it at once, for I think the time must be getting on."

"May I come back, too?" inquired Maggie, wistfully. There was something in this beautiful, defiantly unhappy bride which interested her deeply.

"No! you had better not. First impressions go a long way, and I am not mistress of myself to-night. Let me go to rest now, and I shall see you again in the morning."

"Good-night, then, dear Lady Ethel!" and Maggie's eyes glistened whilst she held out a timid hand.

The best of Lady Ethel's nature came to the surface. She was a woman, after all is said and done, and she had a heart, however she might upon occasions refuse to listen to its dictates. At the present moment she acted just as it prompted her to do, and, as Maggie rose, rose also, and kissed her on the face.

"Good-night! I think that I shall like you; but don't judge of me as you have seen me now. We will begin afresh to-morrow."

CHAPTER XX.

ACROSS THE MOORS.

Maggie Henderson was down very early on the following morning. She had not slept well, for the interview she had held with Lady Ethel had left a deep impression on her mind, and robbed her of her rest. She felt drawn in an inexplicable manner towards this spoilt child of fashion, the beloved object of her Cousin Thomas's affections; and to be drawn towards her seemed like deserting her own cause, like going over to the enemy against her own bruised little heart. Nature had been fighting against Grace all night long, and a selfish sorrow had nearly gained the victory over charity. Maggie could not help wishing either that Lady Ethel appeared less interesting in her eyes, or that she was not the person of all others she desired to be least interested in; and she was angry with herself for having given vent to the feeling which had come spontaneously to her. Lady Ethel's hysterical emotion was, doubtless, as she had affirmed, due to the fatigue she had undergone, and ought to have been treated like the unreasoning folly of a child. It was impossible, that so lately married, and possessing everything in this world calculated to make a woman happy, she could have any cause for giving way to sorrow.

Maggie concluded that she had been far too quick and ready with her sympathy; had wasted it, in fact, and the thought galled her and prevented her from sleeping.

So, as soon as the world was fairly awake, she rose and dressed herself, and crept softly down-stairs, with the intention of getting out in the fresh air, and walking off the effects of her vigil before she passed under the scrutinising gaze of Aunt Letty.

It was a clear, cold morning, in the commencement of April; but Maggie cared little for the cold. She had been reared hardily, and accustomed to be out in all sorts of weather, and often walked a mile or two across the moors before the elder members of the family had left their beds. And so, wrapped up in her woollen plaid, she stepped briskly out upon the terrace, prepared to take an hour's exercise before breakfast. But, scarcely prepared to encounter Colonel Bainbridge walking up and down, with his hands in his pockets, as though waiting for her to join him. Maggie's first impulse was to retire again. It was hard enough, under present circumstances, to meet him in the family circle—harder even than she had calculated upon—but she felt as though she could not trust herself to speak with him alone. And yet there was no opportunity for retreat, for he turned at the opening of the door, and came quickly towards her, whilst she felt her stupid cheeks flame up at the mere consciousness of his approach.

"Why, Maggie!" he exclaimed, apparently as much surprised as pleased to see her, "are you too bound for a constitutional this fine morning? That's famous, we will go together; I was just longing for some one to talk to;" and as he took her hand, he placed it snugly within his arm.

But the girl drew backward—it was no comfort to her; it was a misery to feel it there. She felt that she could have no part in that support henceforward and for evermore. There are some hearts, so constituted, that they must have all or nothing.

"I never expected to meet any one," she stammered, as she held both her hands before her, and rolled them round tightly in her plaid. "It is so very early, not seven o'clock; I thought everybody would be in bed."

"Everybody except Miss Henderson and *one other*, I suppose," rejoined Colonel Bainbridge, laughing. "Ah, Maggie, my little cousin, have I caught you out? And who is the favoured laddie? Not one of the young Appletons, I hope; for I'm left your guardian, you know, miss, and intend you for something a great deal better than mistress of that tumbledown old place, Horse-ap-Cleuch."

"Oh, it is no one, Cousin Thomas, indeed," replied poor Maggie, who, betwixt the desire to exonerate herself, and the fear lest Colonel Bainbridge should press the question, was scarlet with confusion and distress. "I only came out for a little walk; I often do so before breakfast."

"Never mind, Maggie!" said her companion, affecting to disbelieve her; "we won't say anything more about it; and let me tell you, as one who has had some experience in such matters, that I don't believe he would have come this morning at all, for it's a great deal too cold for that kind of thing, and love is scared at the idea of red noses and frost-bitten fingers. So let us go for a nice little cousinly walk together instead; it is a long time since you and I have had a walk, Maggie. Which road shall we go: round the farm, or down by the river? You had better lead the way, for it is such an age since I was here that I seem to have forgotten all about it."

Thus adjured, Maggie turned silently away from the terrace, and commenced to tread a path which led through the shrubberies of Cranshaws, and across the moorland.

"Now, this is what I call jolly," said Colonel Bainbridge as he paced close to her side. "It reminds me of old days. What a splendid air this is; one seems to draw in a draught of fresh life with every breath. How I wish that Ethel were strong enough to get up and enjoy it with us."

"How is Lady Ethel this morning?" said Maggie, feeling that the allusion called for an inquiry on the subject, though she dreaded introducing it.

Colonel Bainbridge seized the occasion with alacrity, for that he might be able to talk freely of the thought uppermost in his mind, had been his sole reason for desiring a companion in his walk, and his little cousin appeared a very proper person for the infliction. It was a matter of course that girls must feel interested in the sayings and doings of one another.

"Thank you! I am afraid she is not feeling very well, but it will take more than one night's rest to enable her to overcome the fatigue of yesterday. I have told her that she must not get up this morning. By the way, Maggie, I don't suppose my father will be very particular about her appearing at prayers and Bible-reading, and all that sort of thing—will he?"

"For this morning, Cousin Thomas? oh no, decidedly not; he is always ready to make excuses in a case of illness, and I heard Aunt Lizzie say herself, last night, that she thought Lady Ethel ought to lie in bed until she felt quite recovered again."

"Oh! yes!—yes, of course; but I didn't mean that exactly. You see, Maggie, my wife has been reared in a very different style to what you are accustomed here, and all these continual prayer-meetings and psalm-singings are quite novelties to her; in fact, I'm afraid she won't be got to join in them very easily. It's all very well in the country, you know, where one has lots of time, but to people who have been used to a town life it appears perfectly absurd!"

"*Absurd!* Cousin Thomas?"

The awed tone in which the girl beside him let fall this word shamed Colonel Bainbridge into silence. He, too, had been reared, as she had, in the midst of worship, which, if it left scope for longings after a ritual more perfect and soul-inspiring, was at all events pure, both in its direction and intent. And there had been a time also when he would have been ashamed to speak of the means by which his good old father tried to lead the minds of his household heavenwards in any terms but those of respect, and when he had half resolved with himself to give up, once and for all, the World, the Flesh, and the Devil, and to make an open profession of those sentiments which his conscience whispered to him were the only ones worth holding; but he had fallen in with a woman whose feelings were utterly opposed to all religious truths, and having lavished his whole heart upon her natural beauty, forgetful of the shortcomings of her mind, his soul was relapsing into the same indolence as hers.

But the startled voice in which Maggie Henderson repeated after him the word "absurd," in a measure recalled him to himself.

"Well, not absurd, perhaps (I ought not to have said that); but very unnecessary, and can do people no earthly good when their hearts are not in that kind of thing; only I should not like my father to be annoyed, or make a fuss about it, and neither, I am sure, would Ethel, though I have not yet mentioned the subject to her."

"He *will be* very much annoyed if she refuses to attend prayers," said Maggie, quietly.

"But look here!" resumed Colonel Bainbridge, who had an idea, and by no means an erroneous one, that to enlist his cousin's sympathy was to gain his cause. "It can make no difference to him you see, and surely it is better she should stay away than attend unwillingly."

"But why should Lady Ethel be unwilling?"

The question was a simple one, yet he felt puzzled how to answer it. He could not shock her by the information that his beautiful wife was callous to everything connected with religion; that if she said her prayers, or read her Bible, it was in the most formal and unthinking manner; and that she never entered a church except to dissipate the *ennui* by which she was invariably attacked on Sundays. And so he murmured something about not being used to family prayers, and that they had been superseded in the High Church by matins and evensong, and something further about ritual and intoning and the Sacrifice, on which subjects he was very misty himself, but which served to convey the notion to his hearer's mind that Lady Ethel had been used to so lofty a style of worship that she would be unable to pray in the library at Cranshaws.

"Oh, I have heard of that!" exclaimed Maggie, with a kindling eye, "and I have longed—I cannot tell you how much—that my lot had been cast where I might enjoy such privileges. We have many books upon the subject, written by some of the leading Churchmen of the day, and I must confess that sometimes I have been wicked enough to feel discontented that I could only read of it. Oh yes, I am a true Catholic, Cousin Thomas, and so is Aunt Letty; and Scotland will never have the power to shake our faith in the Catholic doctrine. But were we on that account to refuse to join in any worship which is not conducted on strictly Catholic principles, what would become of us? Our places have been assigned to us here, and not by ourselves, and surely God could never intend us to lose the substance whilst we are sighing after what may prove to us the shadow!"

"But Ethel's place is *not* here—at all events not at present," argued her cousin.

"But she might *die* here, Cousin Thomas," was the quiet answer.

"God forbid!" he ejaculated, a look of terror passing over his face; and then he added, quickly, "You have never been accustomed to these things, or you would talk differently."

"But I can imagine them," replied Maggie, humbly. "I can imagine, too, Cousin Thomas," with a little sigh, "how you look in your grand artillery uniform, with all your accoutrements, although I have never seen you wear it, and how proud Lady Ethel must feel to see you riding past the flag-staff on a field-day at the head of your soldiers; but she doesn't love you less, does she, when you have nothing but plain clothes on?"

"I hope not, my child," he answered, laughing. "But what are you driving at, Maggie?"

"Only that wherever we pray, we worship the same God; and though it must make one's heart glow to see His service conducted as we believe He wishes it, yet where it cannot be, where it is impossible—we have an altar, you know—He must be there, and to refuse to go would seem to me like turning our backs upon Him when He was in plain clothes, Cousin Thomas!" with a quiet smile at the homeliness of her comparison.

But Colonel Bainbridge did not smile; her words were striking deeper in his heart than she calculated on.

"But with regard to Ethel—she is very beautiful, don't you think so, Maggie?" breaking off suddenly from his subject with a lover's rapture, and waiting eagerly for her answer.

"Very beautiful!" echoed the girl, with a sharp twinge of envious pain, for which she despised herself, and did penance the next moment by ratifying her assertion. "More beautiful than anybody I have ever seen before, Cousin Thomas; I cannot find a fault in her face or figure!"

"Nor I," he answered, glowingly; "and you 've not seen her at her best, remember—for she looked so pale last night. But her eyes—her hair—the moulding of her features—I have never seen them equalled; and then to think she should belong to *me*," with a low, deprecating laugh—"a delicate, fragile creature like that in the possession of such a great, rough, clumsy brute as I am!" stretching out his muscular arm and large powerful hand. "Why, it seems absurd. One of the six-foot lassies from these parts, with cheeks like nutmeg-graters and elbows like files, would have suited me better, eh, Maggie?"

"O Cousin Thomas! you would never have been contented with mere common beauty!"

"No! by Jove! not after I had seen her, at all events. I am so glad you like her, Maggie" (she had never said she did), "because I want you to be friends with her whilst she is here, and make things smooth. And about these prayers, and regular meals, and all the other fussy rules of Cranshaws. Don't you think you could talk my father over for us?"

"No! Cousin Thomas! I am sure I could not," said Maggie, firmly. "Uncle is more particular about his rules being punctually complied with than anything else; and you must remember how he took Sir Charles Hammond to task before us all, for saying he made a practice of reading family prayers to himself in bed. He never tried to evade them afterwards all the time he was staying with us. And I am sure if you were to represent to Lady Ethel that it is uncle's particular hobby, she would never wish to upset the household arrangements by refusing to appear."

"Oh! of course not—of course not," replied Colonel Bainbridge, who was, nevertheless, anything but sure of his fair lady's dutiful submission to the wishes of her father-in-law, "only I should have preferred her being able to follow her own inclination in the matter." And then he launched forth upon a second edition of her beauties and virtues; keeping poor Maggie in such torture that her morning walk proved but an ineffectual remedy for her sleepless night, and she was thankful when they once more stood together within the hall of Cranshaws.

CHAPTER XXI.

THE COMMENCEMENT OF HOSTILITIES.

NOTHING transpired on the subject of Lady Ethel's absence from prayers that morning except the expression of a general hope that she would be recovered by the afternoon, and towards luncheon hour the young lady, preceded by an unusual bustle, descended to the library. Maggie, who, quietly engaged upon some needlework, was sitting there at the time, thought she had never seen so much fuss made about a single person before. First appeared the German maid, Louise, with a shawl, and a cambric handkerchief, and a bottle of *eau-de-Cologne*, who, after gesticulating wildly in the direction of Miss Henderson and receiving no answer beyond a smile and shake of the head, wheeled Mr Bainbridge's own arm-chair in front of the fire, placed her burthens on the table, and retreated. Then came Colonel Bainbridge, who declared the room was as cold as a cellar, and violently stirring the fire, dragged out a screen which stood against the door to its full length, and disappeared again, grumbling against the draughts in modern houses and the evils of a northern spring as he went. Maggie looked on in silent astonishment at all these arrangements, and was beginning to think that Lady Ethel must really be consumptive or have some complaint of which they had not yet been informed, when the door opened to re-admit her cousin, not bringing his wife on his arm, as a bridegroom might be supposed to do, but following humbly in her train, laden with a French novel and a foot-warmer, made of a stuffed fox, curled round as though he were asleep.

The bride looked still more lovely than she had done the night before, or rather, had it not been for the peevish, discontented expression on her face, she would have done so. She was robed in a morning wrapper of grey cashmere, trimmed with swan's-down, which stood up all round her snowy throat and mingled with the golden tresses of her negligently-arranged hair, and such a costume, though one utterly unsuited to, and calculated to provoke much surprise at Cranshaws, was entirely in accordance with her fair, delicate beauty.

She entered with a lip drawn down, for there had been a little discussion up-stairs between her husband and herself (in which he had come off considerably worsted) respecting her future compliance with the rules of the household.

So Lady Ethel considered herself aggrieved, and Colonel Bainbridge was in greater disgrace than usual, for having presumed to express an opinion on the subject. Though even in these early days of matrimony, unlimited as was her insolence and power over him, she intuitively acknowledged the superiority of the man under whose control she had placed herself, by simply disregarding his wishes, without being able to summon up courage to tell him what she thought of them.

Maggie rose at her approach, and went forward to meet her almost cordially, for the mere sight of Lady Ethel seemed to revive the first impressions she had formed regarding her. But the bride, appearing to have forgotten that any but the commonest courtesies had passed between them, chilled her advances with an indifferent "Good morning," and immediately sunk into the arm-chair that had been placed to receive her. She was too much occupied at that moment, thinking of her own imaginary grievances, to have leisure to remember anything else.

"I don't want it, Colonel Bainbridge," she said in a petulant manner, as he stooped to place her feet into the foot-warmer; "I told you so up-stairs."

"But your feet are so cold, my darling," he urged, affectionately. "You had better use it for a little while, until they are warm again."

But all the answer his assiduity received was in the speaking fact that Lady Ethel kicked the sleeping fox to one side, and placed her slippered feet upon the fender instead. Even this did not seem to annoy him, however, although he made no remark upon it, but drew a chair close to her side, and sitting down after a while, laid his hand caressingly on some portion of her dress or hair.

"I do wish you would leave me alone," Maggie heard her say, with an impatient sigh; "you do fidget me so. Aren't you going out for a walk this morning?"

Doubtless he did fidget her, for nothing on this earth can

be more wearisome to a woman than the attentions for which she has no desire; but then Lady Ethel ought to have remembered that she had brought them on herself.

She had gambled away her pretty humanity and her time, and a score of other trifles, for the sake of maintaining her injured pride; and now that the day for "paying up" had arrived, she was, like many others of her sex in the same predicament, uncommonly averse to fulfilling her part of the agreement. And being in the first weeks of marriage, and in the hands of a very indulgent master, she was allowed for the present to have it all her own way. How long such a state of things would last, however, it was difficult to calculate.

Colonel Bainbridge seemed rather hurt at his second rebuff, if one might judge by his leaving his seat, and taking possession of the newspaper and a chair on the opposite side of the hearthrug; but if he gave the feeling a name, it was only to hope that Maggie would not take his wife's words for more than they were worth.

His cousin, on her part, was more annoyed than himself, for she felt honestly indignant at seeing him repulsed and treated in so curt a manner, and wounded for his sake that she should have been witness to his discomfiture. She took up her work again, and retired to the further end of the room, and brooded silently and sadly on what she had heard. She thought in that moment that she never could fancy again that she should like Lady Ethel, however beautiful or fascinating she might prove; for if she was rude to *him*—if she did not value *his* affection, or care to make *him* happy, there could be no good thing in her.

Meanwhile, Lady Ethel did not even seem to observe the defection of her little acquaintance of the night before, but, listless and unoccupied, reclined in her easy chair in front of the blazing fire, with a screen held up before her face, and her large eyes languidly fixed upon the ceiling. She did not look like an ordinary mortal—so Maggie thought as she stole furtive glances in her direction—in her elaborate and fanciful morning dress, but more like some of the characters she had seen portrayed upon the stage when visiting the theatre during her occasional visits to Birmingham.

It seemed so unnatural to see the pensive, indolent beauty, in her cashmere and swan's-down, reclining in the library at

Cranshaws, and to remember that she was Cousin Thomas's wife—really his own property, who could never again be separated in thought or deed from him—that Maggie wandered off more than once in a dream of things quite different from what they were, and had to recall herself with a sigh to the reality of life.

It was not long before the news that Lady Ethel had descended to the library spread through the house, and Mrs Bainbridge and Miss Lloyd hastened to offer their congratulations on her re-appearance. Anxious to make the best of everything, they had tacitly agreed to ignore the unfavourable impression of the night before, and came in brimful of cordial greeting and kindly solicitude,—Mrs Bainbridge being even brave enough to address her daughter-in-law by the familiar appellation of "my dear."

"Well, my dear! and how do you feel yourself by this time? Our poor Thomas has been quite anxious on your account; but I hope you are none the worse for your journey."

The good, affectionate creature, who would have taken a dairymaid who was honoured by her son's love to her arms, came forward briskly, with the evident intention of folding Lady Ethel in a maternal embrace, had not the look with which she was saluted driven all such presumptuous ideas into the background.

The occupant of Mr Bainbridge's arm-chair, whilst her husband rose immediately to his feet in deference to his mother's presence, opened her big blue eyes at the greeting as though it considerably surprised her, murmured something in reply about being "exceedingly obliged," and "much the same as usual," and—retained her comfortable position.

The want of politeness was too marked to pass unnoticed. Every one looked uneasy, and poor Mrs Bainbridge, who was the humblest nature possible, and the last person in the world to exact unnecessary homage, perceiving the slight shown her, turned red, and immediately directed her attention to her son, who, flushing up to the roots of his hair, began to talk very loud and very fast in a loyal attempt to cover an action which had discomfited them all.

All, that is to say, except the perpetrator of the deed, who remained perfectly passive and unconcerned amidst the general confusion, only interrupting the conversation every now and then to peevishly desire "Colonel Bainbridge" to stir the fire, or bring her a footstool, or perform any one of a dozen little offices which she could have done just as well for herself, though he never would have permitted her to do so.

"Will Lady Ethel come in to luncheon?" demanded Mrs Bainbridge, as the meal was announced. The question was put to her son, she did not venture to address the bride again.

"Oh, I think so! You will come, my dearest, will you not?"

"No, thanks; I will have it in here. It is not worth while to leave the fire."

"Of course not, if you prefer to remain here," acquiesced Mrs Bainbridge, readily, "and the servant shall bring it in to you, my dear."

"*He* can bring it, thank you," said Lady Ethel, with a careless nod in the direction of her husband, who immediately replied that of course he would, and giving his arm to his mother, led her to the dining-room.

"My dear, is it necessary you should take that trouble? could not James do it as well?" remonstrated Mrs Bainbridge a few minutes later, as she watched her son making a collection from all the daintiest dishes on the table to carry on a tray to his wife.

"I would rather do it myself; Ethel likes me to wait upon her," was the rejoinder, as awkwardly lifting his unaccustomed burden he disappeared from the room.

Mrs Bainbridge looked across the table at Miss Lloyd, and sighed. They would have preferred to see Colonel Bainbridge's young wife running gaily about the house upon errands for her husband: it did not tally with their ideas of his dignity and worth to see him turned into a fetcher and carrier.

"Is her ladyship not out of her room yet?" demanded Mr Bainbridge, who had only entered the house at the summons of the luncheon bell. "No wonder she looks so pale and delicate if she lies in bed till this hour every day."

"Oh yes, uncle, she has been down in the library for more than an hour," replied Maggie.

"Then why doesn't she come in to luncheon like other people?"

Mrs Bainbridge shrugged her shoulders.

"I don't know, my dear. You should ask Thomas. I am afraid he has chosen but a weakly wife."

"Or a capricious one," rejoined her husband; and to this remark there succeeded an eloquent silence.

Meanwhile, Colonel Bainbridge, who, with the tray in front of him, made a sad bungle of opening and shutting the library door, and let a draught blow straight in upon Lady Ethel, as she took good care to let him know, had reached his wife's side and deposited his load in safety on the table.

"And now you must let me see you eat something, my dearest," he said, anxiously, as he sat down beside her.

"If you are going to sit there and stare at me all the time, I am quite sure that I shall eat nothing," was the discouraging reply. "Pray go back to your luncheon; your people will think it so strange your remaining here."

"I don't care what they think," he answered. "O Ethel, if you only knew what a delight it is to me to sit and look at you, you would not grudge me the indulgence. It is not much to ask, my darling, is it?" and he placed his hand under her chin and turned up her face to his.

She jerked it away impatiently.

"Ethel! you are unkind."

"Am I? But I have told you so often that I hate to be pulled about. Is it impossible to perform one's duties in the married state without it? I suppose people are differently constituted, but if you want to make me happy, you will leave me alone."

He sighed heavily and moved a few steps further from her. And then, after a slight pause, he said seriously:

"You *know* (and God is my witness) that I *do* wish to make you happy; it is my one great desire, and I suppose I must try and be content not to see it fulfilled in my own way. So long as you love me, Ethel—love and trust in me, dearest—the rest matters little. And so I will leave you now to take your luncheon in peace;" and with a cheerful nod he returned to the company in the dining-room.

As soon as he was gone, Lady Ethel jumped up from her seat, and rushing to the window, gazed on the still, cold, wintry scene outside. It looked like her present life to her.

"I cannot bear it—no, I *cannot* bear it," was the passionate language of her heart; and her knitted brow and clenched hand attested to the strength of that language; "this horrid place—these horrid people—it is more than any woman can bear. But what can I do? where can I go, away from *him?* Oh, heaven! what a fool I have been. I wish that I was dead!"

And then there came a shower of hot tears, which she wiped away as quickly as possible, lest her discomfiture should become patent to "the people" in the other room; but the traces of which, being detected by the anxious eyes of her husband, drew down a loving rebuke upon her, which drove Lady Ethel to her own chamber for the best part of the afternoon.

CHAPTER XXII.

LADY ETHEL IS TAKEN TO TASK.

It may be remembered that Miss Lloyd, when speaking to Maggie Henderson of Colonel Bainbridge's amiable qualities (in those days when they both thought the girl would have been her cousin's choice in marriage), said that "Thomas" was so good and steady as to be competent to be the guide of any young woman; and that they had no doubt but that he would render his wife happy.

And so far as Colonel Bainbridge's true character went, the trust was perfectly justifiable. Moral, from a sense of right as well as refinement; just, because his honour was founded on a rock; firm, because he possessed both sense to form an opinion and courage to maintain it, his was a mind on which a weaker mind might lean for support, and never fear to find its prop give way beneath it. His muscular frame and splendid *physique* were but types of his strong will, as well known in the army as he was himself; and those who saw him intimately could never doubt but that he would be always master in his own house as he was amongst his soldiers. At the same time, no one assumed less power (the really powerful seldom do assume it), or was more silent on the subject of management, or the difference between the intellects of men and women, than Colonel Bainbridge. On the contrary, a stranger might well have imagined that all his convictions leant the other way.

Good-tempered and unselfish to a degree, and conscious of his superior strength, he was just the sort of man to permit the woman whom he loved to go any length with him; as a huge Newfoundland or mastiff may often be seen quietly suffering the impotent attacks of a snappish little terrier, without thinking it worth his while to do more than smile at them.

"The woman whom he loved," I said, but I ought to have added, and whom he imagined loved him in return; for with all his great honest nature, overflowing with the capacity of devotion, Thomas Bainbridge was too proud to cast down his heart to be trampled on for ever, let the feet be never so small, and white, and delicate, that crushed its life out.

He loved well and he loved blindly; but, for that very reason, it would be a more dangerous game to attempt to tear the bandage from his eyes than from those of other men, for he had not hands that could be easily persuaded to tie it on again. And, therefore, had Lady Ethel at that period had any true friend by her side, he would have warned her that in fencing with those two weapons, coldness and caprice, she was sounding the death knell of all future happiness—both for her husband and herself. But she was friendless, and he in no condition to be easily alarmed, for at this time his life, strange to say, appeared to him a paradise. He was too much in love even to perceive her coldness.

To reconcile this statement with the common sense attributed to him (if any excuse is needed for the vagaries of a lover), it must be remembered that Lady Ethel's acceptance of his offer had come on him as such a glad surprise, and so short a period had elapsed since that circumstance, that he had hardly yet realised to himself that they were really man and wife, and had certainly never thought of exerting any marital influence or authority over her. He was still her most willing slave and ardent admirer, who would have gladly served for her as Jacob did for Rachel, and who, on finding himself in sudden and unexpected possession of his coveted treasure, without having had the opportunity to make any love to her before marriage, was taking it out in the most reverential devotion afterwards.

Absurd as most newly-married men make themselves, before custom and companionship have turned their angels into commonplace women, Colonel Bainbridge excelled them all; and his conduct was the more remarkable at Cranshaws, where the whole female community had been used to wait on and make much of him.

But now the times were changed, and if he were not less grateful for the attentions of his aunt and mother, he took less notice of them, for his whole soul was wrapt up in the contemplation of his idol. He waited on her like a servant, watched her every look lest she should require something, stood lost in silent admiration of her person when she was not speaking, and hung upon her words when she condescended to open her mouth. All that afternoon he had been going on like an enamoured school-boy, pursuing his father to the study, his mother into her own room, Aunt Letty to the garden, and poor hapless Maggie everywhere, in order that he might forcibly extract from them, over and over again, the assurance that his wife was the handsomest woman they had ever seen, or that her figure was most graceful, and her taste in dress perfect.

But more than this the honest folks of Cranshaws could not be prevailed upon to say, for they rigidly respected truth, and not even to flatter the proud bridegroom (whom one and all dearly loved) would they praise Lady Ethel's manners, or disposition, or affection for himself. For short a time as she had been amongst them, and unwilling as they were to believe any harm of her, they could not but be already painfully aware of the fact that whatever end Lady Ethel had had in marrying her husband, it had not been the end of loving him. And it galled them that it should be so, it outraged their feelings of affection and respect for the son of the house, the man to whom they looked up as their future head and ruler, who even now possessed the strongest mind as the strongest arm amongst them, and for whom they had imagined no woman could be really good enough. And the little conclave that discussed the behaviour of the bride that afternoon was a very grave one. It was evident that disappointment reigned at Cranshaws. But with the evening things looked brighter, for Lady Ethel reappeared at dinner, having shaken off much of her ill-humour, and if not sociable, had at least forgotten to be glum.

Perhaps she was tired of sulking (it is a very fatiguing *rôle* when kept up for many hours together), or perhaps the genuine, unaffected compliments of her husband on her appearance had softened her heart (for however she may dislike more particular attentions, a woman's breast is seldom impervious to flattery); any way, she looked more animated, and gave longer answers than she had done the evening before, and Colonel Bainbridge in consequence was uplifted to the seventh heaven, and could scarcely take his eyes off her all dinner time.

This improved state of affairs, whilst it inspired the others with content, had the strange effect of making Maggie's spirits sink down to zero. She had been employing herself actively all day, studiously avoiding any opportunities of confidence with Miss Lloyd, and hoping to go to bed as bravely as she rose; but now a deep depression unaccountably took hold of her. She ate her dinner almost in silence, and as soon as it was concluded, and the ladies had adjourned to the drawing-room, flew to her harmonium and took refuge in instrumental music.

But here, in a few minutes, she found that Lady Ethel had pursued her. She raised her eyes, and sickened at the sight of that perfect beauty, set off by lace and delicate muslin, and hung with the ornaments her husband had chosen for her, and Maggie turned her gaze away, almost with a shiver, and bent down closely over the pages of Beethoven.

But her cousin's bride was evidently disposed for conversation.

"How well you play! Have you had a music-master?"

"Only the organist at Mindon, and a few lessons occasionally when I have been at Birmingham," replied Maggie, with a desperate effort to be agreeable. "Do you not sing or play, Lady Ethel?"

"No! I have learned, of course; but I left it off—I didn't care for it; I don't care for anything!" with a sudden, deep-drawn sigh.

"O Lady Ethel! how can you say so?"

"It's the truth! One gets so soon weary of everything in this world;" and the same expression came over Lady Ethel's face that had so powerfully attracted the sympathy of Margaret Henderson the night before—an expression of having utterly finished with all the good that life held for her; and the generous impulse that had prompted her actions then rushed over the girl's heart again as she eagerly replied—

"But you have begun to be weary at the wrong end of life, dear Lady Ethel."

"Yes? Do you find it such a delightful thing to live, then?"

"Oh no;" and Maggie's face flushed crimson. "I suppose no one really does that—it was not intended; only there is always so much left to do, so many duties that involve the happiness of others, that I have thought of late—that is, I sometimes think"— with a stammering, blushing pause, on finding she had lit on such a subject, with such a listener.

"What do you think?" inquired Lady Ethel, struck by her manner.

Maggie had ceased playing now, though she retained her seat at the harmonium.

"I think," she continued, in a low voice, lest she should be overheard by Mrs Bainbridge and Miss Lloyd, "that it is best when we are not too happy in this world; that possessing all that our hearts desire must be so apt to make us cling to this life, and look upon death as an evil instead of a blessing. Don't you find it so?" with a timid appeal in the direction of her companion.

Lady Ethel yawned.

"Oh! for the matter of that, I don't think it much signifies whether we are dead or alive. Do play something lively; I don't like that organ-thing half so well as the piano:" and walking away from the instrument, she turned over the books that lay on the drawing-room table, until the entrance of the gentlemen made the conversation general.

But as the evening progressed, Colonel Bainbridge became manifestly uneasy, and as ten o'clock struck he was almost nervous. Lady Ethel looked up from a book of photographs on which she was employed to watch the footman placing a row of chairs in regular order at the other end of the room, and demanded, sharply—

"What is all that arrangement for?"

"For prayers," said Maggie, softly, remembering the talk she had had with her cousin on the subject that morning. "We always have prayers at ten o'clock, but they won't take long!"

Lady Ethel laughed.

"It is a matter of perfect indifference to me whether they take an hour or ten, for I am going to bed. Good-night!"

"Oh! *do* stay," said Maggie, earnestly, "uncle will be so vexed."

"Ethel! my darling!" remonstrated her husband, in a low voice. But the pleading tones irritated her, and she rose from her seat at once.

"What *nonsense!* As if one could not do as one chose in

such a matter. Colonel Bainbridge, be so good as to light me a candle, will you?"

The old-fashioned silver candlesticks stood in a row upon a table outside the door, and seeing that his wife was resolute, he fetched one, and placed it in her hand.

"Where are you going to?" demanded Mr Bainbridge, as Lady Ethel advanced towards him with the lighted candle.

"To my own room," she replied, haughtily.

She knew that the question denoted opposition, for the bed-room candlestick was evidence of her design.

"But we are just going to have prayers," he said, quietly.

"I know that, thank you! but I have no desire to be present. Good-night."

His sole reply was gently, but firmly, to take the candlestick from her hand, and blowing out the candle, to place it on the mantel-piece, whilst Lady Ethel was too much astonished to oppose him.

"What do you do that for?" she said, angrily, as soon as she had found her tongue.

"My dear," replied the old man, "I don't think the rules of this house are very hard rules; but such as they are, I must have them complied with. Nothing but sickness can justify a person from not being present at family worship. I cannot compel you to serve God from your heart, but, as long as you remain at Cranshaws, you must keep up the appearance of doing so. Here are the servants, you see! Now, go back to your husband like a good girl, and remain quiet until prayers are over. I shall not detain you a quarter of an hour at the outside."

Perhaps Lady Ethel had never been spoken to in such a manner in her life before. She had been opposed and fought against, but to be completely set down and ordered to do a thing, as though she had been a child, was a complete novelty to her. Amazement at the boldness of her father-in-law, and a gentlewoman's innate desire to avoid anything like an *exposé* before the lower orders, forced her back in silence to her seat, where she sat out the prayers that followed.

But it is doubtful if one word of them reached her ear, far less her heart.

She was almost lost the while in rage and indignation,

brooding angrily on the affront she had received, and wondering in what way she could resent it.

Her husband, who was disposed to be almost as offended as herself at his father's curt way of speaking, viewed her acquiescence in his wishes with the greatest surprise, wondering what had come to his high-spirited darling that she should be so meek. But he was not long left in doubt. They had scarcely risen from their knees, and the train of servants had not yet filed out of the room, when Lady Ethel, casting a withering glance upon Mr Bainbridge (which fell perfectly harmless, as the old gentleman was busy placing the markers in his books), and without a single parting salutation to the rest of the company, swept from the apartment. Her husband of course rushed after her, and then the domestics also disappeared, and the Cranshaws' party was left to itself.

"O Mr Bainbridge!" exclaimed his wife, in a tone of vexation, as soon as they found themselves alone, "what can have induced you to insist upon Lady Ethel remaining to prayers this evening? I am sure that you have very much offended her, and our dear Thomas into the bargain. Such a pity, so soon, too—and upon their wedding visit. I do think our guests might be allowed to judge for themselves in these matters."

"Then you think very wrongly," was the determined reply. "I never interfere with the amusements of our guests; they may neglect me as much as they choose, but as long as they remain here they must respect their Maker outwardly, if not inwardly. And I believe, after all, that's the best way to make them respect me, too."

"But Lady Ethel has never been used to these things," pleaded Mrs Bainbridge, "and she is so young, and"——

"She is as old as Maggie, isn't she?" returned her husband, sternly. "Elizabeth, it is of no use your attempting to argue the matter with me. When I see a godless young woman—especially the wife of my own son (more's the pity), it is my duty to remind her of hers upon the very first opportunity. How can I tell that I shall live till to-morrow to remind her of it, or she, to hear me speak? And as for offending Thomas, that is quite a secondary consideration; he ought to be ashamed of himself, for having lighted the candle for her.

A man who does not know how to guide his wife aright has no business to be married at all."

Here the discussion ended, and though neither bride nor bridegroom reappeared that evening, it was not renewed amongst them.

Lady Ethel continued to attend family worship whenever she was down-stairs; though she seemed to take delight in behaving as badly as she possibly could during its continuance; and the slightest reproof from the lips of her husband, or father-in-law, invariably made her worse instead of better.

Yet, she never forgave the old man for the rebuke he had administered to her pride—not, that is to say, until her forgiveness, as far as this world is concerned, was, to all intents and purposes, valueless.

CHAPTER XXIII.

A NOBLE RESOLUTION.

It was two days after this event that Aunt Letty, going unexpectedly into Maggie Henderson's bed-room, was surprised to find her in a deluge of tears.

Surprised, because during those two days, whilst Lady Ethel had been barely polite to Mrs Bainbridge and herself, and pertinaciously disrespectful to her father-in-law (a circumstance which the old man felt more than he cared to acknowledge), she had been even cordial in her manner towards Maggie, much more so than she was to her husband; and Miss Lloyd had begun to hope that a friendship between the two girls might help to eradicate all feelings of jealousy from the mind of her niece.

But she was crying now, as though her heart would break, as though hers were the weakest nature possible, and she had never made that heroic resolution to take up her cross and bear it manfully.

"Maggie, my dear, is it anything new?" demanded Miss Lloyd, half fearfully, as her footsteps were arrested by the sight of the girl's grief.

"Oh no! Aunt Letty. Why did you come here to catch me just now? I bear it so badly—so very badly—I am quite ashamed of myself!"

"Badly, my darling! and when I have been thinking you so brave!"

"That is because you don't know how wicked I am—what evil thoughts I have," said Maggie, mournfully, as she lifted her swollen eyes to her aunt's face. "Dear—I am sure you will despise me for saying so—but I wish sometimes that I could hate her."

"O Maggie! is that really true? You seem to get on so nicely with Lady Ethel, better than any one else in the house."

"Yes, I know; and I *do* like her, or rather I *should* like her if she were anybody else; and that makes it worse, because

I feel so mean. But, aunt, I didn't know—I couldn't realise what it would be to see them together, and all day long, and I shut out from everything—it seems so hard!" and here the girl broke down again, and the small table on which she leaned shook with the violence of her emotion. Miss Lloyd was a good comforter; she knew when to speak and when to hold her tongue; and on the present occasion she sat down in silence by her niece's side, and waited patiently until she should renew the conversation.

"I don't know what you can think of me," said Maggie, presently, making an effort to keep down her choking sobs, "after all I said about this, and the fine resolutions that I made; but to act as though I were indifferent to what is going on around us, is more difficult than I thought it would be."

"You were quite right to make the resolutions, my child," replied Aunt Letty, quietly; "but I should have been very much surprised if you had kept them without a single drawback; in fact, I should have been disposed, in that case, to doubt whether you had not deceived yourself in fancying you entertained any affection for your cousin. There has been a great strain on your mind during the past few days, and this is the inevitable reaction. You will go on all the more bravely for a little relief."

"Oh! what comfort it is to tell you anything, Aunt Letty," said Maggie, with a grateful smile struggling through her tears. "You always seem to put matters straight again. But I have not told you half my wickedness yet. If I only disliked her, or was jealous and envious of her, however wrong, you know it would still be natural, but it is much worse than that! I actually feel annoyed with myself because I *can't* dislike her, and because, in spite of all her rudeness to uncle and aunt and cousin Thomas, and her careless way of speaking of everything serious, I feel my heart drawn towards her in an inexplicable manner; just as though it were possible that we ever could be friends."

"And why is it impossible, my dear?"

"Oh! I don't know!—but it can never be, Aunt Letty—it is against nature."

"Granted, Maggie! but I thought that you and I had pledged ourselves to fight against nature It will be difficult, perhaps, and sometimes very trying; too trying to endure if you depend upon your own strength—but it is not impossible."

"She does not need me," murmured Maggie. "She has *him*—she has everything!"

"I cannot echo your words, my dear, for I think that poor Lady Ethel may have great need of you, and that her coming here, and taking a capricious fancy for you alone out of all her new relations, may just be one of those mysterious and inscrutable means by which He furthers His designs. One cannot help seeing what she is—careless, irreligious, and wedded to the things of this world—without that strong love for her husband which might prove her safeguard whilst passing through it. May not God have thrown you two together (who are so well suited by sex and age to become friends) in order that you may exert a wholesome influence on each other; she by fortifying your strength under trial, and you by showing her that under no circumstances can a Christian's life be an unhappy one?"

"O aunt! you expect more of me than I am able to perform."

"Not so, Maggie, for I expect you to do nothing by yourself."

"But, Aunt Letty, I know that He is always ready to hear and answer prayer; but these petty feelings, these wretched paltry jealousies, and mean heart-burnings at another's gain—they do appear so utterly opposed to everything we have heard of Him; so foreign to His purity and sanctity of life, that I feel sometimes as though it must be a desecration of His holiness, even to name them to Him! It is impossible that He can sympathise in the grosser passions of this earth."

"Maggie, my dear, think what you are saying. You are actually contradicting the Bible, which teaches us that we cannot have one feeling which He has not felt before us."

"But, Aunt Letty, you don't mean to say that you suppose"——

And Maggie's reverence was too great to allow her to complete the sentence.

"I suppose nothing, dear; but I believe what I have read. Although the details given us of our Lord's life are few, I know that He was perfect Man, as well as perfect God, and tempted in every point, like as we are, though without sin. And are not these trials of the affections, Maggie, amongst the commonest temptations that fall to men? There is not a man in the world, let him be the greatest saint that ever lived, that has not had, in some shape or other, to struggle against the impulses of his heart, and often to fight long and hard; to die, sword in hand, before he could overcome the enemy. And is it probable that He, who bore all our sins and griefs in His own person, should have escaped or overlooked what is to His creatures, perhaps, their deepest source of trouble?"

"I never thought of that," said Maggie, softly; "but 'tis very sweet to believe that He has felt it, and can make allowances. Aunt Letty, you have made the burden lighter. He has lifted up the other end again. I can go on now."

"My child, I know you will, and bravely. And what about poor Lady Ethel, Maggie?"

"Why should you call her 'poor?' She appears so rich to me."

"Because, just now, you are not capable of judging. To me she seems the poorest creature I have met for many a day. She has just—nothing."

"I am sure that she has all *his* heart."

"And values it as much as you would that of her maid. Maggie, I must repeat it, with all her wealth and beauty and nobility of birth, and the affection of her husband, Lady Ethel is a pauper."

"If so, she is a willing one; for she has but to put out her hand and grasp it all."

"That does not follow, because love is not compulsory. How should you find it, Maggie, were you to give yourself in marriage this very day to one of the young Appletons, or any man to whom you were equally indifferent?"

"But, aunt, you know that I couldn't; that, under present circumstances, it would be impossible to me."

"Yes, dear, I do know it; but to some women it is not impossible, and in that fact may lie a solution to the mystery."

"But that is a very, very sad suggestion on your part, Aunt Letty. I never thought it could be quite so bad as that."

"Remember that I know no facts, my dear, and that I am only speaking upon supposition. But of one thing I am certain, from whatever cause it may arise, Lady Ethel is not happy. She is an orphan, who does not appear to have any regrets for the home she has left, and certainly is disappointed with the one she has come to, and there seems to be but little confidence between her and her husband. There is only one person here with whom she feels disposed to make friends, and between that person and herself there is a barrier; a natural barrier, though not an insuperable one. Maggie, my darling, I daresay for a while it will make your trial harder to you; but if you could resolve, as far as in you lies, to be a friend to this poor girl, I believe that you might do her good, and in the end you will feel happier for it. It may not be the precise way in which you anticipated suffering, but when you promised to carry your cross cheerfully, you made no bargain as to which road you should go."

There was a short pause, during which the girl was gazing straight out of the window, and striving to make up her mind.

"I do resolve," she answered presently, in a firm, low voice; "I will put no further restraint upon my impulses, but let my heart open as wide as it naturally will towards her, and try to gain her confidence in return."

"It is a noble resolution, Maggie," said Miss Lloyd, "and it will bring its own reward. In trying to sound the depths of another suffering heart, you will forget to look so closely upon the wounds of your own."

CHAPTER XXIV.

MAGGIE PLEADS HER COUSIN'S CAUSE.

MAGGIE kept her word; and during the next few days, by reason of following freely the dictates of her frank nature, made such progress in her intimacy with her cousin's wife, that Lady Ethel, selfishly unobservant of the feelings or wishes of others, kept her constantly by her side, and in a patronising manner openly expressed to her the dissatisfaction she experienced with everything at Cranshaws.

Indeed, Maggie, and the German maid, Louise (who, to Mrs Bainbridge's great dislike, she would continually send for to attend upon her in the general sitting-room, where they carried on lengthy conversations in German, intelligible to none but themselves), were the only individuals with whom Lady Ethel condescended to exchange more than the commonest civilities of social life.

But Maggie, notwithstanding the interest she took in everything that concerned her cousin, and her desire to please him, found enforced friendship with his wife to be no sinecure, and had it not been for her resolution, and the encouragement she received from her Aunt Letty, would often have felt tempted to retreat to her former standing-ground.

For, in the first place, Colonel Bainbridge, whose eyes were beginning to be opened to the fact that Lady Ethel might conduct herself with greater civility towards the members of his family, was so charmed to find that, notwithstanding her behaviour, one of them, at least, continued cordial with her, that he took to thanking Maggie for her kindness, and imparting little confidences to her concerning his bride and his devotion to her, which were naturally very painful for the girl to listen to.

And, on the other hand, Lady Ethel so often made remarks derogatory to her husband or his relations in Maggie's hearing, which she felt herself compelled to comment on, that more than once their intimacy had been on the point of being ruptured; for, notwithstanding the fancy she had taken for her, my heroine's inclinations were subservient to her pride, and it often cost her young friend more pain than any one but herself could calculate, to summon up courage to utter the remonstrance which she felt she had no right to withhold. And yet, though Lady Ethel was often indignant, and more than once seriously offended at her boldness, after a few hours she invariably came back to Maggie's side again, with the petulant declaration that she was the only creature in Cranshaws fit to speak to.

When Sunday came round, the bride refused to go to church with the rest of the family. This was not so remarkable a circumstance, because the church was three miles distant, and the road to it a very rough one; but whilst discussing the subject with her husband in Maggie's presence, she spoke so rudely and bitterly to him, that Colonel Bainbridge, who had kept his patience wonderfully thitherto, suddenly flushed up to his temples with displeasure, and quitted the room without another word.

As the door closed behind him, Lady Ethel laughed.

"He 's in a nice temper, isn't he, to go to church? I hope his psalm-singing will do him good. I am sure he needs it."

Maggie did not know what to reply. She was standing at the window, in her bonnet and shawl, waiting for the carriage to come round; and she had been shocked to hear the tone in which Lady Ethel spoke to her husband. Colonel Bainbridge had turned once and appealed to her; and the look of pain in his face had been so great, that the tears had rushed to her eyes at the sight of it, and prevented her from answering. And still, she was feeling the disgrace and the shame to him so deeply, that she could hardly trust her voice to say what she thought of the scene which had just taken place.

"Well, Maggie! are you sulking up in that corner? Why don't you speak? Which side will you declare for, Colonel Bainbridge's or mine?"

"I never will declare for a wife against her husband, Lady Ethel, and especially so good a husband as my cousin is to you."

"Dear, dear!" exclaimed the bride, sarcastically, though she changed colour and looked uncomfortable at the rebuke, "you quite affect me. Under whom have you been studying the duties of married life so closely?"

But sarcasm was a weapon with which Maggie Henderson

had no idea of fencing; it was so completely opposed to every phase of her character: and she answered Lady Ethel's retort by coming suddenly to the spot where she was sitting, and kneeling down beside her—

"Dear Lady Ethel! you will think me very bold to say so, but you know that you have been wrong. Why do you not love him more? What has he done that you should make him so unhappy?"

The wet, innocent brown eyes, with their true expression, were gazing earnestly into hers, and Lady Ethel forgot, or was too much astonished, to be angry. But she turned her own eyes uneasily away.

"I don't mean to make him unhappy. I have a right to say what I think. Colonel Bainbridge and I perfectly understand each other."

"But why claim your right when you see it hurts his feelings; he is so good, so tender, and so gentle with all weaker things" — here the speaker's voice slightly faltered, but quickly recovered itself—"and he loves you so much that I am sure there could never be the shadow of a disagreement between you, if you treated him more kindly."

"Kindly! what nonsense you are talking, Maggie! What do you know about such things?"

"I can see that he is not happy, Lady Ethel—and neither are you."

It was a desperate thing to say to such a woman; but Maggie felt as though the case were desperate, and her words had a totally different effect to what she anticipated.

Lady Ethel's white teeth closed cruelly upon her under lip, and the tears rose to her eyes, though she dashed them impatiently away.

"If it is the case, it is not my fault," she answered presently, in a husky voice.

"Oh yes, it is! in a great measure," replied Maggie, emboldened by the mood of her companion; "for instance, Lady Ethel, the name by which you call him, it sounds so strange—so unlike what most wives do."

"I care nothing about most wives," rejoined Lady Ethel, growing colder as Maggie entrenched upon the privilege she had gained; "it is his proper name, I believe."

"No, not for you! *you* who are the person he cares for

most in all the world. And he would be so pleased if you were to call him 'Thomas!'" with a coaxing little smile; "you will, dear Lady Ethel! now, won't you?"

But this was going a step too far.

"Indeed! I shall do no such thing; a nasty common name, only fit for stablemen and ploughboys. I hate the very sound of it! If his parents wanted to hear his name called all over the house, they ought to have given him a decent one."

"It was his grandfather's," said Maggie, indignantly.

"Yes? I didn't know he had had a grandfather," was the bride's reply.

Maggie was silent for a moment, and then the full force of the sarcasm striking her, she coloured violently, and rising to her feet, retreated some distance from her companion.

"O Lady Ethel! you are cruel," she said, in a low voice, "you are worse than cruel—why did you ever marry him?"

"Maggie, my dear, the carriage is round, and your uncle is waiting," said Miss Lloyd, putting her head in at the door; and, without another word, the girl joined her friends, leaving Lady Ethel to answer to herself, as best she might, the question she had put to her.

CHAPTER XXV.

SISTER MARGARET.

THE drive to church that morning was not an exhilarating one, for Maggie was unusually silent, and Colonel Bainbridge, who rode on horseback by the side of the carriage, scarcely opened his lips.

Neither of them could shake off the depression occasioned by Lady Ethel's words, and yet each was loyally afraid to confess it to the other by so much as a look.

The church at Mindon was one of those unpretending structures which are to be found plentifully scattered over the land of Scotland, where, although the liturgy of the Church of England is ostensibly performed, it has become so imbued by the example of Presbyterianism on one side, and Dissent on the other, as to be little superior to the services of those communions. Everything about it, in fact, had gone to sleep. The building itself, fast-locked from Sunday to Sunday, was so damp and cold when it was opened, that none but the strong and hearty ventured to worship in it; the village choir was ignorant, unruly, and constantly disorganised; and, worse than all, the incumbent was an old man, of the old school, who took no interest in trying to improve the reigning state of things, but thought that what had satisfied their forefathers should satisfy them, and that the less alterations that were made or primitive customs revived in the service of the church the better. And yet he was a man of lively temperament, who had a keen curiosity for learning all that went on in the world, and rubbed his hands with satisfaction whenever his newspaper informed him of some new discovery in science, some idea brought to perfection, or patent put within the reach of all; and chuckling to his wife, would say, "*that* was the way to do it; *that* was the way to get on;" and the world was a very different world from what it had been when he was young; yet when his eye lit on reports of Ritual Commissioners, or accounts of the actions brought in various quarters by those industrious fleas, the members of the Church

Association, he altered his tune altogether. Improvements in steam-ships, electric telegraphy, or underground railways, were all right—they were for the use and convenience of man, and to further the commerce and comfort of this precious world in which we live; but to toil and spend money, and endure persecution for the sake of making the love of worshipping God come more home to the senses, and take deeper root in the hearts of sinners, was quite another thing in the eyes of the incumbent of Mindon, and directed his thoughts perhaps too rudely to the damp little church from which he derived his income, the rough choir, who sung all out of tune, and the old sermons, now yellow with age, which, year after year, he monotonously poured into the ears of his sleepy congregation without making the least palpable difference in its behaviour.

"Foolish fellows! foolish fellows," he would exclaim, meaning of course, *not* the Church Association party; "why cannot they be content to leave matters as they have always been? Well, my dear! for my part, I cannot feel sufficiently thankful that I am out of all that kind of thing!"

And in like manner, doubtless, many of the friends of those "foolish fellows" who were martyred for the faith, of old, congratulated themselves also.

But unsatisfying as were the Sunday services at Mindon Church, Maggie Henderson delighted in them. She saw so little of congregational worship, and so seldom had the opportunity of claiming the gracious promise attached to it, that it was a pleasure to her simple soul merely to find herself amongst her fellow-creatures, and to feel that they depended for their salvation on one common hope. And when her cousin sat next her in the pew, and the same words left their lips at the same time, the pleasure was greatly enhanced.

As Mindon was the only church for several miles round in which the English service was performed, the congregation was generally composed of families who came from some distance to attend it, and it was a great rarity to see a stranger there.

Maggie could not imagine, therefore, what ailed the people when first she had leisure to notice them that morning; for they were bobbing up and down in their seats, and whispering together in a most unseemly manner; until her cousin touched her arm, and, turning her head in the direction intimated, she saw, in the pew of their neighbours the Appletons, one of those women who, by their spirit and example of self-sacrifice, are doing so much to raise the standard of religion in the Church of England—a Sister of Mercy.

There she sat, in her white head-dress and black robe and veil, attired so sombrely and yet with a face so full of cheerful, sweet content, dead to the world, but who should live when the world dies, and apparently quite unconscious of the commotion she was causing.

There was something in the sight of her that powerfully affected Maggie, for she knew the Sister's mission and its cause; and the tears rushed to her eyes, as a sudden new hope sprung up in her heart, that a vision of her own possible future had been granted to her. She gazed at the interesting stranger until the service commenced, and then experienced quite a difficulty in tearing her mind away from her and fixing it on the solemn work she had in hand.

But Maggie did it; for to control her inclinations had been one of the earliest lessons instilled by her Aunt Letty, though the last-named lady, guessing the cause, was quite amused by the eagerness her niece evinced to get out of church as soon as ever the service was concluded.

"The Appletons, aunt," she whispered. "Don't let them go without our speaking to them. I do so want to know who it is they had in their pew to-day." But Maggie need not have been in such a hurry; there was little chance of her being disappointed, for the opportunities for gossip were too rare in that part of the country for neighbours to separate after church before they had spoken to each other. And the Appletons, who were not quite easy at appearing there in company with a friend dressed in so unusual and striking a manner, considered they should only be doing what was due to themselves, by apologising to their acquaintances for the fact.

"How do you do, Mrs Bainbridge? I hope I see you quite well, ma'am! My cousin, Miss Thomson" (indicating the Sister, who smiled pleasantly and held out her hand)—"Sister Margaret, as I suppose I should call her," with a shrug of the shoulders and a look half deprecating, half amused; and then Mrs Appleton lowered her voice and became confidential. "A good creature, Mrs Bainbridge—

thoroughly good and honest, I believe—but sadly mistaken in her views, as you must see."

"Oh, I hope not!" murmured Mrs Bainbridge, drawing her shawl closer around her as some vague fear of the infection of Popery flitted through her mind. "I heard that those kind of ladies did so much good amongst the poor, and were so amiable."

"I'm sure it is most kind of you to say so," replied her neighbour, returning thanks for the united Sisterhood of England. "Ah! well! we must not judge! and she has been ill, poor thing; over-worked herself, I believe, in night-schools or some of these extraordinary new institutions they have got up in London, and has come here for a few weeks to recruit her health. Miss Maggie and she seem to be getting on wonderfully together. I have just been telling your good aunt, Miss Maggie," she continued, raising her voice again to attract the notice of Maggie Henderson, who was already talking eagerly with Sister Margaret, "that my cousin has been ill lately, and has come to Horse-ap-Cleugh to try what Scottish air will do for her."

"Oh! it will do her good! I am sure it will!" replied the girl, quickly raising her bright sympathetic eyes to the stranger's face; "it is so fresh and invigorating. Shall you stay here long?"

"I don't know, but I hope not; that is to say, I must go back to my work as soon as possible."

"And does your work take up much of your time?" Sister Margaret smiled.

"All of it—every moment—I have not one to spare!"

"But that must be very trying; no wonder it tells upon your health; and you do not look strong enough for hard work. Are you not often tired?"

"No, indeed! I sooner get weary where I have nothing to do. When one is constantly employed there is no time to think about one's self."

"And you do it all for love?"

"Oh, no! My Master pays me well," returned the Sister, brightly, and the words met with a ready echo in her hearer's breast.

"How I envy you!" she cried, enthusiastically.

The stranger looked at her. Yes! there were on her face

the traces of suffering, unmistakable to those who had also suffered—marks that the soul had received its baptism of woe, the gold been dipped in the refiner's fire; and her interest in the young girl was immediately awakened.

Sister Margaret must have had great experience in grief to have guessed the truth so quickly, for Maggie's sorrow had not destroyed the freshness of her beauty, as it had done that of Lady Ethel; and the signs of it were only to be met with in the chastened glances of her eye, and the pensive tremulous expression of her mouth.

She was suffering; but not so deeply as my heroine, for there was no bitterness nor self-reproach mingled with her grief, and she had experienced help throughout it, of which Lady Ethel knew nothing. And probably Sister Margaret guessed something of that truth also.

"Perhaps I may see you again, whilst I am at Horse-ap-Cleugh," she said, cordially, as the parties were about to separate. "I shall be glad if it is so."

"Oh! may I come and talk to you? Then I will come to-morrow," replied Maggie, eagerly—so eagerly that Miss Lloyd laughed, on their way home, at her new-born enthusiasm for Mrs Appleton's cousin.

They were walking together arm-in-arm over the moors, in the style that Maggie loved; for the day had turned out so bright and pleasant, that they abandoned the carriage to Mr and Mrs Bainbridge, and preferred to find their way home on foot—Colonel Bainbridge having ridden forward long before, to gain the presence of his beloved tormentor.

When Miss Lloyd began her gentle quizzing, Maggie only squeezed her arm tight, and pressed up closer to her. There never was greater love nor confidence between women than existed between these two.

"I confess I have taken a great fancy for her," she said, laughing; "but you needn't be jealous, Aunt Letty; there is no occasion, for I think it is Sister Margaret's dress that attracts me, quite as much as herself."

"Oh! my dear, how can you say so? I think it is the most unbecoming costume I ever saw."

"And her name, too," continued the girl, musingly, "Margaret—the same as mine—it seems so curious that it should be so."

"But, Maggie, there is nothing particularly strange in that; it is the commonest name possible in this country."

But Maggie did not answer.

"O auntie!" she burst out passionately, after a brief pause. "How I wish that I could be the same as she is. A life like that would cure me. To be always working for the suffering and the poor; waiting on them, and nursing them, and teaching them—there would be no time left (she said so herself) to brood over one's own petty troubles. Oh! how I wish—I wish that I could throw off every trammel that binds me to the world—that I could feel that I had renounced everything like comfort and luxury for ever, and go forth amongst the sick and needy, as He did, and spend the rest of my life with them."

"Do you think you would be any the happier for it?" quietly demanded Miss Lloyd, after a short silence.

"What! doing His work? Aunt Letty, I wonder you can ask the question!"

"But *would* it be His work, my child? That is the point I should like to hear you settle for yourself."

"It has always been considered so," replied Maggie, dubiously.

"Yes, for some people—some who seem especially called, by loss of friends and consequent exemption from home ties, to make God's family their own. But you could never imagine that a woman was obeying God's voice by leaving her father and mother (for instance) against their wishes, to go and wait upon the father or mother of somebody else—would you?"

"No; I suppose not."

"Therefore, whilst we have duties at home, waiting for us to fulfil, I don't think we should even let our minds dwell too inquiringly upon a condition which is not likely to become ours, and which in all probability we should relish no better than our present one, if it did."

"I shall never be able to do anything more for Him than I do now, at that rate," said Maggie, heaving a deep sigh.

"Don't say that, my dear. Wherever we are placed we must strive to progress, daily and hourly, in the fulfilment of our duties, both towards Him and our neighbours."

"But, oh! aunt, I have been dreaming such a heavenly

dream. I thought it would be so grand to rise up, and, shaking off all this sorrow that oppresses and keeps me down, to go forth into the world and succour those who have been tried as I have. It looked so easy—so delightful; and now you say that it can never be!"

"No, Maggie, I did not go so far as that. I only said (and I am sure that Sister Margaret would be the first to uphold my statement) that we must not imagine we can serve God better, by forsaking the duties He has placed before us, in order to perform others which we think will be more conducive to His glory! He knows best about His glory: all we have to do as servants is to obey Him."

"Then don't you think that women are ever right to leave home and become members of a sisterhood? Do you think that Sister Margaret could possibly please God better than she is doing now?"

"My dear, I know nothing about Sister Margaret; I was speaking only of yourself. You would like to run away and desert us all—(we value you more than ever, you know, Maggie, now that your cousin seems lost to us)—and break your poor old uncle's heart, as I verily believe you would, in order to add your mite of work to the hundreds of hands—hands that perhaps have no one dependent on them—labouring amongst the poor."

"Oh no! Aunt Letty, that is not true," cried Maggie, warmly; "you know I would never desert you. I would sooner die."

"Well, darling, you must do something more. You must try and believe that since you have been placed and given duties *here*, it would be impossible, under present circumstances, for you to serve God so well anywhere else."

"I *will* believe it," replied the girl, in a low voice.

"I can quite understand your feelings, my dear," continued Aunt Letty, affectionately. "You have had a great and mortifying disappointment, and you would like to shake off, not only the grief, but all remembrance of it; to change place and work and companions; to change even yourself, if that were possible. But, consistently with duty and gratitude, it is not possible, Maggie, and therefore you must not even indulge yourself by dreaming of it. No one could honour the noble sisterhoods of the whole Catholic Church more than I do.

They are a glory and blessing to the nations to which they belong, and I doubt not will receive an exceeding great reward when their work is completed. But, at present, my Maggie, your place is not amongst them. We should sorely miss our little Sister of Mercy at home."

"You say 'at present,' Aunt Letty. Do you think, then, it may *ever* come to pass?" inquired Maggie, earnestly.

"If your life is spared and you continue in the same mind, my dear, there is no saying what may happen during the next fifty years. But I wouldn't speculate about it. Speculation even is a want of faith in Him who will order all things according to His will."

"But if He ever wills it, auntie; if He opens the way for me, and makes all things smooth, *you* would not keep me back from it, would you?"

"Keep you back, my darling? You might as well ask me if I would keep you back from entering Heaven. No, Maggie, when all you speak of comes to pass, I will be the first to put that great ugly flapping cap and black veil upon your dear little head; and I don't think I could give you a greater proof of my complete resignation than that, my sweet bonnie girl!" and betwixt laughing and crying, the two women stopped upon the moor, and held each other in a long and fervent embrace.

CHAPTER XXVI.

A SWORD-THRUST.

THERE was a slight coolness between Maggie Henderson and Lady Ethel during the remainder of that day. The bride chose to resent the last words that her husband's cousin had spoken to her, although her heart told her that they had been well merited, and Maggie felt that she could not conscientiously profess to be sorry for having said what she should be compelled to say over again did the opportunity recur. And so she left Lady Ethel that afternoon to the company of Colonel Bainbridge, and, taking her book into her uncle's study, sat on a footstool at his feet, with her head resting on his knee, and alternately read and conversed with him, until the gong sounded a summons to dinner.

She thought, once or twice, during that evening, that she caught Lady Ethel looking rather wistfully in her direction, as though she wanted to be friends again, and her tender heart reproached itself with being hard; but when she tried to say or do something to show that the occurrence of the morning was forgotten, the remembrance of the insult cast on her cousin—on *him*—and on her cousin's family, rose up to prevent it.

And so they parted for the night with the most ordinary salutation, and Maggie began to think she should be very glad when Lady Ethel's visit had come to a conclusion.

The next day was favourable for a walk, and having ascertained that Mrs Bainbridge was going to drive to Borthwick, and would not require her attendance, Maggie's desires turned towards Sister Margaret and Horse-ap-Cleugh, only she was not sure whether, after the conversation she had held with Aunt Letty, it would be right to indulge herself by going there.

"You know, dear," she said frankly to Miss Lloyd, "that we shall be sure to talk about her work and the rules of her

Sisterhood, and all the other delights, and I shan't be able to help wishing just a little; and so if you think it best for me not to go, I will send an excuse instead."

"Will you promise me, Maggie, if you should see Sister Margaret, and indulge in that sort of conversation, that you will repeat to her faithfully what you told me yesterday, and my remarks upon it?"

"Oh yes, aunt! I should have no objection to do so."

"Well, then, go, my dear, by all means, for I am quite sure what she will say, and that her advice will do you more good than mine."

And so, mounted on her pony, and accompanied by two or three favourite dogs, Maggie set off for Horse-ap-Cleugh directly after luncheon.

She did not see Lady Ethel before starting, for, either from laziness or ill-humour, the bride had lain in bed again that morning; and when she descended to the luncheon-room some time after the meal had been announced, she found it deserted by all except her husband, who, with his hands thrust into the side pockets of a loose velvet coat, was lounging moodily upon the hearthrug. There had evidently been some difference between them that morning; for though Lady Ethel entered the dining-room with some clatter, and one or two outspoken complaints against the domestic arrangements of Cranshaws, he did not even move from his position, but with sad eyes and gravely-fixed mouth, continued to gaze stedfastly into the fire; for though men will be taken in and gulled over and over again by the women who profess to love them, where there is not even a profession made, it does not take them long to shake off sleep and rub their eyes and see. Love, unresponded to, may drag out its existence, but it is quite impossible that it should thrive. The bride did not appear to admire remaining unnoticed. She settled herself pompously in her seat, made raids upon various dishes collected round her, declared there was nothing on the table fit to eat, and then, suddenly throwing down her knife and fork, turned round on him like a little fury.

"Why on earth don't you say something? Sticking there, before the fire, and thinking of no one but yourself. You have no more manners than a bear!"

But the only answer that he made her was to move towards the door.

"Colonel Bainbridge!" with an impatient movement of her foot, "where are you going? You might have the civility to reply when you are spoken to?"

Then he halted, came half-way back into the centre of the room, and raised his reproachful eyes to hers.

"I should hardly have thought you took so much interest in my movements, Ethel; I am going with my mother to Borthwick."

"To Borthwick—what for?"

"To see an old friend!"

"What friend?"

"No one, I think, that you would care to hear about—my god-mother, Mrs Hodson."

"And who is she—a grocer's wife?"

"No, she is not a grocer's wife," he answered, calmly disregarding the insolence of her remark, although he flushed painfully as she delivered it; "she is the widow of a general in the army."

"Oh, dear me! what aristocratic company we are getting amongst. But I am afraid the general's widow must wait for the pleasure of seeing you. You can't go this afternoon, because I want you!"

"O Ethel, dearest!" he exclaimed, his eyes lighting up with excitement; "I wish I thought you *did* want me—that my presence were in any degree necessary to your happiness; but you know that it is all caprice, and that if I stayed at home to please you, you would probably shut yourself up in your room for the whole of the afternoon!"

"That is as it may be," she answered, indifferently; "but anyway you must remain at Cranshaws!"

But he would not allow her to press her advantage.

"I am sorry to say that I cannot do so, Ethel; I have already promised to attend my mother."

"And you set you mother before *me?*"

"I do not, either in love or duty, as you know well; but in this instance I must keep to my word. In the first place, I asked you to accompany us this morning, and you refused"——

"As if I am going to visit all the farmers' wives for ten miles round!" she interposed.

"Very well! I did not press it—only I cannot permit your fancies to interfere with what I consider to be my duty. I have not accompanied my mother yet to see any of her friends—it pleases her as well as them—and from this lady I have received a great deal of kindness ever since I was a child. Nothing could have given me greater pleasure, Ethel, than to have introduced you to her."

"*Milles rèmercimens, monsieur!*" she interrupted, with a scornful curtsey; "but I prefer to remain where I am, and that you remain here also."

"That is out of the question," he said, firmly, as he turned upon his heel.

"Colonel Bainbridge! you *shall* stay—I insist upon it," in a heightened voice.

"Do not be so foolish, Ethel! Do you intend to make the whole house cognisant of our quarrel?"

"I don't care if it is! I don't care if the whole world knows how disrespectfully you treat me! You ought to be ashamed of yourself!"

"Oh! my darling! my darling!" he exclaimed, with the vain hope that his love might touch where his determination failed, "for God's sake don't cut up all our happiness in this way! You know that I would do anything in reason for you, Ethel—that my life and everything that belongs to me is at your service; but this is not reason, my love; this is a mere child's fancy that you have taken into your silly little head," and returning to her side, as though it were not worth his while to quarrel seriously with anything so young, and soft, and fair as she was, he put his kind arms round her girlish figure. But she shook herself free from his embrace, as though it had been that of a serpent.

"Don't touch me!" she cried angrily, and in her anger unheeding what she said, "don't dare to touch me, or to speak to me! I *hate* you!"

As the assertion struck his ear, he changed colour, his arms dropped listlessly to his sides, and, without another look, he turned away, and left the room.

It was the first time her unkind words had hit him mortally. Former ones had come and gone, settling on his heart for a moment, and wounding as they settled; but their pain had been but transitory, like that occasioned by a stinging fly.

But these, when taken in connection with the tone, the look, the action, that accompanied them, were as poison dropped upon his soul, the effect of which, though salved over, was never entirely eradicated.

CHAPTER XXVII.

GALL AND WORMWOOD.

Colonel Bainbridge left the house without speaking to his wife again, and as soon as the carriage containing his mother and himself had passed the dining-room windows, from which he kept his eyes carefully averted, Lady Ethel, considerably nettled to find her power was not quite so great over him as she had imagined, shook out her ruffled plumes, and went into the drawing-room with the intention of making Maggie Henderson a sharer in her indignation.

But here she was disappointed, for the apartment proved to be empty. Miss Lloyd having left the house on a round of cottage visits, simultaneously with the departure of her niece.

Lady Ethel rang the bell, and hearing that every one was out, threw herself into a chair and commenced to turn over the freshly-cut pages of the various magazines and papers with which the Castle was always liberally supplied. But they did not interest her; for, though she pretended to be completely indifferent to the scene that had just taken place between her husband and herself, in reality she was not only piqued but a little bit unhappy on the subject; added to which there was a nasty uncomfortable feeling knocking at her heart which bore a strong resemblance to fear lest she might have gone too far with him; and on discovering which, she experienced quite as much surprise as Colonel Bainbridge would have done. She kept glancing at the clock and wondering how long it would take him to call on "that old fogy at Borthwick;" and whether he would return home in a better humour than he had left it; and if he did not, what she could do, without compromising her dignity, to bring him round again.

As this thought flashed through her mind, Lady Ethel smiled consciously to herself; for she knew, well enough, how he had been caught and entangled by the wondrous light in her liquid eyes, and the golden meshes of her hair; and that she had but to exhibit one or other of her many charms to bring him back, adoring to her feet.

Yes, Lady Ethel, it works well for a certain number of times; but there are limits to all things, and some wounds are more than skin deep—and not even to be healed by beauty.

She was ruminating much after this fashion, when the door opening roused her from her reverie, and looking up, expectant of the entrance of Maggie or Miss Lloyd, her eyes encountered the trim, old-fashioned figure of her father-in-law.

Now there was no one at that moment whom Lady Ethel would not have sooner seen than Mr Bainbridge; for since the evening that he had compelled her to remain to prayers, she had felt a mingled dislike and fear of the old man, which was quite as patent to him as to herself; and on the present occasion, the grave and almost stern expression of his face seemed to warn her that their interview was not to be a pleasant one.

She guessed at once that he had entered with a purpose, for he was never known to occupy the drawing-room during the day-time; and yet now, first closing the door carefully behind him, he came deliberately forwards, and took a seat by her side; whilst Lady Ethel, recalling the loud tones in which she had spoken to her husband, grew a shade paler and moved her chair away.

"You have no need to be afraid of me, my dear," quietly remarked the old man in a tone which was very offensive to her pride. "I have a few plain words to say to you, it is true, so I am glad that I have found you alone; but I shall make them as mild as I feel to be consistent with my duty."

Lady Ethel stared at the intruder as though she had never seen him before.

"I am not aware what you can have to speak to me about, Mr Bainbridge," she replied, haughtily; "but whatever it may be, it is not likely to have the effect you seem to anticipate."

"Well, we shall see, we shall see;" said her father-in-law, in no wise disconcerted by her address. "I have little desire to wound you, and therefore, if I can point out your faults without doing it, so much the better!"

Point out her faults! hers! Lady Ethel Carr's? (Lady Ethel never thought of herself by any other name) What would the vulgar, low-born old man dare to do next?

She did not say this. She only thought it, as drawing herself up majestically in her seat, she answered with cutting politeness:

"I am sure I am infinitely obliged by your solicitude. Pray go on. I am quite impatient to hear the list of my iniquities."

Mr Bainbridge turned and looked at the petulant beauty with a strange yearning expression in his gaze—a gaze, which, in its tender compassion, passing over all her attractions, and even her faults, saw only the young spirit at war with the world and itself, and sorely standing in need of friendly counsel.

"My dear," he said kindly, "it is a misfortune that you should have been left without a father at the very time when you were about to take upon yourself the most important duties of your life."

But an allusion to her father, and from Mr Bainbridge, was more than Lady Ethel could stand just then. The tears rose behind her burning eyeballs, but with a strong effort she repelled them; and the violence which she thus did her feelings, made her voice sound harsh and discordant.

"I will thank you not to mention my father to me, sir. You were not acquainted with him; his life or death can be a matter of little consequence to you."

But Mr Bainbridge saw that he had touched her, and he pressed the question.

"Had he been here, Lady Ethel! could he have heard you speaking to your husband in the dining-room this afternoon, what comment would he have made upon the circumstance?"

Her mind rushed back pell-mell to the darkened chamber with its maroon hangings; the handsome emaciated face patiently reclining on its pillows, and the dear faint voice recommending the man whom she had married to her merciful consideration.

Well! she *had* married him! But what right did that give this old farmer, in his leathern gaiters, and rough coat, and rougher words, to come and forcibly remind her of one of the bitterest memories of her life?

Her spirit rose against it; she was indignant at his presumption, and the feeling was apparent in the tones of her voice as she replied:

"I was not aware that eaves-dropping was considered to be a virtue at Cranshaws. I have always been taught to look upon it as a vice."

"There was no eaves-dropping, Lady Ethel! You spoke so loudly and with the door unclosed, that the whole house might have heard you. To me, sitting in my study, it was impossible that the sounds should not reach."

"You were quite welcome to hear them. I am not ashamed of what I said," she answered with an assumption of indifference.

"*Not ashamed!* My dear, think twice of what you affirm. Not ashamed of telling the man to whom you have been married scarcely two months—who is entirely devoted to you, and whom you have sworn solemnly to honour and obey—that you *hate* him? Surely, upon reflection, you will retract your words."

But Lady Ethel tossed her head in the air and was silent.

"Perhaps I should not have taken upon myself to speak to you," continued the old man, "were it not that you seem very friendless; and that I know you hold the happiness of my only son—my only child—in your hands. He has been a very good son to us, Lady Ethel! from a boy I cannot remember that he ever wilfully disobeyed his mother or myself, and, as you may suppose, all that concerns him is of the deepest interest to us. He is very much attached to you; his whole heart appears to me absorbed in the admiration of your personal appearance" (here Lady Ethel with a smile of self-satisfaction slightly turned her face towards the speaker). "Yes! yes, my dear! I know that you are very beautiful—I am neither too old nor too vulgar to perceive that" (at this allusion the girl coloured)—"but your beauty will be of little avail to you in the sight of men, and none at all in the sight of God, if it is not joined to a meeker and more tractable spirit. You have the face of an angel; but if you were to die to-night, my dear, do you think that would make you fit to take your place amongst the company of heaven?"

"I don't know anything about it," she returned, brusquely, "and I don't care. If you have any more pleasant truths to tell me, Mr Bainbridge, you will oblige me by doing so at once, for you interrupted me in my reading, and I shall be glad to return to it."

"The reading can wait," said her father-in-law, as he laid a sacrilegious hand upon the number of "Temple Bar" she was holding before her face, and laid it quietly upon the table, "for my business is of greater importance. I must warn you, Lady Ethel—both for my son's sake and your own—against the course you are pursuing with him. He possesses a noble temperament, kind, generous, and long-suffering; but if you out-step your privileges—if you once thoroughly rouse his jealousy or destroy his faith in you—you will find his is a nature that does not easily forget. At present you might do anything with him, for he loves you far too well for his own peace of mind, and is blind to your faults; but if you repeat the game you were playing with him this afternoon—you will do it once too often, that is all!"

Lady Ethel's cheeks were flaming, and her foot was beating an impatient tune upon the hearthrug.

"And if I do, it is my own concern, and no one else's."

"Pardon me! It is not only his happiness but ours which you seem bent upon destroying!"

"I was not aware that in marrying Colonel Bainbridge I had married his whole family."

"And yet it is the usual thing, surely, when you enter a family to consider it as your own. Lady Ethel, I have felt anxious more than once lately, to learn what reason you possibly could have had for marrying my son!"

She started from her seat, and turned upon him eyes of fire.

"Not to be insulted by his father, Mr Bainbridge."

"Only to insult himself, I suppose! Well, my dear, I daresay you consider you did us a great honour by condescending to assume our name; but if you do not love your husband (and I cannot reconcile your words this afternoon with the belief that you do love him), all I can say is that I would rather he had taken a dairymaid to wife, who looked up to and reverenced him as he deserves," and Mr Bainbridge drooped his head upon his breast in a very despondent manner.

"I will not stand this language any longer!" exclaimed Lady Ethel, angrily. "As if it were not sufficient that I should have lowered my father's noble name by marrying beneath my station in life, I am expected to stand by quietly and hear his daughter compared at a disadvantage with a dairymaid. I wish to Heaven your son *had* married a dairymaid, sir; he would in that case, have taken a wife from a condition more equal to his own; but since"—(with a gasping sob) —"I have committed the irrevocable folly of linking my fate with his, I can at least refuse to subject myself to the indignity of having the fact hourly cast in my teeth by one whose age, if not his knowledge of the requirements of polite society, should have taught him better. I shall leave Cranshaws to-morrow!" And sweeping past her father-in-law, as though she feared he might contaminate her, Lady Ethel flew to her room, and left Mr Bainbridge to his own reflections.

CHAPTER XXVIII.

THE WEDDING VISIT IS ABRUPTLY TERMINATED.

It was a real effort to Colonel Bainbridge to make himself agreeable during that visit to "the old fogy at Borthwick;" for whilst he was receiving congratulations on his marriage, and answering inquiries, all his thoughts were with the rebellious girl whom he had left at home; and his faithful heart was aching with the remembrance of the last words she had said to him.

At first he almost believed that they were true, and was tempted to despair at the idea; but as time lengthened, and their cruel echo beat less distinctly on his memory, he tried to persuade himself that he also had been in the wrong, and provoked his darling to an exhibition of impatience for which perhaps she was already grieving as deeply as he was himself.

He knew that she was capricious, and at times unreasonable; it was the fault of those who from her childhood had surrounded her with flattery and adulation, and he who was so much the stronger, and bound over to protect her, should have been more careful to shield her from the temptation of yielding to such weakness.

And after all, had not her temper risen because she was disappointed at his leaving her; because she did not like to be separated from him, though but for a few hours; and felt a twinge of jealousy, foolish child! at his apparent preference of the society of others.

As this soothing view of the case struck Colonel Bainbridge's imagination, he forgot his previous pain, and even the bitter truth which had occasioned it, in his anxiety to reach home, and assure his dearest girl that he had no pleasure in life except when by her side and ministering to her wishes.

So distorted becomes the judgment of men whose eyes are blinded by a passionate attachment.

The old coach-horses seemed to creep back to Cranshaws on that afternoon, and the rugged road to be more tediously impassable than ever, whilst he sat by his mother in the close carriage listening to her uninteresting remarks on what they had seen and heard at Mrs Hodson's, and longing with his whole heart that he could fly back to the presence of his wife, and read in her eyes that all was right again between them.

They reached the Castle about seven o'clock, just as the dinner-gong was sounding, and Miss Lloyd and Maggie Henderson, dressed for the evening, were passing through the hall.

Colonel Bainbridge, having handed his mother out of the carriage, hurried up the staircase to Lady Ethel's room, expecting to find her in the midst of her toilet.

But what was his astonishment, on opening the door, to see her clothed in a white dressing-gown, with her long hair rippling down her back, quietly seated by the fire; whilst Louise, surrounded by her mistress's travelling-cases in every stage of preparation for a journey, was receiving and obeying the directions given her.

"My dearest Ethel!" he exclaimed, stopping short upon the threshold, and forgetting everything he had intended to say to her, "what does this mean?"

"It means that I am going back to town to-morrow," she answered, curtly. "Do come into the room, Colonel Bainbridge, if you are coming, and shut that door behind you; you are letting a most horrible draught blow right upon my feet!"

He did as she desired him, and took up his position on the hearthrug, just in front of her.

"Going back to town to-morrow?" he repeated, "you must be joking, Ethel, surely."

"I consider it anything but a joke to be insulted."

"Insulted? Who has dared to insult you in this house?"

"The owner of it!" and then turning to her maid with a few words of German, she dismissed her from the room.

Colonel Bainbridge could scarcely believe that he had heard aright.

"My father, Ethel! You must be mistaken."

"Mistaken! when I heard him with my own ears. I tell you that he has insulted me most grossly, and without the slightest provocation; and I refuse to remain in this house an hour longer than is necessary."

She looked so beautiful, with her heated face, and in her

simple undress—so like Colonel Bainbridge's mundane conceptions of an angel, and his affections were so entirely hers, that even though his father were the supposed offender, all his sympathies were enlisted on her side, and he replied, warmly——

"Tell me about it, dearest. I am not going to have you annoyed in this manner for all the relations in the world!"

He threw himself down upon the hearthrug as he spoke, and clasped his hands about her waist, and Lady Ethel suffered it. It would not have been politic in her to repulse him now, for her pride demanded she should be permitted to quit Cranshaws, and she knew she could not do so without his consent.

"Your father has insulted me most bitterly," she went on, quickly, and trying to avoid the passionate gaze he fixed upon her face; "he came into the drawing-room this afternoon as I was sitting alone, and told me that he had overheard what we said in the dining-room (he must have been listening at the door), and that I was a mass of faults, and not so good as a dairymaid, and he wished that you had never married me, with a great deal more in the same strain that was equally polite. And I decline to be subjected to such an indignity again!"

"He mentioned you in the same breath as a dairymaid!" exclaimed her husband, indignantly. "Ethel, my dearest, can it be possible? he must be mad! My own girl! my own noble, peerless, beautiful girl! *I* know, if no one else does, what an incalculable honour you did me by becoming my wife!"

"I *must* leave this place," she went on, unheeding his address; "I cannot stay here after all he said to me—it is impossible. You will let me go back to town to-morrow—*won't you?*" with more appeal in her voice than she had ever used to him before. The tone electrified him.

"Let you go! Of course I will! Do you think I would wish you to stay one hour in a house where you have been made uncomfortable? My queen! you little know me! I can't imagine what my father can have been thinking of to dare to speak to you in such a manner. It would not have happened if I had been at home."

He raised himself up slowly as he spoke, until his lips met

hers, and, as they did so, almost timidly, husband and wife both coloured.

This fact alone would have betrayed to an observer the footing on which they stood to one another. That was not the full frank caress of happy married love, but to Colonel Bainbridge it was a glimpse of paradise.

"My darling!" he whispered, presently, "tell me only that what you said (you remember!)—those dreadful words—say they were not true—that you did not mean them!" and his dark eyes sought hers for an answer. But Lady Ethel leaned back in the chair, and closed her own.

"Of course not! Haven't I told you, lots of times, that you are never to believe anything I say!"

"They were too cruel," he murmured; "they rung in my ears the whole afternoon. O Ethel! you don't half know how much my happiness is bound up in your affection! If I thought for a moment that what you said could really be the case, I should feel tempted to destroy myself! Oh! what fools you women make of us!"

He seized both her hands in his, and carried them to his lips, and she, unknowing what to answer, and longing to be able to release herself without offending him, was on the point of making some unnecessary excuse for changing her position, when, to her relief, a tap came opportunely on the door, and Colonel Bainbridge, with all an Englishman's dismay at the idea of being caught love-making, sprang to his feet, and stood on the opposite side of the fire-place.

But no one entered: to their invitation there only responded the cheerful voice of Maggie Henderson, with a message from Aunt Lizzie to the effect that the second dinner-gong had sounded for some time, and that they were all waiting for Cousin Thomas and Lady Ethel.

"Tell them not to wait," shouted Colonel Bainbridge from the hearth-rug; "I shall be down directly," and then he turned to his wife, inquiringly—

"And you, my darling?"

"*I* am not going down, Colonel Bainbridge. They can send me up some dinner here, or they can leave it alone, just as they please; but I would rather starve to death than sit at the same table with your father again."

"I shall certainly demand some explanation from him of

his conduct," said her husband, as he walked away into his dressing-room.

The small show of complaisance which he had so unexpectedly received from Lady Ethel had completely enrolled him on her side; and when, shortly afterwards, he descended to the dining-room, it was with a lowering countenance and in a very undutiful state of mind.

"Is your wife not coming down this evening, Thomas?" demanded Mrs Bainbridge in surprise as he entered the apartment alone. "I hope she is not poorly."

"She is not quite well," he replied, with grave courtesy, "and she prefers to keep her room this evening," with a glance towards his father, who, conscience-stricken, buried his face in his soup-plate; "so perhaps you will be kind enough, mother, to have her dinner sent up to her."

"Of course I will; but, dear! dear! this is sad work, poor Lady Ethel being so often laid up. Is she always so delicate, Thomas?"

"She is never robust—I don't think any of the women in her sphere of life are. You must take her bringing up into consideration. And—and"—after a moment's hesitation, "this place is too bleak for her. I should not have brought her here."

"Oh! I hope you don't think it has done her any harm?" said Mrs Bainbridge, anxiously.

"Not yet," he answered; and most people might have seen he was only making an excuse to prepare them for what was to follow; "but it would have been better to wait till the spring was more advanced; and I am doubtful now whether it will be prudent in me to keep her here much longer."

"Well, of course you must do as you think best, my dear," rejoined his mother; "for Lady Ethel's health is of the first consideration to you." And then conversation seemed to flag, for no one dared to advocate, and no one cared to deprecate, the proposed departure. But after the ladies had left the room, Colonel Bainbridge drew his chair closer to his father, with whom, during dinner-time, he had scarcely exchanged two words, and plunged at once into the subject that was vexing him.

"Father, I am going to take my wife back to town tomorrow."

"Well, Thomas, I am not surprised to hear it, for from what you said at dinner, I concluded you had some such project in your brain."

"You spoke to her this afternoon in a manner which greatly wounded and irritated her. She is a high-spirited girl, who has not been used to brook control, and your language appeared to her insulting. After which, it is quite impossible that I should ask her to remain in a house where she no longer feels at her ease."

"Had Lady Ethel been truthful in repeating to you what took place this afternoon, Thomas, you would not speak of it in the terms you do. If any insults passed between us, they did not proceed from me. I never insulted a woman in my life, and am not likely to begin with my son's wife."

"But I think what passes between married people, father, should be sacred. Let them make up their little differences in their own way. It is not likely but that Ethel would resent the interference of a third person between her husband and herself."

"I spoke for my own sake as well as yours, Thomas. The 'little difference,' as you call it, was carried on so publicly as to be patent to the household."

Colonel Bainbridge bit his lip.

"She is hasty, I know, but it is soon over. She meant nothing."

"I am glad to hear it; but, in that case, Lady Ethel should be taught that others may misconstrue her unmeaning words. I said nothing to her, Thomas, which, under the same circumstances, I should not have said to my own daughter—that I should not repeat to-morrow did the occasion for it arise."

"I can take care of my wife myself, thank you, father," rejoined Colonel Bainbridge, hastily.

"I hope you can, but you will find a difficulty in it."

"Of course you are set against her on account of her birth; but she is no more responsible for that than I am for mine."

"You are quite wrong, Thomas. I may think *you* have committed a mistake in bringing a woman of noble birth into our family; but the mere fact can never raise or lower Lady Ethel in my estimation. No, no! my objection to my daughter-in-law consists in something of far greater importance. It is, that she is both careless and irreligious."

"Well, you will not have her bad example set before you much longer," returned Colonel Bainbridge, drumming impatiently on the table with a spoon.

"It would not much signify if I did; but you have bound yourself to pass your life beneath it. Oh! my dear son, you refused to take my previous warnings; but, as you value your wife's welfare and your own peace of mind, do not despise the advice I give you now—in all cases gently but firmly to insist upon her doing what you know to be right. I am quite aware that in your present state of mind my counsel may appear unpalatable, perhaps unnecessary, but you know that I have never yet interfered in your private affairs without a sincere desire to do you good."

"I know that, father, and I thank you for the interest you take in me," returned Colonel Bainbridge, whose heart felt sorely divided between its affection for his parents and his wife; "only it is not to be expected that every one should feel the same, and—it is better we should go; is it not?"

"If Lady Ethel is bent upon going, most decidedly," replied his father. "The day may come when she will wish to return to Cranshaws; but, whether or no, this home is always open to you or yours, Thomas."

Colonel Bainbridge grasped his father's hand, but he could not speak. With all his blind idolatry for Lady Ethel, he believed in this instance she might have been the one in the wrong.

The news of their intended departure did not create the amazement in the drawing-room which he had anticipated, for Mr Bainbridge had related the incidents of the afternoon to his wife, and she had already prepared Miss Lloyd and Maggie to hear of some change.

All the remarks that met his announcement were polite regrets for the sudden termination of the wedding visit, and hopes that when the weather was warmer they might see Lady Ethel there again; but Colonel Bainbridge missed from their voices the ring of genuine sympathy which usually accompanied all their comments on his actions; and sick at heart for want of it, he urged the fact of having preparations to make for the morrow as an excuse for quitting their company early.

The day-mail passed through Borthwick during the forenoon, and the travellers were obliged to leave Cranshaws by nine o'clock. Lady Ethel, holding to her determination not to speak to her father-in-law again, refused to appear at breakfast, and the carriage was standing at the door when, having parted with Miss Lloyd and Mrs Bainbridge on the upper landing, she descended to the hall.

Maggie Henderson was there, superintending with Colonel Bainbridge the packing of the luggage. Her eyes were heavy, and her face pale, for she had been grieving not only for her uncle and aunt (who felt the sudden departure of their son acutely), but for her cousin, who was scarcely less distressed than his parents; and in her loyalty towards these three, so dear to her, her feelings for the capricious creature who had been the cause of all their annoyance, were anything but friendly.

Yet, when Lady Ethel stood on the last step of the staircase and called her by her name, the old attraction came so forcibly upon her, that Maggie could not help answering with alacrity—

"Yes! here I am. Can I do anything for you?"

"No, thank you; Louise has done everything. I only wanted to give you this." And Lady Ethel thrust a large gold cross into her hand.

Maggie did not know what to answer; but she was sure that she could not accept it.

"Oh! no!—pray don't—it is not fit for me—I must not take it, Lady Ethel."

"What nonsense! If it is not fit for you I am sure it is still less so for me; I have not much to do with such things!" with a little grating laugh; and then, as her companion stood silently regarding the ornament with a perplexed expression of countenance, she added, hurriedly, "Don't forget me, Maggie! I feel as though I should be safer if you think of me sometimes in your prayers."

She was going forward then, in obedience to a summons from her husband, when she hastily returned, and casting her arms round Maggie's neck, kissed her three or four times upon the cheek. The girl looked up, half-startled by the action, and saw that tears were standing in Lady Ethel's proud blue eyes. That fact was quite sufficient to melt the thin ice upon

Maggie's heart, and, opening her arms, she folded her cousin's wife in a warm embrace.

"I won't forget you! I will pray for you every day," she whispered. "God bless you: try to make him happy."

"Ethel! my dearest, everything is ready!" exclaimed Colonel Bainbridge. And Maggie fled away to hide her wet eyes in the dining-room.

As Lady Ethel passed the threshold, Mr Bainbridge stood upon it.

"My dear!" he said, almost humbly, "you will not refuse to give your hand at parting to an old man who may have blundered, but had not the intention to offend you!"

She was a different creature then to what she had been a moment before. She placed her hand in that of her father-in-law, it is true, but no forgiveness shone out of the cold face she turned upon him.

"Of course she won't, father!" exclaimed Colonel Bainbridge, promptly, trying to make up by his own heartiness for the shortcomings of his wife. "Ethel knows as well as I do that you meant it for the best!"

But the old man did not heed his son's remark. He was still holding the small gloved hand she had delivered to him, and gazing up earnestly into her beautiful unmoved face.

"May God Almighty bless you," he said, solemnly, "and make you a blessing to your husband and your children, if you have any; and grant that we may meet above, my dear. Good-bye!" and abruptly dropping her hand, with a farewell grasp to his son, he turned away and walked slowly back into the house.

Colonel Bainbridge, having watched his figure till it disappeared behind the study door, put his wife into the carriage, and got in after her.

"The dear old man," he said, musingly, as they drove away, "I am sure he didn't mean to be rude to you, Ethel. He has a blunt way of speaking, but it is mostly due to his country manners."

She did not immediately reply, and he thought she might have been touched by the last words of his father.

"Don't you think so, my dearest? Can't you make a few allowances for an old man who has seldom had to do with such a dainty bit of goods as you are?"

"It is of no use your speaking to me whilst we are jolting over these horrid roads, Colonel Bainbridge. I can't hear half you say, and have enough to do to keep myself from being shaken to pieces."

He sighed heavily, and turned his attention to the view from the opposite window.

CHAPTER XXIX.

LET SLIP THE HOUNDS OF WAR.

THE house in Curzon Street, which had been taken and furnished for the bride and bridegroom by the liberality of Mr Bainbridge, was nearly ready for their reception; and after a few days spent at an hotel, they entered on their first experiment in housekeeping.

It was now the end of April. London was filling fast, and between the excitement of meeting former friends, and setting her new residence in order for the season, Lady Ethel shook off much of her previous lethargy, and appeared more like herself than she had done since her father's death. She had not visited town since that time; and reviewing old scenes and reviving old memories, lent her, for the moment, a false stimulation which might well be mistaken for happiness by those who were unacquainted with the secret of her heart.

She never appeared tired of running about from shop to shop to select ornaments for the decoration of her drawing-room or herself, or of returning the visits of her numerous acquaintances; whilst Colonel Bainbridge, delighted at the welcome change in her demeanour, permitted her to do exactly as she chose.

He had not forgotten—far from it—the disagreeable circumstances attendant on their journey north; but as the merest allusion to Cranshaws appeared to revive his wife's ill-humour, the subject was seldom mentioned between them; and he tried hard to banish the unpleasant memory, as she seemed to have done.

Meanwhile, there were few amongst the unmarried portion of her female acquaintances who were not disposed at that juncture to envy Lady Ethel for the possession of one of the prettiest houses, the best-appointed equipages, and the most indulgent husbands in town.

The six months' leave which Colonel Bainbridge had obtained upon his marriage, extended over the season, and consequently he had nothing to do except to frequent his club and dance attendance on his lovely wife, though Lady Ethel thought that she would have gladly dispensed with the latter obligation, had she been able to do so.

There had been some talk at Cranshaws of his selling out of the army and settling down quietly at home; but love for his profession, and a great horror of idleness, had prevented him hitherto from taking any steps in the matter. It would be time enough, he thought, to come to a decision when his present leave had expired.

For Colonel Bainbridge, though he spent thousands yearly, was, with the exception of his regimental pay, entirely dependent on his father.

He was as sure of receiving his annual income as though it had been legally his own, but every shilling of the money he expended had been coined by the sweat of the paternal brow at Birmingham; and though he accepted it from the paternal hand with as little scruple as he had done half-crowns when a boy, yet he had all an Englishman's pride at the thought of resigning the last scrap of independence he possessed.

At his father's death he knew that all would be his own to do with as he thought fit; but until that event took place, he did not relish the idea of relinquishing his profession. Even to think upon the subject was an evil day, which he put off as long as possible; he had nothing to do in the present but to enjoy himself.

April slipped unconsciously into May, and Lady Ethel's moods of excitement deepened daily. She would go out driving in the park every afternoon, and return home with a bright carmine spot in either cheek, and eyes of unusual brilliancy; and her husband, without guessing the reason of it, saw only that it made her look more beautiful, and knew by experience that she did not like to have the alteration noticed. But attributing the change to her increased content, he only trusted that his darling would not over-fatigue herself, nor injure her health by too much exertion.

Meanwhile, Lady Ethel was awaiting, with mingled dread and longing, an event which she knew to be imminent—the advent of her step-mother in London. Would she be accompanied by *him?*

At last it occurred. Towards the middle of May, the *Morning Post* announced that the Countess of Clevedon had arrived at her town residence for the season; and Lady Ethel knew that if the courtesies of society were to be kept up between them, it was imperative that she should be among the first to pay the compliment of a call in Park Lane.

She dressed herself most carefully for the occasion, returning again and again to her glass to be certain that her bonnet was becoming, and not a lock or braid of her hair out of place; and that she looked just as a happy bride ought to do; so that when she descended to the carriage, her husband, who accompanied her, was loud in his approval of her general appearance. They found Lady Clevedon at home, and alone.

Bewitchingly attired in the faintest of half-mourning, and with her rich coils of hair arranged in the most girlish fashion, the Countess did not look a day older than one or two and twenty; and Lady Ethel, who had braced herself up to the point of meeting her successful rival amidst a crowd of chattering guests, grew deadly pale as she submitted her face to the undivided scrutiny of her young and radiant-looking stepmother. Lady Clevedon was loud in her commiseration of her appearance.

"My dear Ethel!" with uplifted hands; "what *have* you been doing with yourself? why, you are a perfect ghost! I declare I shouldn't have known you in the street."

At this remark Colonel Bainbridge became seriously anxious.

"Do you *really* think she looks so ill?" he exclaimed, and fixing his gaze upon the pallid features of his wife. "I did not consider she was at her best in Scotland; but she seems to me to have improved so much since her return to town!"

"Well, my dear Colonel! she may have improved—I don't deny that—but there must have been room for it. She looks quite shocking to me."

"I am perfectly well, nevertheless," said Lady Ethel, with all her old *hauteur*, for she read the meaning which underlay her step-mother's compassionate remarks, "and never felt better in my life. When did you arrive in town, Gertrude?"

"Last Thursday. I ought to have been here sooner, only Victor—you remember your old friend Monsieur de Lacarras—was suddenly called over to Paris; and his departure rather delayed me in my preparations."

Her grey eyes were staring Lady Ethel full in the face as

she delivered this sentence; but the blue ones which they encountered were a match for them, and if the girl's teeth clenched beneath her firmly-closed lips, no one was the wiser for it but herself.

"Indeed! I suppose Temple Grange has been very full of company this spring!"

"Pretty well! Oh, we managed to enjoy ourselves," with a smile of secret satisfaction. "And you—you also have been very gay, I presume, at Cranshaws Castle!"

"Well! I am afraid poor Ethel can scarcely say that," interposed Colonel Bainbridge, smiling; "for my father and mother are a very old-fashioned couple, who live in the depths of the country, and have not much opportunity to give their friends more than a hearty welcome."

"We did not go there for society," interposed his wife.

"Ah! solitude was no detriment in your eyes, I daresay, Ethel. We all know that newly-married people think no company so charming as that of each other."

At this Colonel Bainbridge coloured and laughed, and looked shyly at his wife, in the stupid way that even sensible men adopt when twitted on their most sacred feelings; but she was occupied, apparently, with examining a photograph upon the table.

"How is Alured?" she said, presently. "I have not asked after him, Gertrude!"

"Oh! your dear little brother! How could I be so forgetful?" ringing the bell; "of course you must see him;" and then, as the servant appeared, she gave the order for Lord Clevedon to be brought down at once; and the subsequent arrival of his lordship, in a highly embroidered and blue-ribboned condition, turned the conversation into another direction.

"Oh! you have changed his mourning!" exclaimed Lady Ethel. She still wore mourning herself, although she did not dress exclusively in black; and that the heir to her father's titles and estates should be permitted to discard it before the usual term had expired, appeared to her neither right nor reasonable. Lady Clevedon coloured.

"Well! he is but an infant, you see!" she replied, apologetically; "and under the circumstances—and with the season coming on—my friends thought—that is, I was advised, to put off his black with the cold weather."

"I daresay it is more consistent you should do so," said Lady Ethel, quietly, as she lifted the child upon her knee.

She had never evinced much affection for her infant brother, for beyond the fact of being her father's son, he did not appear to have any claim upon her; being the image of his mother, and bearing no resemblance whatever to the Carrs.

"Well, Alured," she said, as he turned his full grey eyes upon her, "have you quite forgotten me?"

The youthful Earl of Clevedon, who, amongst other maternal virtues, had inherited the gift of a very long tongue, was able to make himself perfectly well understood in reply.

"I don't know who you are."

"Why! I'm your sister, you ungrateful little creature! Don't you remember me at Temple Grange?"

"I remember Temple Grange, and Victor. Mamma," raising his voice, "when is Victor coming back?"

"Soon, darling, very soon!" exclaimed Lady Clevedon, in the midst of a conversation with Colonel Bainbridge, and the knees which supported the little questioner trembled beneath him.

"And so you have forgotten Sister Ethel altogether?" resumed the quivering lips.

"Yes! I suppose so!" with amusing earnestness; "but perhaps I could remember, if I tried. Did you ever give me bonbons? Victor used to give me large boxes of bonbons,—*so* large!" clasping both his rosy hands together.

In another moment, greatly to his surprise, he found himself deposited upon the carpet.

"Colonel Bainbridge! I think it is time that we were going."

"Just as you please, my love," he answered, rising to his feet.

"So soon!" exclaimed the Countess; "why, this is quite a formal visit. You must both come and dine with me some evening—quite by ourselves, you know; and I'll get one or two of Ethel's old friends to meet you. But you must really do something to put a little colour in your face, my dear, or we shall have people saying that the Colonel hasn't treated you well."

Lady Ethel turned upon her cheeks of fire.

"She doesn't look pale now," said Colonel Bainbridge, eagerly.

"No!—but that is not natural; perhaps the room has been too warm for her. I advise you to go into the park, my dear, and get a little appetite for dinner. I am sure you cannot eat enough."

Her remarks went home to Colonel Bainbridge, and though Lady Ethel stoutly denied their truth, he could not shake off the impression they made upon him, and as soon as they were in the carriage he alluded to it.

"Ethel! my dearest! Lady Clevedon has made me so unhappy! Is it really true that you are not feeling well? Let me look at your face!"

But she was sitting with her back towards him, gazing out of the opposite window, and refused to yield to the gentle force with which he tried to turn her round.

"What nonsense! Do leave me alone! You heard what I said to her. I am as well as ever I was in my life!"

"But people are not always the best judges of their own health, Ethel. And now I come to think of it, you do not eat so much as you ought to do. How miserable I should be if you were to fall ill."

"I have already told you that I am not ill."

"But why, then, do you look so thin?"

"I always was thin."

"Oh, no! I am sure you were not so when I first knew you. And you are paler than you used to be. And I know you do not sleep well at night."

Lady Ethel returned no answer to his anxious remarks. She kept her eyes determinately fixed the other way, and had bitten her lip till the blood came in her endeavour to keep down the emotion which she felt gaining the mastery over her. Her interview with Lady Clevedon, and the allusions which had been made during the course of it, had revived her old pain more bitterly than she had calculated on. At last, her husband became alarmed at her long silence.

"Ethel! I am sure that you are concealing something from me; and if you refuse to tell me what it is, I shall send for Dr Chalmers as soon as we get home, and ask him to find out the truth; for you are much too precious to me to have your health trifled with in the slightest degree."

But the mention of Dr Chalmers' name was just the feather needed to overbalance the woman's tottering strength of mind, and turning quickly from the window to the centre of the carriage, she hid her face in her hands, and burst into a storm of tears.

"O Heavens!" she said impatiently, between her sobs, "what have I done that I am to be worried—worried—worried—in this way, and never allowed to have a peaceful moment to myself? I hate it—I am sick of it—this constant *surveillance;* not to be able to eat a little more or less, or to hold one's tongue for five minutes together, without being brought to book for it, like a child. You'll kill me, Colonel Bainbridge, if you go on in this way; no woman on earth could stand it. It's enough to make one wish one's self in the grave!"

So she declaimed, with her impetuous little tongue, whilst her heart was weighing a very different matter; and he, deeply wounded by her manner, and still more by her words, sat quietly in his corner of the carriage, till she should have concluded.

When that occurred, she expected that at the least he would have reproached her; but still he sat silent, though his countenance was very grave.

At last, she lifted up her head, disclosing an inflamed and tear-swollen face, on which the traces of violent emotion were but too evident. They were driving, then, towards the park.

"Don't you think we had better go home?" remarked her husband, quietly.

"Yes," said Lady Ethel, in a low voice. She wished that he would fly out at her in return; she did not understand having her turbulent passions treated with so much coolness; and she was almost reproaching him with his indifference during the course of their drive home. Yet he did not relax in any of his usual attentions to her; but having handed her out of the carriage and into the drawing-room, summoned Louise to her assistance before he ventured to leave her alone. But then he walked off to his club, and did not appear again till dinner-time, during which interval Lady Ethel found it exceedingly dull, and had occasion more than once to miss the manifold services of love with which of late her life had been surrounded.

"He doesn't care for me!" she murmured, with female inconsistency. "No man who cared for a woman would walk out of the house in that way, on a horribly dull afternoon, and leave her to look after herself. They are all alike! There is not one of them better than another. I wish to goodness I had never set eyes upon a man at all!"

CHAPTER XXX.

A SCENE AT THE OPERA.

COLONEL BAINBRIDGE, far from reproaching his wife for the burst of temper she had exhibited towards him, did not even allude to it; but spent his evening as usual by her side, and made no difference either in his manner or his words.

But this was no proof that he had not felt the circumstance. Sorely against his will, he had been forced of late to acknowledge that Lady Ethel was not the perfect creature for which he had taken her, nor responded to his love as he would have her do; but still his generous heart framed excuses for her on the score of youth and faulty training, and hoped against hope that her indifference was only "manner." For (so he argued), without caring for him, what reason could she have had for becoming his wife?

Her momentary impatience in the carriage he attributed, upon reflection, to the fact that it was the first time she had visited the house in Park Lane since her father's death; and her attachment to his memory, no less than the painful truth that he had left one who was more than a stranger to her (for the mutual dislike of Lady Ethel and her step-mother, though not its cause, was well known to Colonel Bainbridge), in the position which she ought to have occupied, seemed sufficient reasons in his lenient judgment for rendering her a little irritable and unwilling to have her silence broken in upon.

He wished, with a deep sigh, that his dearest girl could love him well enough to turn to him in all her doubts and difficulties, but he trusted that the day might come when she would do so; when patience should have her perfect work, and Lady Ethel would find that his unfailing sympathy had become one of the necessaries of her life.

How little he thought that, far from grieving for her dead father, whose absence from a world which she found so bitter Lady Ethel had already learned to rejoice at, every nerve of her soul had been quivering at the fresh wrenching asunder of wounds, whose edges, though unconsciously to herself, had already commenced to close beneath the balm of his affection.

He treated her that evening much as one treats a child that is a little out of sorts—that is, without inquiring further into the cause of her distress, he petted and coaxed her whenever he had an opportunity; and, persuading her to go early to bed, sat for a couple of hours by himself, buried in thought as to the best method by which he could procure her amusement and distraction.

Acting on the decision he arrived at, he sallied forth the next morning, and bought her what she had more than once expressed a wish to have—an opera-box for the season. But it was a small box on the second tier, and by no means came up to Lady Ethel's ideas of what was befitting her rank and circumstances.

"Why couldn't you have let me know before you got it!" she said, fractiously; "men always make some stupid mistake when they undertake to do things they know nothing about."

"My darling, there is not a box on the grand tier to be had; this is the best procurable, I can assure you; and I had no end of trouble to get it."

"Well, your trouble has been thrown away then, for I'm not going to sit in it."

At this Colonel Bainbridge frowned, and looked gravely at the bit of paper representing so many wasted pounds, which she had tossed to one side. He was beginning to think Lady Ethel's caprice might be carried a little too far.

"Very well, then," he rejoined, coolly, "I will give it to some one who will. Only I'm not going to buy two boxes in a season, remember."

She glanced up quickly; he had never presumed before to use so authoritative a tone to her; was it possible he could be in earnest? In her dread of it she so far forgot her pride as to stretch out her hand and place it on the paper.

"That I am sure you sha'n't," she said, half defiantly; "it is mine, Colonel Bainbridge; you gave it to me."

He smiled at her vehemence; for, to see her interested in anything was pleasure to him, and his eyes and tongue told her so.

"My dearest Ethel, you know that everything I have and

am, is yours. How could it be otherwise? But what is the use to you of an opera-box in which you declare you will not sit?"

"I cannot sit on the second tier, and so far from the stage. I should never see anything that was going on, and the gas-lights make my head ache. But you can exchange it for a couple of stalls."

"Would you really rather have two stalls?"

"Yes, since this box is too small to admit any but ourselves."

"I thought it would be so cosy," lamented Colonel Bainbridge. He had not been married long enough to mind being shut up alone with his wife for two or three hours.

"Too cosy, in my estimation," rejoined Lady Ethel. "It would be as hot as a furnace. And sitting there alone, too, night after night; fancy how stupid."

He did not answer her directly, he was gazing dreamily at the table-cloth.

"Well, Colonel Bainbridge," impatiently; "are you going to change this box for me or no?"

"*Colonel Bainbridge* will do nothing for you, Lady Ethel," he said, gently; "but your husband will, if you ask him."

Her persistence in calling him by his surname had become a source of great distress to him; for, unable to blind himself longer to her indifference, the cold appellative stung him to the quick each time she used it. But, as yet, he had failed in persuading her to abandon it; and as he alluded to the custom now, she turned her face away from his scrutiny.

"*Which* of us is to go, Ethel?" he continued, playfully.

"*You* are."

"And who am I?" coming round to her side.

"Yourself, I suppose;" and then the complaint burst from him almost without his meaning it.

"Oh, my darling! why can't you be a little kinder? You know how I am longing day after day to hear you say you care for me."

She sat down on the nearest chair, and put her feet up on the fender, and was silent.

He stood by her for a moment, expectant of an answer; but none coming, he went on passionately—

"Say something, *anything* to me before I go."

"I *have* said something—I've told you to change that opera-box for me; and when people profess to be so *very* fond of one another, they generally care to do the things that are asked of them."

He seized up his hat and gloves, thrust the offending bit of paper violently in his waistcoat pocket, and, turning on his heel, left the room without another word. He was desperately in love, but he had some pride as well as herself.

The stalls were procured, and from that day Lady Ethel, although not particularly fond of music, was to be seen at the opera at least three times a-week.

Her husband was astonished at the pertinacity with which she went there, the excitement she betrayed in going, and the extreme langour which attacked her coming home, and more than once remonstrated with her seriously on the amount of fatigue which she encountered; but Lady Ethel, as usual, was not well disposed to listen to any counsel that ran counter to her inclinations.

She was living at this time under a continual fear of meeting the Marquis de Lacarras again, and yet there was nothing that she desired more than to meet him.

She did not know how much Lady Clevedon might not have revealed to him of the feelings she had discovered in herself, nor to what motive he attributed her hasty marriage, and she longed by her conduct to make him believe that she had grown utterly indifferent to the claims he once had upon her. At the same time, she could not be sure how far she might trust her pride and courage in seconding her will, and she thirsted to have the ordeal over, and feel that she was safe. It was only the first sudden meeting that she dreaded, for after intercourse she could depend upon herself. But day succeeded day, and neither at the opera nor in the park did she see anything of the Marquis, and she could not bring herself to ask her step-mother when he was expected to return.

One evening, Lady Ethel was particularly pale and languid, so much so that her husband entreated her to give up the opera and remain quietly at home; but she persisted in going, and had not been seated in the house many minutes, before, overcome by the heat and glare, she fainted away.

She did not even have any warning of what was going to happen to her, but quietly lost consciousness whilst sitting by her husband's side, and remembered nothing more until she found herself supported in his arms in the crush-room, with some one standing over her with a glass of water.

"Where am I? oh! where am I?" she exclaimed, in the vague manner in which people always put that question on first coming to themselves.

"Here, dearest, with me! you are quite safe," replied Colonel Bainbridge, whose face with alarm was almost as pale as her own.

"You have been ill, my dear," interposed the unwelcome tones of Lady Clevedon; "you fainted in your stall, but it is all right now, and the carriage will be here in a minute to take you home."

"Lady Ethel's carriage is already in waiting," replied a voice, the sound of which thrilled through her languid nerves like an electric shock; "and if she will permit me to offer her my arm, I will have the pleasure of conducting her to it;" and looking up, almost with horror, Lady Ethel encountered the dark eyes of Victor de Lacarras.

"Yes! do, Victor," said Lady Clevedon, familiarly; "the sooner she gets home the better; such a strange attack, and so very sudden!"

"Thanks, monsieur," answered Lady Ethel, coldly, as she attempted to rise from her recumbent posture, "but Colonel Bainbridge's support will be sufficient for me;" and she turned towards her husband, who eagerly responded to the appeal. But she had miscalculated her strength; her weakened frame was as yet unable to sustain her without further aid, and Colonel Bainbridge was compelled to demand for her what she had refused for herself.

"I must ask you to support Lady Ethel on the other side," he said to the Marquis, "for she is quite powerless to stand by herself;" and then, as between them they conducted the sinking girl down stairs, and placed her in the carriage, he added, "I am sure I am infinitely obliged to you for all the trouble you have taken; I scarcely know what I should have done without your assistance."

The Marquis only answered by raising his hat respectfully to Lady Ethel, and as they drove away from the opera-house, the last thing she saw was his figure, standing bareheaded on the pavement.

She lay back on the cushions with closed eyes, passively leaving the hand which her husband had clasped in his where he had placed it, and was silent. She never asked where the Marquis de Lacarras had come from, or how he happened to be there; she felt too weak to enter upon that, or any other subject. But the next morning, when, by the advice of Dr Chalmers (whom Colonel Bainbridge had insisted upon summoning), she kept high holiday in bed, her husband came and sat by her, and told her the whole story.

"You frightened me most dreadfully, my darling," he began, in his fond way, as he played with the long tresses of hair which lay upon her pillow, "for I was occupied with the stage and what was going on there, when down dropped your dear head upon my shoulder, and you looked just as if you were dead. I didn't know what to do with you at first, when the Marquis de Lacarras leapt over the front of his box (he was in one on the ground tier with Lady Clevedon), and came and helped me to carry you out. But you made quite a sensation, I can assure you. There was not a man in the stalls that didn't want to help too. I never liked De Lacarras in the old days, Ethel, but I suppose that was only because I fancied he was in love with you, for he seems a very nice fellow. You can't think how good-natured and active he was last night; it was raining hard, you know, but he went out in it all to look for the carriage, though Lady Clevedon seemed to be in a great state of mind lest he should come to harm. Is there anything between those two, Ethel? They appear very intimate with one another."

"You had better ask Lady Clevedon yourself if you are curious on the subject. *I* am not in her confidence."

"Ah! well, I shouldn't wonder if there were, for it looked like it. By the way, Lady Clevedon expressed so much surprise at your fainting. She said it was so unlike your usual habit, and that when you entered the theatre she thought you looked so well. You went off just as she was pointing you out to the notice of De Lacarras."

"Indeed! a remarkable coincidence. Colonel Bainbridge, I think if you were to leave me to myself a little while that I could sleep."

Sleep! that was a strange sleep that attacked Lady Ethel as soon as she was left alone, as with a burning head and throbbing eyeballs she turned restlessly on her uneasy pillow.

So, by an unhappy accident, she had failed (without connivance on her part, for she had been quite unaware of the presence of the Marquis de Lacarras in the opera-house) at the very time to which she had been looking forward to display her courage, and her pride quailed at the thought of the construction which would be put upon her conduct, both by the Countess of Clevedon and her lover.

Fainted! dropped off lifeless—at the moment when *his* eye was first directed towards her, when he might reasonably suppose she also had caught sight of him, and in the centre of a crowded theatre. As Lady Ethel reflected on it, she thought that fate must surely be against her.

CHAPTER XXXI.

THE TELEGRAM.

But she was not a woman to sit down quietly and cry over misfortune. Temporarily worsted in the engagement with her step-mother she acknowledged herself to be; for physical weakness and an unavoidable *contretemps* had for a while placed her at a disadvantage, but so long as she had power to rise again and renew the encounter, the calamity was not irremediable.

When she arrived at this conclusion, Lady Ethel became all anxiety to leave her room and return to the arena she had quitted; and, notwithstanding her husband's entreaties and Dr Chalmers' prohibition to the contrary, she was down stairs again on the day but one after the accident had occurred.

The first things that met her eye on entering the drawing-room were the cards of those friends who had called to inquire after her health, conspicuous amongst which naturally appeared the names of the Countess of Clevedon and the Marquis de Lacarras. Lady Ethel tossed them contemptuously to one side, thankful only that their owners had not reserved the expression of their deep interest in her welfare until that afternoon, by which means she ran the chance of gaining a little strength before meeting them again. But it was with different feelings that she opened and perused the contents of an envelope in the handwriting of her step-mother, which set forth, on highly-scented paper, that the Countess of Clevedon would be "At Home" upon the following Thursday. Lady Ethel knew by experience what these "At Homes" meant, and that the familiar invitations, scribbled in apparently so off-hand a manner, usually resulted in some of the most brilliant gatherings of the season, comprising all the beauty and fashion and wit of Lady Clevedon's wide-spread circle of acquaintance.

It had been amidst the clamour and confusion of such a gathering that her father had breathed out his soul—in such a scene that *he*, the Marquis, had dared to outrage her by a false profession of his love.

At this remembrance Lady Ethel drew herself up, and resolved, at all hazards, that she would be present at the forthcoming assembly. They might say that she had been overcome at the first sight of her lover; but they should not have it in their power to cap the falsehood by the assertion that she was afraid to trust herself in his presence. It was there he had insulted her, and there was the most fitting place for him to hear that she defied his inconstancy to interfere either with her happiness or peace of mind.

She would go: with her husband by her side, and brilliant as it was possible for art to make her, she would challenge the world to detect the traces of tears upon her cheek, or a false ring in the lightness of her laugh.

Her heart's language, unlike that of jealous Guinevere, "Tell her she shines me down," was rather a determination to shine down not only her rival, but every woman she should meet that night, forcing him who had rejected her to acknowledge that she was the fairest of them all.

The idea excited and lent her a new strength; it was a fresh trumpet-call to battle, and Lady Ethel was eager for the fray.

But when Colonel Bainbridge became aware of her intention, he was very much annoyed. It wanted but two days to Thursday, and Dr Chalmers had warned him that if his wife were not kept quiet for a little while she might be seriously ill.

But what availed advice to Lady Ethel? Opposition to her wishes only made her more determined to follow them; and her husband, seeing that his attempts at persuasion were worse than fruitless, consoled himself with the idea that he should be by her side, and ready to warn her if she went too far.

Her bridal robes, which she had never used since the wedding-day, were prepared for the occasion; a professional *coiffeur* was engaged to dress her hair, and as upon the night in question Louise put the finishing touches to her mistress's toilet, the mirror had certainly never flashed back on any one a lovelier reflection of womankind.

The soft white satin and rich lace, without power to

detract from the fairness of her skin, drooped in easy folds over her slight figure; brilliants flashed upon her bosom, and amid the flowers in her hair, contrasting strangely with the innocent and natural-looking love-locks which lay upon her forehead; whilst a heightened colour on her cheeks, and brilliancy in her eyes, though both false and fleeting, added in no small degree to the marvellous effect of her general appearance.

She was looking at herself with interest, not conceitedly, for she cared nothing for the weapons apart from the use she was about to make of them, when a tap sounded on her door.

She thought it was her husband, who, after dinner, had sauntered over to his club, promising to be back in time to dress and go with her; and gave the command to enter with alacrity. She was eager to have his opinion added to her own, to receive the burst of applause with which he was certain to greet her appearance, and hear him say that she had never looked so handsome. Not because she loved his commendation (or thought she loved it), but that it would be satisfactory to know another thought her armour fitted well.

But the comer was not Colonel Bainbridge; it was only a servant with a large, long envelope in her hand.

"A telegram, if you please, your ladyship, for my master; and he's not home yet," she said, in a half-frightened manner, for telegrams are alarming, even when we have no reason to anticipate misfortune—they come so suddenly and unexpectedly, and it is such a time before our trembling fingers can open the fast-closed end of the official envelope: with most people, that is to say; but Lady Ethel at that particular juncture was so perfectly easy with regard to the fate of all the world, that a dozen telegrams would not have had the power to disturb her equanimity.

"Is it paid?" she demanded, supinely, of the servant.

"Oh, yes, my lady! I believe so!"

"Very well, then. Leave it on the table!" and the woman, having deposited the paper as she was desired, disappeared.

At first, Lady Ethel seemed supremely indifferent as to what the envelope might or might not contain; but, after a while, having turned from one side to the other to afford Louise readier access to the upper portion of her dress, she moved her hand slowly towards the table, and taking up the paper which was directed to her husband, deliberately opened it and read the message it contained. It was as follows :—

From MRS BAINBRIDGE, CRANSHAWS,

To COLONEL BAINBRIDGE, CURZON STREET.

"Your father is seriously ill; come to us as soon as possible. The carriage shall meet the mail train at Borthwick to-morrow morning."

The mail train! and if her husband went by that, he must quit home as soon as he had entered it; must start at once, leaving her to go to Lady Clevedon's alone, or to give up the triumph which she contemplated; neither of which prospects suited Lady Ethel's inclination.

As she took in the full consequences of the message sent, all her indifference vanished. She started, flushed deeply, knit her brows, and finally crushed the telegram between her hands.

"It is *impossible*," she said to herself; "he cannot start off in this manner at a moment's notice. It is unreasonable to ask him."

She thought of the ill-natured comments which would be made on her appearing without her husband at the first large evening party she had attended since her marriage; and of the malicious exultation which her step-mother would experience if she stayed away altogether: of how she would deplore her weakness and its cause in the ears of her dear Marquis, and call him a "dangerous fellow," and a "sad naughty man," for having broken the heart and ruined the happiness of her "poor pretty step-daughter; her dear Clevedon's legacy," &c., &c.

Lady Ethel ground her teeth over the probability of such an ignominious mention of her name, and then she glanced at her reflection in the mirror, and considered if it were possible that she could waste all the trouble she had taken, or consent to throw away the opportunity for which she thirsted.

And that it should be her father-in-law who thus threatened to interfere with her plans, was an aggravation of the evil in her mind, for she had never forgiven the old man for his plain speaking to her. She had not mentioned the fact to her husband, or any one else; but it was quite sufficient for Colonel Bainbridge to allude to Cranshaws or his own family to stop all conversation on his wife's part, and consequently the subject was seldom mooted between them.

Yet she felt sure that if he received the telegram in time, no entreaties from her lips (even if she stooped to entreaty), would prevent his obeying the summons of his mother.

And Lady Ethel, with a heaving breast, and a heart not entirely at ease, told herself that he was her property, not Mrs Bainbridge's, and that his first duty lay towards his wife; and crushed the unwelcome messenger more and more between her fingers as she did so.

She was still uncomfortable, still undecided, still flushed and palpitating with uncertainty, when a second tap upon the door was followed by the intrusion of her husband's head.

"Lots of time, darling!" he said, cheerfully, in anticipation of a reprimand for being late; "I sha'n't be ten minutes dressing," and then, struck by the appearance of his wife, he came further into the room. "By Jove, Ethel!" he exclaimed, as, with eyes glowing with admiration, he surveyed her from head to foot, "you *are* a success! I never saw you look so well in your life—you are a perfect picture. I pity the poor wretches you dance with to-night," with a happy chuckle over his own good luck; "you will take the room by storm!" and then he stooped down, like a foolish lover, and kissed the white arm which hung by her side, in the hand of which was crushed the telegram entreating him to fly to the bedside of his poor old father.

"You *will* be late," she answered, "if you do not go at once!"

"If you only knew how hard it is to tear one's self away from you, you little witch!" he said, laughing, as he left the room.

His fervent praise, which had given her proud heart more pleasure than it would acknowledge, decided the fate of the telegram from Cranshaws. No, she could not give up the prospect of the evening before her—it was impossible! If there were any real danger, which with a fat, red-faced old man, like Mr Bainbridge, was most improbable (so Lady Ethel argued), they would be sure to send again, and then it would be quite time enough for her husband to go to them; meanwhile what should she do with the obnoxious paper?

There was a fire burning in the grate, for the evenings were still chilly, and, without further thought, she threw the telegram upon it. Her conscience did just give her an uneasy twinge as she watched the ready flame seize, scorch, and shrivel it to nothing, but she had been too much used to have her own way in everything to feel much alarm at the thought of the probable consequences of what she had done!

At all events, it was gone—there was an end of it; she could not recall her act, and it was no use crying over spilt milk. And in another quarter of an hour she was seated in the carriage by her husband's side, and driving rapidly towards the residence of the Countess of Clevedon.

CHAPTER XXXII.

LADY CLEVEDON AT HOME.

PERHAPS it is scarcely necessary that I should halt at this portion of my narrative in order to assure my readers that notwithstanding their apparent intimacy, the Marquis de Lacarras had no intention of marrying the Countess of Clevedon. It is true that he spent much of his time in her society, called her by her Christian name, and treated her generally in a very *nonchalant* and familiar manner; but undue licence between man and woman is not always the token of impending marriage; on the contrary, it oftener means that nothing further is wished for or intended.

It meant so with the Marquis de Lacarras, although Lady Clevedon was hard to be convinced, and hoped against all hope.

The intercourse between them had always been more upon her side than on his, for it was she who invited him to her house; breaking, without scruple, all engagements that interfered with meeting him, and set him the example of an address, which naturally he copied, but would never have presumed to originate.

Without doubt he liked the attentions of the Countess; it was pleasant to have the habitual *entrée* of a good establishment, with a pretty woman at the head of it; pleasant, too, when he had no higher game in prospect, to be caressed and flattered by such rosy lips as Lady Clevedon's; and, what the Marquis perhaps valued more, there was a pleasant *prestige* for him amongst his fellow-men, in being known as the recipient of so much favour, to which, at the best, he was but tolerant.

Yet still Lady Clevedon believed that success would eventually be hers; it seemed so improbable that a man who made her the *confidante* of all his pecuniary and amatory difficulties, and was to be seen day after day hanging about her opera-box and drawing-room, should learn to live without the sympathy with which she never failed to greet him. But the net for his feet was spread in vain; for Victor de Lacarras was not a marrying man, and if he had ever entertained the idea of throwing himself away, it had been before Lady Ethel Carr had committed a similar error—though her step-mother continued so blind to the truth, that she persisted in drawing his attention, in a derisively compassionate manner, to the supposition of the girl's hopeless attachment for himself.

Yet, though men can be very hard against the obstinate faith of women for whom they never cared, or have lost their first fancy, the case assumes a different aspect where their own hearts are concerned, or rather where their vanity is flattered.

And Victor de Lacarras was exceedingly vain, more so than the generality of his sex (which is saying a good deal for him),—and the notion that a woman, who promised to be the belle of the season, was dying of love for him, was very soothing to his feelings; it was more than soothing, for, added to the little uncertainty respecting his former regard for her, it almost made him think that he was ready to return her love.

So, conceited and fastidious with his hostess to a degree, he was awaiting Lady Ethel's advent that evening with an unusual amount of eagerness; and when, in all the pride of her youthful beauty, she entered the room leaning on the arm of her husband, and he heard every stranger asking who she was, and all those who knew her remarking how beautiful she looked, he started forward to demand her hand for the dance, as though, above all others, he had a right to claim her preference.

Lady Clevedon advanced to meet her step-daughter with an affectation of welcome and congratulations on the restoration of her health, which ill disguised her envy. Her quick eye, taking in at a glance every detail of the bride's costume, noted how admirably it suited her, and how much handsomer it was than the grey *moiré antique* and black lace that she wore herself; and she became jealous accordingly, and with her jealousy a little tarter than was quite politic.

Victor de Lacarras noticed the change in the Countess's manner, and smiling insolently to himself, resumed his attentions to the new-comer, whilst Lady Ethel, opposed to both her antagonists at once, felt as though every joint and buckle of her armour had been tightened. She had studied well her part before venturing to appear before them, and the result did credit to her powers of acting.

"How blooming you look, my dear!" cried Lady Clevedon, as she saw the bright smile with which Lady Ethel greeted her. "I am sure no one would suspect you of mysteriously fainting away at inopportune moments."

"So stupid of me, wasn't it?" replied the girl, as she placed one hand cordially in that of her step-mother, and extended the other to the Marquis de Lacarras, "and to have you both waiting on me, too, when I had no idea that you were even in the house! *Monsieur!* I embrace the opportunity of thanking you for the trouble which my husband tells me you took on my behalf, though I trust it may be for the first and last time. A waltz?" glancing at the programme which he tendered for her acceptance. "Yes, certainly, with the greatest pleasure. Is it commencing now? Here, dearest!" turning to her husband, who started and coloured at the unusual appellation; "just hold my flowers for me, will you?" and in another moment Lady Ethel Bainbridge was spinning round the room in the embrace of Victor de Lacarras.

The Marquis was astonished; in fact, he hardly knew what to think of her ready consent and cheerful volubility; above all, the terms in which she had addressed her husband.

From the representations of the Countess he had expected to meet a depressed and love-sick girl, covered with confusion by his presence, and trembling at the sound of his voice: but here she was, the woman supposed to have contracted an unhappy marriage from despair at his neglect of her, bright and smiling, and waltzing as though she had not a care in the world.

The circumstance piqued him; he felt unaccountably injured by the liveliness with which Lady Ethel carried on a conversation over his shoulder on all that she had seen and done since quitting Temple Grange. It was not what he had expected of her, and the higher her spirits seemed to rise, the more silent did he become, until, as after the third or fourth round, they stopped to breathe themselves, and scanning the crowd, she said, with assumed anxiety—

"Where is my husband? Can you see him anywhere, *monsieur?*"

The only answer that he made her was—

"That seems a strange question for you to put to *me*, Lady Ethel; at least, there was a time when I should have said so."

At these words Lady Ethel's heart gave a great thump,—a thump of excitement and agitation, rather than of love, although she may have mistaken it for the latter feeling. It was so familiar to her to hear the measured tones of his voice, and meet the meaning glance of his dark eyes, that on being for the first time brought again beneath their influence, she may be pardoned for having mistaken the ghost of the past for the spirit of the present. Yet she restrained herself, and answered, lightly—

"Times change, *Monsieur le Marquis*, and indeed it is almost longer than one cares to count since you and I last danced together."

"Too long for you, perhaps," he whispered, "but as to myself, it has been counted for me, in days and nights of pain."

But here remembering what she had witnessed between him and her step-mother, Lady Ethel frowned, and slightly drew herself up. The man must be cautioned not to go too far.

"Shall we proceed, *monsieur?* I am quite rested." And as he passed his arm round her waist again, she thought she heard something like the word "*cruelle*." "Whilst we are on the subject of marriage," she said, with an attempt at a laugh, as they continued their dance, "will you allow me, as an experienced person, to recommend it to your notice, *monsieur?* I hear that for some time past you have been shivering on the brink, but you do not appear able to make up your mind to take the final plunge. But, as an old friend, let me advise you not to waste any more time. It is like the measles, one takes it so much more favourably whilst young."

"I shivered on the brink too long, Lady Ethel, and the bank gave way beneath me. I shall never take the plunge you speak of now."

Was it possible she had heard him right, or did he dare a second time to dupe her? Lady Ethel believed it was the latter case, and made a desperate attempt at an indifferent reply.

"What nonsense! You cannot deceive me, for I know all about it, excepting the day fixed. And did I question Lady Clevedon on the subject, I dare say she could tell that too."

There was no balcony to retire to on that evening, for the season was not sufficiently advanced to leave the windows open; but as Lady Ethel made this bold assertion, her partner suddenly stopped dancing, and, placing her upon a sofa, sat down beside her and looked her in the face.

"What do you mean by that?" he demanded, in a low voice, and speaking his own language, which he always used with intimate friends.

"Just what I said, *monsieur;* it has been made no secret."

"That I am about to marry the Countess, your step-mother?"

"That you are engaged to her," replied his companion, turning away her head.

"And *you* can believe that, Lady Ethel?" he responded, earnestly.

Her heart was throbbing violently, her head confused, her thoughts flying at a tangent, anywhere, and she upon the point of crying out, "No! No! *I* might have known it was false! O Victor! we are lost to one another!" when the remembrance of the night on which she had seen those two together, the attitude and look of her step-mother flashed again upon her mind, and turning fiercely round upon the Marquis, with eyes brilliant and replete with scorn, she replied, firmly—

"*Of course* I can. Did not I see you sitting upon the sofa together at Temple Grange? How easily you must think I am to be deceived."

"At Temple Grange!" he repeated, musingly. "Yes, I remember it—but too well. *It was about a month before your marriage, Lady Ethel.*"

She coloured, and was silent; then felt that she was losing ground, and resumed the attack vigorously—

"It was, but that matters nothing. I understood from Lady Clevedon at the time that you were engaged; and considering the circumstances, I was not surprised to hear it."

"Ah! the circumstances! But who was to blame for them, I wonder? It is a delicate matter to handle, but has a man the option to refuse attentions which are lavished on him gratuitously?"

"*Monsieur*, pray think of what you are saying. You are calling in question the character of your hostess—and your betrothed."

"Of my hostess—yes; and, as such, I humbly ask her pardon. Of my betrothed—no. And if this rumour has become public, Lady Ethel, I must beg of you to contradict it. The subject of marriage has never been canvassed between Lady Clevedon and myself."

Lady Ethel was thunderstruck; she did not know how to proceed with the conversation.

A month before she would have been overwhelmed at the thought that by her unnecessary rashness she had for ever severed all possibility of union with the man who sat beside her; but now, though she felt flattered to hear that he had not forsaken her for her step-mother, the news did not seem to waken any great emotion in her mind, and she was as amazed with her own tranquillity as with the Marquis's assertion.

"You surprise me, *monsieur!*" she said, after a moment's pause; "I have been looking forward to the event as a certainty."

"You are the last person in the world who should be surprised, Lady Ethel," he replied; "I do not possess the control over my memory for which you seem to give me credit."

The dance was ended by that time, and other partners were already claiming her attention. The Marquis de Lacarras, with a long, lingering gaze, relinquished her to their care, and refusing to yield to the Countess's solicitations, that he should join in the galop just commencing, took up his station in a corner whence he could observe Lady Ethel's movements, and throw a hot sigh or a pensive look after her every time that she approached him.

Meanwhile, Colonel Bainbridge, leaning over his amiable hostess, was being instructed in the secret of true happiness—suspicion!

"How wonderfully well our dear Ethel is looking!" she exclaimed, as together they watched the graceful figure and lovely flushed face of the girl gyrating round the room; "she seems to have perfectly recovered her little attack of the other night."

"Well, I am afraid a great deal of it is excitement," replied Colonel Bainbridge, gravely; "for she was so weak this afternoon, I was quite alarmed at the idea of her coming here."

"Dear me! She would have been much better in bed, I dare say."

"So Dr Chalmers thought, but she was determined to come."

"I am surprised at that, for there is not much attraction for her, one would think, to-night. What does Chalmers say about her fainting?"

"He considers it entirely due to the lowness of her nervous system. He says she is weaker than she ought to be, and must keep quiet, but he does not appear at all anxious about her."

"And she wouldn't stay at home to-night? How foolish of her! It was curious her fainting just at the time she did."

"Just as we had entered the theatre?" he said, interrogatively.

"Well, just as I had pointed her out to the notice of my friend there, Monsieur de Lacarras. He is an old flame of Ethel's, as perhaps you know, and I had but that moment said to him, 'Look, Victor!'"——

But Colonel Bainbridge did not appear to be listening to her words—he was craning his neck to obtain a view of what was passing at the other side of the room. "She is going to dance again," he said, in reply to Lady Clevedon's looks of inquiry. "I wish she would sit down this time; I am afraid she will be so tired!"

"Why not tell her to do so, my dear Colonel?" suggested the Countess, as though, in her ideas of a wife's duty, to be told was to obey.

"It is too late," he said, laughing, "she is off again!" and as he spoke, Lady Ethel passed them in the mazurka. She was dancing for the second time with the Marquis de Lacarras.

Lady Clevedon watched them with a frown.

"I really must speak to Victor," she exclaimed; "he knows how delicate she is; it is unreasonable in him—and" (after a slight pause) "not the best thing in the world for her. By the way, my dear Colonel, whilst I think of it, don't let that dear girl make herself at all conspicuous this season; for she is very thoughtless, you know; and a young woman gets so soon talked about, and"——

"Well, I hardly know, my dear lady, how I am to prevent her being either 'conspicuous' or 'talked about,'" he replied, with a glowing smile, "whilst she continues to be the prettiest woman wherever I take her—present company excepted, of course."

"You foolish fellow!" said the Countess, playfully, "I do really believe you are in love with your own wife. But, jesting apart, I mean what I say. Ethel is a dear creature, as we all know; frank and high-spirited, and generous; but she is not over fond of being controlled, and the Marquis, though an excellent fellow, and a great friend of our family, is apt to be rather careless about such things."

"He will let her overheat herself—yes, that is just what I am most afraid of," replied Colonel Bainbridge, innocently; "if you will permit me I will go and fetch her cloak." And he left the room for that purpose.

"The man's a fool," thought Lady Clevedon, as she watched his retreating figure, "and there's that girl flirting under his nose, as though she had never been married at all. It's perfectly disgraceful—I will not have such things going on in my house, and shall take good care to let Victor know my mind on the subject."

But Lady Ethel was not flirting, or at all events in the manner her step-mother ascribed to her; she was only keeping up an appearance of great hilarity in order to mislead the Marquis as to the real state of her feelings. For the news he had told her affected her more than she dared to let him see, and she was curious to hear the climax of his story, to learn how far she had been deceived, and if he never cared for any but herself (there was triumph in that thought for Lady Ethel), why he had hung back from offering her his hand! Her cheek was flushed, and her eye sparkling with the excitement of the discovery she had made, and yet it never struck her that she did not feel so miserable at its futility as she ought to have done. That revelation was reserved for a later and more momentous occasion.

Only one other opportunity had the Marquis of speaking to her privately that evening, and he made good use of it. It was in the supper-room that they found themselves alone altogether.

"I don't think that Lady Ethel Bainbridge half credits

what I told her," he said, softly, as she was engaged in taking the refreshment he had brought her.

"It is difficult to do so," she replied, as she turned her burning face away.

"Where is the difficulty, Lady Ethel? To believe that no woman can ever again engage a tithe of my attention; or to comprehend how a man could commit so fatal an error as to fear to speak his mind? Fatal, because defeat could not have placed him in a worse position than he stands at present; and success—success, Lady Ethel," in a low voice, and looking quickly away from her, "would have turned this life into a paradise for him."

She could not profess to misunderstand his meaning.

"You must not speak to me like that," she commenced in an agitated voice, and her husband entering the room at that moment in search of her, she ran up to his side with great relief.

"Yes, yes," she said, hurriedly, in answer to his inquiry if she were ready to go home; "I have had quite enough. I am tired out; let us return at once," and with a nervous bow in the direction of the Marquis, she suffered Colonel Bainbridge to lead her to the carriage.

CHAPTER XXXIII.

THE SECOND TELEGRAM.

LADY ETHEL BAINBRIDGE reached her own home in a very fervid condition. All the old doubts and difficulties which she had trampled under foot (as she thought) months before, had commenced again to surge within her breast and sway her mind; and though (unperceived by her) the passionate regret which used to mingle with them had disappeared, they were sufficiently interesting to disturb her whole being by their unexpected recurrence. Was it possible, she asked herself, as, released from the attentions of Louise, she reclined in an arm-chair before the fire in her dressing-room—possible that, after all, she had been mistaken; had judged him too harshly, too hastily; and that Victor de Lacarras, as insinuated by himself, had permitted her to slip through his fingers from sheer want of boldness to declare his wishes? Was it her step-mother who had been their enemy; and by her forward intervention, prevented their reading each other's hearts more clearly? or was it the fault of her own pride which had made her shrink from anything that looked like affording him the opportunity for which he had been sighing?

Lady Ethel could not say; perhaps she did not care too closely to inquire. She seemed to have forgotten the long months during which the Marquis de Lacarras left her in suspense and uncertainty as to his intentions regarding her, and the weeks they had passed together in which he had made no sign. The sight of his eyes, looking as they had done of old, before the blight of disbelief in him had fallen on her heart, and the accents of his voice, lowered for her ear alone, had revived so much of her former feelings, that her soul was fast becoming absorbed in a sentimental pity, not for her own loss, but for that of the man whose ill-fortune had been revealed to her. In fancy she pictured the long life which lay before him: unlighted by the possession of her love, or of herself; a miserable, lonely existence, which could never be freed from the sting of regret; and then to think that he had missed his happiness by a mere chance, a stroke of ill-luck, which could never be remedied—a lost opportunity, which could never be recalled. Poor Victor! poor Marquis de Lacarras, with the reproachfully sad eyes! Was it possible she was the cause of all this misery? that she alone was to blame for his unhappy life? He seemed to think so, and that she might have saved him from it. And yet all the while her heart had been full of the most bitter reproaches. Should she, *could* she ever forgive herself?

Profoundly wrapt in some such reverie, with her pretty face supported by her hand, and her eyes mournfully fixed upon the fire, Colonel Bainbridge found Lady Ethel still sitting up, when, having finished his last cigar, an hour and more after their return to Curzon Street, he sought his bed-chamber.

"My dear Ethel," he exclaimed, "not yet in bed? Why, do you know what time it is, darling? past six o'clock! What would Dr Chalmers say?"

"Oh! don't tease me," she answered, fretfully.

She had just arrived at that pitch of mental fervour, when having discovered that both her happiness and that of the Marquis had been ruined for evermore, she decided that thenceforth they should pass through life with sunken cheeks and sad eyes, taking part in the hollow amusements of the world, it is true, but testifying to each other by their appearance and demeanour that they were devoured by regret for their irrevocable loss. And it was annoying, to say the least of it, to have a romantic reverie like this broken in upon by the common-place remonstrance of a great, strong, muscular, everyday husband, as to why she did not go to bed and to sleep, like anybody else, whose heart was not broken.

Colonel Bainbridge recoiled at the tone in which his wife addressed him. He had been so elated by the one term of affection she had unexpectedly used to him at Lady Clevedon's *soirée*, that he had been calculating on its effects ever since. But though her answer threw cold water on his joy, it had not the power to make him retaliate. His was too generous a nature to return evil for evil.

"I did not mean to tease you, dearest," he said, gently; "but this fire is nearly out, and you will take cold. Shall I make it up again; or—would it not be better if you came to bed? You must be very tired."

She was very tired, and her musing had been interrupted, so Lady Ethel resolved for once to follow the advice given her, though long after her husband had fallen asleep, she continued too excited to close her eyes, but lay awake, believing herself to be the most unfortunate and miserable woman in the world, as with false sympathy she pondered on the revelations which had been made to her.

When at last she fell asleep, it was to slumber profoundly for a few hours—so profoundly that on being roused again, she sat straight up in bed with a start, having forgotten everything that had occurred the night before. It was broad daylight then; the sunshine was streaming through the closed blinds of her windows; and as she rubbed her eyes she became conscious of a gentle tapping on the bedroom door, which had been the cause of her awaking.

"Colonel Bainbridge," she said, quickly, "there is some one knocking at the door."

Her husband did not answer, and she turned to where, flushed and warm, with one arm beneath his head, he lay beside her, wrapt in a deep sleep.

How handsome he appeared—better than handsome—how manly, how powerful, how big! Night and forgetfulness had smoothed away the lines of thought which impressed his brow by day; his face was tranquil and careless as a boy's, and his huge muscular limbs were stretched out in perfect rest.

"What a Goliath!" thought Lady Ethel, as she regarded him; and yet a proud feeling of possession ran through her, as she laid her little hand upon his broad shoulder. It lasted but a moment—that feeling—though it endured to all eternity!

"Colonel Bainbridge!" she repeated, with as vehement a pinch as her fingers could accomplish, "there is some one at the door!"

"Is there, my darling?" he replied, as with a sudden movement he jumped out of bed, threw on his dressing-gown, and turned the key in the lock.

"What do you want?" he demanded of the servant who was waiting there.

"A telegram, if you please, sir! I thought it best to bring it up to you, in case it should be of importance."

"Oh, yes; of course—all right. Thank you!" and without

stopping for further inquiry, Colonel Bainbridge closed the door, and walking to one of the windows, pulled up the blind, and tore open the official envelope.

As he did so, there rushed back upon the mind of Lady Ethel, who was still sitting up in bed, all the circumstances of the previous evening: the telegram which she had destroyed; the buzz of admiration which had greeted her entrance to Lady Clevedon's drawing-room; and then the Marquis, with his sad reproachful eyes, and his assurance that he had not, and never had had, the least intention of marrying her step-mother—of marrying any one except herself, whom, by ill-luck or treachery, he had lost.

And as all this came back on Lady Ethel's memory, she sunk down on her pillows with a deep-drawn sigh. She had just remembered that her heart and the heart of Victor de Lacarras were both broken, and that there remained no happiness in this world for either of them again.

The reception of his telegram seemed greatly to disturb Colonel Bainbridge, for he read it more than once, and had his wife been watching him, she would have seen his hand tremble.

"There must be some mistake here!" were the first words he uttered, as he violently pulled the bell.

"What is it about?" said Lady Ethel, with affected languor, though naturally she guessed the news it must contain.

"My poor father is ill—dangerously ill. I doubt if I shall ever see him again alive," he replied, in a broken voice; and then, as the servant's knock resounded on the door, he put the question—

"When did this telegram arrive?"

"Now, sir! not ten minutes ago; I brought it up directly."

"But it is the second that has been sent me; at least it says so. Have you seen anything of another?"

"Not since last night, sir."

"What do you mean by 'last night?'"

"The telegram that came for you, sir! just before you started. You were not at home, so I took it up to her ladyship's room."

"Ethel! did you receive it?" he asked, quickly appealing to his wife, but she had turned away her face from observation.

"Oh, yes, sir!" interposed the woman, who feared to incur blame from the transaction. "I gave it into her ladyship's own hands myself."

"You did no such thing," replied Lady Ethel, tartly, "you put it on the table."

"That will do," said Colonel Bainbridge, who saw there was something wrong. "Tell James to take the Bradshaw into my dressing-room at once, and look out my things for travelling. I shall start for the north as soon as it is possible to do so;" and then he shut the door again, and came round to the other side of the bed.

"Ethel! where is that telegram? and why did you not give it to me?"

His voice was firm and decided; it had lost all the winning sweetness with which he usually coaxed her to do a thing; it was a voice not to be trifled with; and his wife chose to resent the tone he had assumed.

"I'm sure I can't tell you where it is; in the dust-hole I conclude, as I put it on the fire; and I didn't give it to you, because if I had done so it would have prevented our going to Lady Clevedon's." Her nonchalant manner roused his ire.

"But do you know what it contained?" he said, indignantly.

"Of course I do; I read it!" Colonel Bainbridge took a step backward.

"You read it!—read that my father was dangerously ill—that my immediate presence was required at Cranshaws—and burned the message? Ethel! how *dared* you?"

His voice was more than firm now; it was stern, and she shrunk before it; but she was true to her feminine nature—that unworthy little nature that, knowing its impotency is its safeguard in the hands of a generous man, will claw, and spit, and hiss like a cat when beyond reach, sooner than say one word that shall acknowledge it is in the wrong.

And, with the falsehoods of Victor de Lacarras ringing in her ears, Lady Ethel had worked herself up to that pitch of self-commiseration which makes every rebuke, however well-deserved, assume the appearance of injustice.

"*Dare!*" she exclaimed, springing up in bed, "I dare everything; I would burn it over again to-morrow if I thought fit to do so. It is you who dare too much in speaking in this way to me."

"Come! come! I am not going to have any nonsense of this sort," replied Colonel Bainbridge. "If you were aware of the contents of the telegram, you did a very cruel act in destroying it, and one which may never be repaired. My father will most likely be dead before I reach Cranshaws."

She was a little shocked at the idea of what she had done then, but still she carried it off with a high hand.

"It's not my fault!" she murmured. "If they had made themselves a little more agreeable to me whilst I was under their roof, I might have felt better disposed to give up my amusement to satisfy their whims."

"Whims! you call it a whim in a dying man to wish to see his only child again?"

"How could I tell he was dying?"

"You knew that he was seriously ill—and that he wanted to see me; and you were unwilling to relinquish a few hours' pleasure for the sake of permitting a father and son to meet for the last time upon earth. You are heartless—cruel—unwomanly! Ethel! I thought better of you!" and sitting down upon the nearest chair, Colonel Bainbridge covered his face with his hands.

The action, instead of softening, seemed to irritate her.

"Who told you to think better?" she demanded, sharply; "and what have you ever seen in my behaviour to lead you to suppose that I was so particularly interested in your father's feelings, or your own?"

"Nothing—God knows!" he answered, bitterly; "your conduct whilst at Cranshaws was a source of the greatest pain to me; but since you are my wife, and my father has become yours, a sense of duty might"——

But his speech was interrupted by her shrill laugh.

"Duty! Is it not sufficient that I should have consented to marry *you*, without being called upon to show filial duty towards a man who"——

Colonel Bainbridge rose from his seat with a lowering brow.

"Have a care, Ethel! You had better be cautious what you say to me just now!"

"Oh! you don't frighten me, I assure you. No one could have behaved more rudely to me than your father did."

"No one could have taken your rudeness to him and my poor mother, in a spirit of greater patience and charity."

"That is your opinion, perhaps. I say I did you enough honour by accepting the offer of your hand, without being expected to adopt all your relations into the bargain. And if I had known—if I had known"—— growing suspiciously hysterical.

"If you had known what?" he asked, sternly. "Do you mean to insinuate, Ethel, that you were unaware, before our marriage, that my family was not on an equality with your own?"

"Oh, yes! I knew that too well."

"What then? Have I been fool enough to marry a woman who does not care for me?"

"I should think you might have answered that question for yourself. You have received ample proofs of the truth," she said, scornfully.

"Perhaps you will go further, and inform me that you cared for some one else."

"And what if I did?"

He did not answer her; but he advanced to the bedside, and Lady Ethel saw that every one of his strong limbs was shaking.

"Are you insinuating the truth to me—or a lie?" he demanded, hoarsely.

She was frightened at his manner; she knew that she had gone too far; and yet, with a bravado with which the weakest of her sex is at times familiar, she threw the apple of discord in his face.

"The truth—of course! How dare you accuse me of anything else? What motive on earth do you suppose should have induced me—*me*, the daughter of earls, and connected on every side with the purest blood in England,—to lower myself by marrying into the family of a tradesman—yes! you needn't look at me in that way, for you know perfectly well that your father was nothing but a tradesman—unless there had been some reason—some deep and miserable reason," with a sob, "that I should try to forget who I was, or that I had ever been;" and Lady Ethel buried her face in her hands.

"And the 'deep and miserable reason,' madam; I am waiting for that," he said.

"My heart was *broken*," continued his wife in a burst of

tears; "my life was wasted; I had lost everything I cared for in this world; or rather I thought that I had lost it."

"And the fragments were good enough for a tradesman's son," replied her husband. "I am vastly indebted to you for your condescension, Lady Ethel. One word more, and I have done. What is the name of the man in the face of whose loss, real or supposed, you were pleased to throw yourself away upon me?"

"I shall not tell you," she said, quickly. She already regretted, though she little foresaw the effects of the folly into which she had been betrayed.

"But I intend to hear it," was the decisive reply; and as he spoke Colonel Bainbridge took her two hands prisoner in his, and forced her to look him in the face.

She might as well have tried to struggle against a pair of handcuffs.

"I shall not detain you long!" he said, solemnly. "You have but to speak the word, and you are free. What is his name?"

The influence of his glance subdued her even more than the powerful grasp of his hands.

"You know it," she answered, sullenly. "*Victor de Lacarras!*"

"And you care for him?"

She made no reply, but her eyes flashed up at him indignantly, and were cast down again.

"And married me because you could not marry him?" continued Colonel Bainbridge.

"*Yes!*" with a desperate effort to get free; "if you *will* have the truth, and nothing but the truth, there it is for you."

He let her go as she spoke; and she twisted away from him, and buried her head in her pillow.

But once more his hands—those kind, strong hands that had never handled her before but with the tenderest, gentlest touch—came about her face, and turned it to confront his own.

Turned it to meet two hungering, despairing eyes, the gaze of which haunted her for many a lonely day and night succeeding; and a sad drawn mouth which seemed to ask what he had done to be requited by such treachery.

He looked at her, perhaps for a full minute, which appeared to her guilty conscience like an hour; and then he dropped his hands, turned suddenly away, and left the room.

The iron had entered into his very soul.

As he gained his dressing-room, he was greeted by the intelligence that there was no train by which he could travel north, before eight o'clock in the evening.

"Very good!" he replied, with easy indifference; "then there is no hurry. Pack my portmanteau, and meet me with it at the King's Cross Station at a quarter to eight."

And having dismissed his valet, Colonel Bainbridge dressed himself, and left the house before Lady Ethel had appeared downstairs.

CHAPTER XXXIV.

WHY IT WAS SENT.

Things had been going on very quietly at Cranshaws, between the time that Colonel and Lady Ethel Bainbridge left the castle, and the occasion for sending that first telegram to Curzon Street.

Spring advanced but slowly in that northern climate, but each day Nature unfolded something new and fresh and beautiful for the contemplation of her admirers; and the final demolition of the frost brought plenty of work for those who wanted it, both in-doors and out. The season for ploughing and sowing had arrived; for the housing of young lambs, and counting of apple-blossoms; for calculating how long the winter stores would last, and how soon the upspringing grass would afford pasture for the increasing flocks and herds. And Mrs Bainbridge found almost as much occupation as her husband, for she permitted no one to superintend the poultry-yard but herself, and held daily conferences with the old hen-wife, for the purpose of mutual congratulation on the successful efforts of young pullets, or the happy hatching of large broods. In the house, Miss Lloyd was employed in ransacking the linen presses, calling over the roll of preserve jars, and giving Maggie Henderson loving little lectures; whilst for the girl herself, perhaps this was the bitterest phase of the trial through which she was passing.

It may be remembered that, on the day Lady Ethel resolved to leave Cranshaws, Maggie had gone to pay a visit to Sister Margaret, at Horse-ap-Cleugh.

The interview, as her aunt prophesied, had done her good. The gentle sympathy she had met with, the calm counsel received, and, above all, the assurance with which she had been impressed, that whatever was right and best for her in the future would be brought to pass without the help of any violent effort on her own part, had left a sense of trustful expectation on her mind, which was the best feeling she could carry back to lighten the duties to which she was bound.

She had often seen and talked with good women before; she had been brought up under the example of her aunts, who both led humble and religious lives; yet, until she met Sister Margaret, Maggie had never known what it was to read in another's eyes the complete happiness that springs from the surrender of one's life to God.

From that hour she felt her own vocation fixed; not assuredly to be a Sister of Mercy, not even to labour amongst the sick and suffering, if He did not so will for her; but to be His faithful servant to her life's end.

She had dreamed of such a service before; she had longed for, and, in part, adopted it; but now she felt as though it were impossible to keep back anything for commoner use; and gave herself to Him body and soul, to do with as He thought fit; believing, as Aunt Letty had taught her, and Sister Margaret had endorsed, that true religion consists not in *what* we do, but *how* we do it; and less in great efforts than in complete obedience.

And so, when her new friend left Horse-ap-Cleugh (which she did not do without a promise to keep up their intercourse by correspondence) Maggie returned to her uneventful life with a firm determination to perform everything, however trivial, that came to her in the shape of duty; and, for His sake, to perform it well.

Thence her existence should have been all sunshine, rest, and quiet; blissful in the satisfaction of an easy conscience, and changed from dark to light, by the hope of her reward; yet it was not so—not, at all events, in this stage of her recovery.

The path of wisdom is not always a happy path, let Solomon say what he will. It is a hard path; sometimes it is bitterly, cruelly hard, stained with the blood of feet unused to tread it, and the tears of eyes that have wept themselves blind before they found it; and, since it is so, we have no right to say it should be otherwise.

For, though hard and bitter, it is the furnace that purifies the gold, and there is another fact to be borne in mind: it is the only sacrifice we have it in our power to render up to Him who has done all for us. This sacrifice of self, our tears and sighs, fierce resolutions, and ultimate victories—gifts of His own though they be—are the sole offerings He can take from our hands; because they only typify our love and whole submission to Him; and we have nothing else to give. Nor are they lost in His immensity; we all know that. He sets our tears as jewels in His crown, and gives us in exchange eternal smiles.

Shall we have time to think about them then? But betwixt "then" and "now," how wide a difference, He who was human knows.

With the excitement of her cousin's and Lady Ethel's visit over, and the solace of Sister Margaret's company past, Maggie Henderson sometimes felt as though her mere existence were a calamity too heavy to be borne. She was neither despairing nor jealous; she no longer gave way to violent bursts of grief; she did not even desire things to be other than they were; yet all the lightness and the sunshine seemed to have died out of her life, and left her stranded on the barren shore of her dull thoughts—from which she often had not strength to rise to prayer or praise. She went through her routine of little duties carefully—being even more punctual, solicitous, and affectionate, than usual; so that Aunt Letty was deceived by her demeanour, and Mrs Bainbridge did not once question the fact of her complete contentment.

But one person did: one who (though unknown to himself) was drawing near the confines of the other world, and had his sympathies perhaps quickened by the unseen influences he was approaching; and that was her uncle. Mr Bainbridge had never been quite himself since the departure of his son. He had gone about his farm as usual, it is true; settled bargains with his drovers, checked his bailiff's account-books, and determined what works were to be set in operation during the ensuing season. And yet he, like Maggie, had lost the cheerful activity which characterised all his former movements, and the girl perceived the change and attributed it to the disappointment he had experienced in her cousin's marriage. She knew what his hopes had been, and the knowledge drew her closer to him, so that these two became very sympathetic and near friends during the last weeks of their companionship together. Not that Maggie ever told her uncle of her trouble, nor he express what he felt to his niece ; but whenever the day's labour left an interval of quiet, the girl was to be found by the old man's side; walking with him hand in hand, or sitting at his feet, or leaning with her head upon his shoulders ; and they both felt happier and more contented when it was so. Afterwards she took it as a sign of God's good will, that she had been left so sweet a legacy of love, by him who had stood in the place of her own father to her.

One afternoon in May, the same day on which Lady Ethel destroyed the telegram, Mr Bainbridge, to the consternation of the household, was suddenly taken with a stroke of paralysis—found prostrate and helpless on his study floor, and unable to articulate more than the word "Thomas" as he was carried to his bed. In this dilemma, by which both Mrs Bainbridge and Miss Lloyd were overwhelmed, Maggie proved the guardian angel of the family. It was she who despatched a messenger post haste for medical aid, who wrote and sent the telegram to Curzon Street, and then took up her station at the sick man's side, ready to interpret to her aunt each feeble action by which he strove to make his wishes understood.

The doctor came and stayed all night, during which the feeble flame of life was flickering to and fro, and keeping them in miserable suspense, and by the morning Mr Bainbridge was so much weaker that it was considered doubtful whether he could survive to see his son again.

But he was still alive when the carriage went to Borthwick to meet the mail train, and returned to them—empty ; no Colonel Bainbridge having arrived by it.

His mother was almost in despair. She insisted that Thomas must be ill himself, unable to quit the house—perhaps his bed ; for nothing else would have detained him from his dying father ; and she was about to lose both of them at once.

It was in vain that Maggie represented to her that in such a case, they also would have had a message ; and that by far the likelier solution of the mystery was that her cousin and Lady Ethel were away from home. Mrs Bainbridge was quite certain she was to be rendered childless as well as widowed, and divided between her desire to rush off to town to see after her son herself, and the duty which kept her at the bedside of her husband.

"It is useless to attempt anything like argument with your good aunt," observed the doctor, confidentially, to Maggie; "but if Colonel Bainbridge is to see his father again alive, you must send another telegram at once."

And so the second telegram, which was still more strongly worded than the first, reached London about noon, and the same evening saw its recipient on his way to Cranshaws.

CHAPTER XXXV.

TOO LATE.

Colonel Bainbridge alighted hurriedly from the hired vehicle which had conveyed him to his father's door, and without inquiry passed at once into the dining-room. There was no one there but Maggie Henderson. She was looking pale and tired, for she had sat up for two nights at her uncle's bedside; and as she came forward and placed her hand in Colonel Bainbridge's, he guessed at once that he had arrived too late.

"O Cousin Thomas, I am thankful you are come! Aunt Lizzie will be so glad to see you—but it 's all over!"

His presence had no power to make her blush or tremble then; but her sad, compassionate eyes rested calmly upon his, as though he had, indeed, been the brother to her which he called himself.

Colonel Bainbridge broke away from her kindly grasp, and, sinking into a chair, for a moment concealed his face from view.

"All over!" he muttered, hoarsely; "all—quite—*quite* over! It seems too hard—and yet it is but what I expected. When did it happen, Maggie?"

"This morning at four o'clock," she whispered. "He went so happily; so full of faith, and hope, and love. Had you been here you could never have forgotten it. He said he had but one wish left ungratified."

"And that was"——

"To see yourself. O cousin! why did you not come as soon as you received the telegram?"

"I did not receive it," he answered, brusquely; "I was at a party that night, and still asleep the following morning when your second message came to hand. I started as soon as it was practicable."

"And your servants never gave it to you on your return? How very careless of them! If they had only known the consequences involved in their neglect!"

"It is of no use talking of it," he said, moodily. "How is my mother, Maggie? How does she bear all this?"

"Oh! she has been in despair, cousin; and when the carriage came back from Borthwick yesterday without you, I thought she would have gone wild with fear. She imagined something must be wrong. But since—since this morning, she has been much quieter; and when I went upstairs about half an hour ago, was fast asleep upon her bed. Poor soul! she has not closed her eyes once before since uncle was taken ill; and she is unused to fatigue, you know. But shall I tell her you are here?"

"By no means, Maggie. Let her sleep while she can; and, to speak the truth, I don't feel equal to encountering her just yet. I fear to read reproach for my tardiness in her eyes."

"O cousin! you will never do that; she loves you too fondly. She will feel at once that it could only have arisen from a mistake."

"It is an awful shock," he continued, presently. "Your message did not prepare me for so sudden a termination, Maggie."

"Not the third one?" she inquired.

"Was there a third one?" he replied, indifferently.

"Of course there was. I despatched it about three o'clock. It must have reached Curzon Street before you started. The first was necessarily worded with some uncertainty, but directly Dr Mackenzie pronounced him to be sinking, I sent another to prepare you for the worst. Did you not receive that either?"

"No."

"But at what hour did you leave town, cousin?"

"By the eight o'clock train."

"And it had not reached your house before that time?"

"I do not know—I was from home," he said, uneasily; and then, after a pause, "the fact is, I left Curzon Street at one o'clock, and did not return there again."

"Oh!" replied Maggie, thinking the proceedings sounded unusual, but ignorant what remark to make upon it. Then there was the silence of a minute between them, during which the clock upon the mantelpiece ticked as though it had been the only live thing present.

"Won't you have some breakfast, Cousin Thomas?" she inquired, timidly, as the servant appeared with the tea and coffee; "it is quite ready now."

"No, thank you, my dear; I have no appetite."

"A cup of coffee," she said, coaxingly; "you really should

try to take something after your long journey. Remember how much there will be for you to do and think of. Aunt Lizzie will depend on you to do everything."

"Well, a cup of coffee, then," replied Colonel Bainbridge, though he made no attempt to leave the arm-chair into which he had thrown himself, and approach the table.

"He suffered no pain," continued the girl, softly, as she took up her station behind the breakfast equipage, and tried to think of something that should console her cousin. "Dr Mackenzie, who has been with him from first to last, and only went to lie down about an hour ago, told me himself that in all his practice he had never seen a more peaceful death-bed, and that thought ought to be a comfort to us, cousin."

"Yes!—I am thankful to hear it!"

"And in several conversations that dear uncle and I had together, previous to his being taken ill, he told me what a consolation it was to him to leave Cranshaws and—us—that is, Aunt Letty and Aunt Lizzie, you know—to the care of one whom he felt would look after them just in the same way he should have done himself."

"Eh?—what?—I beg your pardon!" exclaimed Colonel Bainbridge, starting from a reverie.

He was evidently not listening to her; and presently Maggie tried if another subject would rouse him from his mood of despondency.

"Did you observe the country as you came along, cousin? It begins to look very green and lovely."

"Very lovely, Maggie!"

"But I suppose the trees are more forward with you south than they are here."

"Yes! I suppose so."

His face looked so dark and so despairing as he sat there, supporting it upon his hand, that the girl's heart bled for him. He must not reproach himself too much for a mere accident. What could she say to recall his mind to happier thoughts? In her anxiety to comfort, she probed the wound which agonised him.

"I hope"— she began, with some degree of hesitation—for Maggie had not yet learned to speak the name so freely as she should have done,—"I hope, cousin Thomas, that you left Lady Ethel quite well."

But had she been prepared for the electrical effect of her words, she never would have uttered them.

Colonel Bainbridge, with a violent expression (she was not quite sure what it was), started from his chair and rushed towards the window, as though he were going right through it.

"For God's sake!" he cried, vehemently, "don't mention her to me."

At this outburst, so unexpected and apparently uncalled for, Maggie turned white with apprehension. What horrible tragedy could have happened in that establishment, the mistress of which she had often been weak enough to envy? She regarded her cousin in silent dismay.

"You will think me a great fool," he said, presently, passing a handkerchief over his clammy brow; "and so I am—the greatest fool that was ever born—but I would rather discuss any subject but that of my wife at present. And now," returning to the table, "let me have the cup of coffee you promised, Maggie; after which, as I am not to see my mother yet, I will go up to my room."

Perceiving how he had alarmed his cousin (for Maggie's hand shook as she poured out the coffee for him), he tried to converse more calmly after that, and entered into several details concerning his own journey and his father's illness; but she was quite unable to imitate his affected ease. She could not shake off the remembrance of that sudden ejaculation, and the tone in which it had been uttered; it penetrated even the sad subject on which they were engaged; and full of forebodings for his happiness, and dread of forthcoming revelations, she sat almost in silence, until relieved by the entrance of the doctor, who had been informed of Colonel Bainbridge's arrival, and on whose appearance she slipped out of the room.

Dr Mackenzie was an old man, who had known the Bainbridge family for years, and his greeting to the son of the house was as cordial as the circumstances under which they met permitted.

"How do you do, my dear Colonel! very glad to see you," —with a prolonged shaking of hands,—"though you have only come in time to hear bad news."

"I was prepared for it, doctor, and have at all events the comfort of feeling that since you were here, nothing further could have been done for him."

"You are very good to say so, my dear sir, very good," was the doctor's reply; "and I think I may affirm, that no amount of skill could have saved your father's life. His constitution received so severe a shock in the first seizure, that had he not been a remarkably hale man, he could not have survived to have a second, which he did yesterday afternoon. It was a pity you were not here—a great pity!"

"It was impossible," said Colonel Bainbridge, brokenly. "I have been explaining the circumstances that detained me to my cousin. I would have given worlds to be present."

"Well—well! we must look upon the bright side of things. He died easy in mind and body, and we shall be lucky if our friends can say as much for us by and by—eh? Cranshaws is looking very pleasant, sir, just now!"

"Very pleasant," was the mechanical reply.

"You will find plenty of work up here, Colonel, both for hands and head. It's a fine estate! I suppose you'll be for selling out of the army now, and settling down as a county gentleman, eh?"

"I don't know; I have had no time to think about it."

"Ah! I expect that is what the old gentleman intended you to do, though. But perhaps you would not care to bury yourself in the country just yet, Colonel! You'll wait till you've got half-a-dozen boys and girls to pull the house down about your ears for you. How is her ladyship? well, I hope!"

Colonel Bainbridge winced, but answered, firmly—

"Quite well! I thank you!"

"Ah! she's a beautiful creature; it's not often we see the like of her in these parts. And so she keeps her health, eh? Very gay up in London, I suppose?"

"Very gay!"

"Dancing all night and sleeping all day, eh? Not quite the best thing to preserve good looks, though. Is it, Colonel?"

"I suppose not!"

"You must bring her ladyship here again as soon as the season is over. Nothing like Scotch air for setting one up. No prospect of a family yet, Colonel, eh?"

But here the Colonel, who had been on thorns for the last ten minutes, and looking round wildly for some means of escape, opportunely heard the voice of Mrs Bainbridge on the staircase.

"My mother!" he said, quickly, "I must go to her," and in another moment he was folded in her arms.

CHAPTER XXXVI.

COLONEL BAINBRIDGE MAKES UP HIS MIND.

It was so sweet, so good to have him there, and to have him there alone; that though he came in an hour of deep distress, Mrs Bainbridge felt as though half her grief were lifted off her shoulders as she gazed into his face.

"My son! my dear, dear son! my own Thomas!" she repeated over and over again, clinging to him as the weaker clings to the stronger, and pouring the story of her sorrow into his sympathising ears.

"Oh, if you had but been here, my dear! He asked so often for you. The only word he uttered upon being seized was your name; and, afterwards, I am sure the door never opened but what his poor eyes turned in that direction, hoping it was you."

"Oh, don't! mother, don't!" he urged, imploringly. "I cannot bear it! I wish to God I had come sooner!" And then he placed her in a chair, and sat down by her side, whilst she sobbed for a few minutes in her handkerchief.

"You see, my dear," she continued, presently, through her tears, "it is best that you should hear all this. It may be painful now, but it will be a comfort to think of hereafter. Your father loved you very dearly, Thomas; he was a good father to you, and a good husband to me. We have sustained a great loss in him."

"Heaven knows we have!" her son replied.

"But we need not make it worse by unnecessary self-reproach. Maggie has told me all you said to her this morning on the subject; and of course your absence could not have been helped. It was an accident, and nothing more."

"But did *he* think it so? That is the doubt that will haunt my lifetime."

"We must hope he did, my dear! At all events, he knew your circumstances, and how much engaged you are; and doubtless made allowances for the delay. He could never have thought you would refuse to come to him."

"I hope not. He little knew me if he did."

"Oh, no! He had perfect faith in your affection. Even of late—during the last few months—since your marriage, that is to say (you know, my dear, without my telling you, that he was just a little disappointed at your choice)—he has always expressed himself as completely satisfied with all you did, or were likely to do after his decease. I think now that he must sometimes have had a kind of inkling he was not long for this world. O Thomas! what are we to do without him?"

And Mrs Bainbridge relapsed into a natural but very distressing exhibition of feeling, which made her son thankful of an excuse to quit her presence, for the purpose of procuring the refreshment of a bath and change of linen after his night's journey. It was a melancholy meditation that he indulged in as soon as he found himself alone. There he was, master of Cranshaws, and the bulk of his father's prodigious fortune—the richest man, perhaps, in the army—as rich a man, certainly, as is, ordinarily speaking, to be found there; yet the poorest, he felt, shuddering—the poorest wretch that traversed this wide earth; than whom a beggar clothed in rags, but warmed by love, lived, by comparison, in affluence.

O Lady Ethel! what a ruin you have created here!

He threw his thoughts back to that time last year, when he had first seen and become enamoured of her; and remembered, with set teeth, how *that man*—the one whose name she had mentioned to him—had been always hovering about her, and he had felt jealous of him even then.

But her treatment of himself at Temple Grange; her altered manner, warm caressing glances, and preference openly confessed to: had it all been a falsehood, a delusive maddening dream, from which he had but just awakened, to find that in order to avenge herself she had cruelly made shipwreck of his hopes?

Yes; it had been a dream, and he had wakened from it. He recalled her flaming looks upon the morning that they parted, her taunting speeches and insulting words, and felt that what she said then was the truth—the woman he adored had never loved him. Oh! it was hard to bear; harder than any other trial could have been to him, for his pride was great as his love, and both were sorely wounded. He had wasted all the strength of his passionate nature on this woman, and she had turned and mocked him for his folly. He had given up everything he possessed to her—name, and wealth, and happiness; almost the affection of his family—and she had thrown them back into his face, telling him openly that she had used both him and them as tools—mere instruments wherewith to carve out her revenge.

The deed was as wicked, and far more cruel than that of savages, who sacrifice a life to appease the supposed anger of their gods; and he did not feel the torture less because it was administered by fair soft hands that seemed too delicate to crush a heart, and feet too light to trample on it.

He was crushed as he sat there—unmistakably crushed—body, soul, and spirit, and he did not care to deny it, even to himself. He acknowledged freely that the world, or what constituted in his eyes the world, was over for him.

And it was for this woman—this false, forsworn, and evil nature, who could marry whilst she despised him, and after receiving all he had to give her, cast in his teeth as accusation what was no fault of his—that he had refused to listen to the advice so affectionately tendered by the father who now lay lifeless in the room next to his own; had brought her home to be a cause of misery and strife in the house which had never been the scene of anything but domestic happiness till then; and finally, by her chicanery, had missed the farewell blessing, without which he now felt as though he never more should know the name of peace. Would he subject himself to be the occasion of her insolence again? Would he bring his wife to Cranshaws, to wander through the apartments which had been his parents', and abuse their memory at every turn; place her in his father's chair, at the head of his mother's table, only to encounter the bitter truth whenever her jeering lips chose to deliver it, that she had lowered herself by marrying a tradesman's son in order to excite the jealousy of an aristocratic and more favoured lover?

No, he would perish first: and Cranshaws might go to rack and ruin before he would install Lady Ethel as mistress there. On one point his mind was made up—he and she would never live in the same house again!

Yet—"how to take last leave of all he loved!" Oh! the golden hair, the 'wildering blue eyes, and marble skin! Even in that hour of dark despair, before he had looked upon the corpse of his father, or realised that he was indeed gone from them for ever, such trivialities commenced to haunt and vex him, like a swarm of gnats about a wounded man. The force of a great blow stuns us into silence, but it is these small extraneous memories which goad the brain to madness. Yet, as, an hour later, Colonel Bainbridge stood by his dead father's side, gazing through tears which he was not ashamed to brush away, upon the closed eyes that would never again meet his own, the sealed lips that never more could bless him, and the folded hands that had responded for the last time to his pressure, he felt that had Lady Ethel been twice as beautiful, and he had loved her twice as much, it would still have been the same, and he could not have forgiven her for wantonly depriving him of the consolation of being present at his parent's death-bed.

He was a tradesman, it was true (and here the son, regarding the figure stretched upon the bed, involuntarily drew himself up), but he had given him life, and no one who despised him, or his honourable calling, should fatten on the produce of his labour.

From that moment Colonel Bainbridge's resolution was fully taken.

CHAPTER XXXVII.

"MAGGIE, I WANT TO TELL YOU SOMETHING."

THE next few days passed much as such days usually do. Every window of the castle was closed and blinded, and chance visitors to Cranshaws, glancing up half fearfully at that of which the sash was raised a couple of inches, whispered to each other that the corpse lay there.

Colonel Bainbridge passed most of this time in his own room. There was plenty of business to be transacted with lawyers, bailiffs, and undertakers, which all devolved upon him, and therefore his seclusion appeared neither unnecessary nor strange.

At stated periods the family assembled for meals, at which the conversation, if it could be called such, was stilted and unnatural, and seldom turned upon any but the most indifferent topics. Consequently, he had not so much to endure from the mention of Lady Ethel's name, or his future intentions with respect to her, as he had anticipated.

Indeed, the subject of his domestic life was seldom alluded to at all. His mother, when her first emotion at meeting him was spent, had spoken of his wife, and asked a few particulars concerning her; but Colonel Bainbridge answered curtly, and the theme, not being one on which they had much sympathy, was soon discarded.

No one, therefore (excepting Maggie), had a suspicion that his evident depression was due to any cause but their general affliction; and only noticed it to praise his filial duty, and say he bid fair to make as good a man as his father was before him.

But Maggie knew better. Maggie, remembering the look and gesture with which, on the morning of his arrival, he had commanded her to avoid the mention of his wife to him, felt there was a deeper shadow than the shadow of death resting on his soul, and her own yearned to administer the sisterly comfort which she almost felt competent to do. For she had so far schooled herself that her cousin's presence was no longer an active pain to her. To hear his voice, and meet his glance, and watch his movements, knowing, meanwhile, that so to hear, and meet, and watch, was all the part she evermore could bear in his existence, made her heart feel heavier, perhaps, but had no power to quicken it.

The first stage of nervous suffering was past for Maggie Henderson. She had prayed so much that she might be enabled to regard her cousin as something altogether beyond her reach; and she had striven so hard to attain the blessing which she confidently expected to receive, that it had come to her; as sooner or later it does come to all who trust and pray.

The fever and passion of her grief were over; and though much weakness remained, much despondency, and, at times, even want of faith, yet she was out of danger and on the road to convalescence—thanks to the Physician who never fails to heal.

And even now the first token of her reward was appearing in the hope that she might be the means of comforting her cousin in his secret distress. But how to introduce the topic after he had so violently disclaimed it, Maggie knew not; yet she watched patiently, hoping that an opportunity might occur. When it did, it was himself who broached it.

The funeral was over; the will—by which, with the exception of a couple of thousand a year to his mother for her lifetime, and trifling annuities to Miss Lloyd and Maggie Henderson, Colonel Bainbridge was rendered sole possessor of his late father's fortune and estates—had been read, and the castle being cleared of lawyers' clerks and undertakers' men, the blinds were drawn up to admit the cheerful sunshine, the windows thrown open, the rooms set in order, and the family re-assembled to look each other in the face and ask what they were to do next.

"I suppose, my dear Thomas," remarked Mrs Bainbridge, "that you will not take possession of Cranshaws before the summer is over; or shall you move into it at once? Either plan will be equally convenient to me, you know. And with respect to the house in Curzon Street, shall you retain that as it is? I am afraid you will find no room for the furniture here, for your dear father disliked nothing so much as a half-furnished room. But I suppose you will require to be in

London until you have settled something with regard to resigning your profession?"

Such questions Colonel Bainbridge hardly knew how to parry.

"My dear mother," he would reply, "the very last thing I should wish you to do would be to hurry out of Cranshaws. Make it your home for as long as you like; altogether, if it pleases you to do so."

"But, my dear Thomas, that would be quite unreasonable both on your part and mine. You have Lady Ethel to consult in these matters, remember; besides, dear as you are to me, I should never feel comfortable whilst living in another person's house, and have long made up my mind if I should be so unfortunate as to survive your father, to go and settle near my own friends at Birmingham. It was there he met me, my dear, and married me" (with a little sob), "and I would rather die there than anywhere else—only you'll promise, when that happens, to bring me back, Thomas, and lay me by his side in Mindon churchyard."

It was after some such conversation as the above that Colonel Bainbridge called his cousin abruptly to his side.

"Come here, Maggie, I want to tell you something."

It was a bright, beautiful morning the day after the funeral, and they were sauntering on the terrace which ran round the castle.

"Well, cousin, I am all attention."

"My mother seems to imagine (you heard what she said at breakfast just now) that I am about to throw up the army at once, and settle down at Cranshaws. Now, I am not going to do any such thing, and you must break it to her."

Maggie's face fell; she guessed his resolution had something to do with Lady Ethel, and knew how great a disappointment it would prove to Mrs Bainbridge.

"But, Cousin Thomas, if you don't live here, and Aunt Lizzie goes away to Birmingham, who is to look after the place?"

"I don't know—the bailiff, I suppose; he can manage it much better than I could—I am totally ignorant of farming matters."

"But the house, the garden," said Maggie, as the tears rose to her eyes, "all the little improvements which dear uncle took such pride and pleasure in, because they were for you—are they to go to rack and ruin for want of use and supervision, cousin?"

"If they must, they must," he answered, moodily, "for I am quite resolved not to live here at present."

"If it is only Lady Ethel's wishes that you are considering," continued Maggie, timidly, "I do not think she could object to Cranshaws as a summer residence. It is very pretty in the summer, you know, Cousin Thomas, and you will always want to shoot over the preserves. And residing here for half the year would be better than not at all."

"It is my profession that stands in the way," he replied, evading her question as they turned into the shrubbery together. "I have no wish to leave the army, and whilst I remain in it I must work. It is not improbable that I may have to go out to India again."

In her astonishment, Maggie, with clasped hands, stopped short before him in the path.

"Is it possible? oh, you cannot be in earnest? What reason should there be for you, under present circumstances, to return to that horrid climate? Who would do so, excepting of necessity?"

"Well, *I* would!" he answered, with a short laugh. "Any place appears preferable to England in my eyes, just now."

"But Lady Ethel," urged his cousin, "would she accompany you? or could she bear to be left here, all alone? and so shortly after marriage too! You must consider her."

"Oh, I think she would prove amenable to reason," replied Colonel Bainbridge, with an affectation of indifference. But Maggie was not to be so deceived.

"Cousin Thomas!" she exclaimed, eagerly, as she laid her hand upon his arm, "I am sure that something dreadful has happened between you and Lady Ethel! oh, what is it? Do tell me the worst! It is terrible to see you suffer thus."

Her plain speaking, no less than her earnest manner and that pathos in her tone which the French call *larmes au voix*, touched the overstrained chord in the man's heart and snapped it. Receding from her, he threw himself upon a bench coiled round a tree hard by, and covered his face with his hands, and in another moment, the girl who stood beside him was shocked to see the tears trickle through his fingers.

"O cousin! cousin!" she pleaded, in a voice which trembled with emotion, "what have I said—what have I done to cause this? Pray, pray forgive me; but I cannot understand how anything short of her death or her desertion should make you feel like this."

"It is worse than death, Maggie."

"Worse than death?" Maggie could only repeat his words, and attend their explanation.

"Yes, a thousand times worse! She doesn't love me, Maggie! she never loved me! and I have been but as a tool in her hands."

"And she dared to tell you so?"

The indignation of the heart which *could* have loved him so truly and faithfully, had it fallen to its lot to do so, was too great to check the exclamation.

"She would dare everything! she has no more fear of me, than she has of breaking my heart. And, Maggie, I loved her so. God is my witness how I loved her."

"And how you love her still," replied the girl, with trembling lips. "Cousin Thomas, this is but a quarrel; you will make it up by and by. All will be right again between you."

"*Never*, Maggie; it is kind of you to say so, but it is quite impossible. I have made up my mind, we shall never live together again."

"Never live together," she echoed, in her consternation; "but she is your *wife*. Cousin, think of what you are saying."

"I have thought of it," he replied, "bitterly and often enough, Heaven knows. Would you have me go back to the arms of a woman who has told me to my face that she never cared for me; that she lowered herself by marrying a tradesman's son to accomplish her own revengeful purposes; and that she despises me no less for my folly and short-sightedness, than for my birth?"

"She *could* not have intended it," said Maggie, earnestly; "she could never be so cruel; she is sorry for her words now, depend upon it."

"*Sorry!*" he repeated, with a gesture of incredulity, "you have not seen her as I have, or you would not say so. And I have not told you the worst yet, Maggie, though that shall remain locked in my own breast."

She did not know what comfort to give him then ; it seemed too dark and terrible a grief to be meddled with, even by hands as loving as her own. So she remained silent.

"The long and the short of it is," exclaimed Colonel Bainbridge, after a moment's pause, as he jumped up from the bench and stretched himself, "that I intend to serve Her Majesty for some little time longer yet, under which circumstances, if my mother declines to live at Cranshaws, the dear old place must consent to be shut up for awhile and look after itself. And what I want you to do for me, Maggie, is to bring my mother gradually round to the idea. As soon as I am gone—I return to town to-morrow—let her know positively I have no intention of selling out of the army at present, and when I have left England you may tell her the reason why. It will reconcile her to my absence more than anything else would do."

"But when you have left England, cousin? Surely that is only a contingency."

"It is more than that, Maggie," he replied, in a low voice. "I have already effected an exchange with one of my brother officers, and I start to join his battery next week."

She answered nothing, but her tears fell fast upon her sombre mantle.

"It could not be otherwise, my dear; it would be impossible for me to stay in England now. I should cut my throat if I did. I must have change! Don't cry, my dear girl! perhaps we shall tread these old paths together yet, when we are both grey-headed—who knows?"

"With your grandchildren running on before us," she answered, with sweet wet eyes, that tried to smile at him.

"My grandchildren! No—never!—or, at least I hope so! The fewer children that enter the world the better, Maggie, for there is nothing but misery on all sides for them to inherit."

"With a great hope to brighten it, dear cousin, and make it bearable."

"Is there any hope extant?" he answered, gloomily.

Maggie, thrusting her hand down the bosom of her dress, drew thence a little crucifix which Sister Margaret had given her, and held it up before him.

"There is always *this*," she said, with a bright upward look.

"For you, perhaps, Maggie; not for me."

"For all of us," she rejoined, quickly. "O cousin, what would *he* have said to hear you speak like that?"

"Or to see me as I am! I don't know, Maggie! I have felt thankful sometimes during the last few days to think that he can never see or hear me speak again."

"But are you sure of that?" with an earnest, searching look.

"Why! do you imagine that he can?"

"I *imagine* nothing," she replied; "but I cannot believe that glorified he has less powers than he possessed on earth, or that if in the service of his God he ministers to the heirs of salvation, the interests of those who are dear to him would not be nearest to his heart. And if you believed, Cousin Thomas, that he was watching with the deepest anxiety every working of your spirit and action of your life, would it not make you more desirous of walking worthy of a love which death had had no power to overcome?"

"Perhaps it might."

"And is not our Lord then watching you with as much intensity of purpose, and a far more enduring affection? O cousin, you have forgotten that!"

He walked on silently, pulling his moustache.

"If—if"—continued the girl, "your happiness has vanished, which I cannot quite believe, there still remains your duty, which no sorrow authorises us to shirk. It will be harder than it used to be, but not the less imperative."

"Maggie! you talk like a child, or rather like a very innocent woman. Your theory may be good, but you would find it rather difficult to put in practice. What should you know about a grief like mine! Try it, and then prate about accepting duty in the stead of love."

"I did not say that," she answered, modestly; "but only that the loss of love does not release us from the obligations of our duty. And—and—I am not quite so ignorant of the matter as you seem to think, cousin! I have had my little troubles as well as you, and I do not recommend what I have not tried myself."

"Have you?—poor dear child!" said Colonel Bainbridge, affectionately, as it struck him for the first time that Maggie's face was not quite so round, nor her eyes so full of mirth as they used to be. "How I pity you—but it is the same with every one—sorrow is the common lot."

"You need not pity me," she answered, softly, "for I have left off pitying myself, Cousin Thomas."

"You have got over it, I suppose, Maggie! Well, it will be a long time before I get over mine."

"No! I have not," she said, stopping suddenly and laying her hand upon his arm; "I have not got over it, Cousin Thomas! I did nothing of myself: it is all His work."

"*Whose?*" demanded Colonel Bainbridge. But as he put the question, he read the answer in her reverent gaze.

"He did it all," said Maggie, whilst tears of love welled up into her eyes. "He made me see that sorrow borne with Him is better than happiness without Him; and that if we would be numbered amongst His servants, we must bear the mark upon our foreheads, of His blood-stained Cross—the baptism of woe. We must all pass through it. Cousin, perhaps He is just calling you to yours; be true—don't shrink from it; and, however events turn out, they must come right in the end. I know it from experience!"

She looked inspired, as her eyes eagerly sought his for an answer to her words; but none came.

"Your advice is very good advice, my child," said Colonel Bainbridge, in a tone of voice which made her relax her grasp upon him, with a sigh; "but it comes a little too late. My lot is fixed, Maggie, and in another fortnight I hope to be miles away from England."

And then they fell to discussing less important matters, and Maggie had no further opportunity of speaking to her cousin on the subject of his wife.

CHAPTER XXXVIII.

IS IT TIME YET?

"Well, I must say I am disappointed in your cousin Thomas! very much disappointed!" said Miss Lloyd, shaking her head in a methodical manner. It was about a fortnight after the conversation detailed in my last chapter, and she was sitting with Maggie Henderson in the library at Cranshaws.

Colonel Bainbridge was, as he had anticipated, on the sea, and hundreds of miles away from his native land; and the unexpected news of his departure, although accompanied by every expression of filial love and gratitude towards herself, had descended on his mother's heart, still quivering beneath the effects of her recent affliction, as a second and almost severer blow.

She had filled the house with lamentations over her loss, wondering why her poor husband need have toiled half his life to lay up wealth if it were to bestow no greater benefit than this on his survivors; and why Thomas could not have followed his father's wishes, by selling out of the army as he was desired to do, or should ever have married if he intended to desert his young wife three months after the wedding-day.

The affectionate letter that she had received from Colonel Bainbridge, and in which, whilst prophesying (for her sake) a speedy return to England, he assured her that everything that was necessary to be done with respect to her money he had placed in the hands of one far more competent to conduct it than himself, and begged her to use Cranshaws as though it still belonged to her, during the term of his absence, had no effect in stemming the flow of her regret, nor her indignation at his leaving Lady Ethel. In short, so much disposed was she to cast all the blame upon the shoulders of her son, that Maggie, taking advantage of his permission, partially enlightened her aunt as to the reason of his departure; and the explanation which had taken place that morning, although it had no power to comfort Mrs Bainbridge, had, at least, turned the torrent of her displeasure in another direction.

And it was in commenting upon this subject (after having received a few extra particulars concerning it, from the mouth of Maggie Henderson), that Miss Lloyd gave vent to the exclamation with which this chapter opens, and expressed herself very much disappointed in Colonel Bainbridge.

"It is not so much his fault as hers," said Maggie, warmly, for she felt hurt that every one should be in league against her cousin. "I was sure she did not love him when they were down here together. Oh! what a foolish thing it is for people to marry in such a hurry."

"He was blinded," replied her aunt. "If he had not been, he would have thought twice of his dear father's proposal to him! Ah! Maggie! he would have had a different kind of wife in you!"

Maggie blushed, but only to hear herself praised.

"Perhaps so; yet it does not follow he would have had a better one."

"My dear! but you would always have loved him!"

"I hope so, Aunt Letty; but it is impossible to tell. You see I used to think so very much of him, and it has struck me more than once lately, that on a nearer view he might not have come up to my expectations."

"What used you to think of him, Maggie?"

"Oh! at one time—about a year ago, you know, Aunt Letty—I really thought there was no one in the world to compare with Cousin Thomas. He seemed so brave, so honourable, so wise; I believe I would have trusted my very soul in his hands in those days."

"And you would not trust it now?"

The girl shook her head.

"Good, he is—that I am sure of; it would be strange if, coming of such a father and such a mother, he could be otherwise than good; and honour is involved in goodness. But is he brave or wise, Aunt Letty? Is it bravery to run away directly he is attacked by disappointment? or wisdom to leave his young, beautiful wife alone, without even the safeguard of her love for him? to say nothing of his poor mother, who needs his help so much just now! I could hardly have believed it of him!"

"Then you have quite altered your opinion with respect to him, Maggie?"

"No! I don't think that so much as that my opinion is altered with respect to myself. I was not competent to pass judgment on my cousin. He remains the same as he was then; but I can see more clearly. He is a dear, good fellow; he will always be very dear to me; but he is an ordinary man, neither better nor worse than the generality of his fellows."

"But don't you think that must be the end of most inordinate affections, Maggie? that the scales falling from our eyes, we perceive the glitter which we took for gold is only the reflection of our own love—partly of our own wishes—and that our idols are but clay?"

"I daresay it is, Aunt Letty; but it must be a dreadful thing to wake up and find one's self bound to that which is not what we took it for. I have suffered, as you know, but 'tis nearly over now; and I have been so thankful lately to feel that I have taken on myself no other ties than those which nature gave me."

"Why, my darling?" demanded Miss Lloyd.

"That I may devote the remainder of my life to those for whom He laid down His. O Aunt Letty!" (with clasped hands and an appealing face;) "you don't know how much I have thought and dreamt of it lately. You said, you remember, on the day that we first saw Sister Margaret, that if the time ever came when I might conscientiously enter on that vocation, you would not hold me back from it! And has not the time come now?"

"Do you think it has, dear Maggie?" said Miss Lloyd, gravely.

"Why should I not, Aunt Letty? Uncle is gone; I can be of no further use to him; Cranshaws is to be vacated, and Aunt Lizzie goes to her own friends at Birmingham. And you, my own sweet aunt, you love Him far too much yourself to grudge Him the service of His meanest creature."

At that moment their conversation was interrupted by the entrance of Mrs Bainbridge.

"I could not think where you had got to, Maggie," she said, in a complaining voice. "They say that old Hetty is worrying to see me, and that Mr Dobson has come over from

Borthwick with an authority from your cousin to look over the stables, and really I have not the heart to speak to them. I wish you would go and see what it is all about. I am sure," sinking into a chair as she spoke, "if people only knew what an exertion it is to me to give my attention to business, they would be a little more merciful. It all falls upon me; there is no one to do it but myself."

"There is always Maggie," said her sister, pointedly.

"Ah! true! and she is the greatest comfort a woman ever had. Well, go, my dear, and get it over quickly;" and as her niece left the room, she ejaculated, audibly, "God bless her! I don't know what we should do without her!"

In a few minutes Maggie re-appeared, having executed her commissions satisfactorily, and then Mrs Bainbridge asked her if she would take a turn in the grounds with her.

"It seems quite an age since I have been round the flower-garden, and I think it would do me good. Thank you, my dear," as Maggie readily acquiesced in the proposal; "you are just like a daughter to me: you are all I have left me in the world. I will be ready to accompany you in five minutes."

As Mrs Bainbridge quitted the library to put on her walking attire, Miss Lloyd looked Maggie Henderson in the face.

"Well, my dear, do you think the time has come yet?"

"No, aunt," replied the girl, meekly, but there was a shade of sadness on her countenance as she spoke.

"You are disappointed, darling," said Miss Lloyd, affectionately; "but were you to follow your inclinations in opposition to your duty, you would be more so. Remember what you preached to your cousin, and don't fall short in your own practice. The path of duty is generally straight before us; but we are too fond, even when most in earnest, of looking for it in the far distance, or in some almost impracticable by-way. It is so hard to convince beginners that grace is not always where most sensibly felt."

Maggie did not answer. She was standing by the window with something very like a tear in her eye; it was so difficult to believe that any one could go wrong in a hearty and sincere effort to please his Master.

"You think that Aunt Lizzie won't want you at Birmingham, Maggie," continued Miss Lloyd; "that in a strange house and place she will not miss her husband's voice and her son's kind attentions so much as if she stayed at Cranshaws, but I think you are mistaken. I think, were you also to propose to leave her now, that she would feel as though she were bereft of all for whom she cared at once. But you are your own mistress, my love, and must therefore take my counsel for just as much as it is worth."

"I am not my own mistress, aunt," replied the girl, "and I never wish to be. I see that you are right; the time has not yet come."

"And suppose it never comes, Maggie?"

"Then I must be content."

"Content to do the will of Him that formed you! Were it to live crippled in a garret for the rest of your life, child, it would come to the same thing in the end. Our love to Him is not shown forth in what we do, so much as in what we suffer!"

"Suffer with Him and reign with Him," responded Maggie, smiling.

"Suffer with Him for love of Him, without calculating on the reigning. The first is too much honour for such poor weak wretches as ourselves. Suffer with Him in Birmingham, my child! His heart knows yours, and beats to the same measure; and He will do your work in London (or wherever in the future it may lie) until you are freed by His will to take it from His hands."

"O aunt, you are such a blessing to me," cried the girl, enthusiastically; "you seem to put everything in the right light."

"Not more a blessing than you are to me, my darling. I have often prayed, Maggie, that I might be enabled to counsel you aright in this particular; for it is very selfish pleading, my dear! I can't yet think what home would look like to me without you."

"You shall never see it so, dear aunt, without your free consent. I don't think I could go myself, unless you promised to go with me."

Miss Lloyd laughed at the idea, and shaking off a few bright tears that had gathered on her eyelashes, released Maggie from an affectionate embrace, just as the door opened to admit Mrs Bainbridge.

CHAPTER XXXIX.

THE WIDOWED BRIDE.

LADY ETHEL BAINBRIDGE did not feel very comfortable after her husband had left her, on the morning of their quarrel. There was a cold, sickening, palpitating sensation about the region of her heart, which bore a strong likeness to remorseful fear, though she would not have acknowledged the feeling.

She knew that she had gone too far—much further than she wished or intended; and believed the probable consequence of her gratuitous information would be an entire separation between herself and the Marquis de Lacarras; but, strange to say, notwithstanding the interest she still professed to take in that gentleman and his proceedings, the prospect of never seeing him again did not give her nearly so much uneasiness, as the idea that Colonel Bainbridge would revert to what she had told him, and reproach her with it. Surely, if she promised never to speak to Victor again, it ought to appease his anger.

"Men are always so unreasonable," she thought to herself, as she lay coiled up in her luxurious bed, with rather an anxious face pressing the lace-trimmed pillows; "so jealous, and exacting, and fussy; it is only necessary to mention the name of another man to have them looking drawn daggers at you at once. As if a woman could be expected never to speak to any one but her husband. Such nonsense! Or to marry her first love—particularly when she's——not bad-looking. Does the man imagine no one thinks me pretty but himself? Absurd! And then to stare just as though he were going to eat me! Scottish manners, I suppose. And, after all, what did I say that was so very atrocious?"

But here, a faithful memory bringing two or three expressive truths back to Lady Ethel's mind, caused her to turn restlessly upon her pillow, whilst the uneasy sensation at her heart proceeded with redoubled violence.

Pooh! what folly it was to think twice about the matter;

she had much better go to sleep again, and it would be all right by the evening.

But she could not sleep; she had been too thoroughly roused; and after ineffectually lying with closed eyes for a longer time than was agreeable to her, Lady Ethel vacated her couch and rang for Louise to assist her in dressing.

When she descended to the dining-room, it seemed very bare and empty; breakfast was laid upon the table, but had not been touched; and three unopened letters addressed to her husband, and which in the anguish of his spirit he had overlooked, were placed beside his plate.

Yet he did not appear.

"You had better tell your master that breakfast is ready," said Lady Ethel to the servant in waiting.

"The Colonel has gone out, my lady," was the reply. "He left the house about a couple of hours ago."

"Oh! very well!" in a querulous, discontented voice; "remove the covers then."

And the covers being removed, disclosed their respective dishes in precisely the same condition in which they re-covered them when the meal was concluded, her ladyship attributing her want of appetite to the fatigue she had undergone the night before.

A weary afternoon upon the sofa; then a solitary drive round the park, which she accomplished mostly with closed eyes, and Lady Ethel returned to Curzon Street in time for an eight o'clock dinner.

For this meal she waited rather more than half-an-hour before she rung the bell to inquire if anything had yet been seen of Colonel Bainbridge; but the only answer she received was, that he had not re-entered the house.

"Where is Russell?" she demanded, sharply, alluding to her husband's valet.

"He is gone to the King's Cross station, my lady, with my master's portmanteau and hat-box. He started rather better than an hour ago. I believe he expected to meet the Colonel there."

"Very good!" replied his mistress, flushing, nevertheless, with disappointment. "I shall not wait any longer. Let the dinner be served."

The dinner did not prove a much greater success than the

breakfast had been; and, after lingering in the drawing-room till nearly midnight, Lady Ethel betook herself to bed in a highly excited and indignant frame of mind. She had forgotten her fears of meeting Colonel Bainbridge again by that time, and only felt greatly injured by the slight put upon her.

"The *idea* of his starting for Scotland in that manner, without even telling her his intentions, or the train by which he meant to travel; leaving her in perfect ignorance of his plans, and making her a laughing-stock to her own servants. He ought to be ashamed of himself; he would have no further need to talk about good or bad behaviour, after the rudeness with which he had treated her. But that was just what came of marrying a bear; it was not likely that any one reared in an out-of-the-way country hole like Cranshaws, would know the meaning of the word 'politeness.' It was her own fault; she had brought it all on her own head; she had no one to thank but herself. She was the most miserable, desolate, insulted woman in existence!"

And here Lady Ethel shed a passing shower of hot, smarting tears, which she brushed away proudly, calling herself a natural and an idiot to care two straws if the man went and hung himself, or no. If he left her, and in peace, so much the better. Thank Heaven, she was not entirely destitute of friends, and would manage to enjoy life as well without him as with him, perhaps better—who knew? *Vive la bagatelle!* And so, when the next day, and the day succeeding, and the day after that, came and went, without bringing her a letter from her husband—not one line of entreaty, reproach, or explanation—Lady Ethel's spirits rose, apparently, to the very highest pitch. Wherever she could go alone, she showed herself in public, laughing, talking, and flirting, just as the fancy took her, and but too often, to the disgust of Lady Clevedon, with the Marquis de Lacarras in her train.

The sober portion of the fashionable world shook their heads, and began to ask each other where was Colonel Bainbridge? but Lady Ethel lightly disposed of all inquiries, by the announcement of her father-in-law's illness, and her determination to take a little more out of the season, before she retired into crape and bombazine.

The Countess of Clevedon appeared to regard the matter

in a far more serious light, and it was edifying to hear the prudent cautions she thought fit to administer to her volatile step-daughter at this juncture, and the sudden and deep interest she evinced for the feelings of Colonel Bainbridge.

"I really *do* think, my dear Ethel," she said, in a most maternal manner, "that you should keep at home during this melancholy period of uncertainty respecting old Mr Bainbridge's health. Why, he may be lying dead at this very moment, and just consider what your dear husband's feelings would be, were he to return home to-night with the mournful tidings, and find you dancing at Lady Taunton's ball. It does not look well, indeed it does not."

"I do not care one straw about looks, Gertrude; you are so *over* prudent that you see these things in too serious a light. Please to remember that I am a married woman, and supposed to be competent to judge for myself. And as for my father-in-law being dead, he is much more likely eating a hearty dinner; only he 's so selfish, he won't let Colonel Bainbridge return to London."

Though at this moment, as I have related, old Mr Bainbridge was actually gone, and in the face of the announcement of his death, which appeared in the *Times* shortly afterwards, Lady Ethel, unable longer to deny the truth, was compelled in decency to remain in-doors until suitable mourning had been provided for her.

But still she received no intimation that her husband thought of or regretted the misunderstanding that had arisen between them; and in spite of her affected gaiety, her heart was daily becoming heavier beneath the influence of a suppressed longing to see him again, and a growing fear that her conduct might produce more serious consequences than she had anticipated.

It was but a few days after her re-appearance in society, that, as she was reclining, a most fashionable mass of bugles and black crape, upon the cushions of her open carriage, the block which usually takes place in the Row every afternoon during the season, brought her to a standstill alongside of Lady Clevedon.

"Well, my dear; so you have got your husband back again. I congratulate you," exclaimed that lady, who, with the baby earl, got up in a manner regardless of expense, by her side, and more than a suspicion of rouge on her cheeks, was attracting, as she desired, universal attention.

Lady Ethel's heart gave a rapid bound, but no one would have guessed it from her manner.

"Where did you see him?" she demanded, as though she had just parted from him herself.

"Down by the Horse Guards, about an hour ago. I stopped the carriage to speak to him. You find him a little altered, do you not? I thought him looking remarkably dark and thin. You should have persuaded him to drive with you. The air would do him good."

"Colonel Bainbridge doesn't like the Row," murmured Lady Ethel, evasively.

"Few men do—married men, that is to say. I wonder when we shall be able to move. Have you seen Victor today?" with a searching glance.

"He looked in for half-an-hour after breakfast."

"Ah! very sociable and friendly, but not always so safe. He'll have to give up some of those free and easy little habits, my dear, now that your lord and master has returned. Well, here we are actually making progress at last. Good-bye. I shall look in upon you in the course of a day or two," and the next moment, to Lady Ethel's infinite relief, the carriages were separated.

He had come back then; was in London, most likely in Curzon Street at that very time; and sick with impatience to meet him again, and have an explanation regarding her conduct and his own, as soon as she was satisfied that her step-mother was no longer witness to her proceedings, Lady Ethel pulled the check-string and gave the order to be driven home at once.

Arrived at Curzon Street, she had hardly descended the steps of her carriage before she put the eager inquiry, "Any one called?" to the servant who received her, and an answer in the negative made her spirits sink to zero.

"He was trying her too far," she said, indignantly, to herself, as, without waiting for the assistance of Louise, she tore off bonnet and mantle, and cast them impetuously upon the bed. "It was all very well for a man to show he had some pride—she knew that she was esteemed rather proud herself—but when it came," pulling a glove off inside out, and flinging it to the other end of the room, "when it came to treating her with utter contempt—walking about the place openly, and speaking to her friends, before he had even advised her of his return," here flew the second glove after its fellow, "she would let him know pretty plainly that she was not going to stand such behaviour." And, sitting down upon the strength of it, Lady Ethel fanned her heated face, while she impatiently tapped the carpet with her foot.

But, notwithstanding her ire, she took care to make a most becoming toilet for that day's dinner; and to issue an immediate command that she was "at home" to no one for the afternoon or evening.

Could Colonel Bainbridge have read her wilful spirit and appeared to take advantage of it, he might have sealed his happiness from that hour; but there was no angel near to presage his good fortune to him. The only angel that sat brooding on his heart that night, was the prophet of sorrow amounting to despair.

When the dinner had been served, and cleared away again, Lady Ethel's excitement vanished with it, and she lay on a sofa in her drawing-room, listening with strained ears to every cab-wheel that rattled in the street, to every footfall that sounded on the pavement, and trying to cheat herself out of the knowledge that time was passing rapidly away, and he had not yet come home.

At length, it was nearly ten o'clock, and the last postman commenced to give his double knocks all up the street. As he stopped at their door, Lady Ethel thought little of it, for her correspondence was, like that of most ladies, voluminous; but when the servant, bringing up the tea-tray, handed her a letter in her husband's writing, all her demeanour changed. "He was not coming then—he passed a night in town and not at his own house—he chose to write instead of speaking to her—well," with a heaving breast and something which felt very uncomfortable just at the top of her throat, "we shall see, Colonel Bainbridge, which loses the most by that proceeding."

"No, I don't want any tea; you can take it away," she exclaimed, with such uncalled-for energy, to the servant in waiting, that he beat a hasty retreat again, and she was left alone with her unwelcome messenger. The door had scarcely closed, before she had torn open and devoured it.

CHAPTER XL.

TWO LETTERS.

BUT, as she did so, standing tremblingly beneath the gaslight, her cheek paled and paled until it was as white as the flowing robes she wore.

"How am I to address you" (so the letter ran) "after the bitter truths with which you have acquainted me? You know by this time that my father is dead; that, thanks to you, he died without the small consolation of seeing me again; but for which, now, I feel almost thankful. It would have been too hard, perhaps, for me to stand face to face with him and death, and to conceal what all the world must soon guess—that you have destroyed my happiness.

"I have no intention of reproaching you. I ascribe the error to your artificial rearing, and the little sanctity with which, in these days, marriage is invested, more than to yourself; but you must forgive me if, under the circumstances, I find it impossible to live with you again. Could you have loved me, if only with a friend's affection, I would have laboured to procure your happiness to my life's end; but my spirit rebels against being further subjected to the avowal of your scorn. I have thought it better, therefore, both for yourself and me, that we should not meet again, and, with that intention, have made arrangements for joining a battery of artillery in India.

"I start to-morrow; and, if fortunate, may never return to provoke unfavourable comparisons in your mind again. But do not imagine I have forgotten what I owe to you, or neglected to make arrangements for your comfort in my absence. There is no rival in my thoughts of you, nor will there ever be.

"Cranshaws is ours, as you will surmise, and if at any time you have a fancy to spend a few weeks there, you have but to write to the steward, and give orders that it is prepared for your reception. But, as a residence, you will prefer the house in Curzon Street; and the management of your income (which will be the same as it is now) I have placed in the hands of my solicitors, who have advices from me to give you all the assistance in their power.

"If, in my hurry, and the confused state of my mind, I have overlooked anything which is necessary to your well-being, you need but apply to those gentlemen in order to procure it.

"I met your step-mother to-day and spoke to her; and, fearful of the gossip that is certain to arise from my sudden departure, I have written for your sake to tell her that I am unexpectedly ordered back to service in India, and, not having yet made up my mind to resign the army, we have decided on a brief separation. Whether to carry out or deny my pious fraud, I leave to yourself. I had not the courage to confess the truth. And now I must close this; for I dare not trust myself to speak to you of what I have lost in losing the conviction that you loved me. You married me (I had it from your own lips) for your convenience; and my fatal money was the means of bringing down this curse upon me.

"Well, then, take my money. I shall never bear the sight nor touch of it again; and thank me for removing myself out of your presence! However unwillingly, I could never prove anything but a shame and a reproach to you.

"THOMAS BAINBRIDGE."

So the letter ended. She stood with it in her hand, shaking—shaking like an aspen-leaf—feeling as though she should fail upon the ground, and yet too proud to cry, even though she was alone. But an hour later she was still standing there—still gazing at the letter in her hand—still slowly reading it over and over again, and trying to comprehend all the consequences that it involved; to extract all the supposed insult that it contained, and to fortify her pride by the conviction that it had been penned with the hope of making her suffer in return for the suffering she had entailed upon him; of giving her back indifference for indifference, scorn for scorn, and slight for slight. And it was this self-deception that for a while sustained her. Woman-like—because the man had felt so keenly in the construction of those sentences, that he had not dared to trust himself to use one affectionate expression—she judged that they had emanated from a spirit heartlessly cold and severe. She had no power to interpret the proud, despairing tone which breathed in every word; which forbid his making any fresh appeals to a love which he did not believe existed for him; which betrayed that, although mortally wounded by her cruelty, he was resolved to die and make no sign.

She only searched eagerly, from one sheet to another, for the familiar forms in which he had been wont to tell her he adored her; and, disappointed at failing to find them, assumed, or chose to pretend that she assumed, that her husband had never really cared for her.

"No more than I have cared for him," she exclaimed, as ashy pale she started from her reverie, and tearing the paper into a dozen pieces, scattered them upon the floor. "So much for your letter, Colonel Bainbridge. You hope, perhaps, that I shall not enjoy my life so much without the protection of your presence. You will live to find yourself wonderfully mistaken." And she was about to quit the room.

But as she stood upon the threshold, she turned her head, and two weary eyes rested lingeringly upon the morsels of paper cast upon the ground.

Was it advisable to leave them there, for any servant who was curious to place together in their original position, and peruse? The credit of her name was involved in such an accident. So, slowly retracing her steps, Lady Ethel gathered up the fluttering fragments and conveyed them to her room. And when Louise had left her to herself, she drew out needle and thread, and carefully stitched them all together again.

It would be as well, she thought, to preserve a written record of the man's barbarity.

Could she have read a hurried scrawl from him, which about the same time reached the hands of Margaret Henderson, Lady Ethel would surely have altered, if not her whole opinion, at least that final substantive.

"I write to you on the eve of my departure," it commenced, "and in great distress of mind, so pray forgive all but the intention with which these words are written. Maggie, at this moment, when there is no possibility of changing, I am haunted by a miserable doubt whether, in deciding to leave England, I have acted either wisely or well. To live again with her under present circumstances, appears impossible to me; but perhaps I ought to have sacrificed my own feelings, in order to afford her the protection of the love which she has trampled under foot. She is so young, so beautiful, and so admired! If any harm comes to her, I shall never forgive myself. Dear Maggie! my sister more than my cousin, I entreat you, by the memory of the affection of our childhood, to befriend my darling, should it ever be in your power to do so. She appeared to like you. I think you are the only person in our family she was ever intimate with; and, though it seems improbable, a dread oppresses me that the day may dawn when she will look round for a woman-friend and find none. Should she be sick or in trouble (though I pray God to protect her from every ill), and express the least desire for your presence, I depend on you to go to her. This is my last charge, Maggie, and should it be the last I ever make, I shall be a happier man than I am now. Cheer up my mother by every means in your power; and be, as you have always been, the good angel of our household. I have no sweeter memory to carry into exile than that of the affectionate solicitude which in your person is associated with every incident of my life, and every individual of my family."

This letter, scribbled during the last hour that Colonel Bainbridge spent in England, was marked "private;" but Maggie had no secrets from Aunt Letty.

"What do you think of it?" inquired Miss Lloyd, as she returned the epistle to her niece.

"It is much more than I deserve," said Maggie, with glistening eyes.

"We won't argue about that, my dear, and it was not what I meant. What do you think of the prospect of new work carved out for you? Ah, Maggie! and you were afraid that you would be so idle!"

"It is scarcely a prospect, Auntie."

"My dear," said Miss Lloyd, seriously, "it is more than enough for prayer to turn into a certainty; and something tells me it will come to pass. Lady Ethel is very wilful, Maggie; but she is not utterly heartless. It will be a grand thing to bring those two together again!"

"Oh! if one but could!" exclaimed the girl, clasping her hands; "it would make him so happy."

"And half repay you for the past, my child."

"*Half*, Aunt Letty? It would be full measure; pressed down and running over," replied Maggie Henderson.

CHAPTER XLI.

OPEN WAR.

When Lady Ethel rose from her bed upon the following morning, she was quite convinced that she had been much ill-treated by her husband, and resolved to let the world see his absence had no power to affect her happiness, to which intent, it being the day on which she usually received her friends, she attired herself with the greatest care (for she knew a woman's dress is taken as index of her mind), and was in her drawing-room, lovely, languid, and complacent-looking as ever, ready to receive the first visitor who arrived.

The first was Lady Clevedon, who, red-hot from the receipt of Colonel Bainbridge's letter, appeared full thirty minutes before the hour of reception.

"My dear Ethel," she exclaimed, "I have come early on purpose that I might speak to you alone. What is this extraordinary freak on the part of your husband? Is he mad, or have you quarrelled with each other? We shall have all London ringing with the scandal before another day is over."

"What scandal?" demanded Lady Ethel.

"My dear, you know what I mean as well as I do. Why, Colonel Bainbridge running away from you in this manner before you have been married four months. What on earth is the reason of it?"

"I understood Colonel Bainbridge to say that he had informed you, Gertrude."

"He wrote me a few lines to say he was ordered at once upon foreign service; but I want to know why he went. He has money enough to buy up half the regiments in England. Why did he not sell out of the army when you first married him?"

"I should think that was his own business. A man may surely be allowed to judge for himself in such a matter."

"But to leave you here alone so soon after marriage, and in the height of the season; I think it is perfectly improper;

and if your poor dear father had been alive, Colonel Bainbridge would not have dared treat you in so nonchalant a manner."

Lady Ethel flushed.

"*Dared*, Gertrude! what daring is there in the matter? One would imagine he had gone without consulting me."

"You should not have let him go; you should have persuaded him to stay at home," said Lady Clevedon, hotly, for she was by no means pleased to see the way paved so completely for the attentions of the Marquis de Lacarras.

"That is a subject for argument," replied her step-daughter, as she played with a fan.

"No one will believe but that there is something wrong between you."

"Is that the case whenever a married officer has to join his regiment? It must cause a good deal of awkwardness," was the laconic reply.

"Don't talk nonsense, Ethel! You know how widely Colonel Bainbridge's circumstances differ from those of most people. He has no need to remain in the army at all."

"Not from a mercenary point of view, perhaps; but he dislikes a country life, hates an idle one, and is fond of his profession. I should think that was reason sufficient for his doing as he pleases."

"People will say he ought to be fonder of his wife," remarked the Countess, in a tone of malice.

"People always say so much more than there is any occasion to do. They might leave that question to be settled by his wife."

"But how do you like the prospect yourself, Ethel? You will have to keep very quiet during Colonel Bainbridge's absence, you know."

"Yes? In what way?"

"Why, you can hardly go about to theatres and balls as you have been doing, surely!"

"My husband has laid no restriction on me."

"But I suppose you will go into the country—to Cranshaws, or to his mother, will you not? You would never think of staying in Curzon Street alone."

Lady Ethel opened her blue eyes.

"And why not? Is there any chance of my being devoured by the natives?"

"Colonel Bainbridge could never desire you to reside in town and mix in the gaieties of the season without the safeguard of his presence," exclaimed Lady Clevedon, with virtuous indignation. The idea of her step-daughter reigning there in solitary unprotected beauty, and throwing wide her doors alike to simple and noble (Victor de Lacarras included), was gall to her. At any risk, the scandal must be prevented, and the rapid advance in propriety and morals which the thought occasioned in the Countess's mind, was almost as wonderful to behold as the Indian juggler's mango-tree, which grows as you gaze upon it.

"Did he tell you so?" demanded Lady Ethel.

"No; how should he be aware of the customs which obtain in *our* sphere of life? But modesty, and decorum, and a womanly sense of what is right to be done, Ethel, no less than a knowledge of the world (*our* world), warn me that you are contemplating an act which will be ruinous to your character, both for propriety, and attachment to your husband."

"Dear me! I had no idea it was so much as all that!" said Lady Ethel, with provoking coolness. "But if the world knew that Colonel Bainbridge had especially desired me to remain in Curzon Street, perhaps it would alter its opinion, and give me instead some credit for conjugal obedience."

"It is not possible he can have done so!"

"It is more than possible; it is true!"

"Well! I could not have conceived he had so little sense!" replied Lady Clevedon, who was trembling with vexation; "and you must forgive me if I cannot uphold his decision. I confess that I have been reared to see things in a different light, and I should not think I was following the wishes of your dear lost father, if I countenanced his daughter in a step of which I am certain he would have disapproved. When your husband was with you, Ethel, I was always glad to see you at my house, as you well know; but, without his protection, I should not consider I was doing my duty in asking you there. Balls and parties are no fit scenes for a young wife separated from her husband; and if you cannot see that for yourself, I am the proper person to point it out to you."

"How extremely obliged I am to your ladyship for the tender solicitude you show for my good name!" replied Lady Ethel, sarcastically. "To be excluded from your *réunions* will be a terrible trial to me; but I will try to bear it with all the fortitude of which I am mistress, sooner than cast the slightest slur upon your hitherto spotless character."

"Ah! you may laugh!" exclaimed the Countess, who had risen to her feet, "but what I tell you is the truth! You have chosen to make a thorough *mésalliance;* to lower yourself to the level of a tradesman's daughter-in-law; and it behoves you, in consequence, to be more particular than others what you do or say, lest the world should think that you have lost the power of rising above your surroundings."

At this bitter taunt, Lady Ethel, who had also risen to her feet, turned deadly pale. She could cast a sneer herself at the family of her adoption; but it was not in human nature to take it quietly from stranger lips, and those the lips of her step-mother. She flew at Lady Clevedon with her own weapons.

"A *mésalliance?* And if I have, who did all in her power to hasten its fulfilment? who urged me on to it, by goad and taunt? who *tried* to take my lover from me? There are no secrets between us, Lady Clevedon, though we may not have had the opportunity to give them vent."

"*Tried?* What are you talking of?"

"I am talking of you and the Marquis de Lacarras, who will never be more to you than he is now, for all the trouble you have taken to ensnare him."

"I shall not stay here to be insulted!" exclaimed Lady Clevedon, as she moved towards the door.

"I have no wish that you should stay at all. There has been war between us long enough. Let it be open from this time henceforward."

"I believe that you are mad!" replied her step-mother, too angry to know what to say.

"I daresay that I am," said Lady Ethel. "Four months' close companionship with a tradesman's son must be cause sufficient in your eyes to turn the strongest brain. And, therefore, perhaps you will the more readily excuse the eccentricity of my avowal that I have little desire to see you here again. Though I conclude that the customs which obtain in your sphere (I have quitted it myself, please to remember) would prevent your visiting the tradesman's daughter-in-law, whom a stern sense of duty prevents your inviting to your house in return."

And with a sweeping curtsey, Lady Ethel Bainbridge bowed her indignant step-mother out of the room.

Who could have guessed that saw her half an hour afterwards, sipping chocolate with her numerous visitors, and dispensing small talk on every side, that she had just fought so sharp a battle in her husband's cause? Victor de Lacarras was amongst the number of her guests; Lady Clevedon had passed him in the hall, and, to her great annoyance, been quite unable to persuade him to turn back and drive in the park with her instead. Here he was, lounging in his easy, half-insolent fashion over the sofa of her step-daughter; by look and manner daring any one to take his place.

Regarding him as the proximate, though unconscious agent in her present trouble, Lady Ethel would have felt most disinclined to make him welcome, had it not been for the interview through which she had just passed. Each glance or word from Monsieur de Lacarras, recalling, as they did, the anger and the coldness of her husband, made her feel uncomfortable; but Lady Clevedon's insolent truths were ringing in her ears, and she could not afford to give the Marquis his *congé* just yet.

Her step-mother should not have it in her power (so she thought) to point at her for being deserted by lover and husband at the same time; she should not say that she had attempted to number Victor de Lacarras amongst her ring of satellites, and failed to do so; but she should live to see his attentions—those attentions for which the Countess would give all that she possessed—pressed on her, and cast away as less than worthless. For that was the estimation at which she had learned to hold them. Pride, and the love of revenge, were still busily at work in Lady Ethel's heart, prompting her to trifle with her character—with the good name of her husband—and, if she went too far, even to make shipwreck of the happiness which still remained to her.

But it was an excitement—a distraction from the troubles which, though unacknowledged, pressed heavily upon her heart; and Lady Ethel went in for it as heedlessly as the soldier rushing into battle shuts his eyes to the probability of being wounded, or left dead upon the field.

She laughed and talked that afternoon, in her soft rippling way (one of her great charms was that, unexcited, she never laughed or talked in a loud voice), as though she had been the most contented creature in existence; and when her guests alluded to her husband's sudden departure in terms of pity or surprise, was ready with an answer, calculated in seeming to set all things right.

His absence was not to be for long; Colonel Bainbridge required change; his father's death had been a shock to him; and for her part she was glad to know he was not compelled to remain in London. To pass through the remainder of the season would have been an aggravation of his trial, and he could return when he chose.

"But did you not *long* to be able to go with him?" inquired one lady, who considered separation from her husband to be living death.

"Colonel Bainbridge would not allow me," was her hostess's reply; "the climate, the hurried journey, and probability of his early return, were all against such an idea!"

"I suppose so! But how you will count the hours until you see him again."

Lady Ethel turned her face away; the old sickly sensation had crept over her as she listened to her friend's remarks. What would she not have given for such happy confidence!

"Must we resign ourselves to miss you at the opera?" whispered Victor de Lacarras.

"Why should you? I shall probably go oftener than before."

"What a pleasure to hear you say so! you do not intend then to shut yourself up from all society?"

"Most certainly not! Do you consider me addicted to solitary confinement?"

"And your friends may sometimes claim the honour of being admitted here?"

"My friends are always welcome," replied Lady Ethel, though she thought, a moment afterwards, that she might have made him a more prudent answer.

And accustomed to be courted by insinuations and innuendoes, the Marquis de Lacarras took her words for much more than they were intended to convey.

CHAPTER XLII.

THE MARQUIS DE LACARRAS HEARS THE TRUTH.

It was June when Colonel Bainbridge started for the East. London was as full as it could be, and the season considered at its height.

Déjeuners, botanical fêtes, "at homes," dinner parties, and dancing parties, followed each other in rapid succession; every hour of every day was filled up by the fashionable world with some fresh scene of folly; and wherever mirth was loudest, and youth and beauty most abundant, was to be met the bride and belle of the season—Lady Ethel Bainbridge.

Everywhere, that is to say, with the exception of Lady Clevedon's *réunions*,—and as the two ladies had refused to speak to one another since the day of their quarrel, it was not surprising that the Countess rigidly adhered to the resolution which had been the primary cause of it.

Her firmness had its drawbacks, however, for she found, to her annoyance, that the Marquis de Lacarras could be as obstinate as she was; and because her fair step-daughter ceased to grace her assemblies, too often absented himself from them also, in order to spend the evening hanging over Lady Ethel's stall at the opera, or dancing attendance on her at a ball.

Indeed, the constancy with which he adhered to her society had already provoked comment from half the town.

To her he proffered gladly attentions that no other woman had ever had the power publicly to extort from him—transforming himself into a holder of bouquets or carrier of mantles, into a conversationalist or a dummy, a partner or a wall-flower, just as the humour struck his companion that he should be.

Yet, though Lady Ethel professed to enjoy his society, though she took false pleasure in exercising her airs and graces on one hitherto considered invulnerable, and letting her friends see how she could turn and twist him at her will, she was actuated by no warmer feeling in the pursuit of her amusement than a desire to annoy Lady Clevedon, and let her husband hear (as sooner or later she was certain he would hear) that the indignities he had heaped upon her were powerless to affect her equanimity.

People talked, of course.

All the women of her acquaintance (and especially those who had set their caps at the Marquis and failed to attract him) were properly scandalised at her behaviour; and even men—those lenient judges when a pretty woman is put into the prisoner's dock—began to say it was a great pity that Bainbridge should have no hint given him of how affairs were going on at home.

And if the public was impertinent upon the subject, the Countess of Clevedon was perfectly furious.

To watch the attentions of her admirer, dwindling day by day, until they resolved into mere commonplace politenesses—shadows of their former selves—was in itself sufficient aggravation; but when she saw her rival monopolise, without making the least effort to retain them, her rage knew no bounds. To have seen Lady Ethel pass through the agonising gradations of hope and fear, and uncertainty and suspense, that she had done herself, before she could allure the Marquis from her side, and to know that her efforts, if finally successful, could only culminate in her ruin, would have been some sort of consolation to Lady Clevedon's wicked heart; an alleviation, though a nugatory one, of the disappointment she was enduring.

But, happily for my heroine, there was no such solace in the future for her step-mother, and the Countess was quick enough to perceive that though some secret burden evidently weighed at times on Lady Ethel's mind, it was no longer connected with Victor de Lacarras, whose pertinacious attentions she treated with perfect *sang-froid*, and returned far oftener with frowns than smiles. But the Marquis had arrived at that stage of his amatory fever when repulses had no effect except to render his pursuit more ardent; and had Lady Ethel cherished a desire to be revenged upon him for his former conduct to her, she could have found no better opportunity than this to take it in; but her thoughts at that time were all directed in another quarter.

She was neither well nor happy. Day after day she forced herself to drive, and walk, and talk as usual; and evening after evening she dragged her tired limbs through the routine of fashionable pleasure (so called) that awaited them, but half the time she would have been thankful to remain quietly at home instead.

And yet she could not rest at night: weary as her life made her, and few the hours that she spent in bed, she generally passed them waking; she was full of nervous fancies and uneasy sensations, and her appetite seemed to have vanished with her powers of sleep. The German maid Louise became quite alarmed on the score of her mistress's health, for Lady Ethel had fainted several times during the past month, and grown so thin and weak, that more than one consultation had been held in the servants' hall as to the propriety of giving Dr Chalmers a private hint upon the subject.

Still, the object of their solicitude was not anxious about herself. She knew that she felt ill at times, and was oftener fatigued than not, but she attributed the unwelcome change to the heat of the weather and the life of excitement she was leading; and often affirmed that as soon as the season was over she should be quite well again. She was accustomed at this period to keep her bed till about noon, a circumstance which was not entirely attributable to the late hours she indulged in. The fact being that, when down stairs, Lady Ethel missed, and sometimes to a degree that was insupportably painful to her, all those little fond cares and attentions by which, since the moment of her marriage, her life had been surrounded.

She missed the bright genial glance, too often disregarded, that had welcomed her at every fresh meeting; the chair and foot-stool set for her convenience; the news, political or otherwise, which she was too idle to glean from the papers for herself; above all—oh! remorseful—bitterly remorseful memory!—above all, the kind arm round her waist, or hand upon her shoulder, and the warm kiss laid upon her lips.

On how many occasions had she jerked that hand away, or turned her own face to one side; and how much would she have given now to feel herself a prisoner in his grasp.

She did not say so, but she felt it, and it required but one more turn in Fortune's wheel to make her openly confess she was enamoured of her husband. And Fortune's hand was on the tire.

It was a warm, hazy, sleepy afternoon towards the close of June; the heavy air that stole into the house, laden with the scented breath of flowering stocks and mignonette, had no power to stir the smallest atom of the canvas-awnings stretched across the windows; the whole town seemed slumbering; the noise of wheels had ceased; dogs even found it was too hot to bark; and the pleasant dripping of the water-carts upon the burning pavements was the only sound which made itself apparent.

Lady Ethel having denied herself to visitors, was lying clad in a white muslin wrapper upon a sofa in her drawing-room, but neither book nor work was in her hand.

She had been up late the night before, at a brilliant entertainment given by some of her aristocratic friends, where she had looked so beautiful, and achieved so great a triumph, that one of the highest personages in the realm had singled her from every woman there, and, dancing with her half the evening, appeared unable to tear himself from her society.

Yet it could scarcely have been of this flattering circumstance that Lady Ethel was dreaming now; for as her head lay back upon the cushions of the sofa two tears had stolen from under her closed eyelids, and were standing on her cheek.

How silent everything appeared, how solitary! She wondered what o'clock it was in India, and if the sun could possibly shine brighter there than he was shining over London.

What nonsense! As if it signified!—Colonel Bainbridge had been gone a month; by that time he must be in Bengal. What a distance! They could have no legitimate reason thenceforth for complaining that they troubled one another!

She had received no communication from him since he quitted England; but she had not expected it! What could he have to say? She supposed he never would write to her again.

If she died—(and she often wished that she were dead! there would be an end of trouble then, and all this fretting jealousy and suspicion!)—he would read it in the *Times*, if the servants were sharp enough to put it in. "Ha! ha!—and if *he*—if anything were to happen to him—if they were never to—to—to." And here the twin tears, finding themselves dislodged from their position by a couple more, rolled slowly down her cheek and settled in the corners of her mouth.

At this juncture the drawing-room door was cautiously pushed open.

"Pray, don't let me disturb you," said the soft voice of the Marquis de Lacarras.

Lady Ethel sprung to a sitting posture. She had considered herself secure against all witnesses, and the present intrusion did not seem to please her.

"I told the servants to say 'Not at home,'" she uttered hastily; the tears still glistening on her eyelashes.

"Not to *me*, I hope," replied the Marquis, who was quick to notice the traces of her agitation, "but if my presence is unwelcome to you, Lady Ethel, I will go."

Common courtesy forbid she should dismiss him.

"It does not signify, *monsieur*. Pray, be seated; but I hardly expected that any one would take the trouble to call on so oppressive an afternoon."

"You cannot be in earnest when you talk of trouble to me," he said, as he drew his chair beside her couch; "but what are those tell-tale drops I see upon your cheek? I must have interrupted a reverie, Lady Ethel."

"Perhaps you did," she answered, dashing her hand across her wet eyes.

"A pleasant one?"

"*Cela depend!* People have such different opinions, *monsieur*."

"Shall I divine its subject?"

"If you can."

"You were dreaming of the absent."

Lady Ethel coloured; she had not imagined that he would really guess her meditations.

"No harm if I were," she answered lightly, as her thoughts flew to Bengal.

"*Harm!* who says so? Not myself, most certainly! I should be the last person in the world to blame you, Lady Ethel."

"Indeed! Have you become an advocate for constancy, then, *monsieur?*"

He bit his lip.

"I feel that my one unfortunate mistake will never be forgiven in your eyes, or assume a different colouring to that with which it was first invested by your fancy."

But this was a topic which had become distasteful to his hearer.

"Excuse me, *monsieur!* It has been both forgiven and forgotten long ago, and we have agreed to be good friends. There is no occasion to revert to it."

"And yet it has left its sting behind it, Lady Ethel."

"If so, it is a sting totally unconnected with itself," she answered proudly, "and one of which you probably know more than I do."

"You cannot deceive me thus," he exclaimed eagerly. "Ethel! you know that you are not happy; you cannot deny the truth to me."

"I have no wish to deny it."

"And that I am the cause; the base and unpardonable cause."

"I am glad you have come to view the past in its true light, *monsieur*. But I have sufficient reasons for my unhappiness (if you will have it that I am unhappy) without laying the blame on you. My present position is attributable to my own fault."

"But from the consequences of which I would rescue you at the peril of my life. Ethel, there must be no further misunderstanding between us. We have missed our happiness once; let us secure it for the future. For your sake, and in order to retrieve my folly, I would brave everything and dare everything. Only say that you will accept the protection of my love against the horrors of the pit in which my blindness plunged you."

He rose from his chair as he was speaking with the intent to gain her side; but she rose also, and as he concluded, and his eyes met hers, he read at once that he had made an error.

Lady Ethel was strongly agitated; but it was the emotion consequent on anger rather than on love, and by look and gesture she forbid him to approach her nearer.

"Monsieur de Lacarras," she ejaculated at last, "I think that in this matter you have made a slight mistake."

Her tone of irony galled him.

"You may say so, Lady Ethel," he replied, "but I am not bound to take your word against my own interests. Mistaken, when I have had opportunity to interpret your every word and look for a month past, and the knowledge that no one amongst your numerous admirers has been so honoured by your open preference as myself!"

She covered her face with her hands: trembling hands that almost refused to be held in that position.

"Oh, you are right," she answered, mournfully, "you are quite right, I have nothing to complain of; I have brought this on myself."

"How could love err?" he said enthusiastically, "or fail to read the heart that beats for it? It is no such easy matter to conceal our feelings, dearest; spite of ourselves, they shine out of our eyes. I *knew* you loved me."

"Oh, no, no, *no!*" she exclaimed, retreating further from him with each word. "Indeed you are quite wrong. I care for—for *no one!*"

"Except *myself*," he answered, with a smile of confidence; "come, my dear girl, you have teased me long enough. My memory is not so short that I have quite forgotten a certain balcony in Park Lane, where the only woman that I ever cared for told me she loved me in return. You have but to repeat the same words."

But the sacrilegious hand he tried to lay on her was arrested by the expression of her face.

"How dare you mention it?" she said, indignantly.

"Is it so bitter a remembrance, then?"

"The bitterest I have," was the quick answer; "though not for the reasons you attribute to me. Listen, *monsieur*. I do not blame you for the insult of to-day, because I acknowledge I have brought it on myself; but you shall not leave this house until you learn the motive that actuated my behaviour."

She turned very pale then, and for a moment almost seemed as though she would faint; for to humble herself before another was a new and difficult position for Lady Ethel Bainbridge.

"I confess," she went on presently, whilst silently he waited for her explanation; "I confess that in my desire to triumph over Lady Clevedon, and for—for one other reason,

I have permitted you to associate more familiarly with me of late than I should have done; but I never dreamt you would presume to go so far as this."

"You thought, in fact, that I was made of stone, or any other substance not generally considered inflammable," he said sarcastically.

"I am afraid I thought very little about the matter, or if I did, it was not in the direction you imagine, *monsieur*."

"May I ask in which, then?"

She did not immediately reply, and from the rapid manner in which her bosom rose and fell beneath the flimsy materials of her dress, he understood how great an effort it was to her to speak.

"I am going to tell you," she said presently. "When—when you deserted me, *monsieur*, yes—*deserted*—there is no other word for it—and I rushed heedlessly into my destiny, I took as much misery to scatter broadcast in the family I entered, as you had endowed me with—and that was no small amount, as I have little need to tell you."

"You loved me *then*," he exclaimed, triumphantly, thinking he perceived his advantage.

"Excuse me," she replied, "I *despised* you then; the *love* died on the evening that I saw you with my step-mother."

"Ten thousand curses on her—" he commenced; but Lady Ethel went on without heeding the interruption.

"What treatment should you say that, under such circumstances, I deserved? What treatment would *you* have given me had I become your wife, in order to revenge the slight cast on me by another? The treatment I have received, Monsieur De Lacarras, is unmitigated love and tenderness."

"You call it love that leaves you by yourself—alone and unprotected—to be the subject of scurrilous reports, and the object of universal admiration! Love guards its treasure, Lady Ethel, in a better way than that!"

"But it is my own fault I am so left," she eagerly rejoined, "I dared him to it. I goaded him on by sneers and imputations; I said I did not love him; that I had married him for mere convenience. I said that—that—— Oh! my God!" cried Lady Ethel, as suddenly breaking down, she buried her face in her hands and burst into tears; "I have lost him—my dearest and my best—for ever; I shall never, *never* see him any more!" and for a few moments there was no sound to be heard in that apartment but her unrestrained and choking sobs.

Victor de Lacarras seized the hat which he carried in his hand, and vigorously commenced to smooth the nap beneath the influence of his kidded palm.

"This is deeply interesting!" he observed, presently, when Lady Ethel's emotion having partially subsided, he thought he had some chance of being heard. "I had no idea that *Monsieur votre mari* had made such an impression on your heart, or I might have hesitated to convey the sentiments of my own to you. But you are doubtless in the right, Lady Ethel; to profess devotion to the man she has married is always the most respectable, if not the most pleasant, course for a woman to pursue; and in your case, I should think respectability was as much as you could aspire to."

The coarse insinuation did not escape her notice, and love made her equal to the emergency of meeting it.

"If your conduct is noble, *monsieur*," she exclaimed, angrily, "heaven save us from more than that which is respectable! But if your words are intended to convey a reproach towards that man—in whose presence you are no more worthy to sit than my footman is to take his ease before me in this drawing-room—I tell you that I would not change my husband—little as you think of him—for the bluest blood that runs in Christendom. He is not noble in your acceptation of the word—looking on you, and on my step-mother, and others like you, I can say, thank God, he is *not* noble—but he has the noblest body, the noblest heart, the noblest soul, of any man who walks the earth this day. And I love him! Heaven is my witness that I love him as much as ever he loved me! and I have wronged him, and driven him away; and I am the most miserable woman that God ever made! *Fancy! how much* I love him," she exclaimed, in a sudden torrent of eagerness, as with clasped hands she started forward, and regarded the Marquis in the face; "fancy! to what a pitch of despair this parting has reduced me, that I can humble myself before you to-day, regardless of everything but to preserve my faith to him!"

Yes; it was true; Lady Ethel had humbled herself at length; and from that hour she commenced to rise.

"I am sure I am only too glad to hear it," returned Victor de Lacarras, in a voice of the most studied politeness; "but under the circumstances, what can I do but offer you my heartfelt congratulations? I could scarcely be expected to pursue and bring him back again."

"But you can remove yourself from my presence," she said, nettled at the continued sarcasm of his tone, "and I would be alone, *monsieur!* Your visit has agitated me, and I feel ill."

"I have no pleasure except in following your wishes," he answered, "and for the same reason, Lady Ethel, I shall not trouble you again;" and with a courteous inclination, he left the room.

"He is gone!" she said, in a hysterical manner, as the slam of the hall-door reached her ear, "they are all gone now. There is not one left"—and then, with a bewildered look and the sharp cry, "Oh, my love! my love! will you never come back to me?" Lady Ethel, after making one or two feeble efforts to maintain her equilibrium, sunk fainting to the ground.

CHAPTER XLIII.

A WONDERFUL DISCOVERY.

It was fortunate that Louise, desiring to learn her lady's wishes with respect to the trimming of a ball-dress, knocked at the door a few minutes afterwards, and, receiving no reply to her appeal, ventured to pass the threshold, and found her mistress stretched upon the floor.

Else Lady Ethel's illness might have been attended with very serious consequences, for though the German maid quickly procured assistance and conveyed her to her room, unlike her former attacks, she did not regain consciousness from this till Dr Chalmers was sitting by her bedside.

The first things which became patent to her returning senses were the pressure of his fingers on her wrist, and a general perception of strong odours, and being very cold about the head and breast.

"What is the matter?" she said, in a frightened manner, as she opened her eyes and attempted to quit the recumbent posture.

"Nothing—nothing," replied the calm tones of the physician, as with gentle force he replaced her on the bed; "you have been a little faint, that is all, but you must keep quiet for an hour or two."

Lady Ethel threw herself back upon the pillows with a sigh.

"I feel terribly weak. Have I been worse than usual, doctor?"

"Not that I know of; but you should have told me of these attacks before, to which your maid says you are very subject. Why, what have you been doing with yourself?"

"I am sure I don't know. Just the same as other people."

"Have you been dancing much?"

"Yes, pretty well."

"And keeping late hours?"

"Of course. Who keeps early ones in London?"

"And exciting yourself in other ways?"

"Perhaps so. But what has that to do with my fainting?"

"Everything; and I am going to lay strict orders on you to give it up."

Lady Ethel's eyes opened to their widest extent.

"Give up balls, and dinner-parties, and going out altogether! What nonsense, doctor! It is not the end of June yet."

"If it were the beginning of May, my dear Lady Ethel, it would be the same thing. Your health requires perfect rest, and you must observe it."

"It is impossible," she said, querulously; "you might as well tell me not to eat at once. It would kill me to remain shut up here all alone."

"It may kill more than one if you are obstinate," replied Dr Chalmers, gravely.

"More than one! What do you mean?"

"I mean, Lady Ethel, that if, against my advice, you persist in pursuing this constant round of gaiety, you will be answerable, not only for your own life, but that of your child."

"My Child?"

The motherless girl, who had never known what it was to hear that sacred title from a woman's lips, who had been denied the blessing of brothers and sisters, and (with the exception of the Countess of Clevedon's son) not even brought in contact with the holy influences of childhood, did not seem at first as though capable of comprehending the prospect opened out before her by the doctor's words.

"My Child?"

A picture rose before her mental vision of tiny hands to clutch and cling to her; pure eyes to gaze into her own; and trembling feet to toddle by her side; of something very indistinctly traced, it is true, yet helpless, loving, and dependent, which should belong to her alone, and call her by the holy name of "Mother," and that at that thought the evil spirit that had so long possessed her heart spread wings and flew away, and the woman shone out in her true colours.

"O Dr Chalmers! are you quite—*quite* sure that it is true?"

Springing up in bed as she spoke, with crimson cheeks, dilated eyes, and parted lips, she seemed to demand some further proof of this wonderful revelation at the physician's hands.

"Yes, quite sure," he answered, soothingly; "have you not suspected it? Come, Lady Ethel, you must lie down again; I cannot allow you to excite yourself like this."

But, to his surprise, she turned upon her pillow, and burst into a flood of tears. Oh, where was *he* who would have been so proud to hear this news; who would have encompassed her with solicitude and care, supported her courage when it drooped, and nursed her with more than woman's tenderness? where was the father of her child? She sobbed so bitterly as the wide gulf which stretched between them, mentally and physically, became apparent to her understanding, that the very centre of her being seemed to be stirred by the violence of her emotion. And mixed with the hopelessness of their re-union, there came another feeling, a lower, narrower, yet still natural sense of profound shrinking from the trial which inevitably awaited her; for, born and reared in sensuousness, Lady Ethel had never yet been taught that self-control is virtue, and was a very coward in the face of pain.

Dr Chalmers had had too much experience in the treatment of feminine weakness to attempt to check her tears; but as soon as they had given place to low gasping sobs, and she had turned her pallid stained face to the light again, he held a cordial to her lips and bade her drink it.

"That's a good girl!" he said, in a paternal manner—(he had known her almost from her birth)—as she submissively swallowed the contents of the wine-glass; "and now I must have you lie quiet and try to go to sleep, or you will be ill."

"But, one word, doctor," laying her white hand on his; "will it be very soon? I feel so horribly afraid."

The question made him smile.

"Pooh—pooh! there's nothing to be afraid of, and it's a long while to look forward to yet! I shall have you as strong and saucy again as ever before it happens. I see that Colonel Bainbridge has arrived in Calcutta. Is any time fixed for his return?"

"I don't know—I believe not," she answered faintly.

"We shall have him home fast enough when he hears the good news, I warrant. And, meanwhile, I cannot allow you to live any longer by yourself. You must have some woman to stay with you."

"I have Louise; no one could be kinder."

"Kindness is all very well in its way; but you want company, Lady Ethel, and you must ask some lady—one that is young and cheerful and will keep up your spirits, to come and remain here until your husband joins you again. Now, who shall I send for?"

"Oh! I'm sure I don't know!" with a despairing little sigh.

"Lady Clevedon?" suggested the doctor.

"Most decidedly not. We never speak to each other."

"Never speak to your father's widow?—that's a bad sign, Lady Ethel. Your aunt, then, Lady d'Eyncourt."

"I have not seen her for years."

"Has not Colonel Bainbridge a mother living?"

"Oh! yes!—but I could not ask a favour of her," returned his patient, with a sudden shrinking that was very patent to her hearer.

"No sisters, then, or cousins?"

"No!—yes! though stay, there is one—but I am not sure if she would come to me," said Lady Ethel, as her thoughts lighted upon Margaret Henderson.

"We can but try; and the need is really urgent. Let me have the lady's address, and I will write to her at once. If we are expeditious we shall save the country post."

"Miss Henderson, Cranshaws, Borthwick; but, Dr Chalmers, I really don't feel justified in putting her to so much trouble. I dare say I shall get on very well alone, and—and —it is all my own fault that I am left so," in a lowered key.

Dr Chalmers looked upon the fair, sad face laid upon the pillows, with intense compassion. He had known Lady Ethel Bainbridge, proud, wilful, and determined from her very childhood, and had more than once suspected that her married life was not a happy one; but her present mood was quite a new phase in her character to him. He could not understand the subdued tones of her voice, the softened expression in her face, the tears standing on her eyelashes; she did not look like the same girl whom he had been accustomed to attend; and his heart warmed towards her, so young and fragile and beautiful, and left so utterly alone. Could it be, as she affirmed, by her own fault?

"However that may be, my dear," he answered, "I alone am responsible for the step we have in contemplation. You are under my charge, and I consider the presence of a female friend to be indispensable to you; and if Miss Henderson cannot come we will find some one else. Meanwhile, you must try to go to sleep, and I will look in again this evening."

Dr Chalmers did not write to Cranshaws; for his object being as soon as possible to convey relief to his patient's mind, he telegraphed the news that she was ill and in immediate requisition of a woman's presence, begging her husband's family to let him know at once if Miss Henderson could be spared to nurse her.

And when he visited Curzon Street at ten o'clock the same evening, and found Lady Ethel free from emotion, but still very weak and sorrowful and languid, he showed her the answer which had reached his hands an hour before:—

"Most glad to be of use; will travel by earliest train to-morrow."

When my heroine fell off to sleep that night, the telegram was underneath her pillow.

CHAPTER XLIV.

A SISTER OF MERCY.

Dr Chalmers' telegram found Mrs Bainbridge, her niece, and sister still at Cranshaws, for various delays on the part of house-builders and decorators in Birmingham had prevented their vacating the Castle as speedily as they had intended, and for the moment there were divided opinions on the advisability of answering it in the affirmative.

That Mrs Bainbridge should feel rather unwilling to part with Maggie Henderson, who was her right hand, at the very time when she most needed her, and for the sake of her son's wife, was not unnatural. She bore no malice towards Lady Ethel, but she could not forget the haughty manner in which she had treated her husband's family, nor that it was due to her misconduct that Colonel Bainbridge was, at that hour, an exile from his native land.

And it was hard to believe the message had been dictated by the wishes of her daughter-in-law. She had not cared for them in health, why should her thoughts turn in their direction when she needed a sick-nurse? and surely, were the case emergent, it were far more reasonable to expect some member of her own family should go to her assistance. Mrs Bainbridge did not like the idea that Maggie should be ordered from one place to another to suit the convenience of her cousin's wife; and perhaps to meet with insult or indifference for her pains. She had half a mind to say she could not spare her.

But gentle Aunt Letty saw the matter in a very different light. Dr Chalmers was a physician of high repute, who would not have needlessly alarmed them; and if the necessity could have been met nearer, what reason had he for incurring the delay consequent on an appeal to them. She was quite sure that it was Maggie's duty to go to Lady Ethel's aid at once; but if her sister felt she could not spare her, why, she would go herself. They could never look in Thomas's face again if they neglected to offer to his wife that assistance which they were ready to extend to every poor woman about Cranshaws.

Upon which Mrs Bainbridge, with somewhat of impatience, said, "if that was the view her sister took of it, Margaret had better settle the question for herself."

And Maggie had but one opinion on the subject: that she should answer—as she did—in the affirmative.

Not that she entertained any strong desire to travel southward by herself, and take up a position in the fashionable circle of which they had heard that Lady Ethel was the centre; on the contrary, the prospect rather dismayed her. She, too, had her painful memories of the wounds this girl had recklessly inflicted on her uncle and her cousin; of the father, who, for her caprice, had drawn his last breath before he saw his only child again; and of the son, driven from England, the comforts of his home, and the embraces of his widowed mother, rendered hopeless and almost desperate by the cruelty of the woman who had sworn to love and cherish him.

These were not the thoughts which, humanly speaking, would have inclined her heart towards Lady Ethel; but, fortunately for both of them, Maggie's conduct was actuated by higher motives than those of this world, and had she been disposed to hesitate, she had but to throw one glance in the direction of Aunt Letty to make up her mind.

"Full measure, pressed down and running over," whispered the elder lady in her ear, and Maggie turned at once to Mrs Bainbridge.

"Aunt Lizzie, if you are willing, I would rather go. He loved her so much, and—and, suppose she should be fretting after him?"

"Little chance of that, I'm afraid, my dear," said Mrs Bainbridge, with a sigh; but she offered no further opposition to the idea. And the next morning Maggie Henderson, with Aunt Letty (who insisted, at all events, upon seeing her darling safe within the doors of Curzon Street), started for London, where they arrived in safety the same evening.

Lady Ethel's carriage had been waiting for them at the station, and when they entered the house Dr Chalmers met them in the hall.

"This is real charity," he said, shaking hands with both of

them ; "that poor young creature upstairs is terribly lonely ; it will put fresh life in her to hear that you are come. May I ask which is Miss Henderson ?"

"This is my niece," replied Aunt Letty, as she pushed Maggie forward. "I only accompanied in order to protect her, and return to-morrow. She is much the same age as Lady Ethel, and I hope may be of use in cheering her."

The doctor looked critically at the fresh, glowing colour, clear complexion, and bright eyes of the country girl, and decided that his application northwards had been a great success.

"Strong constitution," he said, mentally, "cheerful temperament, and plenty of brains, that's the article for my money! Is this a specimen of your rearing, madam ?" he he continued, vocally, "for if so, it does you great credit ! I wonder what some of our London belles would give just now for a little of that bloom ? You are not often troubled with headaches, Miss Henderson, or I am much mistaken."

"Not often," she said, smiling.

"No ! nor heartaches, nor vapours, nor hysterics, nor any of the thousand and one complaints into which our girls dance and dress themselves down here. Poor Lady Ethel is a specimen of the bad effects of over-exertion just now. She is very low, very weak, and very despondent, and your cheerful company will do her more good than any amount of physic or advice. You know how to laugh, Miss Henderson ?"

"When there is occasion for it, doctor."

"Ay, ay ! laugh with those who laugh, and weep with those who weep ! I can read off your character like a book ; you're all sympathy ! But just at present I want you to go on another tack ; Lady Ethel is all tears, and you must be all smiles. Do you understand ?"

"I will try, sir."

"And you will succeed. You are not going to leave us, madam ?" to Miss Lloyd.

"Yes ! I only came to deposit my niece here in safety, and pass the night at the house of an old friend. To-morrow, if all goes well, I will see Lady Ethel before I return. Good-night, my darling !" and with a farewell salutation to Dr Chalmers, Aunt Letty re-entered the carriage.

"Will you come upstairs at once ?" inquired the doctor ;

and, laying aside her bonnet and shawl, Maggie followed him. notwithstanding a certain fluttering at her heart, for she hardly knew what sort of welcome waited her, to Lady Ethel's room.

"I have brought you a present," said Dr Chalmers, gaily, as he pushed the door open, "what will you give me for it?"

"I am sure I don't know," replied a voice, so weak and weary that Maggie scarcely recognised it as that of her cousin's wife. "How does the time go, Dr Chalmers? is it late?"

"Just about time for the Edinburgh mail to be in, I should think," he answered, with a sly look at Maggie.

Lady Ethel heaved a deep sigh.

"I don't think she will come to night; I am trying not to expect her; it would be too much."

"Well! perhaps she had better go back again," he continued.

"Oh! has she arrived?"

A faint colour struggled into Lady Ethel's face, which deepened to a blush as she turned and caught sight of Maggie standing in the doorway. That timid look of shame appealed more nearly to the new comer's heart than any boisterous welcome could have done. It was so strangely different from what she had expected. In a moment Lady Ethel's numerous offences, her pride, her coldness, and unsociability, were blotted from her memory as with a sponge, and remembering only her present weakness and the deep interest which, from the first, and against her inclination, she had taken in her cousin's wife, she sprung forward and knelt by the bedside.

"Dear Lady Ethel! I came as quickly as I could: I am so grieved to find you ill."

Lady Ethel started up to greet her, and Maggie was surprised to see how thin and pale she had grown; still more surprised to feel her arms clasped round her neck, and hear the proud girl sobbing on her shoulder.

"O Maggie! how good of you to come; but it was the doctor sent for you! I never could have done it! Do you know all? Did—did—Colonel Bainbridge tell you?"

"Hush! hush! yes—partly—but you must not speak or think of sad things now."

"I cannot help it! I am thinking of it night and day," she wailed; "I think of nothing else."

Maggie Henderson, afraid lest her emotion should do Lady Ethel harm, looked round for Dr Chalmers, but he had disappeared.

"Try to calm yourself," she urged, as she disentwined the white arms from her neck. "I am come to see if I can cheer you up; but this is a bad beginning! If my company is to be the signal for tears, it will do you more harm than good."

"What is there left for me but tears?" said Lady Ethel, mournfully.

"Faith in God! All will come right in the end if you do but trust in Him! And now, do you know that I have been travelling for ten hours, on nothing but a basket of sandwiches, and feel uncommonly hungry?"

"Dinner is waiting for you," said Lady Ethel, eagerly. "I ordered it for eight o'clock."

"Dinner?" with a comical gesture of distaste. "What! all by myself downstairs? Might I not have a cup of tea up in this room instead?"

"By my bedside? Would you like it so?"

"Of course I would! What have I come for, but to be by your bedside?"

"Oh! that would be delightful!" and Lady Ethel's eyes actually sparkled at the idea; "and you are sure you will not mind?"

"I shall mind very much if you send me away," was Maggie's answer; and then Louise was summoned to show her to her room, and to take the necessary orders for their projected meal.

When Margaret Henderson had changed her travelling dress, and returned to Lady Ethel's side, she was struck by the animation with which she was directing her maid to lay the tea-table.

"Tell Wells to send up some dishes from the second course; and there is no guava jelly. Make haste, Louise!—here is Miss Henderson!"

"I hope you are not making all these preparations for me, Lady Ethel," said Maggie, laughing, "for my appetite is a very healthy one, and will take kindly to anything in the shape of food."

"For both of us," replied the other. "I feel as though I could eat to-night. It is such a comfort to have you here."

And thereupon she commenced to speak of her illness, dwelling on each detail as a woman feels it such a comfort to do when she has been fretting by herself, and drawing on her friend for sympathy at every turn.

"Dr Chalmers says I shall not leave my bed for weeks, or perhaps months. Can you imagine anything more dreadful?"

"Yes—many things!" said Maggie, cheerfully; "to be confined to it for life, for instance."

"Oh! but that would be too terrible—I should die!"

"I don't think you would. There are many who live through it."

"Good people, perhaps; not sinners, like myself! You don't know what I am, Maggie!"

"I can see what you might be, and what it lies in your power to become," rejoined her companion, with a smile. "We are not always the best judges of ourselves, Lady Ethel."

Still, though they talked familiarly and cheerfully together, the principal topic which engrossed both minds seemed by mutual consent to be avoided. Neither had courage to mention Colonel Bainbridge, and even when Maggie spoke of Cranshaws, the sudden flush on Lady Ethel's cheek, the quick drooping of her eyelashes, or nervous motion of her hand, showed that the allusion was a painful one.

They were still engaged over their meal, when Dr Chalmers, peeping into the room, was so surprised to hear the altered tones of his patient's voice, that he jestingly declared that he should discontinue his visits now that Dr Henderson had arrived.

"All that you have to do with this rebellious subject," he said, in allusion to Lady Ethel, "is to keep her quiet, and make her eat as much as she can. And the sooner you can persuade her to go back with you to Scotland, Miss Henderson, the better."

But at this suggestion the subject of it coloured so painfully, that the doctor saw that he had made an error.

"We must neither of us sit up late to-night," said Maggie, when he had departed, "for you have excited yourself more than usual, and I am very tired. Shall I read to you before I go, or will you do that for yourself?"

"Read?" repeated Lady Ethel, interrogatively.

"The Bible," said her friend, as she looked round for one.

"Oh! my dear! don't give me any of that, for goodness' sake! I don't believe I have looked into it for years."

Maggie Henderson stopped short, and earnestly regarded her.

"Not for years!—not when you pray?"

"I never pray!"

The assertion was so defiant that it was met in silence; but after the pause of a few minutes, Lady Ethel, glancing up at her companion's face, saw that it was bathed in tears.

"Have I said anything to hurt you?"

"Not to hurt *me*," said Maggie, in a broken voice.

She was thinking how patiently One must have stood for years at the door of that little careless heart, knocking for admittance, and in vain.

"Who then?"

"*You* know, Lady Ethel! You know as well as I do. There is no need to tell you."

She was right; and in the interval that followed there came no refutation of her words.

"If you don't pray to Him," Maggie went on, presently; "if you never take the trouble to ask Him for what you want, or thank Him for what He gives, I don't wonder that everything goes wrong with you. How could it be otherwise?"

This appeal was made so simply, and with such an air of interest, that it carried no offence with it; but neither did it gain an answer, except such as was conveyed by total silence.

"O Lady Ethel!" cried Maggie, earnestly, as she threw both arms round her; "try to speak to Him. Try to realise that He is here, close by you, ready to listen and to sympathise, and all the remainder will come easy."

"Don't call me '*Lady*' Ethel any more," whispered the other, as she embraced her in return. "I want to be 'Ethel' to you, Maggie! I feel somehow as if a sister had been sent to me!"

And Maggie felt that to have met with no repulse was something gained.

CHAPTER XLV.

INSTALLED IN OFFICE.

LADY ETHEL slept so much later, on the following morning, than she had been used to do, that Miss Lloyd was compelled to return to Scotland without seeing her.

"It is just as well, perhaps, my dear," she observed, after hearing Maggie's account of the glowing welcome which she had received; "my presence could have added nothing to Lady Ethel's pleasure, and might have been the means of reviving disagreeable recollections."

"Then you won't stay in town another day?" said Maggie, wistfully.

"No, darling, don't tempt me. Aunt Lizzie was very good to let you come, remember, and I am sure she cannot spare both of us at once. Has Lady Ethel made no mention of her husband?"

"Not the slightest, after having once spoken his name, in asking if he had told me of their disagreement. Is it not strange? And yet she seems so to shrink from any approach to the subject, that I am sure her silence is owing to the pain it gives her."

"She will speak by and by, my dear, but do not try to force her confidence. With a proud nature like Lady Ethel's, the least encroachment would cause her to retire within herself again. You must wait, and watch, and hope."

"And write all the particulars to my Aunt Letty."

"Oh yes, keep us well informed of everything that goes on here; and if she manifests the least inclination to visit us again, remember how glad your Aunt Lizzie and myself would be to receive her. And don't overwork yourself, my little Maggie; we can't afford to have our right hand laid up on the sofa."

Maggie laughed at the idea.

"Fancy *me* upon a sofa," stretching out her firm round arm. "No, aunt, if I fall sick of anything it will be of too little exercise, like Mrs Appleton's old spaniel. I shall be afraid to walk out in this crowded place alone. It would tire me so to be always trying to keep out of other people's way."

"You will have the carriage, my dear."

"Oh!"—with a shrug of martyrdom—"fancy driving about in state by myself, and all the swells wondering who that red-cheeked, countrified-looking creature stuck up in Lady Ethel Bainbridge's barouche can be?"

"Maggie! I will not have you speak of yourself in that fashion," exclaimed Miss Lloyd; "besides, it is not the truth. You heard what Dr Chalmers said last night, that the London belles would give half their fortunes to have such a bloom as yours."

"All talk, auntie, particularly when they can buy it ready made. And really a natural colour does look coarse. You should see my skin beside Lady Ethel's now. Aunt," with sudden seriousness, "she is *very* lovely; I don't wonder at Cousin Thomas having had no eyes for some one else."

"Nonsense, my dear," replied Miss Lloyd, rather impatiently, for she had not yet recovered from the pain of seeing her darling rejected for another; "looks had nothing to do with it. Beauty is proverbially skin deep, and I am sure it has proved so in this instance. I dare say your poor cousin has often regretted his headstrong choice."

"Oh, no!" exclaimed the girl, earnestly, "indeed, I don't believe it. Whatever she is, Aunt Letty, he loved her; and how could he have done less than ask her hand in marriage? And if I am not mistaken," with a light smile, "Lady Ethel is coming to the knowledge that she loves him too; and when that occurs it will be all right again. What a happy day, Aunt Letty! We shall have no more talk about regretting then!"

Aunt Letty turned and regarded the dear, honest face that was beaming on her for a few moments without speaking.

"O my *darling*," she exclaimed, at length, as she took the girl in her arms, "God bless you!"

It was not much to say, but the three words spoke volumes from one heart to the other.

When Miss Lloyd was gone again, Maggie felt at first a little lonely. Breakfast was on the table, but she had no inclination to sit down by herself, for her ladyship was still asleep, and the large house seemed silent and deserted.

So Maggie sat down to think instead.

She thought of her cousin—banished from this pleasant home which had been prepared for him by his father's bounty—of how much he might be suffering—how much be called upon to suffer—before the discord which had separated him from all he loved was reduced to harmony again.

Yet she felt that with so determined and resolute a character as his, that happy end would never be accomplished until his wife recalled him of her own free will. It was she who had inflicted the wound; from her hands alone could come the remedy. And to effect a reconciliation between them was the great wish of Maggie's heart—the aim of all her present actions.

As she sat there that morning in the very arm-chair her cousin had been used to call his own, she determined to leave no stone unturned that might advance the cause for which she laboured; to bring all her efforts to bear upon that end, and to be patient, watchful, and trusting as her aunt desired her to be. She might lead to the subject as much as she thought fit, but Lady Ethel must be the first to broach it. All she had to do was to invite her confidence, and pray to be enabled to advise her right when she received it.

With this intent it was a happy, loving face she took into the bedroom when Lady Ethel's bell was heard to ring; so much so, that the other asked, with an eagerness that did not pass unnoticed, if she had heard any news?

"None; excepting that the clock has just struck half-past ten, and therefore I hope your ladyship feels refreshed by your night's rest."

Lady Ethel looked disappointed.

"Oh, yes, I feel much stronger, thank you. But is it really so late? I hope that you have had your breakfast."

"No; I waited for you, though I am not quite sure I shall be so polite another morning. May I help you in your toilet?"

"Oh, Louise will do it, thank you. It will be such a trouble, won't it?" with an appealing glance that seemed to beg for an answer in the negative.

"Of course it will be—a most horrible trouble; but all children are that to their mothers. I shall be your mother till you are well, you know."

"You are the first I have ever had," said Lady Ethel, despondently.

"That is a bond between us," replied Maggie.

"Is there no other?" asked her friend. "O Maggie! I dreamed last night I was alone again, and it was such a blessing to wake up and remember you were here."

"Well, let me prove I am a blessing, by combing through this long hair without making you call out. You must let me plait it for you, Lady Ethel"——

"Ethel," interposed the other, quickly.

"*Ethel*, then—dear Ethel, if you will."

"Dear Maggie," said her cousin's wife; and then the girls (both under twenty, remember) threw their arms round each other's necks and exchanged a hearty kiss.

The day passed happily, Maggie taking up her station altogether in the sick-room, and whether she worked, read, or wrote, carrying on her business under Lady Ethel's eye, so that she was constant company.

Dr Chalmers looked in upon them once, declared his patient's pulse to be much stronger, laid a few injunctions with respect to her on Maggie, in whom he seemed to have implicit confidence, and disappeared until the following day. With this exception they saw no one; and Maggie, who had heard so much of the constant round of gaiety in which her cousin's wife engaged, and the large circle of her fashionable acquaintance, was surprised to find that no lady came to sit with her for a few minutes, or to cheer her up with prognostications of a quick recovery. Had she been ill at Cranshaws, every farmer's wife for ten miles round would have jolted over the moors in her spring cart to inquire if the "braw young leddy was no richt yet?"

It is true that people called, for at the close of the afternoon Louise brought up a salver full of visiting cards, but the unflattering comments with which her mistress turned them over, did not seem to intimate there were any she termed friends amongst them.

"Lady Kitchener! and about time she *did* call! it 's a month since she dined here!

"Mrs Carmichael! a disgrace for any one to have her carriage standing at the door!

"Mrs Fuller! of course *she* must know the why and the wherefore of everything!

"Lady Rosa Vokes! oh, the old scarecrow! What a mercy I escaped her!

"Mr and Mrs Trevanion! Thank you, none of that tribe for me!

"Colonel Marshall! What effrontery! I only danced with the man once! Here, Louise, take them all downstairs and put them in the card-basket. I expect it will be a long time before I trouble myself to return them."

"It must be very unsatisfactory work paying calls alone," said Maggie, innocently.

Lady Ethel coloured.

"I think it generally falls to a woman's lot, though. Men always shirk visiting."

"Is Lady Clevedon in town, and your little brother?"

"Yes," hesitatingly, "but I don't often see them."

"He is quite a baby still, is he not?"

"About three years old."

"Oh, what a nice age! Aren't you very fond of him?"

"I can't say I am. You see, his mother and I are not the best of friends, Maggie. Do you know why I am ill? Has Dr Chalmers told you?"

"From over fatigue, is it not, and perhaps a little worry combined with it?" said Maggie, affectionately, as she laid her hand on Lady Ethel's.

"Well—yes; but that is not all. I am going to have a baby."

Maggie had been looking earnestly in her face the while, but at these words she rose and, dropping her hand, turned suddenly away to the window.

"Indeed, dear!" the words were cheerfully delivered, though the voice was rather strained, "that is grand news! How pleased you must be."

She thought she had been reconciled to the marriage of her cousin, but this information staggered her.

Why is it that a woman, by strength of will and steady purpose, can bring herself to contemplate the fact that the man she cares for has preferred another—can even force herself to be a friend, where she has been a lover—and yet have no firmness to look on children, born of such an union?

She can let the man go! If he has lost his love for her, with what object should she seek to stay him? Let him wed elsewhere, if so it pleases him; but let it be a silent house he goes to! She does not say so, perhaps she hardly dares to wish it; but it is the natural language of her heart.

If he finds greater pleasure, warmer looks, more constant love, in the embraces of a stranger, she is content; but may no sweet child seal the unhallowed union to bind their hearts irrevocably to each other. For children are a pledge—a sign—a token of affection—which no other thing can be; and the man who can look upon a woman and forget she is the mother of his offspring, is less than man—he is not deserving of the name. It is a sacred seal set on her which should for ever preserve her from the blight of coldness, unkindness, or neglect; and women, who have faith in the honour of the men they love, know it to be so.

Maggie would not have altered one phase of her existence, if she could; she had no wish but to see her cousin happy with the woman whom he loved; and yet at the thought of this new life on its way, she trembled, and grew hot and cold by turns.

I only tell it to depict her resolution. This was nature, and she was natural from head to foot; but there was a stronger power within to overcome it.

"I am not sure about being pleased," said Lady Ethel, in answer to her last observation, "it came on me as a great surprise, and I think I have been rather sorry since than otherwise."

"Oh! don't say that!" replied Maggie, quickly, as the thought of her cousin's feelings, when he should hear the news, flashed across her mind. "It will be such a blessing when it comes! Think, Ethel, of a little creature"—— here she halted for a moment, but only for a moment—"all your own, to love you and look up to you; there could be no greater happiness!"

Lady Ethel's breast heaved; she was not insensible to the prospect laid out before her, only she was still a little too proud to confess it.

"Well, I don't know! It will be an immense trouble, and I feel very nervous; and—and"— with a quivering lip, "I am all alone, you see!"

"But you will not be alone then," said Maggie, confidently.

Lady Ethel looked away.

"At all events it is inevitable!" she replied, after a pause, "so it's no use grumbling about it, Maggie! Is it not nearly time for tea? I am so thirsty;" and her willing messenger flew to give the required orders.

The days slipped tranquilly one after another. Maggie had nothing but good accounts to send to Cranshaws, and Lady Ethel progressed in strength and devotion to her husband's cousin; yet she was selfish in her gratitude.

Reared in an atmosphere of self-pleasing, and accustomed to regard every thing and body exactly in proportion as it ministered to her gratification, she seemed to imagine that Maggie's constant attendance in her sick-room was amply repaid by thanks and multiplied caresses. She could not go out herself, and therefore it never struck her that her nurse was suffering for want of exercise; and it was not until Dr Chalmers had spoken to her on the subject that she asked Maggie if she did not think a walk would do her good.

Maggie was enduring a slight headache at the moment, for, used to an abundance of fresh air and exercise, she had felt the close confinement to a London bedroom more than she cared to acknowledge; but she declined to avail herself of Lady Ethel's offer till the morrow.

"To-morrow will be Sunday, you know," she said, with a smile, "and then, if you can spare me, Ethel, I should be glad to go to church. I have a friend belonging to the sisterhood of Saint Ermenilda's, and I want to attend service there."

"Saint Ermenilda's!" repeated Lady Ethel; "why, that is our church! we always go there."

"Is not the service very beautiful?"

"Oh, yes! there is splendid music; and a boy in the choir with a voice like a thrush. But horribly hard chairs; I advise you to take a shawl, or something to sit down upon. And you have a friend amongst the sisters? those women with black hoods and things? how funny! I do not know any of them; but I will order the carriage to be ready at a quarter past ten to-morrow to take you there. But not twice a day, Maggie! I can't spare you for more than the morning service, and I'm sure that's long enough for anybody."

And Maggie smiled, and promised not to be encroaching,

whilst her heart beat faster at the idea of worshipping in the same church as Sister Margaret.

Yet, all this while, she had been unable to say a word about her cousin Thomas. A score of times his name had been upon her very lips, but something in the face of Lady Ethel had restrained her. They had spoken of Cranshaws, of London, of the house they lived in, of the child that was expected; and yet the owner, the master, the husband, and the father, was a forbidden subject.

Maggie felt sometimes as though she could not bear it—as though she must transgress all bounds to plead the cause of him who could no longer plead his own—as though she must tell Lady Ethel either to give him her affection or withhold it from herself. It seemed so cruelly hard that of all topics spoken of between them, his name should be the only one forbidden. But the remembrance of Aunt Letty and her last advice restrained her.

Maggie had the utmost faith in Miss Lloyd's good sense and counsel. She had told her not to force Lady Ethel's confidence, and so she waited, patiently and in hope.

CHAPTER XLVI.

SAINT ERMENILDA'S.

"I SUPPOSE I may ask for your pew?" said Maggie, the next morning, as she stood by Lady Ethel's bed, drawing on her gloves, and waiting for the carriage to come round.

"*Pew,* my dear child! you'll get nothing so comfortable as a pew at Saint Ermenilda's, I can promise you. Go and sit down in the first rush-bottomed chair you see, and consider yourself lucky if you have not a dressmaker on one side of you and a housemaid on the other. That's the worst part of these high churches, they let *everybody* in without the slightest regard to one's feelings, and you never know next to whom you may sit."

"The rich and the poor are met together," said Maggie, smiling.

"Just so," replied Lady Ethel, without the least conception of the meaning of that smile, "and I assure you I have sometimes had the shabbiest people possible put next to me. But if you go at once, dear, and get into the front seats, there will not be so much fear of it."

"I am not afraid," said Maggie, as she kissed her friend and went downstairs.

When she found how near Saint Ermenilda's was to Curzon Street, she was almost ashamed to have had the carriage ordered for her; but she was quite ignorant of London, and would have had to ask her way. Besides, the church, which was a large solid structure of dark-red brick, stood back from the dwellings in the thoroughfare it occupied, and by a stranger might easily have been passed by, though its deep bell gave sonorous notice of its proximity. It was approached through massive iron gates, and Maggie Henderson had scarcely set her foot within its court before the stillness of the place fell on her, and her heart said, "this is the gate of heaven."

And if she felt so without its walls, how much more so, when she had entered them! The church was dim, almost dark, for all its glass was stained, and in the chancel, gas was lighted, even for the morning service; but Maggie had no eyes for anything but the numerous worshippers already scattered about the sacred building, and engaged in preparatory prayer. She longed to join them; to feel herself one with them in purpose as she was in spirit; and timidly taking up her station at some distance from the altar, she remained lost to all things earthly, until the rising of the congregation roused her to the knowledge that the stalls were filled with white-robed choristers, and the ambassadors of Christ were ready to fulfil their mission. Maggie had never witnessed such a congregation, and as she stood up and saw, not only the sittings, but the aisles, crowded with eager faces all turned towards the chancel, the verse flashed across her mind: "I was glad when they said unto me, We will go into the House of the Lord."

She had never seen such joyous, anticipating looks in church before; never more solemn ones. The priests knelt; every knee dropped simultaneously upon the stone floor of St Ermenilda's, and for a few moments the silence of death pervaded the vast building. Then commenced the service.

There is no need to chant the praises of our liturgy, which every Church acknowledges to be as nearly perfect as it is possible for human work to be, but Margaret Henderson had not thought it could be rendered as she heard it then.

Rapidly but majestically it proceeded, without hurry and without hesitation, yet with an amount of reverence conveyed by every look, and gesture, and position, which was as unusual as it was apparent.

Maggie listened to it all, as though she had been in some happy, heavenly dream; it was too surprising, too wonderful at first almost to believe: certainly to adopt as one's own rightful heritage. As the two bands of choristers answered each other in the psalms—the glorious organ, whether sad or joyous, plaintive or solemn, tallying with the words they sang—they seemed to acquire a new meaning in her ears; and she took her part in the responses with the keenest pleasure. Then came the Lessons, succinctly and decisively delivered: the glorious Te Deum and the happy Jubilate, the brief practical sermon, the solemn Credo, followed by the still more solemn Celebration.

Maggie had entered Saint Ermenilda's with the intention of communicating, but when the moment came, her courage failed her, and she could not go up to the altar. An awe had fallen on her senses, a sudden new appreciation of the Majesty on High and her own littleness; and she could only fall upon her knees and worship; whilst she prayed to be made more worthy of that privilege. Hot smarting tears fell on the chair she leaned against—tears wrung from her by a bright vision of His love and her ingratitude—and yet tears that thanked Him for their flowing. She had loved Him all her life; yet now, loving Him no less, she glowed and trembled in His presence, as she had never done before.

It was as though she had seen her Saviour lifted from the manger to the Throne—from the Cross to the right hand of God; that He whom she had worshipped in His painful earthly travail had appeared before her decked in robes of glory, making her for the first time fully aware of all His condescension in having permitted her to love Him in return.

What wonder she fell down and worshipped Him!

Let none dream, however, that I imagine outward things make any difference in the soul's interior converse with its Maker; they elevate, but cannot widen it. Were it not so, God help the many who from the cradle to the grave possess no such advantages as those I write of; and had not Margaret Henderson been depicted in her country home as serving faithfully, I might not have dared to draw her feelings upon this occasion. But what she had said erstwhile to Colonel Bainbridge was the truth; she would have scorned to desert His presence on an altar decked in rags, therefore she had earned the rapture she experienced now.

Faithful in a few things, who would grudge her entrance into the joy of her Lord?

When she lifted up her face again—her blistered, tear-stained, happy face—there was a glow upon it, such as may, perhaps, at times have shone on that of His disciples. It was still lingering there as she re-entered the deep porch, where Sister Margaret, who had been apprised by letter of her coming, was waiting to receive her.

The look exchanged between them was significant.

"You like it," said the Sister, as they clasped hands of true fellowship.

"*Like it!*" Maggie's eloquence failed to express all she felt. "O Sister Margaret, I can think of nothing but that I love Him with all my heart, and with all my soul, and with all my mind, and with all my strength. I have seen 'the King in His beauty.' Blessed Saint Ermenilda!" as lovingly she gazed back into the empty church. "Shall I ever forget this day? I am not the same creature that I was on entering these walls."

"When are you going to become one of us?" inquired her companion, smilingly.

"When He pleases, Sister Margaret; I am all His, as you are, and cannot move hand or foot of myself. And just now I have a little work at home," and then she detailed the circumstances of Lady Ethel's illness, and the probability of her being much detained in-doors.

"But you must come and see us before leaving London," said the Sister; and Maggie, promising so much, they separated to their respective destinations.

The happy look that shone upon her face did not escape the notice of Lady Ethel.

"You like Saint Ermenilda's!" she exclaimed, as Maggie went up to her side.

"*Like* is no name for it," said Maggie, enthusiastically; "I am charmed—delighted. I have had such a happy time."

"I thought you would, every one admires it so. Are not the windows lovely?"

Maggie started.

"I don't think I saw the windows, Ethel."

"Not the painted windows with the history of Saint Ermenilda? Why, where were your eyes? They are considered the best things there. And the carved screen too."

"The screen? Is that the part which divides the chancel from the nave?"

"Of course; it is all in marble, and came, I believe, from Italy. What colour did the altar wear to-day?"

"What colour? I do not understand you, Ethel."

"Was it vested in red or green? Red is for the martyrs and saints, you know, but green means nothing. It wears green every day."

"I am sure I can't tell you," replied Maggie.

"What a queer girl you are! I thought you were such a devotee. I suppose you never looked at the altar at all?"

"Oh, yes, I did," said Maggie, eagerly, "and at the painting above it—the Blessed Virgin holding out the infant Saviour to the people. How beautifully it is done; the Child seems almost to stand out from her arms; and the expression of His face, too! I could hardly take my eyes off it."

"The lectern is generally considered to be a very fine piece of workmanship."

"I don't think I observed the lectern."

"What anthem did they sing to-day at the Consecration?"

"I do not remember," said the other.

"You haven't seen anything, and you don't remember anything. Why, what were you doing all the time?"

Maggie was going to reply; she struggled to get out an answer, but she could not manage it, so she stooped down, and kissed Lady Ethel on the cheek instead.

"You might just as well have been at home with me," observed her ladyship, pouting.

"I must go some other day," said Maggie, "and see the things of which you speak. They would give me infinite pleasure, I can assure you. Only this morning—it was all so new, you see—and—I was thinking of something else."

"What else?" demanded Lady Ethel.

Maggie lingered for a moment by the bedside as though uncertain what to answer, and then, without speaking, left the room.

CHAPTER XLVII.

THE ICE BEGINS TO THAW.

The rest of the day passed very quietly, for Maggie was more thoughtful than usual, and Lady Ethel dozed, or seemed to doze, away the greater part of the afternoon upon her bed.

It was dusk when she fully roused herself again; a soft air was creeping in at the unclosed windows, and the figure of her friend was but just discernible in the dim twilight.

Lady Ethel turned upon her heated pillow with a deep-drawn sigh. Something had affected her; she was more low-spirited than usual.

"How long the days are, and how horrible and silent everything appears! Why don't you light the candles?"

"Too soon, is it not? and I thought that they might wake you."

"I have been awake for hours! What are you doing, Maggie? You can't be reading, though you have a book in your hand."

"No! it is too dark. I was thinking, Ethel!"

"Of what?"

"The sermon which I heard this morning."

"What a lively subject!"

"It was very interesting, as you would acknowledge had you heard it. So short, and yet so practical, and to the point. It was on charity, and the erroneous manner in which some people translate the word. The preacher said that, doubtless, there were many women present who, in a moment of excitement, would throw a bracelet into the offertory bag, or bestow the shawl they wore upon a beggar, who would be incapable of resigning the enjoyment of an hour in order to set a good example, or gratify the wishes of another! So true; is it not?"

"I daresay it is," with a yawn; "only I have not much faith in all that self-denying business, and people pretending that it gives them pleasure."

"Have you not?" The remark struck Maggie painfully,

remembering, as she did, how often her cousin had given up his will to Lady Ethel's, and sought no return. "But you must often have seen and admired it, Ethel! There is nothing so lovely as unselfishness!"

"We were not addicted to practising the virtue at Lady Clevedon's."

"And I have seen so much of it!" said Maggie, musingly. "I believe my dear uncle was one of the most unselfish creatures that God ever made!"

To this remark there was no answer.

"I have been thinking so much of him to-day," she went on, presently. "I wanted him in Saint Ermenilda's. He had never attended any but country services, you know, and fancied nothing else would please him; but he was so thoroughly good and unaffected, so ready to believe that, in religion, everybody must be before himself, and so anxious to promote the glory and honour of God, that I am sure he would have altered his opinion. He could not but have acknowledged the grandeur of what I heard to-day, as a fitting tribute to the King of kings, and his heart would have thrilled and melted under it as mine did. Dear uncle!"

Still there was no answer to her observations, but Lady Ethel turned restlessly about, until her face was hid from view.

"Of course I can't expect that you should follow me," continued Maggie; "you saw so little of him, but"——

"I wish you wouldn't speak to me of him!"

The words came so abruptly and so vehemently, that her companion started.

"Not of my uncle? O Ethel! surely you are not cherishing resentment for him still. Remember where he is—and that he can never vex you more!"

"It is not that!" The voice which spoke was broken.

"Not that? Dear Ethel! what have I said to make you cry? You cannot believe that *he* has not forgiven; he who forgave you over and over again, before he died."

"Did he? O Maggie!" and round came the penitent arms to clasp themselves about her neck.

"Don't sob so! dear, don't sob so, or you'll upset my calmness too. The occasion for it is all past. He will never feel annoyance or vexation more."

"But I—I never shall forget," said Lady Ethel, weeping. "His last looks, his last words, they haunt me day and night. Do you remember what they were? 'God Almighty bless you—and—and—your children—if you have any!'"

"Well, dear! and they ought to comfort instead of distressing you. He never mentioned that name lightly. It was a prayer he prayed for you; and you must have belief in its fulfilment."

"But I made him so unhappy! I was so—so—rude—and—uncivil to him. And then he died without my having seen him again. I did not think he would."

"But not without having forgiven you, darling! He talked so often of you during the last few days, it seemed as though he intended you should hear how entirely he had forgotten your behaviour."

"What did he say?"

"That he was sure you had so much sterling worth, beneath the crust of pride raised by your artificial education, that it depended on your husband's judiciousness whether you turned out a good wife or a bad one."

"How little he knew of me! I am not teachable like that!"

"And that the greatest blessing God could send you would be children. Baby hands to pull down your reserve; baby voices to distract your attention from yourself; and baby wants to make you grow less selfish. I speak plainly, dear, as he spoke; don't let me offend you."

There seemed little fear of that, if one might judge from Lady Ethel's low continued weeping.

"But Maggie—do you know—did *he* ever tell you that the reason that he was too late to see his father, was—because—because—I"——

"He did not tell me, Ethel, but I guessed it. It was very, *very* sad, but you could not foretell consequences, and it is all right now."

"All right now?"

In her surprise at the assertion, Lady Ethel stayed her tears to lift a flushed face of inquiry to her friend.

"With regard to uncle. He knows now why his son was absent from his dying bed, and such things have no more power to vex him."

"But he cannot know that I am sorry."

"Why not, dear? I believe he does; and thanks God for his death, if it has been the means of changing your state of mind. Dear Ethel, you don't half know what a loving soul he was. He never had an unkind thought for any living creature—is it likely he would begin now? Why do you cry still? You will be ill if you can't control yourself, and then Dr Chalmers will be angry with me."

Yet still her face was bowed upon the pillow, whilst her trembling frame gave evidence of her emotion, and Maggie felt the time to speak had come.

"Ethel, there is something further. Your self-reproaches are not all for your careless speeches to my uncle. A deeper wound than that is troubling you. Why not give it vent?"

"O Maggie! you must guess what it is. He was angry with me—justly angry; and in my resentment I insulted him upon his tenderest point. I said what was not true, and drove him from his home: and now—now"—with a failing voice—"I am so miserable!"

"But, dear, I thought you did not care for him."

"Not care for him! not *care* for him?" exclaimed Lady Ethel, hysterically, as starting up she threw her arms above her head. "I care for him *as my life*, I would *die* to bring him back again! I am thirsting to hear the sound of his voice or feel the touch of his hand; but I have driven him from me, and I know that I shall never see him again as long as I live. And the child too—the child—I shall never put it in its father's arms. O Thomas! Thomas!" and with hidden face she rocked herself backwards and forwards in her bed.

"Thank God!" said Maggie, solemnly.

"For what? For utter misery?" inquired Lady Ethel.

"For the dawn of hope," replied the other. "If you love him, everything is easy. A word will bring him back to you."

"Oh, no!" despairingly; "you do not know what passed between us, Maggie! I told him that I cared for some one else, and he will never forgive it or forget it. I said I hated him—I *hated* him!—him whom I would have died in the same hour to serve; but it was all my wretched pride, and I am rightly punished for it. O Maggie, my heart is broken; I shall never, never be a happy woman again."

"Hush! hush! no one can say so much as that, no one should *dare* say it whilst he lives."

"But so far off, and in that dreadful climate, he may never return."

"If so, you will not be left alone."

"I may never have the opportunity to tell him I am sorry."

"It will be told him for you, Ethel."

"I may have to pass my life without seeing him again."

"But not without One who loves you far more than Cousin Thomas does; who suffers with every pain experienced by your heart, and echoes every repentant sigh you heave. O Ethel," with clasped hands falling on her knees beside the bed, "do try to believe that He is by you at this very moment, hearing every word, reading each thought, and able by a breath to fulfil your dearest wishes if you make them known to Him."

"I have forgotten Him so long," said Lady Ethel, in a low voice.

"He has never forgotten you, dear."

'But that makes it so much harder. How can I go to Him just because I want something, when I never remembered Him in my happiness? It seems so mean."

"Nothing can be mean, dear, that brings us to His feet. And it is so sweet, whilst kneeling there, to think that He knows everything; there is no occasion even to speak to Him; our tears are all the explanation that He needs."

And then, seeing that they still streamed down the cheeks of Lady Ethel, Maggie bent over the repentant girl, and took her in her arms as though she had been a little child, and sweetly kissed them all away.

"Dear Ethel, don't cry any more. Everything will come right in time; I am sure it will. And now you must let me ring for candles and your tea, or you will have a headache and be unable to sleep."

And assuming a bright, cheerful countenance, she coaxed the invalid to eat and drink until her former composure was restored, and she saw her drop off tranquilly to rest.

But the next morning, as soon as Lady Ethel's toilet was completed, Maggie came dancing to her bedside with pen, ink, and paper, and placed them all before her.

"For what?" she asked, in genuine surprise.

"To write to him, dear. You must write at once to Cousin Thomas and tell him to come home. A word from you will bring him back again."

But Maggie had been too precipitate, and Lady Ethel shrunk from the proposal. In a soft moment she had acknowledged both her fault and her repentance, but she was hardly prepared to put a seal to the confession, and a remnant of the old pride rose to hinder it.

"Oh, no! indeed I could not."

Maggie's face fell.

"You will not tell him what you told to me?"

"Some day, perhaps—when he has written to me; but surely it is his part to write first."

"Do you imagine he will think you care to hear from him?"

"He has not asked me yet. And we have not even received the news of his arrival in Calcutta."

"I know the address of his agents, who will forward the letter to him."

But still Lady Ethel did not attempt to take either pen or paper from her hands, and Maggie saw her errand for the time was fruitless.

"May *I* write to him, Ethel?" she inquired, after a short pause.

"Of course! What has my leave to do with it? He is your cousin."

"Yes! but you know what I mean. May I write and tell him you are ill, and lonely, and in bad spirits, and that he must come home?"

"If you like," after a slight hesitation—"but nothing more, remember, Maggie! Now promise me."

"You shall read my letter," was her answer, "and send or tear it up, as seems agreeable to you. That is a fair bargain, is it not? And now I must go and write it, or it will not be ready for to-morrow's mail."

In another hour she returned.

"There is my production, Ethel," placing two crossed sheets of paper in her hand; "a fearful scribble, but I dare say you will be able to decipher it; and there is the envelope ready stamped and directed. If you don't like my letter tear it up; but if it meets with your approval, you had better send it to the post at once. I am just going round to see Sister Margaret, but shall be back before your luncheon time. Good-bye," and with a kiss she left her.

Lady Ethel regarded the sheets before her with somewhat of dismay. She knew Maggie's energetic character; and felt as though she held her own fate in her hands.

At one time she thought that she would send them to the post unread; but curiosity overpowered the half-formed resolution, and she commenced to peruse them. And as she read, and her own heart was laid bare before her, the tears gathered in her eyes and fell upon the paper.

Maggie had not spared her, had not meant to spare her. She spoke freely to her cousin of the mental anguish he had suffered and divulged to her at Cranshaws; enlarging on his love for Lady Ethel, and his bitter disappointment at the discovery it was not reciprocated; and then she touched upon the present weakness of his wife, her loneliness and need of careful treatment, and begged him to return to England as soon as it was possible to do so. And her allusions and entreaties pierced the very heart of the woman for whom they had been written.

Maggie had dexterously placed a pen and inkstand by the side of Lady Ethel's bed, and as she came to the end of the epistle, where a little slip of fair paper had been left, unwritten on, her longing to have some communication with the man whose hands should touch it next, grew too strong for her resistance, and seizing the pen, she wrote, hurriedly, just below his cousin's signature—"Oh, come! do come! I want you."

The deed done, she felt half ashamed of it. Supposing he should refuse a reconciliation, and desire her to write no more, or taunt her with having made an ineffectual act of humiliation. Alarmed at the idea, Lady Ethel smeared over the words she had transcribed, to render them, as she thought, illegible; but the ink had already sunk into the thin foreign paper, and having disfigured without effacing them, she hastily folded the letter, and enclosing it in the envelope, ordered Louise to have it taken to the post.

"Is it gone?" cried Maggie, when she returned from her visit; and being answered in the affirmative, told Lady Ethel that she would lay her a thousand pounds, if she had them, that in two months' time Colonel Bainbridge would be back in England.

"I don't believe it," said the wife, despondently; "it takes more than a letter to make up a quarrel like ours—besides, two months! just fancy, Maggie, what a time to wait! It seems an eternity in prospect."

Nevertheless, she was much more cheerful after the letter was posted than she had been before, and that evening, when Maggie was bidding her good-night, said, rather awkwardly, but with evident sincerity—

"If you are going to read—you always do so, do you not? —you may just as well read here as in your own room."

So Margaret Henderson sat down again by the bedside, and read a certain gracious promise to the intent that, though a woman may forget her sucking child, there is One by whom we can never be either forgotten or forsaken.

"I cannot remember my mother," said Lady Ethel, thoughtfully (she had alluded more than once of late to the same subject); "but I have heard my father say that the last word she uttered was my name. A mother's love must be a very holy thing."

"Yes, or it would not have been chosen as a type of His. But, I thank Heaven, I have never known the loss of it. Aunt Lizzie has been my mother."

"Is she so good to you?"

"Oh, very good; so sweet, and patient, and forbearing. She has never made the least difference between me and Cousin Thomas, although he is her own child, and she dotes on him. And in sickness or trouble, there is no one like her; except, indeed, Aunt Letty, who is my peculiar property."

Lady Ethel sighed.

"It must be very sweet to have a mother," she repeated.

"You have one, Ethel."

The blue eyes were fixed inquiringly on her face.

"Aunt Lizzie. Who could be more a daughter to her than her dear son's wife? And I am sure that no one would be readier to act a mother's part to you. She would love you just the same as if you were her own. For *his* sake, if for nothing else."

And Lady Ethel fell to sleep with those words sounding in her ears, and a smile upon her lips.

CHAPTER XLVIII.

HOME AT LAST.

THE time went on, until Maggie had nearly been a month in Curzon Street, and Lady Ethel had so far regained her strength as to be allowed to move about the house, and take carriage exercise. But she never cared to drive out in the Park, nor would she go anywhere without her friend. Maggie seemed to have become indispensable to her, and the old haunts distasteful; so, by mutual consent, they made daily excursions into the surrounding country, and spent as little time as possible in the crowded thoroughfares.

Yet even with this precaution it was not practicable for Lady Ethel entirely to avoid the remembrances that pained her. More than once, as she and Maggie Henderson drove out together, they came in contact with a showily-appointed carriage, containing a handsome woman, with a child seated by her side; a woman who, passing Lady Ethel without apparent recognition, stared with supercilious contempt at her companion, eliciting a justly-deserved condemnation from the lips of her step-daughter.

"There is my father's widow, Maggie, and a specimen of courtesy for you. Not that I should blame her though, for I have been rude enough in my day, and have no wish to renew my intercourse with her. I suppose the secret of it is, that true politeness must be founded on some firmer basis than the mere desire to keep up one's character for a knowledge of the requisitions of society. How I wish it were possible to get into the country, without driving through these hateful streets."

And the next moment, as a gentleman in passing lifted his hat to her (a tall slight man with dark eyes, whom Maggie could not help remarking for his elegant appearance), Lady Ethel, flushing scarlet, desired the coachman to turn at once into a by-road and take them anywhere, by any route, so that she might be spared the worry of these constant recognitions.

But that night, when she was laid in her bed, and Maggie stooped to give her a last kiss, she found her cheek was wet.

"Dear Ethel! what has happened to disturb you?"

"Oh—nothing! do not think of it—only that man (you saw him, Maggie) who bowed to me at the corner of Hyde Park this afternoon, he is the occasion of all my misery; it was for him I quarrelled with my husband; and now I hate the very sight of him. I wish that I might never see him more. O Thomas! O my darling! when will you come back to me?"

And Maggie spoke dear words of comfort to her, as she always did, promising a future of happiness if Ethel would but seek it in the way appointed; then crept to her own room, but not without a tear (for if the memory of her past was laid to sleep with holy words, it was not quite forgotten), and soothed her heart by praying that all those she loved might yet be re-united, and at peace.

But Mrs Bainbridge was getting clamorous that Maggie should return to Cranshaws. She was desirous to remove thence, and would not let a case be packed until she had the assistance of her niece.

Her last few letters had been filled with plaintive inquiries as to the probable duration of her absence, and Maggie had experienced no small difficulty in concealing her demands from Lady Ethel, by whom she felt the news of her impending departure would be received with the deepest lamentation. But the country letters generally arrived about the time that they had breakfast; and one morning, as they were sitting in the dining-room together, the intelligence conveyed to Maggie by her aunt was too important not to be inferred from the rapid change of her countenance.

"What is the matter?" exclaimed Lady Ethel; "you have had bad news."

"Oh, no; I hope not," said the other, trying to speak cheerfully; "but my aunt has had a letter from Calcutta."

"From Calcutta?"

"Now, don't be frightened, darling! really it is nothing, only Aunt Lizzie is so nervous and so easily alarmed. She has heard from Cousin Thomas: he was quite well when he wrote (remember that), had made a good passage, and arrived in Bengal safely; but he found orders waiting for him to proceed immediately up country, and could not stay in Calcutta long enough to receive our letters."

"But why—why go up country?"

"Why, his battery is up country, you little goose, and they wanted him. There had been a slight rising amongst some of the hill tribes in the north provinces (they are always rising up there), and Cousin Thomas wrote that he was likely to have some skirmishing, at which Aunt Lizzie says he seems uncommonly delighted; but, of course, like most mothers, she is horrified at the mere name of fighting, and fancies all sorts of coming trouble. But that arises from her overweening love for him."

"*They are going to fight?*"

The voice seemed so unlike Lady Ethel's voice, that Maggie looked up, quickly. There she stood, having risen from her chair, grey as ashes, and trembling in every limb.

"Ethel! you will never be so foolish as to worry yourself for a little thing like this. Would you have a soldier for a husband and not let him ply a soldier's trade! What nonsense! Rouse yourself, my dear! You are worse than even poor Aunt Lizzie."

She spoke sharply; and went up to her as she spoke, and took her roughly by the hand.

"Ethel! you will make me angry in a minute! This is perfect folly! I never should have told you, except as an excuse for the news that I must leave you. Aunt Lizzie wants me to go home again."

But the beautiful, pleading face, that, amidst all its knowledge of the world, had retained so much of childlike innocence in its expression, was lifted to her own; and Maggie felt her powers of resistance ebb away.

"Oh, do not leave me! and just now too. I could not bear the suspense by myself; it would kill me!"

"What can I do, dear? I don't want to go; but Aunt Lizzie has great claims on me, and I have been here a month, and she is anxious that I should return. Do you think I like to leave you, my dear sister?"

"Take me with you," whispered Lady Ethel.

"To Cranshaws? Would you really like to go?"

"If she—his—his mother will receive me. Do you think she will?"

"I do not *think*, Ethel, I am *sure* of it."

"What, after all? Oh! if she would—if she would let me stay near her! I fancy by her side I could be patient, whatever happens. O Maggie!" with clasped hands, "for God's sake, tell me that he will come back again!"

"How can I tell you that, my darling? But of one thing I am certain, that God will give him back to you; and if you have to wait, Ethel, until you meet him in another world, remember that we all deserve less at His hands than we receive. But, now, if you have quite decided to go back to Cranshaws with me, we must write to Dr Chalmers, and ask his opinion on the subject."

The physician caught at the idea: country air was all his patient needed to restore her to her usual health, and he could advise nothing that was likely to do her greater good. The only stipulation which he made was that the long journey should be broken by a night's rest at York, which gave Maggie time to prepare her aunts for the reception of their unexpected visitor; and though she had kept them well-informed of all that had occurred in Curzon Street, and the love which Lady Ethel had evinced for herself, it must be confessed that the proposition of her advent struck Mrs Bainbridge with dismay.

"Lady Ethel coming with her! and when I wanted Maggie just to help us in the packing! This is very awkward, Letty; it will turn the house all topsy-turvy again."

"Oh! I hope not, Elizabeth. You see how affectionately Maggie writes of Lady Ethel; and how well they seem to agree together. I hope we may find her much changed for the better."

"Fond of Maggie she evidently is," said Mrs Bainbridge; "but who could help being fond of Maggie—especially when she had nursed them through an illness? But that, in all probability, will only make Lady Ethel cling to her the more; and, perhaps, monopolise her services and her society. You remember how selfish she was with poor dear Thomas."

"Let us try not to remember it, Lizzie. She was newly married then; had been much spoiled; and likely to be a little overbearing. And now she has felt what it is to be in sickness and in trouble, poor child; and, from Maggie's account, she must behave very differently from what she did then."

"Maggie is always enthusiastic, particularly where her affections are concerned," said Mrs Bainbridge. "Well, of course, I must always feel kindly towards any one whom my dear Thomas loves; but I must say, I should have been better pleased if Lady Ethel had delayed her visit till we were settled in our new home."

"Perhaps she wants to come and help you, Elizabeth, as Maggie does," suggested Miss Lloyd.

"Now Letty! just think of that girl, with her delicate mincing ways, and all her pretty fashionable fal-lals, and say if that is probable. Help me, indeed! she is far more likely to keep the whole house (myself included) waiting upon her."

"She is a fragile creature," said her sister, "and looks as if she had been born to be waited on. How proud Thomas was of her."

"Ay, and think of him now, poor dear, exiled to that horrid country, because of her unkindness. When I remember that, Letty, I hardly feel as though I could receive her in a cordial manner."

"She would not have proposed to come to us, unless she felt the want of our affection. Don't let it be said that by our coldness we checked the first impulse which her heart has conceived towards us. Receive her as a daughter—as if nothing unpleasant had occurred between you (she has no mother of her own, remember)—and you will do more, Elizabeth, to show her she was wrong than any amount of reproaches would effect. But I do not believe she is coming to us in the same spirit that she did before; for I have faith in Maggie's representations, and know that, though enthusiastic, she never exaggerates; nor would she take so great an interest in any one who was not disposed to look kindly upon those she loves."

Yet, notwithstanding all Miss Lloyd's cheerful prognostications, Mrs Bainbridge continued quite nervous at the prospect of seeing her daughter-in-law again; and when the carriage had been sent to Borthwick to fetch the travellers, wandered restlessly from room to room, unable to settle anywhere, and evidently much discomposed by the meeting that awaited her.

"Here they come," cried Aunt Letty, as she pursued her sister to the Library, "the carriage has just passed the brow of the hill, and I can see Maggie's dear round face out of the window. Come, Elizabeth, let us meet the children in the hall."

But Mrs Bainbridge, trembling with anxiety, stood rooted to the spot.

"O Letty! if she should speak and look as she did before, and neither of them here to stand between us! I don't think I could bear it—I don't indeed!"

"Nonsense!" exclaimed Aunt Letty; "you are frightening yourself with shadows, Lizzie. Why, there is Maggie's voice already in the hall. My darling, are you really here at last?"

"'*At last*,' you may say indeed, auntie. Poor Ethel is tired out of her life; she is not yet strong enough for such long journeys." And then as she was embraced by each in turn, Maggie pushed Lady Ethel forward. "Aunt Lizzie, I have brought your daughter to you, who wants all the love that you can spare from Cousin Thomas to console her for his absence, and all the care and petting you can give her for the sake of a little secret of her own. There, Ethel," as she placed the hand of her companion in that of Mrs Bainbridge, "there is your mother, and here is mine," turning to Aunt Letty; "and now that we have one apiece, we shall not quarrel."

Mrs Bainbridge glanced timidly at her daughter-in-law, but one look at the pale harassed face raised imploringly to hers, was sufficient to make her kind maternal arms fly open.

"My dear girl, you look very ill! what has been the matter with you? How miserable my dear Thomas would be to know it."

"O *mother!*" whispered Lady Ethel, clinging close to her, "do you—do you think there is any fear that he will not come home again?"

"Not come home, my dear? what, Thomas? God forbid! But I am very anxious, naturally—and so must you be, until we hear that he is safe and well again at Calcutta."

"I thought I could not bear it away from you and all he cares for," murmured the girl, feverishly; "I should have seen faces that were not there, and heard voices when nobody was talking. It seems so long—so very long—since he went away; and there is so much before me, I don't think we shall ever meet in this world again."

"Maggie!" exclaimed Mrs Bainbridge, in a voice of alarm. "Why does she talk so strangely? My dear, you ought to be in bed."

"I think she is very tired, Aunt Lizzie; but nothing would do her more harm now than to be silent. Let her say all she has to say, and then carry her up-stairs and put her to bed in your own dear comfortable way."

"Yes, let me speak," went on Lady Ethel, hurriedly, "just a few words; I might not live to say them till the morning. O mother! (if I may call you mother), I behaved so ill when I was here before; I was proud, and selfish, and presuming; I did not know how necessary love is to life; and now that I am stripped of everything, I come home to ask it at your hands."

"My dear daughter, you have no need to ask, it has been always ready for you. You had but to stretch your hand and take it."

"And may I stay here until he comes back to me—or I go to him? I feel as though I could not live now except in places with which he has been familiar."

"My dear, Cranshaws is your own. You are the mistress here."

"Oh, no! no!" shrinking backwards, "I cannot feel that; I would rather be your daughter and your guest. And if—if—anything should happen—if he never comes again, you will let me try to be your child instead of him. But I could not live—indeed, indeed, I could not live without him. My heart is breaking now," and bursting into tears, Lady Ethel fell upon the homely breast of the woman she had so despised. Mrs Bainbridge, powerfully affected, could only strain her to her heart, and cry with her, and had not Maggie interposed her authority, the invalid might have been rendered seriously ill.

"Come, Ethel, try to calm yourself. What would Dr Chalmers say to such an exhibition? Aunt Lizzie, make her go up-stairs, and then you can wait on her, and cosset her to your heart's content, until she goes to sleep."

Acting on which opportune advice, Lady Ethel was persuaded to allow herself to be made much of (a proceeding to which the young woman was at no period averse), and Mrs Bainbridge seeing her eat her dinner and made comfortable for the night, had a very happy tearful time of it until she was called down-stairs again by the ringing of the prayer bell.

"Only to think," she observed to Aunt Letty, as, waiting the appearance of the servants, she wiped her moistened eyes, "that that poor darling is fretting for Thomas even more than I am; and would give her right hand not to have offended him. And I daresay he was partly in the wrong; men are so difficult to deal with."

"I do not think Ethel would agree with you there," said Maggie, smiling.

"Ah! she is all sweetness. It is beautiful to hear her speak of him, and of herself, and her expected baby! Who could have dreamt she would be so altered? She is not like the same person."

"Let us thank God for it," said Aunt Letty, as the long train of domestics filed into the room.

CHAPTER XLIX. AND LAST.

"PEACE ON EARTH, AND GOOD WILL TOWARD MEN."

WHILST these events were happening in England, Colonel Bainbridge, in a very restless and unhappy state of mind, was wandering about the north-west provinces of Bengal. For that which, on the eve of his departure, he had written to his cousin Maggie, was the truth. Scarcely had he concluded the terms of his exchange, and paid down his passage money to the East, before he repented that he had been so rash.

To go back to his wife, and without some further explanation of her words, to claim the empty casket whence the gem of love had been extracted, would have been impossible to him; but the thought which haunted him throughout the tedious journey, that in order to save his own wounded feelings, he had abandoned her to temptation and the power of the man for whom she had confessed a preference, nearly drove him mad.

By the time he reached Calcutta, he had almost forgiven her; or rather, absence, and the strong desire to prove her cruelty not wilful, had so softened the remembrance of it, that the thought of all he had loved best in her, her pretty childish ways, her grace, her beauty, and her mock imperiousness, was the predominating thought; and, blaming himself more than he blamed her, he would have returned to England by the next steamer if he could. He was not perfect; this great, honest, short-sighted Englishman, bred of the middle classes; but he was a very fair type of a gentleman who truly loves the woman he has sworn to cherish. There is weakness apparent in his hasty flight, and incapability to stand by and look upon the desolation of his hearth; still more, perhaps, in his quick following repentance and desire to return and "make it up again;" but weakness, where a woman is concerned, is pardonable in the man who loves her, and firmness too often prognosticates an absence of affection. It is so hard to hold out against anything which we can crush at will.

By the time that Colonel Bainbridge had reached his destination, therefore, he had a thousand excuses ready hatched for Lady Ethel. She was so young, so beautiful, so much admired. He had proposed to her too hastily, and without sufficient encouragement, she had never told him that she loved him; he had no one to thank for his gross error but himself. And then, was she quite unimpressionable, that fair, soft, girlish creature? that, instead of attempting to provoke her love, he had deserted, without giving her due warning, and left the field open to his rival. Fool! idiot! madman! The only remedy he could think of was to return at once.

But when he got to Calcutta, Colonel Bainbridge experienced the unpleasant fact that when a man is bound to his profession, saying and doing are two different things.

Despatches waited for him (or rather for the officer in whose stead he appeared there), demanding his immediate presence with his battery up country, where a disturbance had broken out amongst some of the hill tribes, and, unable to do more than write a few hurried lines to his mother (when it came to the point, his courage failed him to address his wife), and leave directions with his agents to forward all his letters, he took the speediest means to reach his destination. Arrived there, he found the mutiny more important than he had imagined; regiments were ordered out in several directions, and he was immediately placed in command, and sent to do duty somewhere in the jungle.

Here Colonel Bainbridge remained for several weeks, seeing no service, with the exception of a few skirmishes and night surprises, which he called child's play, and receiving no hurt, unless a cut across the head from a glancing spear, which he declared too trifling to demand the doctor's aid, could be called such.

Colonel Bainbridge, however (always the last person to look after himself), in this instance proved too careless; for though the wound was not dangerous, the weather was so; and a sunstroke supervening on exposure, threw his already heated frame into a state of fever which threatened his existence. For weeks he lay delirious on his bed; raving of things past, present, and to come; and when his malady was at last abated, and consciousness restored, he was so feeble as to seem desirous of one thing only, and that was to die. He appeared to have lost all memory, interest, or curiosity, and the only occasions upon which his medical attendant could rouse him to anything like energy, was when he mentioned the desirability of his proceeding immediately to England; and then Colonel Bainbridge, with all the firmness of which he was master, would declare his willingness to go to Australia, the Cape, or the Mauritius, anywhere, in short, but to his native land.

"No country but England will set you up again," the doctor urged.

"Then I will die here," was his patient's answer. For during his illness, all the softened thoughts which he had entertained for Lady Ethel on his voyage out, had faded into the far distance, to be replaced by one idea, the indisputable conviction that she hated him—that she had said so—and that he must never see her more. With strength had vanished his powers of discernment, and he could only lie quiescent, and in his feeble way, rehearse over and over again the last sad scene he had gone through with his wife; until he convinced himself that the best thing for her, for him, for both of them, was that he should die where he lay, and never trouble her again. "Yet, O Ethel! O my God! How I have loved her!"

It is this fact that accounts for the circumstance that it was five months before he returned to England. Part of that period he spent up in the jungle, unable to post letters or to receive them; but by far the larger half was passed in apathetic indolence upon his couch, when his mental condition had attained to such a pitch that he refused to open the advices which were forwarded to him; and whilst his friends were thirsting for news in England, really believed himself incapable of either answering or perusing what they sent him.

But the day came when he could feign apathy no longer, when his body sprung from bed, renewed and buoyant; and his mind waking up to action, as at a trumpet-call, he seized on his large packet of hitherto despised despatches, as the famished seize on food, and devoured them!

What a feast he found there!

The first which he tore open was Maggie's long, warm letter, sent from Curzon Street, with the little smeared-over, but still legible postscript, in the hand he loved. Could he believe his eyes, his senses? or was this a renewal of the delirium that had oppressed him? Yet every line of the epistle he held in his shaking hand confirmed the fact; she had misjudged herself, her heart, her feelings. His darling was his own again.

Thank God!

The aspiration as it came bubbling, bursting, welling up from the deepest depths of his great heart, and bringing a rush of scalding tears with it from his yet weak eyes, can never be expressed by printed letters. To be appreciated, it ought to have been heard; but no one heard it but the One to whom it was so gratefully addressed.

After this, the doctor found no difficulty in persuading Colonel Bainbridge to return to England, the difficulty was in preventing his travelling there in such hot haste as to materially injure a frame which was still delicate.

"But I *must go,* doctor; it is absolutely necessary. Affairs of the utmost importance call me home, and if rail and steam can take me there, I spend my Christmas-day in England."

"Well, Colonel, I have not had you for a patient for nothing, and if you must go, I suppose you must. Only, bear in mind that in such an instance most haste may be worst speed."

Bear in mind! Could he bear in mind anything, excepting that his beloved had arrived at the true knowledge of herself, and that he carried a precious letter from her (written after her arrival at Cranshaws) next his heart, and was hastening to rejoin all he loved?

The voyage did him no harm, for expectation bore him through it, and it read him a good lesson upon patience, which he sorely needed; but when he once set foot in England, he hardly allowed himself the time to eat, before he was rushing onward to the north. Oh, how lingeringly, how wearisomely slow the express train seemed to run with him.

"All well?" he inquired breathlessly of the groom who waited at the Borthwick station with a saddle-horse (he had particularly requested in a telegram, that the carriage should not be sent to jolt him homewards at a foot's pace).

"All well, sir," said the man, smiling; and as Colonel Bainbridge took the reins from him, he thought his face looked very bright and cheerful, as though it held some hidden joy.

Yet, why should it not, when joy reigned on every side of Cranshaws? joy at the mere thought of which his own heart stood still.

Not so the heels of the animal he bestrode; for as the idea crossed his mind, he struck spurs into the horse's side, and sent him clattering over hill and dale in a manner to which he had been of late but very little accustomed. Reeking and breathless he brought him to a standstill before the door of his own house and flung himself from out the saddle.

His mother met him in the hall.

"My son! my dearest!" it was all she could find voice to say, "we are so happy."

"She is here—mother—she is well—I can see her? Oh, do not keep me waiting! If you only knew what I have suffered!"

"My dear boy, you shall see her in a minute, but I must prepare you; it was her wish you should not know of it beforehand; that there is a child—a son for you—born this morning, Thomas! and all well as possible. Are you not thankful?"

Is gratitude expressed by sudden pallor, a fixed face and trembling limbs? Mrs Bainbridge was quite frightened at the alteration in her son's appearance.

"My dear! they are quite well, and Ethel is so proud—she only wants you to complete her happiness. And such a fine child, Thomas, the very image of yourself with large dark eyes. Everybody who has seen him says so; and when I took him first to his dear mother"——

But Mrs Bainbridge had to finish her interesting description of the new comer's charms to the hall-table—for darting past her without another word, Colonel Bainbridge had already scaled the staircase and gained the upper landing, where, Maggie waiting, without the least effort to detain or greet him, silently opened the bed-room door, and ushered him into the presence of his wife.

It was through her instrumentality that they had been brought together again: it was fitting she should be the one to turn that handle for him.

Then the door closed, and she was left——outside.

But not *alone.* No! Maggie, dear, generous, faithful Maggie! never again, through life or death——alone!

The room was darkened as such rooms are, and the curtains partly drawn about the bed, by the side of which stood, curtseying, a substantial nurse, who evidently considered that the bundle of flannel she pompously held in her arms was better worth inspection than all the Lady Ethels in the world.

But not so the man who loved her, who, pressing past both nurse and infant, saw nothing but two weak arms stretched out to welcome him, and flew to their embrace, and found his heaven there.

"Oh, love, can you forgive?" was all she whispered, but the inquiry received no answer, and Lady Ethel never pressed for one.

There is a silence more eloquent than words—a silence during which hearts speak to one another, and souls are joined in marriage—and such a silence reigned between them now.

When Thomas Bainbridge unlocked himself from that embrace, he knew that for the future no explanations would be needed—that he and his wife were *one*.

. . . .

It was in November that he reached his home; and with the dawn of Christmas-day, a happy party assembled in the breakfast-room of Cranshaws. Lady Ethel, as beautiful as ever, and become what her husband termed "impudently strong" again (which meant that as usual she gained her own way in everything), was seated between him and Mrs Bainbridge, and engaged in carrying on what appeared to be a most animated discussion.

"Well, you must settle it between yourselves then," said Colonel Bainbridge, as he rose from table, and took up the Englishman's favourite position on the hearth-rug.

"Of course we will," replied Lady Ethel, laying her hand in that of her mother-in-law, "*I* settle it by saying that mother must live with us at Cranshaws, and give up all idea of Birmingham once and for ever."

Mrs Bainbridge looked intensely gratified, but she still held back.

"My dears, it is very good of you to propose it, too good, indeed, but I am half afraid. You will get tired of seeing an old woman like me about the house; I shall be in your way, and you will not like to tell me so. I think it will be best for all parties that I should adhere to my old plan, and go to Birmingham."

"Then I shall adhere to *my* old plan," said Lady Ethel, resolutely, "and refuse to live at Cranshaws."

"My darling, I thought you had quite made up your mind to occupy it for six months in the year?"

"Not without you, mother; I should be lost in this great place all by myself; and do you think I would keep baby here, ten miles from a doctor, and so ignorant as I am of children, unless I had some one to help and advise me? No; I am quite decided. If you go to Birmingham, baby must go to Curzon Street."

"Oh, that would be ten thousand pities, my dear, and when he is getting on so splendidly in this fine air. I am sure he is twice as big as old Hetty's grandchild; and there is only a fortnight's difference in their ages."

"I know it," replied Lady Ethel with mock despondency, "and in Curzon Street, in all probability, he will shrivel up to the size of a prawn. But if grandmamma won't stay and look after him, he must shrivel. O Thomas," with sudden coaxing earnestness, as she jumped up and placed her hand upon her husband's arm, "*make* your mother stay with us. No one can see after baby and me as she can. I should be lost without her. Besides," with rather less assurance and a faint blush, "it was she, you know—she, and dear Maggie—who kept me alive when you were absent, and taught me to be hopeful and patient, and to trust in God. I owe my present happiness to them; it would not seem complete if they were missing."

"Can you resist this pleader?" demanded Colonel Bainbridge, as he raised the sweet face to his own and kissed it.

"Letty, my dear! what *shall* I do?" said Mrs Bainbridge, in a flutter of delight.

"Stay with them, I should say, and thank God for your son and daughter."

"But you"——

"Aunt Letty stays where you do, mother," exclaimed Lady Ethel. "Remember, Cranshaws will be deserted by us half the year, and will want its housekeepers."

"And our home will always be dear Maggie's," added Colonel Bainbridge, smiling.

"Maggie! I should think so," said Lady Ethel, as she rushed to her embrace, "Maggie, my sister—my friend—my dear, dear Maggie! O Thomas, we owe everything to her —our love, our happiness, our very selves. I dare not think what life would have been like if Heaven had not sent us Maggie."

"Heaven will reward her," said her cousin pressing her hand, and as she met the calm look of contentment with which he regarded her, Maggie felt that the reward had come.

"Hark! was not that the sound of bells?" exclaimed Aunt Letty as she flew to the window. "Ethel, my dear, this air will not hurt you, it is too dry and bracing," and as she threw up the sash, the distant chime of Christmas bells came faintly through the frosty atmosphere.

"Peace on earth and good will towards men," said Colonel Bainbridge, as he drew his cousin and his wife towards the window. "Hark, Ethel! listen, Maggie! Peace and good will. My dear girls, how good God is to us!"

. . . .

It was on that same evening that Miss Lloyd surprised Margaret Henderson in a reverie.

"My darling, what are you thinking of?"

"Of Saint Ermenilda's, auntie, and the services they are holding there. How glorious they must be!"

"You wish you could be present."

"I should like it, dear, and so would you."

"Well, go, my child, then."

Maggie stared; Aunt Letty was not used to practical joking, and especially on serious subjects.

"What do you mean?"

"Not that you should start off to-night, my darling, to make one of the congregation in Saint Ermenilda's, but that you should consider yourself, from this moment, free to act in that matter as you think fit. The time has come, my Maggie."

"O Aunt Letty! are you really in earnest?" with a deep-drawn breath.

"Yes, child. If it were the cutting off of my right hand, or my right arm, I must still say so. The time has come.

Your place in Cranshaws is filled up. Aunt Lizzie has procured, through your means, another daughter, and may well spare you to heaven."

"But you, my dearest aunt, to whom I owe so much, can you quite spare me?"

Aunt Letty made an effort to control herself, and then went on, calmly:

"Yes, darling, I have thought of that; I, too, am willing. I shall not loose you more than I should do, if you were married; perhaps less, and I shall always have the comfort of knowing that each step you take will bring us nearer in the end. Maggie! I said once to you 'Stay,' and you stayed most dutifully. Now I say—and quite as earnestly—Go! my child—my blessing—in the name of God!"

. . . .

And in His name she went.

THE END.

PRINTED BY BALLANTYNE, HANSON AND CO.
EDINBURGH AND LONDON

CPSIA information can be obtained
at www.ICGtesting.com
Printed in the USA
LVHW030733230323
742065LV00026B/175

9 783382 127619